THE TIME OF THE LITTLE BLACK BIRD

THE TIME OF THE LITTLE BLACK BIRD

Helen Papanikolas

Swallow Press / Ohio University Press

Athens

Cosmos Publishing Co., Inc.
262 Rivervale Road
River Vale, N.J. 07675-6252
Phone: 201-664-3494

Visit our Electronic Bookstore at
www.GreeceInPrint.com

Swallow Press/Ohio University Press, Athens, Ohio 45701
© 1999 by Helen Papanikolas
Printed in the United States of America

Swallow Press/Ohio University Press books
are printed on acid-free paper ⊗ ™

05 04 03 02 01 00 99   5 4 3 2 1

Library of Congress Cataloging-in-Publication Data
Papanikolas, Helen Zeese.
    The time of the little black bird / by Helen Papanikolas.
       p. cm.
    ISBN 0-8040-1016-1 (cloth : alk. paper). — ISBN 0-8040-1017-X
(paper : alk. paper)
    1. Greek Americans—Utah—Salt Lake City—Fiction. I. Title.
PS3566.A612T56   1999
813'.54—dc21   98-50080

For my husband Nick

Steve Kallos sat at the end of the spacious kitchen that faced a wall-sized window and read the morning paper. Even now, in his early eighties, with thinned, gray hair and a face that looked like an aging boxer's wearing incongruous horn-rimmed eyeglasses, there was a strong male aura about him. His body gave the impression of being solid, immovable, as he leisurely read, with a cellular telephone and a small magnifying glass within easy reach of his right hand.

The mornings were a good time for him: the night's torments were forgotten—the recriminations against his brother Solon, strapped to a bed in a nursing home, and his cousin Constantine, twelve years dead, who had left him their sons to bleed his guts out in the family business. In the night darkness, barely lighted by the icon light in his son's old bedroom, he reviewed old regrets. The past night he had been starkly awakened and saw a tall black figure standing at the side of the bed. "Gotcha," the figure said.

In the morning quiet, he forgot the black figure and the heavy suffocating beat of his heart. He was merely surprised and grateful that he had not died during the night, and with a feeling of well-being he continued to read the newspaper. His vision was better in the mornings, and there was no great urgency to hurry to his office as in his younger years. In the comforting kitchen he sat each morning aware of the faint scent of dried basil and oregano, and the coffee his wife Mary had prepared before going out to her rose garden. He liked the morning peace and always sat facing the big window.

Beyond the window, Mary's rose garden was bright against a fall of dark ivy. Next to the roses were three rows of tomatoes, green peppers, zucchini, and green beans climbing wooden trellises. They constituted his garden; he would go out after his coffee while the morning dew was on the leaves and the earth scent retained the night's moisture.

On this August morning Mary was cutting faded roses and dropping them into a basket at her feet. Steve glanced away from the slender figure with the swollen ankles. He did not want to think of stubby legs—they meant water accumulation, heart problems, the end . . . his mother. Mary walked in front of the rose bushes, set the basket on the grass by a redwood bench, and sat down to gaze at Mount Olympus. Once in a while, Steve would sit with her, but she would not let him talk. "Let's just look and not talk. Let's just rest."

Steve finished reading most of the newspaper, including the editorials, but it was the financial page that was his main interest. He did not miss a single line of it. He read with a satisfied nod that the Stratos Company won a state home-builders award for having sold the greatest number of houses in the past ten years. Theo Stratos was a top builder now and Steve felt a fine pleasure when he read about him. He had had a hand in it. In the middle 1950s, Theo had come to him, an immigrant from the same Peloponnesian village as his father's, and asked him for work. He said he was good with numbers. Steve gave him the job running errands and keeping his office in order, on condition that he give up his crowd of friends. They were a bunch of Peloponnesian toughs from Piraeus who were rumored to use brass knuckles on Americans and fellow Greeks who looked down on them. Steve told him to cut his name from Theophrastos Stratopoulos to Theo Stratos, enroll in night classes to improve his English, and to learn estimating. After finishing his courses, Steve introduced him to his friend George Tsarpalias, a home builder who took him on as an assistant estimator. In a short time—it seemed so to Steve—Theo was out building on his own.

Steve continued reading, still smiling. At the bottom of the financial page in a small paragraph, the name *Kallos* jumped up. The two vertical lines between his eyebrows deepened. Gray hairs bristled from his thick eyebrows. Western Enterprises, he read, had sold its

Block 325 property to the Synoris Communications systems for five million dollars. A multistory building would be built on the site for its national headquarters. According to the president of Western Enterprises, Richard Kallos, the negotiations had been in the works for more than a year. Razing of existing structures would begin immediately.

Using the magnifying glass, Steve read the paragraph again. "Western Enterprises." He whispered the words and lifted his eyes to look at the rose garden. His face was hot. He had never heard of Western Enterprises. Never in all the board meetings of the Kallos family had the name come up. The family had always worked together; it was understood that no one would make individual investments. Getting Block 325 would have taken years, decades, to buy out whatever was already there—old houses, small businesses, empty lots. The Danish pastry he had eaten rebelled in his stomach. He had to tell someone. Two years previously he would have run to his brother Solon. Then one midnight an ambulance took Solon—Solly—to Emergency, where Steve looked down on him, a seventy-nine-year-old man babbling nonsense. He half rose from his chair to rap on the window to catch Mary's attention, but sat down again, surprised at the foolish thought. He touched his hot face thinking he ought to take his blood pressure. Yet he sat there, saying over and over to himself: "How did this happen? We were a family. How did this happen?"

PART 1

I

SIXTEEN-YEAR-OLD Marika stood next to the stranger she was being married to and heard neither the young bearded priest nor the cantor's Lord-have-mercys. Her eyes were fixed on the icon screen, on the black staring eyes of the Virgin; and her hands trembled about the bouquet of green leaves and three red roses. As little clouds of incense rose from the priest's swinging censer, her nose twitched. In the numbness of her head the words churned: *Where is he? Where is he?*

The young priest went on intoning God's blessing of Abraham, opening the womb of Sarah, giving Rebecca to Isaac, and joining Rachel to Jacob. His long hair reached to the shoulders of his rose brocade robe. Marika thought he might know what had happened to her uncle who had sent her the money for passage to America and who should now be with her.

When Marika had arrived at the Denver & Rio Grande Western railroad depot, her smiling, handsome uncle had been surrounded by a group of friends. Some had become his instant friends from the moment they heard of the girl's imminent arrival. A man played a lively leaping dance tune on a stringed *laouto.* Men called out welcomes, elbowing each other to get closer to the girl. Her hair was lank and strands had escaped the knot of braids at the back of her head. She had sat up for three days and two nights to reach the city, and there had been no way to wash her hair during the three weeks aboard ship. Although she had tried to keep her face clean, soot speckled her olive skin, and her clothes were wrinkled. She had been careful with the tag tied to her lapel: To Jim Niakos Salt Lake City, Utah. Even so, the men cheered the young girl with frightened eyes and black smudges of fatigue under them. They followed her,

7

singing distiches, to the midwife's house, where she would stay until her marriage. A big, burly man walked at the side of her uncle, smiling, his face flushed. She understood by this gesture that he was her future husband.

There in the church, with the wedding crown of white cloth flowers on her head, she knew that the man at her side, wearing an identical crown, was not that heavy, smiling man who had walked with her and her uncle to the midwife's house. This man was big-shouldered, but not much taller than she. The priest pushed the silver winecup between Marika's lips. Then as the best man led Marika and the groom three times around the wedding table in the Dance of Isaiah, the lighted candle in Marika's hand shook and the flame flattened and almost went out. With a bound, the small midwife righted the candle to prevent bad luck that would follow if the flame died.

Next, they were outside. The congregation trampled the few feet of grass in front of the small, domed church and positioned themselves for the photographer. Flags stood on stands at either end of the gathering, the blue-and-white Greek on one side, the American on the other. The slight photographer made a great show of his professionalism; he had recently arrived in Greek Town from Chicago, where he had transformed himself from a dishwasher to a night-school graduate with a degree in photography. He waved signals and shouted muffled directions, his head covered with the black cloth of his three-legged camera. The sun was hot; the red roses in Marika's bouquet drooped; and still the photographer changed glass plates and with short, quick steps walked toward the wedding guests, motioning them closer together for another picture. "Enough!" the young men shouted. "We're hungry! Thirsty!"

The photographer grandly waved them toward the church basement. The men jostled each other as they laughingly crowded about the tables, making toasts, drinking from water glasses filled with wine. A group of young men with sprigs of basil in their lapels were shouted at with raised wine glasses: "Bring back brides!" "Bring one for me!" "Leave her mother home!" Flushed, with big smiles, the men would be taking the night train in response to Greece's command that all reservists return. Last year the Greek army had fought the Turks; this year it was fighting both the Turks and the Bulgarians.

Besides Marika, three women were in the crowd. The only children were the midwife's eight, weaving about the raucous men, looking for their godfathers to kiss their hands and receive the usual dime or quarter.

Long tables were set with dishes, knives, and forks, all borrowed from the Acropolis *Kaffenion*. In one corner men were hacking two lambs just taken off the spits in the backyard of the church. Pink grease ran onto the wooden floor. Marika was led to a table, where she was seated with the priest, the best man, the red-faced, laughing groom, his brother, and the three women. The midwife, the *mami,* no larger than a ten-year-old but with heavy breasts, sat on her left, and Andreas, the groom, sat on her right. The other two women sat across the table—one a plump young Cretan woman with heavy black eyebrows and luminous dark eyes, the other plain and thin with yellowed skin, and greatly pregnant. After the priest's blessing of the food, and several long toasts, the lamb and *pilafi* were served by the youngest of the men, who hurried about with dishtowels tied around their waists. Andreas toasted each one. "To your wedding crowns," he boomed, and laughed with boisterous acknowledgment of the men's envious looks. The thin woman leaned back from her plate, away from the midwife's pointed finger. The *mami* ordered her to eat the fat of the lamb to give her strength for her coming ordeal. "I can't," the woman beseeched the midwife.

Marika could hardly breathe; her tight wedding dress, bought by the best man, had been too large, and the midwife had taken the seams in more than necessary. She dabbled at her food. She had hardly slept; she knew people were watching her as she ate; and she was afraid of what was to come. When the groom turned to his best man and said something to him that brought guffaws, Marika moved close to the *mami*. "Where is my uncle?" she whispered.

The *mami* chewed and smacked her lips for several seconds before she answered. "You see, my golden one, your uncle had chosen Barbetos for you, but Andreas offered him five hundred dollars and so he gave you to Andreas. Barbetos went to the coffeehouse looking for your uncle and vowed he would kill him. Barbetos had a house all ready, everything in order for you. Your uncle jumped on the next train to *Tsicago* or *Nea Yorki*." The midwife leaned over her plate, both elbows on the table, and continued eating.

When the tables were cleared, three young men began playing the *laouto, clarino,* and the *lyra*. The best man, young and fat, came forward to lead Marika in the traditional first dance and offered her one end of his handkerchief. She took it and walked carefully in the tight, white satin shoes her uncle had bought. She did well enough, looking down at her feet while the best man led, but when he placed her in the lead, she wobbled and her olive skin grayed. The men called out, "Long life!" and "Next year with a son!"

Long after midnight, Marika, with a box on her lap holding the wedding crowns, the groom Andreas, his brother Heracles, and the two other men who had sat at the table drove in a wagon to the four-room frame *bekiariko,* the bachelor house. The horse clopped along slowly. The musicians followed, singing an old wedding song:

> I'll set out on Sunday to love you,
> To have you on Monday, my ornamented dove,
> To have you again on Tuesday, like an eagle with a robin.
> To have you on Wednesday, like a tree with the one-day-
> blooming lily,
> To have you—

The singing stopped. In the silence, in the bright moonlight, splinters of wood, shards of glass, and uprooted grape plants, the veins of their leaves as stark as in daylight, lay strewn over the dirt yard of the house. While Marika sat in the buckboard, not knowing what to do, the men jumped down, shouting and swearing. "I'll fuck his Virgin!" Andreas screamed, his fist raised. "I'll slaughter him! I'll send him to the devil! Wrecking the house! Pouting because I was the better man and got the girl!"

Dogs began howling; lights went on in houses; a gun shot off in warning. The men threw the debris to one side, making a path to the house, and cursing Barbetos nailed blankets over broken windows and righted the privy. "Come in!" Andreas shouted to Marika. She got down stiffly and walked, teetering over the glass-splattered dirt, to the front door.

"This is our bedroom. The privy's in the back yard. Take the kerosene lamp when you go out."

LIGHT CAME THROUGH the blue blanket nailed over the window. "Get up now," Andreas said. "Make the breakfast. The men are ready to leave for work." Marika sat up. She did not know what to do about the blood that had dried on the inside of her thighs during the night. She remembered that the three men in the adjoining bedroom had snored and farted until dawn. She remembered that she was a lone woman without a male relative to uphold her. She would never speak her uncle's name again. He had left her to the mercy of a stranger.

Andreas instructed Marika on how to make American coffee and showed her the icebox on the back screened porch where a bowl of eggs, a large jar of feta cheese, and wrapped packages were set on shelves. Marika stared, surprise piercing her tired eyes: a block of ice was set in a top compartment. Andreas said, "Make eggs with *feta* cheese for breakfast and a lunch for the boarders, a dry onion, bread, and some of the lamb from the wedding dinner."

While she hurried, the men bantered over their good fortune. "Eh, Marika, for six years we've been taking turns cooking and cleaning up in this *bekiariko*. Now we have you to take over." The men had been introduced to her at the wedding dinner but she could remember nothing about them, except that the youngest of them was Andreas's brother Heracles, who sat eyeing her while passing his palms backward from his temples. A sweetish scent came from his oiled hair. The two boarders stared at her, smiling. Their hair was thin and a light color, foreheads broad, noses pudgy, and teeth as big and yellow as a horse's. They looked nearly alike, except one had a thick scar that led from his ear, down the side of his face, and disappeared into his collar.

After the men left, Marika sat down at the cluttered table. The soles of her shoes, made for her as a wedding gift by a village cousin, grated over the dirty floor. A smell of old cooking odors, sweat, and tobacco reminded her of the men. She thought: Where should I start cleaning? She had seen how Andreas had turned on the water for the coffee. Her shoulders slumped and she closed her eyes.

She dozed and was awakened by a pounding on the back screen door. The midwife walked in with a large pot of stew. She was wearing boys' ankle-topped shoes, a long, plaid gingham dress, and over it a flower-patterned cotton apron—her working uniform. "So, my golden one, I brought this stew so you wouldn't have to cook for them tonight and I came to look at the sheets. Then we can drink a cup of coffee. I see Barbetos did a good job outside." She laughed, a high tinkle.

Marika led the *mami* to the front bedroom and lifted the top sheet. The two women looked at the dried blood. "You bled good all right. No one can say you weren't a virgin. I can vouch for that."

They returned to the kitchen and sipped the strong coffee. "I don't even know who these men are," Marika said, putting her weight on her right thigh to ease the pain low inside her.

"Now—" the midwife said, her small eyes bright, friendly, "there's Heracles, Andreas's brother. Andreas brought him over after he got well settled." The *mami* leaned toward Marika. "He thinks he's too good for us. His shit's better. The other two are the icemen. That ice you have in the *iceboxee*. They deliver it all over town. They're cousins, from an Albanian village in the Peloponnesos."

"One of them has a scar down his face."

"That happened about five years ago. They had a fight with some Italian icemen over their customers. With ice tongs. One of the Italians got him from the ear all the way down his neck. I had a hard time stopping the blood. Gave me fifty cents, the pig." The midwife whistled her coffee and put down the cup with a satisfied smack. "Your man's got a bigger scar on his back. From his neck down to his ass. I saw it when I was cupping him for a bad fever. Got it fighting with an Irish foreman on a railroad *geng.*"

"A long scar?" Marika whispered, then wailed, "I don't know what's happened. I thought I was going to marry one man and I see another man standing next to me in church."

The midwife folded her arms under her big breasts. "You see," she said in a patient tone, "I told you. When Andreas Kalogiannis saw you at the train station, he sent his brother Heracles to your uncle with five hundred dollars for you. That's all there is to say." The *mami* gave a slight shrug of her shoulders at this logical explanation.

"But what about the bans? What did the priest say? Where is the bishop?"

"Eh, Marika," the midwife nodded with a knowing lift of her eyebrows, "you've got a lot to learn about priests and our church in America. A telephone call to the bishop in *San Franchitsco,* a few lies, and Andreas becomes your husband."

Marika clasped her throat. "And what kind of work does my man do?"

"Ah. He owns a *magazy* and sells cigars and cigarettes. I remember when he bought it. Just before he brought his brother Heracles over. He'd been working in the copper mill and had lived on canned pork and beans—he said so himself—to save money for it. He bought it from the third Greek to come to the city. From Corfu. He took his money and went to *San Franchitsco* and is already rich.

"All of us from the neighborhood followed the priest for the blessing," the *mami* snorted. "A crowd of *Amerikanoi* gathered on the sidewalk and gaped and tittered. The priest kept glaring at them while he was chanting. I think he cursed them under his breath. I was surprised your man Andreas didn't wap those *Amerikanoi* with his fists. He's beaten up plenty of Greeks, some *Amerikanoi,* and a few

Serbs and Italians thrown in." The *mami* laughed hard, her bosom shaking. She had arrived in the early 1900s, the first Greek woman, and became the matriarch, no matter that she was still in her twenties. The midwife knew everything about the people in Greek Town.

While Marika sat, looking at her with listless eyes, she described the tobacco shop, the Arcadia, with admiration: white tile on the floor; shelves filled with Cuban cigars, American, Greek, and even Turkish cigarettes. "*Amerikanoi* buy there too. The Greek cigarettes have little cotton squares inside with painted-on Greek flags, or olive trees, the national hymn, all Greek things about our country. Yiannatakina—" here she stopped to describe how wonderfully plump the fat Cretan beauty's arms were. "Yiannatakina sewed hundreds of these squares together and made a beautiful table cover. She knows how to do fine sewing. She learned from the nuns." The midwife went on, talking about the shiny mahogany counter and polished brass spittoons in the closely packed, ten-foot-square little shop, which, when Marika saw it, she thought as grand as the midwife had said it was.

"Now listen, what we have to do," the midwife continued, shaking her finger at Marika, "is get those three bums married off. We have to be cunning. We have to have four eyes." The *mami* got up briskly. "I have to take care of the Evil Eye for a Serb's child, but first I'll help you set this pigpen in order. I would have sent my Hrisi, but I have her watching poor Kyriakoula. You remember, the poor wretch at your wedding. I don't know what kind of a baby's going to come out of her. When her man saw her get off the train, he tried to run away. He kept moaning, 'She doesn't look like her picture.' May he go to the devil!"

The *mami* and Marika washed the sink, scrubbed the encrusted wooden drainboard, and mopped the old linoleum floor. "Those stinking men," the *mami* said while they made up the double bed and cot in the second bedroom. "They never made a bed all the time they lived their bachelor life, now they'll expect to be waited on like Turkish *pashas*."

That night Andreas got on Marika, puffed, snorted, got off, and immediately fell asleep. Long after the train whistles were silent, Marika heard the icemen come in. Their gleeful voices came through the thin wall. "Try the new *poutana*," one of them said. "Her nipples are the biggest I ever saw. As big as oranges." Heracles did not come home at all.

II

[1914]

NINE MONTHS LATER Marika was scrubbing the men's long underwear and cursing Andreas, Heracles, and the two icemen. The *mami* had made a survey: she had questioned the Greek women in the neighborhood, the priest, and the men who came to her for folk cures. All said they knew village girls who would gladly become the wives of Heracles and the icemen. The three men rebuffed the midwife. Heracles said, "And what would I do with a village woman in America?" and the icemen, "Why do we need marriage? We're fine as we are." The midwife fumed and mimicked Heracles, " 'What would I do with a village woman? Can't you see how important I am?' " Then in a low, plodding voice like the icemen's, " 'Why do we need marriage? We have money in our pockets, We go to the *poutanes,* and Andreas's woman feeds us and washes our underwear.' " The midwife slapped the table. "We've got to find some other way."

Kettles and pans of water simmered on the coal stove sending steam to settle on the window and darken the kitchen. Marika had dragged a washtub to a heavy wooden bench and filled it with water from the kettles. One of the men's long underwear was stained; the men did not properly wipe themselves with the Montgomery Ward catalog in the privy. Her face grimaced and she wanted to wither the boarders with a piercing retort. She thought of refashioning the proverb "No matter how rich a peasant, the smell of manure sticks to his shoes," but it would not come out as she wanted. And she knew that if she did have the courage to speak her new proverb, the men might tell Andreas and he would hit her. She had to be careful and bide her time.

A ripping pain seared deep inside her. Water streamed down the inside of her thighs and legs. She left the washtub and ran to the fence, scattering chickens that had escaped the makeshift wire fence the icemen had made.

"Neighbor! Neighbor!" she called. The pretty Cretan woman came running, her thick eyebrows pulled together in alarm. "Neighbor! My time's come. The water broke! Get the *mami*." Marika hurried, swaying from side to side back into the kitchen, looked at the washtub, at the disorder about her. She did not know what to do. Then a wrenching pain shot through her and the midwife was screaming, "Get on the bed! On the bed!" Marika feared the pain would kill her. She begged the Virgin for mercy.

She lived. The baby, a boy, was oiled and swaddled in blankets, which had been warmed in the coal-stove oven. Marika, now the *lehona*, the new mother, remained in bed for the prescribed ten days while the midwife bullied Andreas and the boarders. The midwife sent Andreas on errands, using his Greek surname before it was cut at Castle Garden. "Mr. Kalogiannis, go down to *Tsaysy Penney* and get the *lehona* a robe. The *lehona* must be kept warm." "Mr. Kalogiannis, slaughter your plumpest chicken, I must make soup for the *lehona*. And get some butter and good meat. The *lehona* must build up her strength." Meekly Andreas followed the diminutive midwife's orders, and Marika knew the blessed relief of rest as she lay stretched out wearing an Indian blanket robe from J. C. Penney.

The Greek women in the neighborhood, now numbering eight,

came to pay their respects, drink demitasses of Turkish coffee, eat a baklava or powdered-sugar cookie, and put good-luck coins in the baby's basket. After the women left the house, Marika picked up the coins and hid them in the bottom of a humpbacked trunk that contained her meager dowry linens. She often had frightening dreams of being alone with her child in the silent house and of a dark figure looming in the doorway, watching her—a portent, she thought, that Andreas might die. She had to have money to raise her child in America. She must not go back to Greece a beggar.

As soon as she was up again, Andreas shouted at her when the food was not ready, when shirts were not ironed, when instead she was trying to bring the child's fever down with cool cloths and rubbing alcohol. The *mami* had heard about alcohol from a doctor she helped. After deliveries—for she was called by Italian, Yugoslav, and even Mormon women—she stopped to see her *lehona*. "When your man drives you out of your mind, enough to yank the holy oil of baptism out of you, take yourself to bed. Give yourself a rest while he twists his guts wondering if he will be left with an orphan child on his back." The midwife gave similar advice to all her patients, but not often, because they would face a big accumulation of washing and ironing when they got up from their beds.

Marika did not follow the midwife's advice. For the christening her neighbors helped bake pastries, happy with America's bountiful eggs and cream. Their husbands turned two lambs on spits in the backyard while they sang the dark, ominous songs of the treacherous Turks cutting off the heads of Greeks fallen in battle. The baby was baptized in the backyard, which, almost immediately after Marika entered the bachelor house, had been transformed by the icemen; they added the chicken coop, rabbit hutches nailed together with old boards, and a domed, mud-plastered bread oven on stilts. Marika had spaded and planted a garden against the side fence where Andreas went directly after work, chose a tomato, ate it, then walked into the kitchen with his muddy shoes.

At the ceremony the baby howled, his fury increasing after each of the three dunkings in the new washtub. He was christened Stavros by his fat, red-cheeked, smiling godfather, after himself. It was his prerogative to give whatever name he wished, disappointing Andreas and Marika: Andreas had wanted the baby named after his father, as was customary, and Marika had yearned that tradition would be magically overlooked and her firstborn would carry *her* father's name.

Marika held the hiccuping baby, his hair plastered with holy oil, his swollen eyes looking warily at the men in their black Sunday best who pressed silver dollars into his mother's hands. Later Marika handed Andreas half the money, secreting the rest in her apron pocket. When no one was about the following morning, she stored the silver dollars in her old trunk.

[1915]

TEN MONTHS LATER, Marika had another child, a boy named Solon; she would have two miscarriages before her next delivery; then another before her fourth child's birth. Two years after her marriage, she was still cooking and washing for Heracles and the icemen. All of the midwife's schemes to get them out of the house had failed. The *mami* had let it be known on her travels through Greek Town that men could catch mumps from children in whose houses they boarded and become impotent. Heracles and the icemen merely avoided going near little Stavros with his grotesque, swollen glands. She hinted that certain men who had been infected by prostitutes were being punished by God; the church did not approve of men going to *poutanes*. "What foolishness," the icemen said, when they heard of her talking such nonsense. "Everyone knows men have to go to them at least once every six weeks to relieve themselves or get sick from keeping it in."

Marika had a thought. After Solon, her second son, was born, the men slept in the cellar. In its dankness the two icemen had dug out space for three cots, cemented it, and made a windowless room. Marika thought she would let the irrigation water from the garden flood the cellar room. On second thought she knew it would not work. Andreas would know that she, or little Stavros who helped with the irrigating, had let the water run into the cellar. Then she could be beaten, or—worse—her son would be.

[1917]

THE MIDWIFE AND Marika thought that when the Americans entered the war to fight the Germans in 1917, the three bachelors would be taken into the army and the problem would be solved. Heracles sobbed when his draft notice came, started attending liturgies, pledged money to the Vizas lodge for the care of injured mine and mill workers, and hardly ate. With tears running down his cheeks, he looked at Andreas's children sadly and no longer barked at them.

Marika had more concerns. The Greek import store ran out of olive oil: ships were needed for the war. A repellent corn oil took its place. Sugar and coffee were scarce. American women came to the doors of houses in Greek Town and gave little speeches about saving bacon grease, metal, and rags. Marika and her neighbors had no idea what the Americans were saying, except that it had to do with the war, but they nodded, said, "Come in house. *Kafé?*" The women refused, some with grace, others with a haughty smile. "*Mormonoi* don't drink coffee, tea, wine, or liqueurs," Andreas said. "Remember that and don't make a fool of yourself."

Heracles was rejected by the army for having flat feet and immediately became his old self. The icemen were cheerful about their draft notices, but they were rejected for illiteracy. Marika thought it was her fate to take care of the three men for the rest of her life, yet she continued her urgent appeals to the Virgin, especially toward the end of her pregnancies.

[1918]

LABOR PAINS STRUCK her as she bent over the washboard, heavy with her fourth full-term child. She looked at the children, listlessly hitting wooden spoons on pans within a fence she had made of chairs placed on their sides. With her hands holding up her womb, she hurried to the backyard fence and called her neighbor to send someone for the midwife. Back in the house she ran as best she could to the frightened, crying children. She filled several bottles of milk for them and dribbled a teaspoonful of whiskey into each one. Then she picked up the youngest—not yet old enough to crawl—and put her in the crib on her side, rested a bottle on a folded dishtowel, and pushed the nipple into the quivering, unhappy mouth. Again in the kitchen, she lifted Solon and placed him at the bottom of the crib with his bottle. She put the oldest child Stavros on a small cot.

As the pains came faster, Marika stripped the sheets and blankets off her bed and covered the mattress with a thick layer of Greek-language newspapers, saved both for lighting the stove and for her deliveries. With the midwife screaming at her to get on the bed, she again went into the children's room and stood in front of an icon set on a shelf above Stavros's cot. She lighted the votive taper that floated on a layer of olive oil in a red glass, crossed herself, said the Lord's Prayer, begged the Virgin to spare her so that she could raise her children, gave them a last look, and hurried to undress and get into bed.

Andreas, called from work, tried to read a newspaper in the sparse living room. He was sweat-soaked with foreboding: if his woman died, how would he take care of the children? Neighbors helped during the day of Marika's labor, but if something happened to her? Marika had no family in America. He paced the cold linoleum floor and ventured near the bedroom where the *mami* was shouting, "Push! Push! You've got a baby in there, not a pea!"

Andreas stood at the side of the door where the *mami* could not see him. The men respected her because of her black satchel, like a proper doctor's, in which she kept small bottles of her folk cures: Spanish fly, flaxseed, the makings of mustard plasters, olive oil, cloves, and herbs. Greek Town men knew the *mami* should not be bothered when she was caring for a *lehona.*

"Push!" the *mami* commanded. Straining greatly, Marika complied, and the baby cAme out—a girl.

While washing Marika's hair and cooking the special foods to make up for the blood she had lost, the *mami* alternately cajoled Andreas or lectured him by using the old word *filotimo,* honor. "Mr. Kalogiannis, you must think of your *filotimo.* You must help your woman. We live in a foreign country now. Women don't have mothers, sisters, and cousins to help them. Do you want your woman to become an invalid? No! You do not! Then do some work around the kitchen. Fill the glasses with wine. Cut the bread. Hold the baby and give it its bottle. Those little things, Mr. Kalogiannis, show a man has *filotimo.*" She threw him a dark look from under her eyebrows. "Of course, when those boarders get married and out of the house, it'll be easier for her."

Andreas leaned his head sideways in a cowed gesture. At the same time he glanced at the Superior Ice Company calendar on the wall next to the stove to see how many more days remained of the *mami's* service. The only bad part of Marika's pregnancies for him was having the midwife in the house for ten days each time. He was now the father of four children: Stavros, Solon, Penelope, and the new baby girl.

On the eleventh day after the fourth birth, the *mami* finished her duties to the *lehona.* She had put beans on to soak the night before, dispelled the Evil Eye that had struck the baby with incessant crying, and checked the big earthenware crocks, where Marika had stored pastries she had baked before the baby's birth to serve visitors. The *mami* gave a cry. Only a few pieces of *baklava* remained in one crock. She grabbed Solon by the ear and forced him to admit he had been eating the pastries when her back was turned. Marika reached for the *blasti,* the broomstick she used for rolling out sheets of *filo* dough. She tried to whack Solon, then three years old, but missed. Solon escaped to the back porch, where he climbed onto a backless chair and sniffed dried oregano suspended from the ceiling. A few sniffs and Solon's face swelled with hives. He ran into the kitchen screaming and Marika clutched her hair in hysteria, forgetting his pilfering of the visitors' *baklava*. The *mami* whacked Solon herself, made compresses of flaxseed for his hives, and told him the next time he smelled the oregano, she would force castor oil down his throat.

At the door the midwife said, "Remember, my golden one, not to go beyond your yard. You have three more weeks before the forty days are up. Don't forget and bring bad luck to your house. Go to church and be cleansed and you'll get your strength back. Send Stavros for what you need." Then she left, in time for another delivery in the neighborhood.

The children clustered about Marika, even Solon, scratching the hives on his cheeks. The baby wailed. The basket of men's shirts needing ironing stood in a corner—the *mami* would not iron. Marika whispered, "My little Virgin, couldn't Stavros have been born a girl to help me with the cooking and the ironing." She sighed, told Stavros to watch the children, and began preparing the bean soup.

Andreas was the first to come home. He tasted the bean soup and said in a stern voice that allowed no defense, "Something's missing. Salt or olive oil."

Marika was holding the crying baby. "Why must the boarders still live with us?" she asked, her mouth trembling. "Why can't they live in a boardinghouse or in a bachelor house like other countrymen?"

Andrea's peaked eyebrows rose. "Why? The icemen pay us twenty-five dollars a month! Twenty-five dollars a month each." His voice rose. "It adds up. Just yesterday I bought an old house. Someday it will be worth plenty. Builders are tearing down the old houses and putting up offices. You'll see. It's for our children's future. Do you want the children to work with their hands, like common laborers? Is that what you want?"

Marika turned to the beans and tasted a spoonful, looking ashamed. That night at the kitchen table Andreas announced his purchase and said he bought the house for eight hundred dollars. The icemen's eyes widened, praised him for being smart, a good businessman. Andreas had paid four hundred dollars for the old house and large lot, but he doubled the price in telling about it. He had set the precedent early: whether he bought or sold property, he always doubled the price. His brother Heracles knew the correct sales price—they held a joint bank account—but he said nothing, merely smiled, already dressed to go out for the evening in a new gray suit.

Andreas looked at Heracles and scowled. "How many suits do you need? You should have bought brown. Brown doesn't show stains, like gray."

Heracles, who called himself "Harry," smirked, ran a palm over his sleek, pomaded hair, and said, "Brown's for men like you. You don't know how to live. Gray's for me."

Andreas jerked himself up, sending a splash of soup on the table's oilcloth. The children looked on, wide-eyed. Marika held the baby in one arm and, standing next to the high chair, dipped bread into the bean soup to feed Penelope.

Andreas was shouting, "*I* don't know how to live? Who sent you money all the years I was riding freight cars all over America looking for work? Who sent you to get two more years of school in Pyrgos after you finished the village school? And I sent enough so you could eat *good!* What was I eating? Canned beans and dry onions! I slaved in a slaughterhouse. You wouldn't have lasted a day in that filth! I laid rails! Dug coal! And the Americans hated us! Two times, if I hadn't found a coffeehouse and got help, I would have starved to death!"

Andreas leaned far over the table and glared at Heracles. "You were never hungry! I brought you here! You found the table set! You came straight off the boat, got on a train, and came right here! I bought you a new suit that very first day. I sent you to the nuns to learn English. You never knew hardship. I was a little boy, eight years old when our mother died and our father married again. I took some bread and a bottle of water and walked, WALKED, two days and nights to get to our mother's brothers in Patras. Don't tell me I'm a miser who doesn't know how to live, you *bastardello!* Sonofabitch!" Andreas sat down, huffing, his face red, and finished eating the bean soup with smacking noises. The icemen were smiling at the entertainment.

Heracles put on a straw boater and said he was going to the coffeehouse. Marika told Stavros to bring coal for the stove. Stavros was nearly five and had been bringing in coal since he was three, at first one lump at a time, but now in a bucket. As he walked from the coalshed between the chicken pen and the rabbit hutches, he held the bucket with both hands, his elbows like outstretched featherless wings. One of the icemen walked toward the privy, pulling down his suspenders. "Good boy, Stavros," he said, smiling, showing his big, yellow teeth. "Can't you open the door for the boy?" Marika wanted to shrill at him. Instead she called to Stavros to feed the chickens and the rabbits.

"Why doesn't Solon do it?"

Marika gave her head an impatient shake. "I don't know where he ran off to. Go feed them."

"He never does anything. I'm the one who has to do everything. He just pretends he's sick."

"Leave me alone!"

Stavros threw grain at the chickens, sprinting toward him in their small pen, then pushed carrot tops into the rabbit cages and watched their twitching noses a moment. He returned to the kitchen in time to watch the icemen count their day's cash on the cleared-off oilcloth. Solon sneaked in. The icemen made piles of their coins

—the few quarters, the many dimes, nickels, and pennies. Every few evenings, they would give the children a penny, and at times a nickel. While the counting went on with the adding-up in a dirty pocket notebook, the children waited, looking on to see if that night they would get a nickel, a penny, or nothing. If they got a penny or a nickel, they ran to the Greek Town stores for candy. They got nothing that night.

After the money counting, Andreas and the icemen sat around the table, singing of the treacherous Turks catching the guerrilla deacon Diakos and roasting him alive. Marika sent Stavros to guide the irrigation water into the garden. She had planted rows of spinach, potatoes, squash, beets, and tomatoes. In the dusk, all over Greek Town children were playing. Stavros heard the high-pitched voices of his friends Pericles and Lefterios. The first-grade teacher had changed their names to Perry, Lefty, and Steve on the first day of school. When she found they did not know enough English, she sent them home with notes to learn it and return next year. Neither Andreas nor Marika paid attention to the note. Marika still shouted when the children used an English word: "In the house, Greek! English you can learn in school!"

It was dark when Steve put the hoe away in the woodshed. Solon was on the floor looking though a Montgomery Ward catalog; his sisters were asleep; his father was smoking a cigar in the living room and talking to a Mormon who wanted to buy the empty lot next to the Railroad Hotel, the biggest property Andreas owned. Andreas puffed away and asked the Mormon questions. The bald Mormon leaned back from the clouds of blue smoke.

Marika was talking to herself as she prepared a tray of pastries for the visitor. "He has an office. Why does he bring people to his house to talk business? Why does he torment me? My little Virgin, help me get rid of those three. Strike them dead in that cellar room. No, no, just do something, *I beg You.* Also make him use his office to talk with people, instead of telling them to come to the house."

Andreas's office was a cubbyhole in the Railroad Hotel. He had been using his tobacco shop, the Arcadia, as his office, but he decided to lease it to a village friend. He had accumulated a considerable amount of rundown property, which took all his time to oversee, and Heracles had refused to stand behind the cash register—like a waiter, he said. Andreas and Heracles had bought the Railroad Hotel with a five-hundred-dollar down payment given them by a labor agent for helping break a copper strike in 1912. They had tied all the shotguns they could get to the tops of empty coal cars. The Cretan strikers guarding the mines thought the handful of scabs inside the cars was an army and they slunk off into the sagebrush.

Marika finished the forty days after the new baby's birth, then went to church and was read over by the priest and freed of the biblical uncleanliness. She put Penelope and the new baby in the old wicker baby buggy and, with Steve and Solon trotting on either side of it, left Greek Town for Main Street and the great *Woolwortha*, the ten-cent store. Steve translated for her—she did not realize he knew only a few English words. She knew several herself. The *mami* had taught her to say to the clerks, "More *chip*, more *chip*," and "How much for the *cesh*?" Steve had told her the words were *cheap* and *cash*, and Marika had repeated *chip*, *cesh*. The way he hung his head made Marika think that he was ashamed of her.

Penelope and the as-yet unbaptized and unnamed baby were lulled by the swaying of the buggy, and Marika let Steve and Solon gaze at the Woolworth's marbles in little display boxes. They spoke English words: "Cat eyes," "Steelie," "Agate," "Flint." They counted the pennies and nickels given them by their godfathers and put them on the counter. When they arrived back in Greek Town, other boys ran to see their new marbles. Marika allowed Steve to play a few games in the backyard, made hard and smooth as clay by the gray washwater she threw over it daily.

[1920]

STEVE WAS EXACTLY six years old when he was first sent to the two-
story Railroad Hotel and told to sweep out the rooms on the top
floor. On the ground floor were the Olympus Cafe, Theodore's
Shoeshine and Hat Cleaning and Blocking Shop, and the ten-by-
thirteen-foot office used by Andreas and Heracles. On his first day,
Steve forgot Uncle Harry's ("Don't call me Uncle Heracles!") warning to work quietly because some of the men were on the graveyard shift at the railyards. He had to hold the big broom far down
on the handle and trying to position the dust pan under it, dropped
both with a clatter. Before he could pick them up, Uncle Harry
bounded up the stairs and gave him a backhand that slammed him
against the wall. When he stood up, Uncle Harry hit him on the
other side of his face and he fell back again.

[1921]

MEN CAME IN and out of the Railroad Hotel. Steve tried to work
quietly in the small waiting room with its three spindly, dusty rubber plants. The men talked about labor agents, strikes, incidents in
Wyoming, Montana, Nevada, and Idaho, and the bad times when
they were new in the country and had been beaten by railroad detectives and cheated out of wages by straw bosses because they were
Greek. Three of the men were permanent renters. Steve learned
their histories in the evenings at the dinner table: one used the name
Augustine Sanchez because he had come through Mexico illegally;
Tsimblis had lost all his savings to a Greek who had sold him worthless Nevada gold-mine stock; and Giannis had fled Greece over a
vendetta. They sometimes gave Steve a nickel. On their namedays,
his mother Marika sent them a plate of *baklava*.

While Steve worked, he heard the far-off voices of children playing. He heard them again while he sat in Greek school in the church

basement, dreaming, hoping it would be light enough to throw a few balls with Lefty and Perry before dusk deepened and it would be hard to see. If dusk had turned into evening, they played kick-the-can down the alleys of Greek Town, maneuvering around battered tubs of coal ashes, rusty bedsprings, and cardboard boxes of tin cans and broken glass. The yeasty scent of bread baked in the outdoor ovens was still in the air. Sometimes they chased little girls from beyond their neighborhood, down alleys, and once Lefty was able to pull down a girl's pants before she squealed and ran off.

His father never gave Steve a dime for cleaning the Railroad Hotel, although once in a while he would take him to the Olympus for a creme soda. He sat at the counter and took a long time drinking the pleasantly fizzing soda while the engines in the railyards hissed with steam shooting through their great black wheels, their labored chuggings turned into rhythmic clippings, and billowing gray-black smoke rose to sting his eyes.

When Steve finished his sweeping, he stood in the cramped, dark little office and hoped his father would take him along to see how repairs were going. It was not enough for Andreas that he telephone workers to repair a step, unplug stopped-up plumbing, or replace a broken window, he had to go himself and hover over the workmen. "Eh!" Uncle Harry looked up from a ledger one day, a cigarette drooping from one corner of his scorn-quirked mouth. "What do they need you for?" Andreas jammed his hat on his head. "Because I don't want to be cheated, you fool! *I* don't throw money away!" With a lofty rise of his eyebrows, Uncle Harry adjusted his black shirt protectors and went back to the ledgers.

A few times, Steve accompanied his father to a Greek fruit and vegetable market. The owner telephoned Andreas when something special had been brought in to the Growers Market a few blocks away, especially figs, which Andreas and Marika liked. Figs reminded them of Greece, they said, eating them at the kitchen table in the midst of a chaos of dirty pans and dishes on the drainboard. Next to the Greek's fruit stand was one owned by a Japanese.

Steve looked at the beautiful displays, pyramids of apples and oranges, grapes in little hills, and the vegetables all washed and piled carefully. But the Japanese's displays were better. Steve longed just to stand and look at the stacked shiny-purple eggplants, both round and long, leafy stalks that were like miniature fairy bushes, next to pale, velvety orange fruit or perhaps it was some kind of tomato—he did not know which.

Several times Andreas went to the Japanese farm and told Steve to come along. Steve ran from the dry stink of the hotel rooms that even the open windows of summer could not clean out. They drove in their canvas-topped Ford to the outskirts of the city. Long rows of green converged in the distance, the irrigation streams that ran between them catching glints of the sun's rays. In sheds at one end of the farm the mother and children of the family washed the vegetables, trimmed off wilted and browned leaves, tied them with string, and layered them in wooden crates.

Steve did not know that the peacefulness there came from the order in that greenness, and twice when his father was in the sheds buying lugs of strawberries for jam-making and tomatoes to add to his mother's for still more tomato paste, the *belde,* she made in autumn, he took off his shoes and stockings and put his dirty feet into the gently flowing irrigation stream. His father might have scolded him if he saw him; it all depended on his mood or some kind of sense of what was or was not proper. Still, Steve did not have to worry that his father would catch him: that deep, heavy voice resonated in the sheds. Andreas seemed to think that if he shouted the Japanese farmer would understand what he was saying. When Andreas stepped outside, his voice boomed and gave Steve time to pull his stockings onto his wet feet and tie up his ankle-high canvas shoes, red when they were new, but now blackened.

After the two men put the lugs in the back seat of the car, Andreas would stand at the side of the road and in silence look at the green fields. With his hat set low on his head, in his rolled-up shirt sleeves, his belt cinched above his pot of a stomach, he surveyed the

long, green rows. Steve thought about the green fields while cleaning the Railroad Hotel; he thought of them while falling asleep.

Steve did not always find it good going with his father to business places. His father walked fast, looking angry, especially so when
he hurried down a West Side street one day to the Athens Bakery.
The baker kept saying, "I will not sign a lease on Tuesday." When
Andreas insisted, the fat little man screamed, "It's Tuesday, the day
the Turks became our masters! How could you forget our holy city
Constantinople fell on that day! No one does business on Tuesday!"

"You farting pig!" Andreas shouted. "This is America! Things
like that don't count in America, you sonofabitch horned bastard!"

"No! Only money counts for you!" the fat man shouted back
and flicked the lease away as if it were something dirty. Andreas
began to stamp out of the side door, then turned around and stalked
out of the front door through which they had come. It was bad
luck, Marika often said, to come in through one door and leave by
another.

[1921]

Marika would always remember that evening because she had an
answer to one-third of her prayers. She cleared off the kitchen table
while Andreas, his arms flailing about, described his latest encounter
with the owner of the Athens Bakery. The icemen smiled toothily,
nodding their enjoyment. Heracles was reading the *Atlantis,* the
Greek-language newspaper from New York, when he gave a shout
and jumped up. With the newspaper in one hand, the telephone receiver in the other, he turned the crank on the new wall-telephone.
"What the devil!" Andreas yelled while Heracles asked the operator
to get him the number of the *Atlantis* in New York City. Heracles's
face was a furious red when no one answered. "There is a two-hour
difference in time," the operator said. "Try tomorrow."

Heracles had read an advertisement placed by a woman refugee from the Smyrna disaster of 1921—the Turks had herded the Greeks and Armenians from all over Asia Minor down to the sea. The next morning, early, Heracles was shouting into the telephone as if his voice had to reach New York: "Yes, yes, I am calling about Miss Myrsini! Yes, I am well established! I tell you, very well established! Ask Mr. Stagopoulos, the vice-consul here! I know him very well! I'm not asking for a dowry! Yes, yes, I know women with dowries don't come here! Ask the priest here! He'll tell you I'm an honorable man!"

The baby was rubbing her eyes and murmuring her discontent and Marika was preparing a bottle of milk for her. She added three drops of a new medicine called "paragoric," which her neighbors said was more effective than whiskey and acted quickly. Steve was holding the baby, who pulled at her ears and began to howl. "Shut that baby up!" Heracles screamed. Again on the telephone, he continued heaping praise on himself.

Marika told Steve to take the baby into the *sala*, the small front room. There, his rubber-soled shoes scuffing over the linoleum, Steve walked the angry baby around the room, between the square, wooden-framed sofa with its cracked brown-leather upholstery and a narrow table, covered with a white crocheted cloth, under the window. His parents' wedding picture was set on the table with the photographer's name written in white in English. A moment later, Heracles and the two icemen trooped through the *sala*, laughing, the icemen nudging Heracles as if they were boys at play.

Back in the kitchen, Steve sat on a chair and fed the baby Georgia the bottle of milk. Marika talked to herself while she scraped dishes and cleaned the kitchen: "Thank You, my little Virgin!" she whispered, looking upwards. "I'll finally be rid of him with his airs and his demands. Another woman can scrub his clothes and cook his food. Now help me find a way to get rid of the icemen. Help the *mami* and me get them out of that cellar room.

"We might become friends, this Myrsini and me. We could bake the nameday pastries together, make *belde* in autumn, roll out filo.

I'll be kind to her, a refugee. Her family has lost everything to those Turks. She's searching for a home. The name 'Myrsini,' though, is aristocratic. In the village I worked in the mayor's fields, my little Virgin. His wife's name was Myrsini. Ahh, my little Virgin, Thank You. Thank You for sending this refugee to take Heracles off my hands."

III

[1922]

THE WOMAN CAME immediately—thin, dark, wearing a velvet hat with swooping iridescent blue-green feathers. Andreas, with a cigar in the corner of his mouth, led the way over the new cement walk the icemen had put down a few days earlier—they enjoyed working with cement. Andreas carried two round hatboxes and gave a lift of his eyebrows to the icemen, Marika, and the children gathered on the porch. Marika frowned at him, not knowing what the lifted eyebrows meant. The woman walked behind Andreas carefully, her head up, one black-gloved hand holding up her gray silk skirt as if it were trailing over refuse. Heracles followed, perspiring, struggling with two bulging bags, his face red and puffed.

With her hands folded at her waist, Marika ventured forward. Her voice wavering, she spoke the traditional words, "You've come well."

The woman murmured the customary answer, "I find you well," and looked at Marika in her best dress, a navy blue with white collar she had bought at J. C. Penney, especially for the occasion.

Heracles put down the bags and waved Marika and the children aside. The woman walked through the open door and stood on the square of brown linoleum patterned with yellow roses—also new, the smell sharp. Her almond-shaped black eyes looked deeply set in her sockets because they were small. She quickly took in the cold, potbellied stove in one corner, the sofa, stiff with the cracked leather upholstery, and the several mismatched chairs against the windows. The kitchen table, now set in the center of the room, overpowered it. On the table Marika had smoothed a linen cloth she had woven on a loom while still a girl. The dishes and glasses were new; Marika had taken Steve with her to Woolworth's to buy them. The strange woman then turned an indifferent gaze on the children. Marika had dressed them in their church clothes and had used a curling iron on Penelope's short hair.

Marika asked Myrsini to follow her into the girls' room. They had to move sideways between the table and sofa. Rattling on, Marika explained that the girls would sleep in the kitchen on the boys' cot. In summer, the cot was moved to the back porch. For now, the boys would sleep on the floor of the living room. The woman made no response, carefully removed the tortoise pins from the splendid hat, and arranged it with the feathers spread out on the white, crocheted bedspread that until that day had graced Marika's own bed. She asked where the *apohoritirion* was.

On returning from the privy with her upper lip curled, the woman washed her hands at the kitchen sink wordlessly while Heracles waited, his own hands making washing motions. Myrsini wiped her hands on the towel Marika held out to her. She then followed Heracles into the living room and the dinner began. Marika brought out platters and bowls: rabbit stewed in wine and cloves; chicken oreganon; rice *pilafi;* spinach *pita;* feta cheese; Kalamata olives; and bread warm from the outdoor oven.

Andreas talked loudly, asked about the ship's passage, while everyone else was silent, all, boarders, children, Marika, and Heracles glancing furtively at the stranger, Heracles' soon-to-be wife. That day Steve had picked the first tomatoes from the garden and Marika had quartered them and sprinkled them with olive oil and oregano. The strange woman looked at the stem ends as if they affronted her and with dainty motions began to cut them off. Vivaciously she began speaking about the tomatoes in Smyrna. "Big, juicy, none like them! The grapes, the figs! Achh, Smyrna! You could smell the lemon blossoms all over the city!"

Between the woman's declarations on Smyrna, no one spoke; only chewing and bone-sucking sounds were heard. The icemen smacked their lips even louder than usual, unaware of the stranger's eyebrows lifted in repugnance. The smacking resonated in the crowded room. Steve and Solly looked at each other, snickering, then coughing to disguise it. The chewing and smacking noises went on. At a glare from Andreas and Marika's biting her bent index finger that promised punishment to come, Steve stumbled out of the room, coughing falsely, with one eye on his father's big, powerful right hand.

The pattern had been set. Whenever Myrsini came into a room, a silence followed. She lifted her head in disdain at everyone, but particularly at Heracles. He ran to find a house. "Brick. Six rooms and a bathroom inside," he said proudly at the kitchen table. The house was not in Greek Town, Heracles said, leaning his head toward Myrsini, but not looking her in the eyes. "It's in the good part of town." He ran to buy furniture, to get water and telephone service, to make arrangements for the wedding. Myrsini said she would not step into the house until it was cleaned and painted and the yard taken care of to look like decent people lived there, not gypsies. Two unemployed laborers were recruited from the Open Heart coffeehouse to follow her orders.

In the *grafio*, the office, the cash register dinged throughout the day. Heracles went around puffed up: *he* was not marrying a village woman; *his* wife was educated, he said. Late one night, after Myrsini had made token gestures at helping Marika prepare the wedding pastries and then gone to bed, Heracles came up from the cellar room and examined them. Marika held the youngest, Georgia, in one arm and with her free hand sifted powdered sugar over the butter *kourambiedhes*. Heracles looked at the platters critically and then at whimpering Georgia. "You'll see the kind of children I'm going to have," he said. "My children are going to be refined, aristocratic."

After the wedding, pictures were taken outside the church. Heracles had hold of his bride's upper arm; her head was turned away from him. Then Andreas drove the bride and groom in the new family Studebaker to the Acropolis *Kaffenion* for the wedding dinner. Marika and the children walked. Myrsini looked about the crowded room, her black eyebrows loftily arched as if she might recognize someone she knew. She knew no one. The entire Greek community had come: labor agents, the priest, the newspaper editor, mine workers and mill laborers, small children clustered about their mothers, the midwife, and a newly arrived doctor. Heracles had brought in cases of Canadian whiskey; Steve, Solly, and their neighbors Lefty and Perry studied the wooden boxes in the back room. They knew all about Prohibition. The Feds raided Greek Town regularly. Steve's godfather had made whiskey until he had been caught as an illegal alien and deported. He left his copper still in the woodshed. He'd be back, he said, and told his godson Steve to watch over it.

Steve became Aunt Myrsini's servant. He was always busy: cleaning the Railroad Hotel, helping his mother, and, especially, running errands for Aunt Myrsini. Uncle Harry sent him to buy her groceries, to mail her stream of letters to Greece, to sweep her porch, and to carry trash to the back alley where it would be picked up. She never said a thank-you, only an "All right," by which he knew he was dismissed.

On Uncle Harry's nameday, Myrsini told Steve's mother that the children could not come to the dinner; there was not enough room for them. With a dramatic sigh, Marika at the backyard chickenwire fence, repeated this outrage to her neighbor, voracious for news of the Turkissa, as Greek Town had immediately named her. The news raged through the neighborhood. This woman, this refugee with her nose up in the air, did not welcome children into her house. All Greek Town children ran in and out of each other's houses, but this woman would not allow children in her house. Steve was left at home to watch the younger children.

The midwife often came both to tell and to hear the latest about the Turkissa. Georgia continued to be fretful, and the *mami* used the baby's misery as an excuse in the event Andreas walked in. "She doesn't iron Heracles' shirts," Marika said. "She sends my Stavros to poor Pappina to wash and iron them." They shook their heads in wonder. The midwife always had a sharp word about Heracles and his Turkissa: "Eh, Andreas, so your brother and his woman have a toilet inside the house. It's a miracle. They're so rich, they don't have to go out in the dark to shit."

Not long afterwards Andreas had lumber delivered to the backyard and watched while two carpenters built a lean-to that became an indoor bathroom. The icemen were appalled: "It's disgraceful. A toilet in the same place where food is cooked!" Marika hoped this would send the icemen to pack their cardboard suitcases and leave the cellar room. They stayed and grumbled, and still used the outhouse until Andreas ordered it torn down and filled up with dirt. Marika planted potatoes where it had stood.

The midwife needled Heracles, too. The Turkissa was pregnant and was going to an American doctor, a man! The midwife knew Dr. Hancock; she helped him with deliveries. He was a small man who wore pince-nez and had wavy hair parted in the center and combed sideways into wings. "Heracles, be careful that your baby isn't born wearing eyeglasses," she chortled, and hurried away from Heracles' curses.

Now Marika had another reason to beg respite from the Virgin. Every morning she lit a fresh taper at the icon and complained: "Why can't You relieve me of those two? That tyrant Heracles with his hands in the *grafio's* *cesh registra* and his miserable woman with her airs? Why must I think of her comforts? I'm forced to tolerate them

36   HELEN PAPANIKOLAS

because he's my husband's brother and I have to act like their servant because I'm alone in this foreign country. If my man dies, I'll have to turn to him and he'll be hard on my children. Don't You see that it's not right? Do something. Please, now! And I still have those icemen in the cellar. Please, find them wives or get them out of my house! I beg You, my little Virgin!"

After finishing her complaints and wiping her eyes on her apron, Marika sometimes went into the kitchen and took out one of the bowls of yogurt she made weekly. She called Steve to leave off irrigating the garden, or feeding the rabbits or the chickens. She covered the bowl with a dishtowel. "Take this to Aunt Myrsini and be careful not to drop it," she would say with a grim set of her pale lips.

"Don't take on like a miserable, worthless woman," the *mami* said. "Use your cunning. Fight back."

And so, around the kitchen table, the air heavy with fumes of hot olive oil and tobacco smoke, the family and the icemen ate stews and bean and lentil soups, and Marika would remark on backyard gossip: "Mrs. Mavrakos saw Heracles' wife on the street. She said she looked like a very rich woman. She was wearing a velvet hat with red silk roses and her shoes were black velvet with straps. All the latest fashion—." She finished with a nod of her head as if she knew what the latest in fashions were.

Andreas grumbled. His response to the gossip was to build another lean-to on the house: a bedroom for the boys. When Heracles, resenting Andreas's use of the family Studebaker, bought a new car, Marika said, "Mrs. Mavrakos said, 'Your man and his brother must be making a lot of money. My man says Heracles' new car is very expensive.'" Andreas banged down his glass of wine, spraying it on the oilcloth. "I don't want you talking with those witch neighbors about my brother!" A week later, he had a lean-to built to serve as a dining room. Now the house had a kitchen, living room, dining room, front bedroom, a bathroom, and two nine-by-twelve rooms for the children.

[1923]

THE CASH REGISTER banged open more often when Myrsini gave birth to Constantine. As soon as he began walking, she dressed him in short pants, pongee silk shirts she sewed herself, and flowing red silk ties. Marika sighed, "I wish I could dress my sons like their Constantine." Andreas huffed: "He looks like a little assless school-teacher." Myrsini let Constantine's hair curl to his shoulders and then had a barber cut it, but not above his earlobes. Every spring Andreas shaved Steve's and Solly's hair to make it grow back strong—Myrsini cackled at that. Constantine wore shoes all summer long. Steve and Solly went barefoot until school began in fall.

[1924]

STEVE SAW CONSTANTINE almost every day. He would be sitting on the porch steps when Steve returned from errands for Myrsini. Steve had early noticed that Constantine's mother tightened her lips when he called her "Aunt Myrsini." He hung his head when she gave him orders.

Aunt Myrsini never offered Steve a pastry when he brought the groceries or a bundle of greens from his mother's garden. Marika cleaned and washed the greens and tied them in a dishtowel. Myrsini —the Witch, as Steve, now ten, nicknamed her—took them from him without thanks and set the bundle on the white-tiled drain-board. He knew without being told that he should never venture farther than the back porch.

Several times Steve glimpsed another refugee woman, visiting Myrsini, sitting at the kitchen table, crying. Greek Town had talked about the woman's marriage: She had married a man who could barely write his name in Greek. One day Steve saw the woman had a black eye and he brought this news to the kitchen table as a gift. "He brags in the coffeehouse that he beats her when she puts on airs," Andreas said with a decisive shake of his head, implying Uncle Harry should do the same if he had any sense.

Whenever Steve returned from Myrsini's house, Marika questioned him: what was she doing? was someone visiting her? was there anything new in the house? As Steve was not allowed inside and knew little, she scowled and muttered.

On the next Saint Andrew's feast day, when visitors came to offer their respects to Andreas, Marika brought out several kinds of pastries and demitasses of Turkish coffee. As she handed a plate to Myrsini, she said, "Of course, my pastries can't compare with yours. Someday will you tell me how to make walnut cake?" Myrsini shrugged her shoulders. "There's nothing to it. Any cookbook will tell you how." Myrsini with her black-dyed hair, mascara on her eyelashes, and lipsticked mouth went on eating, her little fingers daintily crooked.

There was a momentary silence: everyone in the room knew that Marika could not read or write. Marika continued serving the guests. The conversation turned to whether the men should join the Greek American Progressive Association, the GAPA, or the American Hellenic Educational Progressive Association, the AHEPA. Andreas thought they should join the GAPA because the lodge wanted to keep the Greek language and customs. Heracles said they should join the AHEPA because it would be better for business with the Americans. The lodge conducted its meetings in English to show the Americans that Greeks could be good American citizens. And it would quiet the Ku Klux Klan that didn't like immigrants. Andreas gave in, lifting his arms and letting them drop. Andreas and Heracles joined the AHEPA and would take turns going to the national conventions. One or the other would always be left to watch over the business. Andreas said he was the older and he would go first. Heracles sulked.

A crowd of boys from Greek Town trooped after Steve, the oldest, to the Denver & Rio Grande Western depot to see Andreas off. He was wearing a new suit and over it a light-gray overcoat. He had set a new, gray fedora sideways on his head, as Heracles wore his hats, and held a big cigar between his thick fingers. At the platform, he waved and then took a seat and waved from the window. The children jumped about, reveling in noisy excitement, and cheered when the train spurted steam between the great black wheels and turned slowly out of the railyards. Solly and the neighborhood boys formed a snake line with Steve in the lead, their hands on the shoulders in front of them, and choo-chooed all the way back to Greek Town.

Two days after his father had gone, Steve came upon his mother on her knees before her open humpbacked trunk. He stood unmoving in the doorway. Marika reached into the trunk. He saw her face in the dresser mirror, a look of anguish pulling her forehead into deep lines. Then with a look of firm decision, she closed the lid and struggled up. Steve hurried into the kitchen, where he was supposed to be tending the younger children. Pulling on her hands, his mother told him to come with her to Uncle Harry's house. She put Georgia, whining, on her hip and threatened Solly to watch Penny or he would eat wood. Solly was terrified of the *blasti,* the broomstick, even though he seldom felt its blows. He was too fast for Marika and she was so busy she often forgot about his latest escapade.

Uncle Harry saw them coming. He was sitting on the porch in the dusk and looked angry, as if he had been put out of the house. "What is it?" he asked, his mouth surly.

Marika stood in front of him with one arm around Georgia, the other hand pulling down the straight gingham dress she had sewed herself. "I need two dollars of the money Andreas gave you to keep for me while he's away."

Heracles peered at her and pursed his lips. "And why do you need two dollars?"

"Andreas forgot to pay the cheesemaker and he told me he had to have the money today."

"I won't give you the money. Let the cheesemaker come back when the man of the house is at home."

Marika raised her voice. "Why should you be in charge of my man's money?" Myrsini came to the doorway and looked at Marika.

"Because I've got balls."

"Donkeys have balls too!" Marika shouted and she turned down the path with Georgia bouncing and screaming on her hip. Steve half-ran to keep up with her. Marika's hands were shaking. Steve held his palms on either side of his head as if to protect it from blows.

When Andreas returned from the convention, Marika was silent. She looked at him from time to time, but Andreas was too intent on telling them about the convention. It was a waste of time and he would never go again. "All of them all dressed up in *tookcidos,* talking English to each other. Most of them with American wives. What nonsense to put in the constitution that they had to talk in English. Trying to act like Americans! Doctors and lawyers and peasants who've made big money! They wouldn't stop to give you a look, they're so swell-headed! One of them told a story about a Greek from a village in our parts and made fun of the way he spoke. You go, Heracles, if you want to! Go like a beggar with your hat in your hand! The horned *bastardellos!*"

Heracles beamed, his lips smug, faintly taunting. "You betcha!" he said in English, then in Greek, "My wife should mingle with the better class. Who has she got to talk to here? The foul-mouthed midwife? Who?"

"The *moderna,*" Andreas said contemptuously after Heracles had gone. "Heracles saves her from the gutter and she needs 'to mingle with the better class.' That constipated, painted-up, fake aristocrat! Comes to the *grafio* as if she's got the right!"

Myrsini often came to the *grafio,* holding Constantine by the hand. Women, to Andreas, had no reason to step into a man's place of business. Steve was sweeping the floor in the disordered office one day when Aunt Myrsini came in with Constantine. Steve did some desultory sweeping while watching a scene as if he were sitting in a movie. Uncle Harry jumped up, patted Constantine on the head, banged open the ornate cash register, took out several bills, and called at the door, "We're going to lunch! If any tenants come in," he said in a clipped, authoritative tone to Andreas, "make sure you write it down in the book."

A pencil resting behind his ear, Andreas made a spitting motion at the closed door. "Leaving the *grafio* to take her to eat! And not at Stellios's place, oh, no. Only the Hotel Utah is good enough for her, the *moderna!*"

The icemen, too, made sport of Heracles. "No more children for Heracles," they laughed. "She sleeps in the front bedroom and he sleeps in the back bedroom." Marika banged pans as she did whenever there was unseemly talk in the presence of the children. "Who told you that?" Andreas asked, chewing on a cigar, his eyes brightening. Marika banged the pans louder.

Steve began to feel sorry for Constantine—having Aunt Myrsini for a mother. When he saw him playing with a new toy, all alone because his mother would not let him play in the neighborhood, he was sad for him, and yet angry that Constantine could have anything he wanted. Constantine would sit on the front porch steps with his elbows resting on his thin knees and his palms pressed on either side of his pretty face—for he was a child with large black eyes, heavily fringed, and a small delicate mouth. Intently he watched Steve rake the small patches of grass in his mother's front yard. No one ever called the house, yard, or possessions Uncle Harry's; everything was Aunt Myrsini's; only the car was Uncle Harry's.

Steve admired Uncle Harry's wine-colored, highly polished Packard. He thought he would have a car like it some day. He already knew how to drive: he'd learned by steering his father's car up and down their dirt driveway.

Steve's friends Lefty and Perry went out of their way to pass Aunt Myrsini's house, knowing Steve would be working there. Lefty, the oldest in his family, had outgrown his overalls; the pant legs stopped above his ankles. Perry was the third son in his family and wore handed-down overalls that were comically large with the pant legs frayed at the bottoms from his calloused heels' rubbing on the ground. Lefty and Perry walked slowly down the road with Lefty's cow, Bossy, ahead of them. Penelope—Penny—took pictures of the three of them as they passed the summer, heads shaved, barefoot, and wearing the old overalls. Her godfather had given her a Brownie Kodak camera on New Year's Day, and she could always get money for film from her father. Andreas looked at each new batch of pictures again and again. When he sent a money order to his father in the village, he always included one or two of the snapshots.

Steve became aware that Constantine watched for Lefty and Perry to come by. One day when they slowed almost to a stop while the cow Bossy continued on, Constantine stood up from the steps, craning his neck to get a better look at Bossy. When she flipped her tail at flies buzzing around her rump, Constantine laughed excitedly.

With their eyes on the front door, Lefty and Perry waited by the picket fence for Steve to finish raking the lawn. Steve asked where they were going, although he knew.

"Taking Bossy to the Salt Flats," Lefty said. It was against the law to raise animals in the city, but the Feds were too busy ferreting out bootleggers to do anything about it. And the sheriff more than once had rattled by in his Ford as Bossy ambled toward the Flats; he didn't even give her a second look. "Come on down and then I'll help you clean the hotel," Perry called.

"See you later," Steve said, not so loud that Aunt Myrsini would hear him. He hurried to finish raking, thinking of his bare, dusty feet in the cool, moist grass of the Flats.

Aunt Myrsini came out to the porch with a book in her hand. "Time for your lesson, Konstandino," she said. She would not let Constantine attend Greek school with Steve and the other Greek Town children. "I know more than that . . . that *teacher*," she had sniffed. Other parents had to remind sulky children that they had to go to Greek school to learn "our" language, but Constantine sat dutifully on a wicker chair next to his mother and read to her in a small voice. He looked up from time to time to his mother's alert black eyes under stark eyebrows and waited for her to say, "Good, very good, Konstandino."

Constantine gazed at Steve as he walked toward the backyard to put away the rake. Rather than leave by the front yard and be seen by Aunt Myrsini with her list of orders, Steve walked down the alley, thinking of the long look in Constantine's eyes.

EACH MORNING his heart beat faster at the sight of the two-story school with its dirt yard. The teachers had put him, the Italian, Japanese, Slavs, and the few Mexican children in the back of the room on the first day of school, and there they remained. Steve's teacher, Miss Wilson, addressed them as "You foreign children." When the "American" children brought cards with red hearts and cupids to school on Valentine's Day and put them in a box to be given out at the end of the day, Steve sank down at his desk, awaiting the awful moment when it was clear he would not get even one Valentine.

One of the boys, Harold Gibbons, gave the teacher a small, heart-shaped box of chocolates. Every day Harold wore wool pants, a white shirt, and a polka-dotted bow tie. His father owned a gas station. Steve described the box at the dinner table. "So she's nice to him," Steve said, although the teacher had never shown much niceness to Harold. The next morning Marika gave Steve a paper sack holding a bottle of wine for the teacher. He hurried to school too early and had to wait in the cold until the principal came out and rang the big brass bell. Out of breath, he reached the classroom first and handed the teacher the paper sack. Frowning, she opened it and lifted the bottle just enough to see what it was. "Hmm. Well, Steve," she said, and put the paper sack on the floor. Steve walked down the aisle to his seat. He was confused and could not pay attention to the story that the children at the front were taking turns reading. By recess he knew for sure that the teacher hated him and he hated her.

A few days later the Ku Klux Klan burned crosses on Ensign Peak and marched down Main Street. Steve, Lefty, and Perry ran to watch them and were beaten by their frenzied mothers. "How many times did I tell you not to leave the neighborhood?" Marika shouted, whacking Steve with the *blasti*. "How many times did I tell you the *Amerikanoi* don't like us? So stay away!" Another whack. "How many times do you have to be told that you could get your head broken?" A final whack.

Young men drove through Greek Town at night, throwing trash at the houses, honking car horns. They tried to burn down a house. "Why?" Marika asked. "They say we send too much money back to our country," the midwife told her. "So, why did we come to this country if not to make money to send to our poor people? They say our men work for less money. Let them tell that to the mine and mill *bossis*. And when our men do go on *strikie* for more money, they say, 'Send them back where they came from.' Achh, it's like living around Turks all over again." The midwife folded her arms under her big bosom. "But, the KuKoukers are going to get it good. All of them, Greeks, Italians, Slavs, Irish, they're ready to fight them." She nodded, eyebrows lifted knowingly. Within three weeks no more crosses burned.

[1926]

THE CHURCH BASEMENT now could barely hold all of Greek Town's people in celebrating their weddings, baptisms, and the Orthodox saints' days. The Greek national anthem boomed out, shaking the basement windows. Toasts were made to "Our country! May we see her soon!" At Greek-school programs speakers admonished the children to learn Greek, the most glorious language in the world, and with hypnotic fervor spoke of the Golden Age of Greece that gave light to the world. The Star Theatrical Company presented comedies, skits, and plays on the great heroes of the revolution against the Turks. In the center of it all was Myrsini.

Myrsini, cold to Andreas, Marika, and their children, was vivacious in the church basement and at nameday celebrations. She told amusing Turkish *hodjas* stories. In all of them, the *hodjas,* the Turkish priest, ferreted out the guilty person by his sly questioning. Sometimes the stories were a little risqué, and the men laughed; the women tittered and looked down at their folded hands. One story was about a *hodjas,* up a tree for some reason, who couldn't control his bladder, and it emptied on the culprit below.

Aunt Myrsini danced gracefully at the church celebrations and, head up, bestowed smiles on those watching. Uncle Harry now danced with care, no longer jumping high, twirling, and calling out "Hopa!" Andreas also became a different person for the church *horoesperidhes.* At home before the event, he made a big show of filling the tub in the lean-to bathroom, shaving with grunts of satisfaction, and putting on a clean shirt and his best suit. In the smoky church basement, the air heavy with the scent of roasting lamb and with children running about, a chicken leg or lamb's rib in their fists, Andreas led the dancers with great dignity. Although he was no more than five foot eight and stocky, he twisted and leaped like an agile young man. Women clapped and men whistled the goat whistles of Greece. His children gazed at him and Marika sat with folded arms and smiled.

Many times, though, Marika and the children, bathed and in their Sunday clothes, waited on the front porch for Andreas. Even on Sundays he met tenants and real-estate people. The children sat on the steps, swung on the fence gate, and looked down the dirt street for his car. Steve walked to the backyard to look at the rabbits. He liked to watch their pink eyes and sniffing noses. Marika had shown him how to wring the necks of chickens, each clutched hand turning in the opposite direction, and to chop off the rabbits' heads with a hatchet. He wrung the chickens' necks without a thought, but he would not use the hatchet. He stood his ground, tears in his eyes because he was defying his mother. His bare feet firmly set on the barren dirt yard, he smelled the dryness of the chicken pen and the green moistness of the rabbit hutches but shook his head. He would not chop off the rabbits' heads, because they *knew*.

Sometimes Andreas did not return home until dark and it was too late to attend the celebration. Penny and Georgie went to bed and cried for a long time. Marika set out Andreas's dinner and made her usual comment on the children's disappointment. "Business comes first," Andreas yelled. One night Steve said, "We should go without you," and his father picked up a heavy piece of kindling and gave him the worst beating he had ever had.

At one of the church celebrations, Myrsini told the priest that the church should have a Sunday school like the Americans. The priest started to object, but Myrsini said she would be the teacher and take care of everything, She often strayed from the biblical text of the day's liturgy and gave lessons in deportment. "Do not say *sh* for *s*. Villagers speak that way. Use the polite address when speaking with older people. Boys, use handkerchiefs! Boys, don't chew gum! Stavros, Solon, Eleftherios, Pericles! Why are you whispering?" She was left with Constantine and girls in the class.

Steve and his friends spied on her through the basement windows. She told the girls not to use vinegar or baking soda paste in their armpits—only village women did that; they should go to the drugstore and buy colognes. They should not look into coffeehouses when passing by. The girls protested they wanted to wave to their godfathers, but she impatiently shook her head. "Truly refined women do not look into coffeehouses, only addle-brained peasant girls would disgrace themselves in that way." Penelope, who was old enough to understand, and Georgia, who was not, immediately told their mother. Marika scowled.

One Sunday morning, when Marika and the children were getting ready for church—Andreas attended only on his nameday and at Christmas, Easter, and the Dormition of the Virgin—Marika came out of the bedroom wearing lipstick, not looking at the children and holding her purse close to her waist. Then she glanced at Steve and with a flustered blink of her eyes hurried into the bathroom. She returned, pink faced, the lipstick washed off.

They walked to church, Steve holding the round loaf of bread stamped with the symbols of Christ. He took it to the side door of the icon screen and handed it to the janitor in his black cassock. Watching his feet, he walked back to a pew on the men's side, on the right of the nave, and joined Solly.

On the women's side, Marika sat with Penny and Georgie. With her eyes staring at the icon of the Virgin and Child on the left of the icon's middle door, she repeatedly made the sign of the cross, leaning far forward and peering as when she stood before the family icon, berating and pleading with the Virgin and Christ about Myrsini, Heracles, the *grafio,* and the icemen. She leaned back, wondering if the midwife knew any of the ways witches used to get rid of people. Not that she wanted the icemen dead, but her years of begging the Virgin had come to nothing. "Forgive me, my Virgin" she whispered, "but I have to try something different."

IV

[1928]

THE MAMI WAS certain that Myrsini had the Evil Eye and could cause mischief, but she and Marika could see no way to get her involved in the conspiracy to get the icemen out of the cellar. Even if Marika cut very small pieces off the icemen's clothing, in places where they wouldn't be noticed, Myrsini would have to intone incantations over them, and of course that was impossible. Still, Marika cut little pieces of cloth from the icemen's shirttails, hoping that *someone* would suddenly appear, take charge, and give her the relief she yearned for.

When this did not happen, she found an opportunity that she prayed to the Virgin would work. On Saint Andrew's nameday, the women visitors, as always, put their coats and purses on Marika and Andreas's bed. While Myrsini was telling an amusing incident she had read in the Greek newspaper to the rapt visitors, Marika quickly went into her bedroom, shut the door, and put the pieces of shirttails into Myrsini's purse. She pushed them to the bottom of the beaded purse where Myrsini would not see them. Marika thought that Myrsini might be so evil that she would not have to repeat witch's words over them—that having them in her purse would be enough to cast a spell. When her plan failed, she looked at the Virgin and said, "Have I sinned that You won't help me?"

By this time Steve had entered the eighth grade. He was a head and a half taller than his father and Uncle Harry, but was also developing their broad chest and heavy shoulders. Their legs, though, were short, and Steve had inherited long legs from his mother's clan of tall men and short women.

At the kitchen table, whenever the boarders had not come home for the evening meal, Marika took to sighing. She now sat between Steve and Solon, instead of between Penelope and Georgia. "It isn't right," she would say, then lift her shoulders, and sigh: "What are people saying? Two boarders in a house with growing girls. No one will want them for daughters-in-law. We'll never marry them off."

"Plug it," Andreas growled, pushing out his lips. "I've got so much on my brain and you complain about silly things. I'm a respected businessman. Fathers will come running to have the girls for daughters-in-law. Stop bothering me!"

What Andreas had on his mind was the building of a row of stores on property he had bought over the years. The boarded-up houses on the lots were torn down, and construction began for one-story brick buildings to house a Piggly Wiggly grocery store, a dry cleaners', a Rexall drugstore, and a shoe-repair shop. Every night he talked with little moans about the problems with the architect, carpenters, plumbers, electricians, and Italian bricklayers. He had acquired them here and there, from friends who knew of them, from advertisements in the local newspaper, and from labor agents who had crossed paths with them. For all his moaning, he was flushed with pride, as was Marika. The property, the *periousia,* was not only growing but becoming *high cless.*

The next time Marika complained about the icemen, Andreas had a washing machine delivered and placed on the back porch. The midwife showed Marika how to use the machine. They whispered while the machine chugged. After a few days, Marika resumed her complaint. With folded arms, her head leaning to one side, she looked at the floor and said, "Ach, Ach," in the same mournful, doomed voice his mother had used when as a small boy he had brought village censure on the family. Fear stunned his face. He raised his eyes heavenward as if something terrible was ready to strike him.

At that moment, the *mami* came to the back door and shouted, "What's the matter with you, Andreas? The whole town is talking about you! Mr. Kalogiannis, the big businessman, considers his daughters no better than dogs! Don't come to me to arrange their marriages! I won't waste my time! Two boarders in the house and two grown-up girls!"—an exaggeration that caused her to blink her eyes. "I'm going right now to the priest and tell him that you are a man without *filotimo!* That's right! You have no honor! You've kept those boarders all these years to make yourself rich buying property! I'll make a rag of you, Andreas! I'll telephone the bishop in San Franchitsco! By the time I finish with you, 'The priest will look like a donkey to you!'" After quoting the proverb, the midwife stalked out, looking enraged, but not before giving Marika a triumphant glance.

Andreas cursed the *mami,* but said he had been thinking anyway that the cellar room was needed for the autumn winemaking. "We can take out the beds, clean it up," he said. "It will be more systematic than using the dirt dugout next to it. More systematic." He repeated the word he had read in Greek-language newspapers, one palm pressed against his barrel chest.

The two boarders took their belongings, including their long underwear and BVDS Marika had been washing for fourteen years, shook her hand, and wished the children a good *tyhi*—a good fate. After they had gone down the road a ways, the children laughed and slapped their hands in the air as if flies were buzzing about, and Marika made them each a glass of sour-cherry drink.

Steve and Solly carried the skimpy beds up the cellar stairs and began clearing out all evidence of the icemen's long, mole-like existence. In the cobwebbed rafters, Steve found an empty bottle with a long black nozzle. He and Solly nudged each other and rolled their eyes; they knew it must be protection against the clap and syphilis that prostitutes gave their customers. When they finished, Solly, without helping deliver the beds and mattresses to a widow whose husband had been killed in a mine accident, disappeared. Steve showed his mother the bottle. "Put it on the washing machine," she said, looking with venom at the bottle, "and wash your hands good." Steve put the bottle on the new washing machine and at intervals looked to see if it were still there. He wanted his father to see it. When Andreas came home, Marika asked in an offhand voice if the bottle should be thrown away as if she did not know what it was. Andreas yelled and cursing the boarders—"those cocksuckers, those *poustes*"—stamped out to the alley and threw the bottle in an ashcan.

The bottle episode, together with Steve and Solly wandering about town in the evening, was the beginning of their mother's constant talk about what happened to men who went to *poutanes:* "Miserable old Andonios, flat on his back in the county hospital. He can't see, and pus runs out of his knees"; "Crippled Demos"—as if her sons didn't know he had been injured in the copper mill; and "Zacharias who—God forgive the sinner—went to the *poutanes* on Good Friday and was struck dead by a car outside their door."

In the eighth grade, Steve began to make excuses when Uncle

Harry ordered him to cut the grass and do Myrsini's errands. He did, though, watch over Constantine, now in the first grade, as he was cautioned to, but it was unnecessary: Aunt Myrsini walked with him to school and at the end of the day waited on the sidewalk to escort him home. No one teased Constantine: one look at his imposing mother and boys left him alone.

Uncle Harry had joined the Masons. An insurance man, the only Greek in the entire chapter, had sponsored him. Marika was shocked: "In our country," she said in a hushed voice, "the Masons were called anti-Christs."

Aunt Myrsini, wearing a long, lace dress with a corsage on her shoulder, and Uncle Harry, in dinner jacket and Masonic fez, attended dances at the lodge. Constantine was left in the care of an American schoolteacher who lived in their neighborhood. Steve's excuses, with growing untruthfulness, came more often and more easily after he saw his uncle and aunt drive by in their Packard: "I've got more lessons. Now I'm in high school and the teacher makes us do more work and in Greek school, too." Steve could look Uncle Harry in the eye while he lied. He was not a good student in public school, and as for Greek school he hardly ever went—then not at all. Marika lectured him and Solly about keeping up the Greek language, the best in the world, but neither she nor their father forced them to go; their sisters, yes, but not them. Steve was still cleaning the Railroad Hotel and took his time doing the errands and odd jobs at the *grafio*.

Uncle Harry tried flipping Steve a quarter after he had cut and raked the grass. Much as he could have gone to a movie or bought a package of forbidden cigarettes with the money, Steve continued making more and more excuses until Uncle Harry gave up and tried to convince Solly to take his place. Solly left the lawnmower in the yard, sometimes only finishing part of the cutting, and ran off. Solly had good excuses. "She makes fun of the way I talk," he said, pretending he had been humiliated. The excuses were logical to Marika. Uncle Harry then hired a neighborhood boy who charged him twenty-five cents each time he cut the grass. "Your sons are ungrateful, miserable wretches," he told Marika.

Now that Steve was beyond her reach and since Solly had never been in her grasp, Aunt Myrsini chose Penny as her target. "Penelope, don't take such big steps. Boys walk like that, not girls"; "Penelope, stay out of the sun. You look like an Indian"; "Penelope, cultured girls do not let doors slam behind them!" Penny often broke a dish or stumbled when Aunt Myrsini was near. Cowed by Myrsini, her mother scolded her: "If you walked slowly instead of clomping like a cow, you wouldn't always be stumbling in that woman's presence. And stop laughing so much when people are around. No one will come asking for you. People don't want a silly daughter-in-law."

For a while, Aunt Myrsini took an interest in Georgia, who was dark like her. She gave her an empty compact with a few pennies inside and the feathered hat she had worn on the day the family had seen her for the first time; Georgie put it on to play house. She often opened the compact and gazed at her big eyes and delicate mouth. "I'm going to be an actress when I grow up," she whispered to Penny, whose face was pale and thin. Penny sniffled enviously over Myrsini's hat. Marika angrily cut off a cluster of artificial red cherries from her best hat and sewed it onto her old brown one—she was in mourning for her father and could not wear anything so frivolous. Marika had had a portent that someone close to her would die: black birds had clustered under the eaves of the house and, soon after, as she stood in the kitchen rolling out pasta dough, a faint breeze swept past her. She stopped her work: someone's soul had passed by. At first she feared it was Andreas, and immediately thought that there were not enough silver dollars at the bottom of the trunk. "I've so much work to do and you cry over a hat," she shouted at Penny.

SUMMER EVENINGS when Steve was in eighth grade were wonderfully free. The sky stayed light until nine o'clock. With Lefty, Perry, and sometimes Solly, they threw the ball over the roof of the house to each other, calling "Andy-I-over." They needed more players for Run-my-sheepie, run, and they let Penny and Georgie into the game. Steve knew they were a little too old to be playing kids' games, but to be out in the cool evenings, scented with honeysuckle or wild rose, with the freshness of water running down garden rows, chores finished for the day, and to be together for fun, was blissful, often joyous.

One evening, Uncle Harry and Aunt Myrsini with Constantine looking through a backseat window, stopped by. Uncle Harry bounded out and hurried into the house from where Andreas's and Uncle Harry's voices rose to great angry heights. Aunt Myrsini looked straight ahead. Constantine watched the group of children choosing sides for the game, his eyes big and dark. "Come on, Con," Steve called. "Come and play. We'll take you home." He knew Con was too young to play with them (he was about seven years old) and that Aunt Myrsini wouldn't let him anyway.

Aunt Myrsini turned her head and glared at them. "His name is Constantine," she said in English.

"Thitsa," Solly said with fake wide eyes—Aunt Myrsini bridled at the word *little-aunt*—"all the Konstandinoses are called Con in English, or Deno, or Gus."

Aunt Myrsini's head shook; her thin lips drew inward. "His name in English is Constantine." Her chest rose and fell. Uncle Harry hurried to the car, jumped in, slammed the door, hissed the word *teras,* and drove off. The children laughed secretly, the girls with hands over their mouths. Uncle Harry had called their father a "monster."

In those late summer evenings, the preparation of dinner was an even bigger commotion than usual: Marika at the stove, Penny at the meat grinder with her lips pushed out sullenly, and Georgie choosing the opportunity to iron. Sometimes she barely heated the iron when she complained of a headache, or hugged herself low down to show she might have one of those wandering spleens the midwife took care of. This absolved her when she left the ironing for Penny and her mother to finish.

The food would be placed on the table, and now that the ice-men were gone, the kitchen was a different place, free from the shouts, commands, and accusations of the day. The smells of lye, soap, and grease had almost faded: rich scents of simmering food filled the room, and the whole house. Protecting their plates with their elbows on the oilcloth, the family ate the stews, the bean and lentil soups, the warm bread from the outdoor oven, all impatient to tell their anecdotes and gossip of the day. Sometimes Uncle Harry appeared and sat with them, giving no explanation of why he was not eating in his own house.

Andreas had more to tell than anyone. Many people visited his office: village friends; other Greeks passing through—fellow workers on railroad gangs in his first American years, men with whom he had "eaten bread and salt," the proverbial words of friendship; the priest; the church president; and New York and Chicago Greek-language newspaper reporters. Oblivious to its being a place of business, they crossed their legs, lit cigars, and leisurely strung out tales of triumph or duplicity. They told of bootleggers outwitting the Feds; the latest on the Greek detective, Milt Valiotis, who had to be paid off by Greeks illegally in the country; intrigue over church politics; and gossip about sheepmen's wives left alone during lambing and shearing. The visitors were especially animated when they carried criticism they had heard about Andreas. They insisted they had defended him as if he were their brother. This interruption of his business duties was difficult for Andreas: he wanted to take care of his business, but he also wanted to hear every detail.

When Uncle Harry gave his news, it was usually something risqué that he pretended the children would not understand. This brought Marika to her feet to bang lids on the stove until he finished. The children took turns, then talked all at once, raising their strident voices and giving valuable information about incidents they had seen or heard. Uncle Harry questioned them like an attorney in a radio play: "And when you saw him coming out of the barber shop was he alone? Did he go to the back door of the barber shop?"

Even Penny and Georgie knew the barber kept a woman in the back room. "All I said was," Steve repeated with just enough contempt so that he wouldn't be slapped, "that he came out of the barber shop with a limp."

Uncle Harry jumped up, and with his mouth full—Aunt Myrsini being absent—walked around the table with a peculiarly distorted limp, affecting a high voice that the limper did not have, "My brother-in-law accused me falsely, falsely I say, that I went to the barber's back door." Everyone laughed, even though they knew it was a lie.

Solly, the vagabond, often had thrilling news: a Feds' raid, an accident in the railyards, and once, most spectacular, seeing the midwife set her oldest son's broken leg right on the street where a car had hit him. The *mami* set the bone while her son screamed, rubbed his leg with olive oil, made a plaster of sheared wool dipped in egg white, and wrapped it all with strips of cotton sheeting.

When Penny told her news, she would laugh and talk at the same time, the laughing overpowering the talking, until Marika said, "Silly girl, stop it!" Georgie would take over and finish the anecdote with gestures and dramatics, making them forget that an hour earlier she had carried on hysterically over some reprimand or accusation.

Mostly the talk was about comic incidents that happened in the neighborhood. Crazy Anna got her breasts caught in the wringer of the washing machine. Bowlegged Soula made eyes at the cheesemaker. Honey-Mouth, a screeching woman who had a child every year, placed a curse on the American grade-school principal: she carved a figure out of a bar of soap and each day poured a kettle of hot water over it to hasten his death. Accidents happened: a child almost drowned in a washtub; a railyard worker's toes were mashed by a handcar. The midwife's exploits were always good to hear, like her tricking a Fed away from a house by pretending she was taking care of a woman in labor.

The evening meal ended with merry good feelings. At times the good feelings spilled over into the living room, where the children sat on the linoleum floor and listened to the new radio. They knew the broadcast times for *Fibber McGee and Molly, Amos and Andy,* and the *Hit Parade.*

Uncle Harry would not sit down one evening until he had said with great solemnity, "The AHEPA is organizing a boys' band. Steve and Solon, go to the church basement tomorrow at six o'clock and get your instruments."

Marika looked at Heracles and then at her sons with a little gasp of delight. "I don't want to play in the AHEPA band," Steve said, his heart bumping.

"What! All the boys will be in it. We have a special teacher, Mister Held, an American. You are going to go!"

"No, I want to play in the school band." Steve had never thought about the school band until the moment Uncle Harry gave his pronouncement. He had heard Ted Lewis on the radio and wished he had a clarinet like his. Here was his opportunity to have a clarinet by playing in the AHEPA band, except it was Uncle Harry's idea.

"You're not going to play in the AHEPA band," Andreas said, in a pique because he had lost the last election for president of the lodge, "and you're not going to play in the school band. You've got enough work to do."

"Let him, Andreas," Marika said.

"Close your mouth!"

"Now, Andreas," Heracles said in a cajoling voice, "you'll be proud to see your sons in the AHEPA band."

"Oh, what the hell, Steve," Solon whispered. "It could be fun."

"I want to play in the school band," Steve said, his eyes steady on Uncle Harry, who raised his arms in disgust, turned, and stamped out of the house.

Andreas shouted, "Look what you've done! Your uncle left without eating. Not another word from you or I'll make you eat wood! You haven't got it for a long time, but keep it up and I'll slaughter you!"

In bed with Solon sleeping next to him breathing noisily through his mouth, Steve lay awake in the shadowed room. A cold, hard resolution finally let him fall asleep. The next day he told Lefty and Perry about his plan. Without telling his father he would talk to the band teacher, who they conceded didn't seem to care if a student came from immigrant parents or not. He would choose a clarinet; Mr. Robertson, the band teacher, let students use the instruments for two weeks to see if they wanted to join the band. Then he would learn to play an old Greek folk song his father and the icemen used to sing, except he could not remember the name and didn't know how to get the sheet music. Perry's sister had a book of Greek sheet music, but first they had to find the right song.

While they were discussing strategy, Steve learned fingering through a book Mr. Robertson loaned him, tan and black with the title *Universal's Follow-up Method for the Clarinet*. He practiced in the Railroad Hotel, blowing so softly that no one on the graveyard shift heard him. Lefty sputtered out the solution: the icemen! After leaving the cellar room, the boarders had moved into a *bekiariko,* a bachelor house rented by two other Greeks. The *bekiariko* was near Lefty's house. "Almost every Sunday, they eat and sing, and if it's good weather they dance in the backyard."

The next Sunday the three hid behind a privy and watched the four men dance in the dirt yard while they took turns rotating a leg of lamb on a small spit. The boys were restless, squatting in the alley behind the privy: someone might see them, and they were hungry themselves. The men carved the lamb, pulled loaves of bread apart, poured wine, and sat down on a table of planks set on sawhorses. They ate, tearing at the meat with their teeth, laughing and talking, and then they sat back. The *traghoudhia tou trapeziou* began —the songs of the table.

Their heads thrown back, the four men began the slow, dark song of an old man who had been fighting the Turks for forty years and was dying. Steve whooped. "It's the song. *Ghero Dimos!*" Perry said his sister had the sheet music for it. They listened to another stanza, then simultaneously howled like coyotes and streaked down the alley.

A week later, at night, Steve sat on the back porch steps, a small electric light switched on above his head, and waited for Andreas to come home. When the car stopped in the dirt driveway, he began playing, a throb in his ears. He knew he was not good, but he hoped his father would recognize the song: the old guerrilla fighter, wounded, ready to die, tells his young comrades he is tired, forty years fighting the Turks. He gives instructions for his casket: wide, roomy enough for two to stand erect, to take cover and reload, and on the right side a window so the birds could fly in and out, the nightingales of Spring.

Steve knew someone was standing behind him in the kitchen doorway and he played the song one more time. Then he stood up and put the clarinet into its battered case. Andreas stepped back to let him pass. He said nothing, and Steve went to bed, unable to become comfortable, his eyes refusing to close. The next morning at the breakfast table, Andreas handed Steve a ten-dollar bill and said, his voice morning-gruff, "Pay for the *clarino*. Bring back the change."

Steve often wore the band uniform to the office and to the Railroad Hotel: black pants, white shirt, a black cape lined with red rayon that one of the mothers had sewed, and one of the gold-braided black caps the bank had donated. Uncle Harry breathed a hiss of contempt that gave Steve satisfaction and inspired him to clean the office and the hotel in a hurry.

He had to get up at six o'clock to be in school by seven. Mr. Robertson insisted that everyone had to be in his seat, the sheet music on the stand, and the instrument in hand by "seven o' clock on the dot." Steve often wanted to sleep in that extra hour, but the band was too important. For once, he had got the better of his father and Uncle Harry.

The band learned to play Souza marches, "The Flight of the Bumble Bee," "O, Sole Mio," "El Capitan," and "Stars and Stripes."

Being in the band made a difference: the grade-school taunts and fights over his Greekness were gone, replaced by remarks like: "Are you taking a white girl to the prom?" Every once in a while he had to use his fists, but he and Solon, Lefty, and Perry took part in school projects like the Harvest Dance.

[1929]

MR. OLSEN, the wood-work shop teacher, asked for volunteers to decorate the gymnasium. Steve, Lefty, and Perry did not raise their hands. Mr. Olsen chose most of the class, then said he needed two or three students to go to his farm to make apple cider for the dance. The three then waved their hands with such excitement, Mr. Olsen said, "I've never seen such enthusiasm over apple cider."

They climbed into Mr. Olsen's old Chevrolet, Steve in the front seat and Lefty and Perry in the back. Lefty sat with his face against the window as if he had never been in a car before. Perry looked worried: he was still going to Greek school and was afraid of being found out. He was small for his age, coming only to Steve's and Lefty's shoulders. He was also quiet.

The sky was blue, with great, rolling white clouds. The acrid scent of autumn was in the air; the passing fields had been harvested: pumpkins in piles, stalks of drying corn, baled oblongs of alfalfa. Seagulls flew overhead and alighted on the burnished fields to peck at the dirt. Other birds were flying south, Mr. Olsen said, and let go of the steering wheel as if to wave them on.

Mr. Olsen's farm was a spread-out jumble of outbuildings in the back of a two-story pioneer adobe house, which had been plastered over with cement. Patches of cement had fallen away and exposed the adobe bricks made by Mr. Olsen's great-great-grandfather. Scraggly lilac bushes grew against the house, and grass in the front yard had grown two feet high. Lefty offered to cut the grass, but Mr. Olsen said lambs were ready to be let loose on it.

Mr. Olsen parked in the backyard of hardened dirt. They got out and breathed the heavy smell of manure and animals and a hint of ripe apples. The sheds had no doors. In one of the larger buildings, pegs on the wooden wall held saws, hammers, and small tools, their handles blackened, blades rusty. Curls of wood shavings littered the dirt floor under the workbench. Chickens wandered about the yard, in and out of the coal and wood sheds. Pink-eyed rabbits looked through the screens of their hutches and imperially eyed pigeons from their cotes.

Mr. Olsen led them to the barn where he kept the apple press and showed them what to do after they picked the apples from the orchard behind the sheds. "Pick the apples that's fallen on the ground, too, unless they're rotten," he said. Evidently, Steve could see, Mr. Olsen did not intend to have the apples washed. "What about the worm holes, Mr. Olsen?" he asked. "Oh, don't pay them no mind. Far's I know, they probably improve the taste."

When they brought the first three bushels of apples into the barn, neighborhood children were waiting with cups and Mason jars. Lefty did most of the pressing, laughing with the children, as they put their cups and jars under the funnel. They worked until sundown. Mr. Olsen drove them back to town while the sky was on fire. Steve told Mr. Olsen to let them off at the Railroad Hotel and Lefty and Perry helped clean it. If they had to answer for their whereabouts, all they had to say was the truth—a teacher needed them. Greek parents respected American teachers.

The three were in charge of the cider at the dance. Students kept coming back again and again with their paper cups. Steve, Lefty, and Perry didn't drink a drop.

Steve stayed with the band until his junior year, when he took a bookkeeping course and began spending more time in the office. On the first day of recording in the ledgers, he compared his father's cramped handwriting—like a child's—with the fancy, curlicued Palmer method Uncle Harry had learned from the nuns.

Andreas did not like writing in the ledgers; he would hand Steve a handful of receipts and tell him to record them. Uncle Harry would put on his hat the moment Steve arrived, ring open the cash register, take out a few bills, and say he was going to see the attorney, or the Greek vice-consul, or the editor of the Greek newspaper, *The Light*.

The first week Steve worked on the books, he lifted his pen a few times and thought about the band, maybe playing amateurish yet recognizable jazz as soon as Mr. Robertson ran off to his sugar-beet farm and left them to practice.

Myrsini and Constantine came to the office at least two times a week. Myrsini and Steve gave each other little smiles. Myrsini looked about, once passed her fingers across the top of the filing cabinet and looked at them for several seconds. "The *grafio* needs dusting," she said, and Steve nodded, then gave Constantine a pen and a few sheets of paper to draw on. Constantine could sit quietly for long periods and with his head bent far over draw amazing creatures, half-man, half-animal, with snake-like arms, and oddly dressed humans with their clothes on backwards. The next day Uncle Harry lectured Steve for being rude to Aunt Myrsini. "You should have got right up and dusted the furniture," he said.

Andreas found it necessary to look into a tenant's complaint whenever Myrsini came to the office. He pulled his hat down until his ears stuck out and in a brusque voice gave Steve orders about what to tell callers if the telephone rang—usually a lie when the truth was easier and better.

Now that Steve was spending more time in the office and learning bookkeeping, he saw its disorder. Together, Andreas and Heracles went to collect rent and lease money, lunched at Stellios's, then continued their rounds. Steve watched them leave the office and despised them: as if the post office would in some way cheat them if the checks were sent through the mail or that the checks would bounce. To pay their own bills, they put on their hats and drove to the water, power, or gas company and paid cash. They paid cash for everything, even for their cars. Only for properties did they sign monthly contracts at the bank. In his first years in America, Andreas did not use banks; he buried his money in tin cans in the back yards of boardinghouses and bachelor houses.

They were still buying properties when the stock market collapsed in late 1929 and the Great Depression began. Uncle Harry had to keep his Packard longer than he had expected and the only properties he and Andreas bought were for back taxes. Of all the disorder in the office, the *ding!* of the cash register opening and his father and Uncle Harry's taking out whatever they wanted, his father frugally, Uncle Harry less so, was most galling. When he and his father were alone one day, he said, "Papa, the business would run better if you and Uncle Heracles had a set salary."

Andreas looked up at him, his face a big red moon. He shouted, "Shit on your mug! We're brothers! The same blood runs in our veins! Brothers trust each other! Get out of my sight!"

Steve reared back. He had not expected this rage; his father had approved of his taking the bookkeeping class. Steve had thought they could sit down, with Uncle Harry out of the office, and discuss setting up a system for the office. He also had thought he could ask his father about Uncle Harry and Milt Valiotis. He was afraid now to speak their names.

Steve had seen Uncle Harry and Milt Valiotis together twice, once in the doorway of the Grill Cafe, toothpicks in their mouths, talking, and once coming out of the Continental Bank together. Milt Valiotis was a Greek from the village next to Andreas and Heracles's. He was ostensibly a detective, working for politicians: he collected from whorehouses, pimps, and bootleggers. His stomach was big; still, he was a handsome man. He wore his hat rakishly on the side of his head, and when he talked, he waved his hand about, making arcs with a cigarette, the diamond on his little finger glinting. Lefty told Steve he had heard that Milt Valiotis used to pimp for his American wife during the World War. He had married her to avoid being put in jail for white slavery.

One night when they had enough money to go bowling, Steve

told Lefty and Perry, "Uncle Harry thinks he's such a big shot and he goes and hangs around with Milt Valiotis. I'm just not going to put up with the way he and my dad do business. I'm going to get a degree in business at the university. They can't tell me to go to hell with that diploma in my hand. I'll get Solly and Con—he'll be old enough by then—on my side." Even before he finished, he was ashamed, as if he had done something dishonorable. He had criticized the family to *ksenoi*—foreigners—as his mother called those beyond the house.

V

[1932]

THE DEPRESSION slid deeper, into stagnation. Andreas bought a brown brick bungalow near Liberty Park. "This is no time to buy a house," Heracles said, with his palm pressed down on the deed Andreas was ready to sign. "We have to have ready cash. Times are shaky. Everyone is behind in the rent."

"Get your hand off my desk!" Andreas exploded. "You want me to stay on the west side with all the Mexicans and the ignorant Americans! You think that's where I belong, whorelicker! I got the house for a bargain. From some poor wretch! See me sign the deed!" Andreas wrote his name with great care.

When the family moved, they left behind the outdoor oven where Marika baked bread, the chicken coop, rabbit hutches, and the big garden, exchanging them for a house with a white-tiled kitchen, a furnace, and an electric stove that Marika gazed at in consternation. They also left behind Steve's childhood terrain. In the backyard of their brick home, he stood on the small square of grass and saw how barren it was.

Two days later, Con pedaled over on a child's bicycle. He was eight years old, but looked small for his age. He propped the bicycle against the steps, but shook his head when Marika told him to come into the house; he sat on the steps and ate two powdered-sugar cookies that Penny brought him. He ate quickly, said his first words, "Thank you," and got on the bicycle. They watched him pedal off fast. "I hope she doesn't notice the sugar on his mouth," Marika said, clutching her hands together. Con made no more visits to the brown brick house.

The house was about two miles from the Railroad Hotel. Now, when he could not get his father's car, Steve had to walk there after school. Sometimes he daydreamed while working on the books in the office, while calcimining the hotel rooms a sky blue, the color of the Greek flag, while throwing the dusty, threadbare rugs on a clothesline he had improvised in the tumble-weeded backyard and hitting them with a wire paddle. He daydreamed about Betty Jo Randall. She was blonde and blue eyed. Students were judged by how popular they were, and those who were singled out were always smiling and well-dressed, even in the Depression. "She's so popular," always followed the mention of Betty Jo's name. Steve would whistle over and over the tune to the words: "Five foot two, eyes of blue, has anybody seen my gal?" He daydreamed of Betty Jo's being his girlfriend, of going to movies and taking her on long drives in his father's aging Oldsmobile.

Steve saw Betty Jo stop in the hall one day and say something to Solly. For just a moment, she smiled and hugged her books. Something like an icicle stabbed through his head. Solly, a year behind Steve, was also popular. He was on the basketball team. He wheedled money to buy the kind of loafers that everyone wanted, or for wool pants that kept their crease. It had not occurred to Steve to ask for loafers and good pants for himself. Solly never ate lunch with Steve, Lefty, and Perry. He ate with other basketball players. Solly would walk by them in the halls or outside and seem not to notice them. "He's pretending he's not Greek," Lefty said, and spat his scorn onto the sidewalk.

Steve saw Solly after school one Friday, talking with several students. He came close to him, wanting to be part of the group, listening while they talked about meeting at the A &W Root Beer stand. Solly paired off with another basketball player, and as he walked away, he looked at Steve and said, "What are you doing here?" Steve turned, his face hot, and walked off toward the Railroad Hotel. He calmed himself by thinking about Betty Jo.

Steve thought he had hidden his fantasy from Lefty and Perry. The telephone rang one evening and he held his breath on hearing Betty Jo's voice. Marika was seated in the kitchen, cleaning bits of rock from a tray of lentils. His heart beat unbearably, his mouth dry, as Betty Jo asked him to meet her for a Coke at the Rexall Drug. He quickly washed his face, slicked down his hair with oil, and hurried to the drugstore. Lefty and Perry were at the counter, slapping their palms on the marble top and pretending they were going to fall off the stools, imitating Perry's sister Sophie's parody of Betty Jo. Steve would not speak to them for days.

Now at the university, where he was studying business, Steve saw Betty Jo often. She smiled at everyone. At the library he listened to three students, sitting across the table from him. One of them said, "Betty Jo finally decided on Chi Omega. I was just going to ask her to my frat dance, but Jim Richards asked her to the Sigma Chi pledge party." Betty Jo walked across the grass with cocky football and basketball players, wearing red pullover sweaters with big white Us on the front. Steve glimpsed her in the College Inn with friends he thought of as society girls, laughing, holding glasses of soft drinks. It was all too different from what he knew: sororities, fraternities that did not pledge Greeks, dances, parties, meetings at the College Inn. Everything he had not thought about came to taunt him: that Betty Jo would not look at a Greek; that she was probably a Mormon, which guaranteed her never doing more than giving him one of her popular smiles. He sneered at himself for thinking of taking her on drives in his father's Oldsmobile, parking at the state capitol where the city lights below dotted the valley, and necking. Moving out of Greek Town and near Liberty Park had not changed anything.

Once in a while, high-school acquaintances stopped to talk with him under the tree-lined, horseshoe-shaped campus, but he felt alone. He wished Lefty and Perry could have enrolled at the university—at least Perry, who had been smart in school; Lefty had barely made it to graduation. As for himself, at the university he made Cs in English, B minuses in American history, and As in economics.

The economics professor amazed him. His thick, steel-gray hair stood out like a porcupine's and his red jowls were mournful; he looked like one of Milt Valiotis's well-fed political friends. The professor called on him often. This gave Steve confidence. Once, before a final exam, the student who sat in front of him stopped him in the library and asked him a question about the stock market and how its fluctuations might affect world trade. Steve would have liked to join the university band and march on the football field with his old clarinet, but he could not take the time. He had to clean the Railroad Hotel and work in the office.

STEVE DID SOMETHING terrible at this time and the memory of it would come back to him at intervals the rest of his life. Years would pass and he would not think about it and then it would be there, stark, stuck to his other memories week after week. Eventually a temporary reprieve would come.

Andreas told Steve to clear out a room where one of the hotel tenants, Old Tsimblis, had died. The body had not had time to stiffen and the odor of sickness and decay hung in the shabby room. As in all the rooms, there were three pieces of furniture: a bed with a metal headboard painted to look like wood, a nicked chest of drawers, and a kitchen chair. The one in Tsimblis's room had a rung missing. The body, dressed in dirty, long underwear, lay atop an old, thin army blanket. The cheeks were sunken; the whiskered face, yellow. The skeletal, blue-veined hands were curled as if they had frantically tried to grab something. The toenails were long, brown, and dirty. The only evidence that someone—Tsimblist—had lived there were bottles of medicine on an orange crate, one with a skull and bones on the label, a water-stained letter from Greece, and an old Greek newspaper, neatly folded and looking as if it had never been read. Two pairs of pants and a brown coat hung on nails at the top of the door, and inside the drawers of the chest were a stained pair of long underwear, a few black socks, and three rumpled shirts.

Steve telephoned the Deseret Mortuary and the body was picked up, to be washed and wrapped in a *savanon,* a burial sheet. The priest and the council president came immediately and watched while Steve went through the drawers. "If you find any money, it belongs to the church," the dapper president said, speaking with that clipped authority that Uncle Harry used. "We're sick and tired of burying these old bachelors who never saved a dime! Spent it all on *poutanes!*"

"We mustn't speak ill of the dead," the priest said, short and fat-cheeked, with a glossy black mustache, and he watched Steve. The president gingerly took down the pants from the nail on the door and holding them by the cuffs, jiggled them. A few pennies and nickels fell on the dilapidated carpet. "Aaa," he said with disgust.

After they left, Steve bundled the few clothes, smelling of sweat and urine, with the bedsheets and blankets. "Burn them all!" Andreas had ordered. "The miserable syphilitic!" Steve carried the bundle to the hotel's backyard and made a fire in a rusty oil drum. A raw, pungent odor rose from the flames.

A teenage girl stopped to watch. She was wearing a faded pink silk dress, wrinkled and oil-spotted. Her high-heeled shoes curled up at the toes. Steve knew she must be one of the thousands of transients riding the freights who hoped to find work in the city. Railroad detectives no longer chased them out with billy clubs: there were too many of them. The girl had tried to arrange her grimy hair in the movie-queen Rita Hayworth style, one side combed back from her ear, the other hanging over her left eye. She took two steps closer and stood on the ground, where stunted tumbleweeds had pushed through the hard crust. "Whatcha burnin'?" In spite of the pathetic attempts to look older, her voice was like a child's.

"Just trash," Steve said, glancing at her quickly, but long enough to see the specks of soot on her throat.

She walked behind him to the door of the hotel. "You got a room to rent? My ma's lookin' for a room to rent."

Steve nodded, and immediately knew he should have said there were none: only men supposedly lived in the hotel. Yet Steve had found that women had been in the rooms: bobby pins on the floor, spills of talcum powder—and one woman had forgotten her slip. Steve looked over his shoulder. "I should have told you only men live here." The girl said that was okay. Steve said it wasn't a good idea. In silence they walked up the creaking stairs to the landing and into the dead man's room. "Well, I have to burn the mattress now."

She said, "It's not bad with a cover over it. We could fix the room up." She came closer, smiling, her eyebrows arched flirtatiously. Steve smelled the unwashed, cheap-perfume smell, and they were on the stained, acrid-smelling mattress. When it was over, she stood up, buttoned the top of her dress, pulled down the skirt, picked up the coins from the floor, and was gone.

Steve dragged the mattress down the stairs and into the backyard. It was too large for the smoldering drum. He built a fire out of dried weeds and old newspapers and placed the mattress on it. He watched it to make certain it would burn black. Instead of returning to sweep the room and take down the curtains for his mother to wash, he hurried home. He took a bath while his mother wondered aloud about this midweek bathing. "The room was filthy dirty," he told her.

"You did right," she said. "Those miserable men. They didn't know why they were living."

He was ashamed to look at the icon: he was unworthy, despicable, but he said the Lord's Prayer, made the sign of the cross, and asked forgiveness.

That night, panic attacked his heart: the girl could have given him the clap or syphilis; he could have made her pregnant; she was underage; his parents might find out; a renter in a neighboring room could have been sick and not gone to work that day or worked the graveyard shift and heard them. His mother—he could see her horrified face in the dark. Next to him Solly slept peacefully; he had been pulling down girls' pants since he was thirteen years old.

AT THE END of the year, Steve said he would leave school. Solly had graduated from high school and would also attend the university. The $85 annual tuition grew in Steve's imagination into a fortune. Marika began making whiskey in the basement of the bungalow, remembering how Steve's godfather had done it before he was deported. The copper still that had been hidden in the cellar of the Greek-Town house began a new life. Steve and Solly bought packages of raisins in grocery stores all over town. Marika fermented the raisins with sugar, wheat, and yeast, then strained and distilled the mash. Her whiskey was high-grade and burned with a blue flame when she put a lighted match to it. She finished by adding a few drops of iodine to give it the amber color and bite that drinkers wanted. Andreas took the whiskey—Marika made about twenty pints at a time—to his office, where he sold some to neighbors, but most of it to uptown American doctors, lawyers, and politicians. Marika said, "Stay in school. I'll get you the money."

Steve objected: "There won't be any business left, the way Papa and Uncle Heracles do business. I've got to quit and be in the office every day."

Marika agreed that the *periousia,* the property, came first. She talked often about the *periousia.* It had to be protected; attention had to be paid to it; they had to have four eyes or it would be lost. The *periousia* then included the Railroad Hotel, the Arcadia Tobacco

Shop, a row of small shops near Main Street, a run-down, two-story boardinghouse where bachelor Greeks rented rooms, three old houses near the church, one of which had been remodeled into a grocery store, four pieces of vacant land west of the railyards, and several tumbleweeded lots on the highway that led to the small airport. Andreas and Heracles had bought the lots and two of the houses for the price of paying the back taxes. Marika and Andreas talked so often about the *periousia* that Steve, Solly, and their sisters thought they were a family of means, even if there was a Depression.

The day he left the university for good, he stood in the entrance to the campus and looked at the white administration building in the center of the horseshoe—a pseudo-ancient-Greek replica. Then he looked at the old brick buildings on either side of it and his gaze lingered on the Business Building. Head down, he walked to the streetcar stop with a dry sadness in his chest that he hadn't expected.

On the day that Steve left for his full-time work in the office, Marika whispered, her head leaning toward the bedroom door where Andreas was getting dressed, "Be careful, your eyes four, so others don't take advantage of the *periousia."* She looked at him with an ominous lift of her eyebrows. Steve knew she meant Uncle Harry and Aunt Myrsini.

When Lefty and Perry learned that Steve was no longer a student at the university, they resumed their old routine of being together often. On weekends, they drove to Black Rock Beach on the shores of the Great Salt Lake, usually in Andreas's faded-blue Oldsmobile. They did a little floating and much gazing at girls in bathing suits with wired tops that pushed up their breasts. And what a surprise! It was easy to get a girl who went all the way.

One evening at dusk Lefty was knocked down by someone's brass knuckles. "That'll teach you to flirt with a white girl," the man said. Then he ran for his life, with Steve and Perry chasing him into the lake. He stood there for hours, waist deep in the rapidly cooling water, afraid to come out. Leisurely, Steve, Perry, and Lefty ate hot dogs bought at the shanty refreshment stand, lay on the rough sand, told a few lies and many stories, and laughed more loudly than warranted. They waited until night, then got into the Oldsmobile and roared off.

One Labor Day they drove to Yellowstone Park in a 1920s Chevrolet that belonged to Perry's uncle. It broke down just over the Utah-Idaho border and Steve had to give up his nine dollars, which was to last the weekend, to get it fixed. They bought bologna, a loaf of bread, and peanut butter. The next, day they drove home without seeing Old Faithful erupt.

VI

[1935]

STEVE'S EXASPERATION with the business never left him; eating, working, in bed next to sleeping Solly, he thought about it and about his father and his Uncle Harry. When he argued about their being more systematic in keeping records, his father told him to plug it and Uncle Harry warned, "You found the table set! You didn't work to establish it!" Steve wanted to tell him that he himself had found the table set when he arrived in America. During the noon hour, he walked to the Denver & Rio Grande Western railroad restaurant to escape. He sat at the counter and watched the trains enter and leave the railyards. It kept him from feeling lonely and adrift.

Steve succeeded in establishing a monthly wage, two hundred each for Andreas and Heracles, and one hundred twenty-five for himself. His father and uncle accepted the wages after much grumbling from his father and cursing from Uncle Harry: "You think you're so smart with your new ideas. Remember when you go shit, your asshole better be big enough."

Steve felt a lift, a buoyancy, over his triumph. He thought it was the beginning; it would lead to other reforms. He did not know that his mother, not he, had been the cause of the monthly wages. Her relentless sighing over Aunt Myrsini's extravagances had finally been too much for his father.

They began to draw wages. It lasted about two months, before both Andreas and Heracles started taking from the till and writing IOUS on little pieces of paper and leaving them in the cash register.

They each had a desk in the cluttered office. The desks were oblong tables with two narrow drawers under the top—no side drawers. As papers accumulated, they put them haphazardly in a file cabinet, wherever there was room, with no attention to subjects. Rental documents could be put in a file under the Greek word for rents, or under the name of a renter, or just be laid across the top of other file folders. When the cabinet bulged, documents and letters were set in untidy piles on shelves that Andreas himself had put up several years ago, all sagging to the right.

Steve tried to get a proper filing system in place and told his father and Uncle Harry that two more file cabinets were needed. "No, siree!" Uncle Harry said in English, which he was using more of lately. Steve's father echoed Uncle Harry: "You're loose with other people's money," he said, then, "Well, all right, go get them. Go to the *cheapie* store." *Cheapie* was Andreas's word for the used-furniture store.

Steve got the old cabinets and had Penny help him file everything as well as possible. Both Penny and Georgie were taking typing classes in high school and they answered the few letters that came to the office. The first time she saw the girls in the office, Myrsini left immediately without a word, but darted a malevolent look at

Heracles. He lifted his shoulders and put out his palms in a beseeching gesture that told of his helplessness.

Andreas and Heracles now no longer bothered with filing any papers. They left letters and documents on their desks and shouted at Steve when he filed them: "I want them here at my fingertips!" They gave him conflicting orders: "Get the Mormon to fix the windows in the *hoteli*." Steve lifted the receiver. "No, better get that carpenter, you know the one with the false teeth." A moment later: "Go look at it yourself. Maybe you can fix it. Save the money."

They sent him on errands they had previously done themselves with peremptory orders in Greek interspersed with English words they had appropriated: "Go to the *builda* and tell the old man Jinkins he has to pay to fix the *eleveta* and he better take care of the crack in the *floori*. When you come back, take the *caro* to the *garatzi* to fix the *brekis*." They made his stomach hurt.

When they left the office, he was relieved. Alone in the small, crowded room, he often had little to do. Hours went by and no one came in to pay rent or to make complaints about plumbing, furnaces, or needed repairs. He read the newspaper and every item in the latest issue of *Public Records:* the list of marriages, divorces, bankruptcies, convictions, court judgments, properties bought and sold, deeds recorded.

When he returned home, his mother made her demands on him. Everything was up to him. Solly was exempt: the supposed scholar, the future army general, their mother believed, impressed with his ROTC uniform. "Studying to be a *stratighos*," she told the midwife. Solly did nothing for Penny and Georgie. All through high school, Steve had been taking his sisters to church and Greek lodge affairs. That was how it was, just as if they were in Greece, he had to be present to keep boys and young men from approaching them in ways that would make them the center of gossip. Marika kept telling him to "look out for your sisters," which meant he was to find them husbands.

Greeks did not let their daughters date. Steve took them to dances, the *horoesperidhes*. Marika saw to it that the girls were dressed well; they did not have many dresses, but she got the money for special occasions from Andreas. She told the *mami* that it was like pulling the money out of his nose. Georgie kept the house in a frenzy when she begged for a dress that cost too much, and if that did not suffice, she sobbed until Marika, grudging, but looking guilty, gave in.

Marika and Andreas did not go to every festivity. If Andreas was off looking at property or meeting a business acquaintance, Marika thought it improper to be seen without him. When they did attend the celebrations, Penny and Georgie stayed at the other end of the hall. Solly, whether his parents were there or not, immediately disappeared and stood outside the church basement, smoking and telling dirty stories with other young men. In his early teens, Con, dressed in a navy blue suit, sat with his mother and never danced.

The pattern of taking Penny and Georgie to dances began with a flurry of excitement as they got ready, a stiff silence as Steve drove them to the hall, and then an amorphous sense of defeat for him almost the moment they entered the church basement. The musicians —three immigrants—would start out playing an old Greek folk song on the *laouto, clarino,* and *lyra.* Penny and Georgie stayed on the side lines, refusing to join the women and girls in the circle dances. After two hours or so of Greek dances, someone would put American records on a portable record player. Dutifully, Steve danced first with Penny, who seemed to him to be dragging an elephant foot, then with Georgie, who squiggled her shoulders. He took turns leading them around the hall. Striated layers of blue tobacco smoke floated overhead and the record player's volume was turned up to contest the raucous noise of the crowd. Steve looked across the room at friends, lounging against smoke-grayed walls, eyeing the girls.

As he danced with Penny, she kept a steady chatter that escalated into shouting gossip she had heard in the rest room. When it was Georgie's turn, she tried to wheedle something out of him, like helping to get their parents' permission to visit a friend in Chicago, or—an almost unthinkable fantasy—to go to Mardi Gras in New Orleans with three women she had kept up with since high school.

Steve pressed his knuckles hard in the small of their backs until they complained: They didn't seem to know that they were on serious business—finding someone to marry them. When that was accomplished, he could get them off his back, out of the office, and silence Aunt Myrsini, who put on insincere looks of concern: "The girls should be home learning to become housekeepers. Once they marry, they'll be out of the *grafio* and other women will have to be trained to take their places." Looking as if she had been reprimanded, Marika ventured to say Penny and Georgie should stay home, but the girls screeched at the suggestion: "So we'll be cooped up in these four walls! Is that all you want us to do—wash dishes, cook, and wait on everybody?" Marika looked perplexed: "Isn't that what women are supposed to do?" Penny and Georgie ran into their bedroom and cried loudly behind the closed door.

One evening Steve managed to be near a group of loungers when the music ended and he bantered with them. They all knew each other from their days at Greek school. Perry and Lefty would not even look at Penny. She had piled her light-brown hair high on her head, following the latest styles in women's magazines. Her hazel eyes looked at the men with the same blandness as Andreas when he was listening to a radio program and not quite catching what was going on. "What are you doing now, Penny?" Pan Daskalas asked. Steve thought Pan might be the one to get her off his hands.

Penny giggled. "Same old thing I've been doing since I graduated. Sitting at a typewriter in my dad's office, getting 'secretary spread.'" Penny giggled again, this time with a nervous glance at Steve, realizing what she had said. No one asked to dance with her, and she drifted to a row of chairs where girls who had been in the choir with her sat and waited.

Steve danced with Georgie. She was wearing a low-cut black silk dress and he wondered how she had got out of the house without her mother's seeing her. Her black hair was piled high like Penny's; her eyelashes were heavily mascaraed; and she had extended the thinness of her lips with a dark red lipstick. Steve was embarrassed at her clothes, her makeup, and her haughty air. Was his mother blind? When they stopped to talk with the young men, Georgie lifted her plucked black eyebrows and looked away as if she were bored.

That night Ted Manopoulos introduced Steve to a cousin from Wyoming; she was staying with his family while she attended the university. Steve asked her to dance, and as they circled the hall, a fine tremble coursed from the hand that held hers and up his arm to his shoulder. The second time they passed the row of seated girls, his sisters were standing in the doorway of the restroom, their arms folded across their waists, their hostile eyes on her, Sylvia. Steve asked Sylvia about school: she was getting a teacher's certificate. I guess, he said, she studied all the time. On Fridays when she had only an eight o'clock class and on Saturdays when she had none, she was the cashier at her uncle's restaurant, the State Street Grill.

Steve wanted to dance with her again, but he knew that if he did, the hall would buzz. The overweight mothers sitting with their arms crossed under their puffed-out breasts, would take note of it. They already had. All eyes were upon him and Sylvia. The girls on the folding chairs were watching. The young men leaning against the wall were smiling.

Until then, Steve had always eaten in the Denver & Rio Grande Western depot restaurant, a block from the Railroad Hotel. From then on, he occasionally ate lunch on Fridays at the State Street Grill. He resisted making it a Friday habit, not wanting to appear too eager. After a few weeks, he began going to the State every Friday at noon. He sat at the counter as close to the cash register as he could and spent most of the time eating and looking at the large mirror behind the counter. On a wooden shelf at the bottom of the mirror were bottles of ketchup, vinegar, oil, and steak sauces, a large glass bowl of small packages of breakfast cereal, and assorted glassware. Above the mirror were signs advertising Hires Root Beer and Coca-Cola. Steve looked at all these items as if they had a deep interest for him. The Grill was small, a narrow entrance with the counter at one side, then at the back, perpendicular to the counter, a larger section with booths on both sides. The ceiling was a sooted pressed tin; the wooden floor was worn to thinness; and the fumes from the kitchen told of frying onions, roasting meat, a faint moldiness that came from decades of cooking, eating, bustling, and something else, sour and greasy like camouflaged dirt. Steve found if he went at eleven thirty, hardly anyone was in the restaurant.

[1937]

HE HAD FANTASIES about Sylvia as he'd had about Betty Jo. This time they were about Sylvia and himself in a home of their own. He glanced at her often. Her long, shoulder-length brown hair glistened under the phosphorescent lights; her skin was flawless, and her eyes were exceptionally dark. This was different, he knew, from blonde Betty Jo. He thought that he would some day marry Sylvia. He wanted to ask if her uncle would let her go out with him, but he did not dare: only engaged couples went to movies and drive-ins together. If he asked Sylvia, and her uncle by some miracle consented . . . but then he had those sisters with no prospects. "Damn Greek customs," he said out loud.

"You should talk. Greek boys get to do anything they want. We know where you go every Friday for lunch," Penny said and gave a theatrical toss of her head. Georgie said, "Can't you find a girl with some pep to her."

"You mean pep like you? With your mascara and your nose up in the air?"

Marika asked, "Pep? What is this word *pep?*" She had given up trying to force the children to continue speaking Greek and had not learned more than the "How much for the cesh?" and "More chip, more chip," but she would catch a word here and there and sometimes understand the meaning of the conversation going on around her. "With some *kefi*," Georgie said, her thin mouth sour.

"Educated women don't make good housekeepers," Marika said. "Don't forget you have sisters to marry off."

Georgie screamed and ran out of the room. "This is America. Let them find their own husbands," Steve said. His mother went to bed with a towel wrapped around her head, and his father lectured him for making her sick, forgetting his responsibilities, and told him to take the girls to the national AHEPA convention in New York. "We can't afford it," Steve said, but Andreas said it was important and took money out of his savings for the girls' dresses.

Steve told Sylvia he was going to the convention. She said, "You don't look too happy about it."

He was not. On the train, he read magazines he had bought to keep from having to talk with Penny and Georgie any more than necessary. He had a coach ticket for himself and a Pullman berth for his sisters. They made him ashamed with their giggling and laughing, their constant walking back and forth to the observation car, stopping to make inane remarks as he sat in his crumpled suit, his neck stiff from trying to sleep sitting up.

Penny and Georgie had also taken well-used magazines with them—they traded with friends—and pointed to models, discussed their clothes, became so involved in excited talk that Georgie asked Steve's opinion on a dress she thought would look good on her. He was about to say, "Get lost," but he knew he had to be careful or the trip would be a waste of money and then he would never be free of them. He was in a bad temper from having had little sleep. He was certain Uncle Harry, Aunt Myrsini, and Constantine had had Pullman berths when they had gone ahead two days earlier.

In Grand Central Station, Steve felt he was herding Penny and Georgie out of the overwhelming, frantic crowd; his heart beat with fear that they would never get to the outside. Then he got them into a taxi, the crowded streets with dangerous, blaring cars and trucks all around, then through the hotel doors and up to their rooms. He was unsure if he had tipped the taxi driver and the bellhop enough. He wanted to be home. Uncle Harry had left a note for him: "You and girls be in big ballroom seven o'clock sharp. Not be late."

Steve showered and lay on the bed, but he was still tired when they took the elevator to the ballroom. Again he had the feeling he was herding his sisters. The ballroom was decorated with swags of red-white-and-blue bunting. The officers of the lodge and their wives sat on an elevated platform at a table with an arrangement of red roses spreading out from the center. Behind them was a backdrop of a large American flag. A Greek flag stood on a stand at the right of the table. Some of the young women were beautiful. They were dressed in flowing satin and tulle and sat with middle-aged parents and younger sisters and brothers. Great bouquets of flowers, the gleam of silver, and tall glassware gave the impression of luxury.

Steve, Penny, and Georgie sat with Uncle Harry, Aunt Myrsini, and Constantine. Uncle Harry and Con wore dinner jackets and Aunt Myrsini a lace dress of chocolate color. Steve wondered if the tuxedos were bought or rented. Aunt Myrsini had cut her hair; in front of each ear was a flat curl. With critical eyes she looked at Steve, Penny, and Georgie in turn, but evidently decided that day to be light-hearted. Gaily, she talked about the wonders of New York.

A few other lodge members they knew had come to the convention. Milt Valiotis was standing with a group of men wearing the wide bands of lodge officers. He came to their table, raised his hand high in greeting, smiled widely, said the girls were beautiful, and he would find them husbands. He did not look at Aunt Myrsini, except to acknowledge her with a quick nod that she returned with a cold smile.

A festive din reached the ceiling. People called out greetings to others at tables both near and far. Steve watched young men make trips to the bar, which interested him because the repeal of the Prohibition Amendment in Utah had brought a brief sale of liquor, then the state legislature settled on 3.2 beer. He thought of going to the bar himself and bringing back drinks, but remembered that one drink and Penny could not stop talking. After the steak dinner, one speaker after another gave orations in English about the AHEPA ideals, many of their words accenting the wrong syllables. Penny and Georgie nudged each other and smirked. Aunt Myrsini's plucked eyebrows pulled together with unwavering censure.

After the banquet Uncle Harry introduced Penny and Georgie to fellow Ahepans and their sons. Penny smiled vacantly, and Georgie lifted her head and looked around the ballroom. They drifted off to the bar. There they began talking with other young women like themselves, overly dressed with only an occasional offer to dance. Penny danced by with a handsome man, talking away at him. Georgie stood with arms folded and scrutinized the dancers.

"What do you think of the meat market this year?" a man nearby, younger than Steve, said to several other young men, who laughed. When he realized the "meat market" meant the girls in the ballroom, he hurried to rescue Georgie. Silently, they circled the ballroom. On one turn, Steve glimpsed Uncle Harry and Milt Valiotis in the foyer in serious conversation. When the dance finished, heavy-set men approached him to introduce their daughters or nieces who hovered close by, but Steve asked none of them to dance. The ballroom became warm, pervaded by the scent of men's shaving lotion and the women's perfumed sweat. It all came to nothing.

On the train going home, Penny and Georgie sat across from Steve in the almost empty coach car and gossiped about the ball, made fun of the speakers, and impersonated Aunt Myrsini who had been scornful of the American wife of the lodge's vice president: She had worn a black satin dress with one shoulder exposed. "'He preens, thinks he's got a prize, just because she's an American. If he had a Greek wife, he wouldn't let her step out of the house in a dress like that.'"

"Goddamn you," Steve hissed. "I bring you all the way across the country, spend all this money and all the good it did! Why the hell do you think I brought you to this convention?" He looked at Penny, wanting to choke her thin neck. "To find you a husband, you stupid moron! You make no effort! You don't lift a finger! You want some guy to appear out of nowhere! One of you is a dope and the other is so stuck-up, no one will come near her!"

Penny and Georgie began screaming that they would find their own husbands. They didn't need him! People turned to look at them. They ran back to their Pullman car, crying revenge: "Wait till we tell Papa."

Steve fumed and looked out the window at the prairie flying past. His stomach tightened and began to hurt. When he got home, he thought of Uncle Harry and Con in tuxedos and Aunt Myrsini in, what looked to him, like a very expensive dress. He said so to his father: "Uncle Harry doesn't seem to worry about money, him in his tuxedo and Con, not yet fifteen, decked out like a bridegroom." Andreas said the family had to be well represented and he should shut his shitty mouth. "I didn't wear a tuxedo," Steve said, and his father's thick eyebrows came together as if he were thinking about it. His mother said, "You didn't try hard enough for your sisters." Steve thought of telling his father about Uncle Harry and Milt Valiotis, but he let it go. His father would shout, bellow, make him look foolish.

Aunt Myrsini telephoned. She complained to Marika about Penny and Georgie. Steve could not believe that his mother was shrilling at her into the telephone receiver. "My girls have good manners! You just want to find fault! And since when did you care if they had husbands or not? Don't tell me I need your help to marry them off! I have my sons now!"

Steve walked outside and down the street, amazed at his mother. *My sons,* she had said. She had also begun to talk back to his father. He thought she had become stronger because he and Solly—all the good *he* would do her—were old enough now to protect her.

On Friday Steve went to the State Street Grill, into the familiar smell of cooking food, grease, and mold. Someone was sitting in his place at the counter, a light-haired young man who talked to Sylvia as she stood behind the cash register. Steve thought she was glad to see him; it seemed her eyes lit up. The young man was almost finished eating, and Steve waited to slide over to his place when he got up.

Sylvia's uncle came out of the kitchen and looked on while the blond man paid his check and Sylvia answered his remarks about the weather and other polite, superficial talk. For a few seconds Sylvia's uncle watched the young man, all the while untying and re-tying the stained apron over his big stomach. As he turned to go back to the kitchen, he noticed Steve and walked behind the counter to greet him. "You go to the convention?" he asked in heavily accented English. "Everybody have good time?"

Steve said they all enjoyed it. "I'm sure your Uncle Harry he enjoy it!" Sylvia's uncle, a glum man, had never come out to speak to him before, and his attempt at friendliness unsettled Steve. In the mirror, he glimpsed Sylvia's flushed, embarrassed face. She looked at the keys of the cash register without raising her eyes. "Nice to see you come in," her uncle said, smiling stiffly and showing a gold tooth in the middle of his mouth. Steve looked at the celluloid-covered menu as if he were studying it. He knew every item on it, and he sensed Sylvia's shame. fathers, brothers, uncles looking for husbands for the women in their families.

Steve did not take the vacated seat. After he had given his order to the waitress, he looked at Sylvia and said, "I feel like I've been gone months, not five days." Sylvia smiled and put on a cheerful look as people paid for their lunch. "Was your lunch satisfactory?" she asked each one.

Steve ate the blue plate special: sliced roast beef, mashed pota-toes with gravy, and green beans. The five days he had been away had cut off the flow of their beginning friendship. He was self-conscious as if they were meeting for the first time. He could not think of what to say. Then he said with a short laugh, "What would you say if someone said the lunch wasn't satisfactory?" She blushed, and her slender fingers played over the cash register keys. He stopped going to the State to eat. He did not know why, except that a faint queasiness lurched in his stomach when he thought about it.

VII

FOR DAYS AFTER the convention, Andreas and Marika ranted against Heracles, Myrsini, and Steve: they had not tried hard enough to find husbands for Penelope and Georgia, then they withdrew into silence. Marika was now stout as she neared forty, and Andreas nearly bald, with a belt that divided his paunch into two parts. Wordlessly they ate, looking disgruntled as if they had been disgraced through no fault of their own. The clock on the electric stove ticked on in the still, heavy air.

One evening Solly arrived in time to eat with them. Marika never asked why he was late coming home for dinner. Solly wore his ROTC uniform, which his parents respected; they had no idea that a hundred and more students at the university wore identical uniforms. The family waited to see what his mood was. It was good that evening; he broke the kitchen's week-long silence with an anecdote about his besting an economics professor in an argument. His parents beamed, then Marika looked sorrowful. "Achh, Solon, you are making your way in the world, but your poor sisters don't have a good fate. They'll remain unmarried. Achh, achh."

Penny and Georgie muttered at their mother. Solon turned to Steve. "What happened? Didn't anything pan out?"

Pandemonium exploded: shrieks from the girls, curses in general from Andreas, cries for her poor daughters from Marika, and shouts from Steve. Solon lifted his palms in a lofty gesture of restraint, and the voices quieted. Andreas said the trip had cost four hundred and fifty dollars and forty-three cents; Marika dabbed her eyes over the possibility of Myrsini's having the Evil Eye; and Steve said, "Next time, you take over, Solly. See how you like it."

"Solon," Marika pleaded, "don't you know any good boys?"

Penny and Georgie stood up and glared at their mother. "Sit down, girls," Solly, the sudden peacemaker, said. "You know what I think?" His parents and sisters leaned forward, while Solly looked at the ceiling, "I think the girls should go to the university."

"What!" Andreas shouted. "In the *Depresh,* girls should go to the university!"

"Nobody wants educated girls for daughters-in-law," Marika protested.

"Things are changing," Solly said.

"Okay by me," Georgie said, and Penny choked, getting ready to cry with excitement.

"It'll elevate them," Solly said, now wholeheartedly taken over by his idea, "and people will come asking for them."

"You plucked that out of the air," Steve said to Solly in English. Solly nodded, giving Steve a wry look.

Late into the night, Andreas and Marika talked in their bedroom and Penny and Georgie in theirs. Steve in his bed caught his sisters' fervid words: "new clothes" and "pleated skirts." It galled him that the family took Solly so seriously when he did nothing for them.

He had to get out of the house; his insides burned up at night. He could not live through evening after evening with his parents and sisters. His friends Perry and Lefty were engaged to girls who had sat on the chairs in the church basement, hoping someone would ask them to dance. One evening on Main Street, Steve was driving the family Oldsmobile and they drove parallel to him, Perry and Fanny in front and Lefty and Goldie in the back. "Meet us at the Doll House," Perry shouted, while Fanny nodded encouragement. Steve shook his head. "I can't." Lefty leaned out the window with his big hands making wild motions. "Get a girl, Steve!" he shouted. The Black Rock Beach days were over.

Penny and Georgie enrolled at the university, and one result of Solly's was good for Steve: they no longer attended the church festivities. Now they went about with their heads lifted; he told them so, but they ignored him. Marika explained to the midwife and visitors that her daughters were learning "things for the house" at the university.

Lefty telephoned him several times to meet at Goldie's house. "Who'll be there?" Steve asked.

"Oh, I dunno. Perry. Some kids we knew in Greek school."

"No, thanks." He knew what they were doing: They had some girl picked out for him.

The stagnant days went slowly by. There was so little business that Andreas sometimes went to the Paradise Coffeehouse in the middle of the day. There he played *barbout* with bachelors who were unemployed or had a few days' work under President Roosevelt's WPA, raking the grounds of the state capitol and the Salt Lake City and County building. Heracles spent little time in the office; he would leave with his fake, serious frown of having burdensome business at the bank or with the attorney or at the properties.

Entire days now could go by without a single person coming into the office to pay rent or talk about a lease. The railyards were no longer noisy throughout the day; trains chugged off only at long intervals. The Railroad Hotel was as quiet as if it were vacant. When Steve had begun working full-time in the office, he had hired a thin, hungry-looking man about his own age to clean the hotel. Elroy had been a Union Pacific freight clerk before he was let go in the early years of the Depression, and had not had a steady job in seven years. He did a lot of talking with the two old Greeks whiling away their life in the lobby. Giannis still faced the entrance, certain that one day a Cretan would walk in and slit his throat over their generations-old vendetta.

At the end of each day, Steve drove his father home and entered the house with dread. The monotony of sitting with the family at the table while Penny and Georgie prattled about school and clothes—who wore what—and his mother and father repeated rumors and gossip sent heat up to the top of his head. He wanted to turn around and drive off, but where would he go?

Lefty telephoned him at the office. "Come on, Steve, come to the lodge picnic at Lagoon. Perry said just yesterday we never see you anymore. Come on. It'll be fun."

"Okay, but I'll take my own car, so I can leave when I want."

"Swell."

Penny and Georgie listened to Steve's inviting them to go to the Lagoon amusement park with disdainful sniffs. Marika told them they were ungrateful to refuse their brother. "Grateful for what?" they said in English. "You ever see Solly at the U?" Steve said, sneering. He could not understand how it had happened that Solly had pledged a fraternity, the first Greek ever asked to, and he wondered how he had got the money for it.

He drove to the amusement park in the Oldsmobile, which besides having lost its shine had accumulated little dents and scrapings. The green farmland on both sides of the road stretched to the slopes of the great mountains. The scent of newly mowed alfalfa was in the air, and men and boys were irrigating fields of corn and potatoes. To the west the sun glinted on a bay of water; birds flew over it and dipped out of view.

He was rested, at peace with himself when he drove into the park. He was even a little excited as he walked toward the tree-shaded tables where the Arcadian lodge was holding its picnic. He avoided Aunt Myrsini and Uncle Harry, sitting at one of the long tables. Aunt Myrsini was holding forth, and the few immigrant women with some education were smiling and nodding. Constantine saw Steve and craned his neck. Steve gave him a short wave and Constantine blushed.

Perry and Lefty got up from a table and came to meet him.

"We've been looking for you," Perry said, and Lefty, who towered over him, guffawed.

"What's the joke?" Steve said.

"Nothing, nothing." Lefty shrugged. "We was just making bets if you'd show up."

"Well, who won?"

Lefty and Perry glanced at each other and Perry said, "He did." Lefty grinned, showing his big teeth, which always reminded Steve of the icemen.

"Son-of-a-gun," Lefty said with a playful jab at Steve's arm, "got here just in time. The speeches are all done and the eats are on."

"God, Lefty, you talk like a hillbilly."

"That's what Goldie says. Now that she's got the ring on her finger, she says plenty."

Steve nodded to people at the tables they passed—the priest, the Greek-school teacher, others of his parents' generation, and a surprising number of young people in their teens. Platters were spread down the center of each table—mounds of sliced roast lamb, tomato-and-cucumber salad, spinach and feta cheese pastries. Perry stopped at a table with several empty chairs and said, "Here, Steve, you sit at the head of the table. Fanny and I are sitting here." Perry sat down at the corner of the table. Lefty lifted his long legs as if he were mounting a horse and took his place on the bench next to Goldie, across from Perry and Fanny.

A girl sat at the corner on Steve's right. He had seen her for years at church celebrations, but had never said even a "hello" to her. Her name was Mary; her father owned a small grocery store, or had; Steve could not remember which. He glanced at Perry and then at Lefty, who were busy eating and not looking at him. Steve remembered Mary was distantly related to Lefty. "You know Mary, don't you, Steve?" Lefty asked, avoiding Steve's eyes, his mouth shiny with grease.

"Well, sure. Don't all the Greeks in town know each other?"

Mary smiled, looked away from Steve, and said, "Hello."

She was not really pretty, Steve could see after a surreptitious look at her, but not bad, either. One eye turned slightly inward. "You should a' been here and heard old Rouhas," Perry said, groaning at mentioning the Greek-school teacher's name. "He gave one of those goddamn orations we used to hear every time we stepped inside Greek school."

Lefty then imitated the teacher, who was no longer dapper, but still thought he was, as if no one could see his expanding stomach and the drooping puffs under his eyes. Anecdotes came one after another; sometimes two people talked at once. Steve ate steadily, so he would not have to talk to Mary. He heard a peal of laughter from Aunt Myrsini and regretted he had not brought his parents with him. Andreas had gone to take a nap and his mother was watering the front yard when he left. Neither he nor Mary added to the liveliness at their table. Perry and Lefty got up to take Fanny and Goldie on some rides, and Goldie said, "Why don't you and Mary come too, Steve?"

"No. I'm too full," Steve said. "I might throw up."

"What a poop-out," Lefty said, and the four strolled away. After a long silence, Mary stood up and walked to the next table to speak with several girls her age, probably three or four years younger than Steve. Steve watched her; she was wearing a long white cotton dress with short sleeves and a tight waist. He saw that she had a good figure.

Soon after that, Steve left, enjoying the ride through the western dusk, the mountains now a deep blue. The last vestiges of an orange-and-red sunset streaked over the horizon. At home, Penny and Georgie wanted to know who had been at the picnic, what they ate, and what kind of engagement rings Fanny and Goldie had. He walked straight to bed and did not mind the dark room, nor Solly's cold feet when he came in around two o'clock.

Lefty and Perry began calling Steve at least once a week to "do something," and he knew Mary would be there. He agreed to go, and usually they sat in the living room of either Fanny's or Goldie's parents, ate popcorn, and listened to the radio, especially the *Hit Parade,* making penny bets on which tune would be the number one for the week. Steve learned through the conversation that Mary and Goldie worked at Woolworth's; that both were helping their brothers through the university; and that Goldie had finished paying for a set of dishes after—she laughed—two years in layaway. Goldie was Cretan; her eyes were black and sloe and her nose came straight down from her forehead, like the ancient Greek statues in their old Greek schoolbooks. Fanny was almost blonde, with blue eyes; she did not look Greek at all. Steve was glad for Lefty and Perry.

Lefty asked Steve if he wanted to go to the Chinese Gardens the coming Saturday.

"Who's going?"

"Just the gang, me and Goldie and Perry and Fanny." A pause, "And Mary."

"Okay."

Steve thought of taking Mary home that night, but her parents might notice she got out of an Oldsmobile and not out of Lefty's Ford.

In the morning Penny and Georgie hurried out of the kitchen as he walked in. Andreas was drinking coffee with a loud whistling and Marika, already having eaten, was sitting with her arms folded against her waist, as if she had been waiting for him. She was wearing an old black-silk Sunday dress that had been relegated to everyday wear. Steve dipped a *koulouraki,* his favorite cookie, into a cup of coffee and waited for his mother to speak.

"Now, Stavro, what's this I hear about you and the Tatsoglou girl Maria?"

"Who told you anything about me and the Tatsoglou girl?"

"The *mami.*"

"You mean Penelope and Georgia." He continued to dip and bite off pieces of the *koulouraki.*

"And, so if your sisters mentioned it, what does it matter who says something's going on?"

Andreas said, "Pour me some more coffee, Marika," and then, "So you're getting friendly with the Tatsoglou girl?"

Steve lifted his cup, then put it down with a hard clink. "What's wrong with that? I'm almost twenty-six. You want me to wait until I'm forty like a lot of these old Greeks who end up marrying young girls?"

His mother shook her head and looked down at the table, "No, no, but your sisters aren't married. It's not right for you to marry first."

"I said I'm twenty-six years old. Am I going to spend my old age in this house?"

"It's your responsibility, like a good brother. Your *filotimo*."

"I've had enough of that *filotimo* business. You keep talking like this is Greece, Mama."

Marika sat up straight. "You could find some other girl. Someone who's not cross-eyed."

"She's not cross-eyed."

"Her family's got nothing," Andreas said "Her father lost his grocery store and works for the WPA."

"Well, who the devil do you want me to marry?"

"The Kitsopoulos girl is nice, modest," his mother said.

"Yes," Andreas agreed with three definite nods that meant finality "He made plenty of money bootlegging and still has it."

Steve stood up and went into his bedroom, where Solly was sleeping off a hangover, sprawled out in boxer shorts. When he thought he had given his father enough time to finish eating, he backed the car out of the garage, and waited for Andreas to get in. On the way to the office, Andreas said, "I guess the Tatsoglou girl is *hokay,* if you think so."

Steve did not answer. At the office, when the new filing clerk came in, a dull young woman with protruding teeth and blotched skin, whom Myrsini approved of, he walked to Schubach Jewelers and bought an engagement ring, a small diamond in a gold setting. Taking big strides, he went back to the office, looked at his bank book, and figured out what he would have left after he bought a car. New ones were selling for about eight hundred and up; he had priced them one day. Since leaving the university, he had been depositing most of his one-hundred-twenty-five-dollar salary. His account had a little over a thousand dollars. He wondered how much it would cost to rent a house and buy furniture.

That evening on the mezzanine floor of the China Gardens restaurant, he sat next to Mary and put his arm on the back of her chair. She smiled at him, and he noticed her looking at him straight on, with no turning in of her right eye. While the young Chinese men, slender in their black pants and white shirts, served them with reserve and very little talk, Steve looked around at the Chinese screens, a large bronze-painted dragon on one wall and red paper lanterns hanging from the ceiling. He felt he had emerged from dull grayness into brightness. He ate as if he had been hungry for days He was solicitous: "Mary, did you get enough to eat? How about that custard for dessert?" Mary, he saw, ate hardly at all, spilled a little of the hot tea, and dropped a fork, which he retrieved and re-placed with one from a vacant table nearby.

At the table adjacent to theirs two young couples gave them furtive glances. Lefty said in Greek, "Look at those *Amerikanoi*. They act like they're looking at animals in a circus."

As if on cue, all of them, except Mary, who looked embarrassed, began talking loudly, laughing with unrestrained hilarity, talking in Greek and English, telling little inconsequential incidents that they found greatly amusing. The two couples at the next table gazed at them, one of the women with open mouth. They finished eating and simultaneously lifted their eyes to see everyone at Steve's table watching them. They got up and hurried out. "That'll teach them to look at us like we're freaks," Lefty said.

Perry, always methodical, figured out the bill and assessed the cost, showing the numbers to Lefty and Steve. Lefty made him go over the bill one more time. Fanny, Goldie, and Mary stood near the stairs, saying how good it was that Steve had joined them. "The

Three Musketeers together again," Goldie said, and looked at the three men going through their wallets and pockets, admiring them as if they were small boys.

"I'll take Mary home," Steve said.

Flustered, Mary looked at Lefty, who said, "Okay," and then in imitation of the black-dressed crones who sat in a row at the church *horoesperidhes,* shook his finger at Steve and said in shrill Greek, "Stavro, watch out! Don't put one finger on the girl or I'll put a curse on you." After whooping, he said in English, "You know their favorite curse? Making a poor guy impotent!" Another loud laughing, bringing the young Chinese to lift their eyes for a moment.

Steve remembered to open the car door for Mary. As he walked around to the driver's seat, he had a brief moment of uncertainty at what he was about to do. It passed as soon as he turned on the ignition. "We had a good time," he said, and Mary agreed: "It was fun." When Steve backed away from the curb, she said, "I live in the alley behind the church."

"Oh, yeah, where Lefty used to live."

Sitting primly, her hands folded, Mary went on, "We're just about the only family left in Greek Town. Our family and the Kamberis family next door."

"I know that alley pretty well. Me and Perry and Lefty used to chase each other down it all the time."

"Yes, I remember. Tessie Kamberis and I used to play hopscotch and had to get out of the way."

They were near Holy Trinity. Steve stopped under a corner light post. Mary leaned forward, one hand on the dashboard. Steve brought out the small blue velvet box and opened it. "It's an engagement ring. Okay?" He handed Mary the box.

Mary stared at the ring, then she turned to Steve, "Yes, I like it," she said, and tried it on. "It's just a little bit too big."

"We'll get that taken care of," he said, pulled Mary toward him, and they kissed for several minutes.

"I'd better go in. Should I tell my parents?"

"Sure. Do you want me to go in with you?"

After a moment Mary said, "All right."

All the small houses were dark except Mary's. A small light burned in the front part of it. "My mother doesn't go to bed until we're all home," she said.

"What happened to your sister Athena? She was in my grade at school."

"Athena," Mary said, and dropped her head, "married a Greek from the old country. She lives in Chicago." Almost inaudibly she added, "He's almost thirty years older than Athena."

"Well, that's too bad. I remember she was pretty."

Mary put her hand on the door handle. Steve jumped out, rushed around the car, and opened the door. He took her hand as they walked up the cracked cement walk to the front door. Mary turned the knob slowly and they walked into a small, dimly lit room. Mary's mother looked up from darning a sock, her eyes opening wide behind small, metal-rimmed glasses. She began to get up, her eyes now afraid. "What? Maria, what is this?"

Maria put out her hand and brought the ring with the small diamond that had slipped around to the front of her finger. "Mama, Stavros and I are engaged."

"Stavros Kalogiannis?"

Her mother stood up and with nimble steps opened the living room door to the hall. While Mary and Steve stood listening, she said, "Kosta, wake up! Kosta! Our Maria is engaged to Stavros Kalogiannis!" A tugging and squeaking of bedsprings, then a whispered, "Just a minute, Kosta, just a minute," and they appeared, Mary's slender mother, her slightly gray hair disarrayed, and her short husband, in an old bathrobe, his sparse hair neatly brushed across his narrow head. Mary's father said, "Bring the bottle, Eleni." He looked at Steve and said in English, "I don't know what this all about, but I guess it's all right." Mary's mother went into the kitchen and returned with a brown, unlabeled bottle of whiskey and a smaller one of pink liqueur. Mary opened a narrow glass cabinet and took out two shot glasses for the whiskey and two dainty stemmed ones for the liqueur. Her mother poured out the whiskey and Mary the pink liqueur. They stood for a moment then clinked all around. "I think I go to bed now," Mary's father said.

Steve got into the Oldsmobile and took several deep breaths. He thought of the small living room, the worn carpet, the table radio, the few pictures on the wall of old-country parents: an old man in a *foustanella,* seated, holding a shepherd's crook, and an aged, wrinkled woman, white hair escaping from her black kerchief, knobby hands folded on her black dress. He thought his monthly salary would be all right.

When he told his parents the next morning, Andreas said, "What kind of business is this? I should have gone to her father and spoken for you. You're acting just like the Americans! See someone once and run off to *Farmington* to *justice of peace* to get married."

"No, we're not going to run off to Farmington. We'll have the usual Greek wedding."

"I think her mother's stuck-up because she can read and write," Marika said. "That's how women from Asia Minor are. Like Myrsini."

"No, she's not. She's plain and does the best she can."

"Did you get a word out of her old man? Or did you have to pull it out of his nose?" Andreas demanded.

"They should be glad their daughter is marrying into a family with *periousia,*" Marika said.

Steve shrugged: Why remind them that there were many sharing the property his mother was so proud of?

Andreas leaned across the table. "Now, who will be the best man? Your godfather who should exchange the wedding crowns is carousing back in the village. Fool to get caught *bootlekkin'*. Because he wouldn't give Milt Valiotis a bribe. Send him to shit and he lost his ass. I guess Solly better do it."

Solly refused. "I don't want to stand up there, all that time listening to the priest."

Andreas's voice roared through the house. "You're his brother and you're going to stand up there and exchange the wedding crowns!"

"Shut the windows, Stavro," Marika shouted. "Don't let the Mormons hear us!" She turned to Solly. "Shame! Shame! I never heard of a brother refusing to stand with his own brother in front of the altar."

"Never mind," Steve said. "He doesn't want to, he doesn't have to."

"Well, Steve, it's just. I don't know, I—"

"Yes, you don't want to. And that's okay by me." Steve hurried out of the house and walked through Liberty Park and down the wide center walkway where great elms formed a dense green canopy. He circled the park and a horrible thought pushed through the heat in his head: what if his father got on the telephone and called Uncle Harry and told him to be his best man? He thought of running back to the house to prevent his father from doing it or anything else so drastic.

Then when he felt calm and accepted this insult, his own brother refusing to be his best man, he walked the dozen blocks to Mary's house. Her godparents were there, stolid and smiling. A merriment shimmered and lit up the small living room. Steve was afraid he might be asked who would exchange the wedding crowns and wished he had told Perry and Lefty about giving Mary a ring: one of them would have asked to be his best man. He was ashamed and did not know what to say if the question were asked. Mary's godfather looked at Steve and said with a proud lift of his gray head, "My boy, I know your godfather can't exchange your wedding crowns. Now, as Maria's godfather, may I have the honor?"

When he returned home that night, his father spat out hard, angry words, "Solly will be your best man," and Steve said curtly, "No, Mary's godfather has asked."

[1939]

THEN BEGAN three weeks of flurried, hectic arrangements. Andreas invited everyone he met, even though Penny and Georgie told him the girl's parents did the inviting. "I hope you're not going to have the dinner in the church basement," Georgie said to Steve. "It's so awful." With Andreas inviting everyone in sight, Steve told Mary that he had rented the American Legion hall without consulting his father.

Andreas took care of the food. He ordered three lambs from a sheepman who summered his sheep in the high plateau near Park City with instructions to deliver them to the Liberty Bakery for roasting. A new baker had taken over the old Athens Bakery: "Now you can do business with that horned Andreas," he said, as he left for San Francisco to run a restaurant. The new baker renamed the bakery in honor of his native Crete that had won its independence from Turkey under the banner *Liberty*. "Bake plenty of bread," Andreas commanded. "We'll be celebrating all day." Next he stopped at Stellios's Stadium Café and talked with the tall Cretan about preparing a tub of *pilafi* and salads. He said he would get the tomatoes, cucumbers, and lettuce from the fruit-and-vegetable stands on Second South. He would bring them himself to the café Saturday before the wedding. He told Marika, "I ordered the *pilafi* from Stellios. I hate to admit it, but the Cretans make the best *pilafi*."

Marika was glad the Cretans made the best *pilafi*. She, the *mami*, and several women who had been neighbors in Greek Town, came daily to prepare the honey-nut pastries and the *kouriambiedhes*, the powdered-sugar cookies. Marika lied to Mary's mother, knowing money was scarce in her family. "No, no, *Simpethera*, you're sewing the bride's dress and that takes so much of your time. And I hear you are also sewing a dress for the neighbor girl Tassia. You have plenty to do. Forget about the pastries. We'll take care of it, the *mami* and I."

Mary's sister came by coach from Chicago with two rumpled, tired children. Her brother Alex helped Steve, Lefty, and Perry sweep the hall and set up tables and chairs. Alex would be one of the ushers. "Don't be surprised if he shows up in his ROTC uniform," Lefty snorted.

Alex, who was dark and thin, wore his uniform even when he should not have, after school and in church. It showed how poor Mary's family was, and Steve did not know what to do about the tuxedos the ushers were supposed to wear. He thought he would pay for Alex's rental, but he did not want to embarrass him, and if he discussed it with Mary, she might be humiliated: he didn't know how she would act. He came to the decision that he would rent the tuxedos for all the ushers, except for Con, who owned one. "Boy, you're sure a sport throwing your money around," Lefty said.

Athena helped her mother with the sewing. Mary asked Goldie, Fanny, her neighbor Tessie, Penny, and Georgie to be her bridesmaids. Goldie and Fanny said they would sew their own dresses, and Mary's mother was to take care of the other bridesmaids' dresses. Mary's neighbor Tessie would be her maid of honor. When the other Greek families moved out of Greek Town in the 1920s, Mary and Tessie—the only girls left—became best friends. Tessie was in charge of the wedding favors—white almonds tied in squares of white net with white ribbon.

For two weeks Steve appeared at Mary's house every evening. The kitchen table, extended with leaves, had been brought into the living room and now supported an old treadle sewing machine. Mary's mother was consumed with her task, said nothing other than a greeting, and concerned herself with a tape measure, patterns, and scissors. Athena's children wandered about, looking as if they would burst into tears at any moment.

Mary and Steve went to a movie one night and to two parties, one given by Aunt Myrsini and the other by Goldie and Fanny. Aunt Myrsini looked like an Egyptian queen in a Cecil B. DeMille Bible movie. She wore her black-dyed hair with bangs across her forehead and the sides straight to the lobes of her ears, where they curved forward. It had been years since the family had visited her house, and as if to prove her superiority not only to Steve's family but also to Mary's, she served a memorable dinner. She had set the table with an exquisite cut-work cloth, tall stemware, and ornate silver. The food was beautifully displayed: squab; wild rice with currants and pine nuts as it was prepared in her native Smyrna; artichokes in egg-lemon sauce; and an array of pastries with Turkish coffee and liqueurs.

Steve's family discussed the dinner around the kitchen table later. Andreas said, "What in the devil is Myrsini up to? All that showing off!"

Marika said, "And did you notice, she hardly gave the bride's mother a second look. And to think they are *patriotisses,* both from Asia Minor."

Penny said, "She had an American woman in the kitchen helping her."

"Uh huh," from Georgie. "She had her bring the dishes to the dining-room door, so we could see her."

Andreas snorted. "I'd like to kick her ass from here back to her wonderful Smyrna." He chewed on an unlit cigar. "And what's this silliness of bringing the dishes from the kitchen already filled up? What fancy airs! Food should be put on the table so people can fill their plates if they want more! That shit-ass!"

"Andreas, watch yourself," Marika said, but looked pleased.

"Of course," Georgie said, folding her arms and looking at the ceiling, "Solly got out of going."

The dinner Goldie and Fanny gave was held in the small dining nook of Goldie's house. A miniature rainforest of rubber plants reaching the ceiling and flowering geraniums spreading out wildly brought the six of them into an intimacy that heightened into exhilaration. Goldie had cooked spaghetti and Fanny had baked a chocolate cake. Lefty told the newest anecdotes he had gathered about old Greek Town; Perry added his in a quiet, measured voice.

They talked about a practical joke they were scheming to play on Ted Manopoulos who had just bought a secondhand car. Ted always left the keys in the ignition. Perry and Lefty decided they would steal the car when Ted went to McCoullough's Arena to watch the wrestling matches and drive it to the Railroad Hotel. They were laughing and slapping the arms of the sofa.

"When are you fellows going to grow up?" Fanny said.

"Well, God O'mighty, Fanny!" Lefty pushed his lips out and frowned. "What else is there to do? We can't just listen to the radio all the time."

"By hell, we had fun when we were kids," Perry said in his slow monotone. "Even when we had to sell all our newspapers before we could go home."

"The most fun I remember," Lefty chuckled for a few seconds, "was when we made the apple cider for the Harvest Dance." He went on to tell the story with embellishments, meandering off on what they saw on the way to the farm, Mr. Olsen's biography, how things used to be, then returning to finish the anecdote.

Perry said, "I can tell you one thing, Steve here, Lefty, and me, we didn't drink none of that cider."

When the men finished laughing, Fanny, who worked at the Denver & Rio Grande Western freight counter, said, "More freight trains are going through. Haven't any of you noticed? They say it has something to do with the war in Europe."

"Oh, yeah?" Lefty said.

"Are you going on a honeymoon?" Goldie asked.

Steve turned to Mary—he had his arm around her. "You know what I think, Mary? I think we could drive to Denver for a few days and take in some baseball games."

"I didn't know you liked baseball, Mary," Goldie said.

"I don't. I've never been to a game."

ON THE DAY of the wedding the commotion in the house expanded, doubling, tripling, noises of all kinds, door slammings, scurryings, impatience from Andreas who had not had a proper breakfast, and shrill orders from Marika: "Who's next to take a bath? Don't use too much hot water or there won't be enough for the next person. Georgia, stop hogging the bathroom! Penelope, be quiet! No, the last minute, you find fault with your dress? Stavro, get Solon out of bed this minute."

"You're grinning like a roasted kid," Andreas said as he dipped a chunk of bread into a cup of coffee.

Steve flushed, then laughed. "Why shouldn't I? It's my wedding day."

The elation was like the high peal of a clarinet in his head. It went with him on the drive to the church and stayed while he stood and gazed at the icon screen, knowing the church was crowded and people were standing at the back.

In front and to the right of the icon screen, Perry's sister played the piano. She had apologetically asked the president of the church about getting an organ, and he withered her, "In the Depresh, you talk about gettin' organ?"

Lefty, Perry, Solly, Con, and Alexander in their tuxedos looked handsome to Steve.

The bridesmaids, carrying bouquets of roses and daisies, were prettily made up, their rose-colored taffeta making swishing sounds as they walked slowly down the aisle. Then the piano banged out Lohengrin's "Wedding March," and Mary's little niece in a beribboned white dress with her basket of rose petals, her hair curled like movie moppet Shirley Temple's, looked ready to cry as she took hesitant steps forward. Mary and her godfather followed. Mary's veil fell from a narrow satin crown; the white satin of her bodice rose and fell rapidly and the fern in her bouquet of white roses shook. In his elation, Steve did not notice the trembling ferns, only realized he should have done something about a tuxedo for Mary's godfather. When they neared him, the gasoline smell in her godfather's well-pressed suit destroyed the scent of incense.

Steve held Mary's elbow as they took a step up to the *solea*. Tessie clumsily lifted Mary's veil with one hand while holding her bouquet with the other. Mary gave Steve a quick glance. Her left eye was turned inward. He reached for her hand, but the short, bald priest frowned at him.

The service inexorably moved on for almost an hour, then came the crowning of the bride and groom with white wax blossoms, the dance of Isaiah in a circle before the altar, and the throwing of rice by relatives and Jordan almonds aimed at Steve by Lefty and Perry.

On the way to the American Legion hall, Mary slid down in the car. Steve patted her thigh. "It's over. Now the good part starts." Mary smiled, her eye now looking almost straight ahead.

In the cavernous Legion hall, the noise thundered: toasts and speeches were swallowed up by it. The food kept coming—platters, bowls, more and more of everything. The ushers and boys were busy taking away empty bottles of wine and bringing filled ones. Liqueurs appeared, and shy teenage girls, thirteen- and fourteen-year-olds, sent by the midwife and Marika, went from table to table with piled-up platters of *baklava* and *kourambiedhes*.

Shouts and cheers greeted the three immigrant men who had been playing for weddings and baptisms since the 1920s. Smiling, nodding, they took out their instruments: the clarinet, the Cretan lyra, and the stringed *laouto*. The gray-haired musicians began playing the sedate bride's dance of the Peloponnesos. Mary's godfather led her in the round dance. Old-country men called out, "Next year with a son!" Penny and Georgie looked at each other with curled lips, and Aunt Myrsini closed her eyes and shook her head. When Steve held out his handkerchief to Mary, Lefty shouted, "Watch your feet, pal! Don't fall on your ass!"

Steve had never been much of a dancer, but he jumped and twisted around the handkerchief he and Mary held at either end, hit his ankle to the shouts of "Hopa!" and twirled dangerously. "Did our daughter marry a carouser?" Mary's father asked his wife, and she, sitting next to her new in-law, Steve's mother, gave a quick glance to see if Marika had heard, but she was beaming, her arms crossed under her breasts. Marika's mouth fell open at Steve's next move. He ran over to the musicians, grabbed the clarinet from its startled owner, lifted it upwards, and blew out "Stompin' at the Savoy." With a burst of clapping and shouting, Lefty led a snake procession around the hall, men, women, and children laughing and shouting.

Later, as Steve and Mary drove through the night to the eastern border of Utah and crossed into Colorado, Steve turned to Mary. "Did I make a fool of myself?"

"No! Everybody liked it. They'll always remember it."

"That's what I'm afraid of."

Steve hummed, talked, talked, talked without stopping while Mary nodded, dozing off and jolting awake at intervals. In Grand Junction they stopped at a motel. "This is far enough for tonight," Steve said, and he carried in the bags. Mary sat on the thin, faded-pink chenille bedspread and looked around the small room that contained a bed, a row of hooks on the door for clothing, and one chair. A limp curtain hung on the narrow window. Steve found that to get into the minute bathroom, the door of which would not open completely, he had to enter sideways. He shut the door. "Oh, my God!" he shouted. "My God!"

Mary jumped up and hovered outside the door. "What's wrong? What's wrong?"

Steve opened the door, his eyes afraid. "Look," he said, pointing to the toilet bowl. "I'm hemorrhaging."

Mary looked at the pinkish-violet water for several seconds. "That's not blood. It's something else, probably something you drank."

"I'll kill them! That crazy Lefty and Perry and their practical jokes! I'll kill them ! They doctored my drinks."

Steve took a shower. Although he had showered before he left for church, he thought he'd better take another one. Then Mary took a shower. Later, Steve heard her murmur in her sleep; or was it like a little chuckle?

PART 2

VIII

THE JAPANESE BOMBED Pearl Harbor on December 7, 1941, and war was declared. Steve's draft card came: he had drawn a low number. Sweat darkened his shirt under his armpits; he forgot to listen when people talked to him; every ring of the telephone, the talk going on about him—it all rattled in his head. He went to the draft board, explained that his wife was pregnant, wanted to plead he was needed in the family business to give him more time, but knew he could not. The board would answer—and he thought of suspicious eyes looking at him—that his father and uncle could take care of the business. The board gave him a nine-month deferment.

After a day and night of labor, Mary gave birth to a baby boy. Steve sat in a chair at the side of her bed and held her hand. He had not left the hospital during the long labor. Perry brought him coffee to keep him awake, and sandwiches from the hospital's cafeteria. Steve's eyelids closed and Mary had just fallen asleep when Andreas rushed into the room, flushed, a big smile revealing his tobacco-stained teeth. "Eh, Maria," he said in a loud voice. Mary opened her eyes. "Maria, I got my boy! I'll be the godfather. Give him my name. Twice as good for the baby, grandfather and godfather. Come on," he ordered Steve, "let's go see him!" With a groan Steve got up and walked to the nursery window with Andreas. "Best kid in the whole goddemn place," Andreas said in English while the nurse held the swaddled, red-faced baby.

When Steve returned, alone, Mary said, "My godfather should really be the baby's godfather, you know. The best man is always the godfather of the first child."

"If the baby was a girl, he'd a let your godfather baptize her. I'll bet anything he's on his way to convince your godfather that he should be the godfather. 'Grandfather, godfather, twice as good,'" Steve mimicked his father.

"Go home now. Get some sleep," Mary said.

"Okay." At the door Steve met Fanny and Goldie and remained a few more minutes. They had brought gifts, Goldie a baby shawl she had crocheted and Fanny a small pot of basil for good luck. "We'll only stay a minute," Goldie said. "We won't even sit down." At that moment Tessie walked in with a sack of salt water taffy and a pair of blue booties. "We'll go now," Fanny said and looked at Tessie. "We know you need the rest, Mary."

Tessie waited a few seconds after Goldie and Fanny left the room and then pirouetted in a red-pleated skirt and a white shirt. "Look, Mary," she said, her dark eyes excited, her full lips spread into a wide smile, "what I got with my first paycheck. I paid eight dollars for this outfit! Isn't that awful?" Steve gazed at her with stupefied eyes.

"You look very nice," Mary said.

"It's so much fun working! Now the men got their draft notices, there's lots of girls taking their jobs. And we go to Woolworth's for a hot dog and a Coke at lunch time!"

Tessie went on, talking about learning to wear her hair with a mass of curls on her forehead like the movie actress Betty Grable. She talked about a movie she had seen. "Oh, Mary, that Clark Gable! I could die, he's so handsome and masculine!"

Steve said, "I'll walk out with you, Tessie. Where do you want me to drop you off?" Tessie gave Mary a longing look as she followed Steve out of the room.

The baby was two months old when he was baptized "Andrew" after his grandfather Andreas. In the cool nave, the votive candles flickering before the icons, the baby was lathed with consecrated oil, submerged three times into the tepid water of the copper baptismal font, and catching his breath screamed and clenched his little fists. His grandfather Andreas smiled, proud and haughty.

Andreas had wanted a big baptismal dinner, but there was no

time in the disorder of wartime: young men of the parish were leaving; mothers, like Mary's, were weeping in front of icons and promising outrageous *tamas*—vows—in exchange for their sons' safe return; the priest was harried.

Afterwards, Steve's and Mary's families; Fanny and Perry; Goldie and Lefty sat in Marika's dining room and ate a bounteous dinner of eggplant *moussaka, dolmadhes,* lamb roast, and honey-nut pastries. The baby Andrew lay asleep in Mary's arms; he was wearing a white cap with visor that Mary's mother had embroidered: on the crown, a dark-blue *V* and inside it the smaller letters *USA*. Underneath the *V* she had used red thread to make three dots and a dash—the Morse code for V, or victory. The sign was everywhere, in store windows, on posters, in newspapers. Mary's mother had seen it in the Greek-language newspaper from New York, the *Atlantis*.

Steve moved Mary and the baby back to her parents' house. They left the sparsely furnished five-room house with the curtains Mary had sewed, the furniture she had polished weekly, and took only her embroidered linens and Steve's clarinet. Steve rented the house to a middle-aged couple from Texas who had moved to Utah to work in the arms plant near the airport.

Mary's old bedroom was so small that only a few inches separated her narrow bed from the baby's crib. The room was wallpapered in faded brown with full-blown pink roses. Steve had moments of despair that Mary and the baby might live there for a long time, but he quickly went about finishing his work at the office. He gave his sisters his Chevrolet coupe on condition that they drive Mary to the doctor and to the grocery store. He talked with his father, and Andreas said he was not to worry: Mary and the baby would be taken care of.

Steve reported to Fort Douglas, east of the city. He was then ready to leave. He boarded a passenger train at the Union Pacific depot that was bound for Camp Roberts in the southern California desert. At the window, he looked at the little group, one of many, Mary holding the baby, her parents, and his parents and sisters. His mother was crying. "My two sons taken from me! Ach! Ach!" she wept. Solly was in New York, a second lieutenant, waiting orders to cross the Atlantic. Steve's face prickled with a chill. He was afraid he would never see the family again. As the train's engine gathered steam, he looked at Mary and Andrew with a fleeting moment of perplexity: were they really his wife and baby?

The soldiers were put two together in Pullmans. Steve shared an upper berth with a sullen young man who had been drinking, snored, and fought enemies in his sleep.

Six weeks later, on the base, a soldier in his barracks took a snapshot of Steve in his military police uniform: white helmet with large black MP letters on the crown, white upper-arm band with the same letters, his trousers tucked into white puttees. He wrote letters full of complaints: the food was awful, the sun was terrible; the classes in the barracks were like ovens. "Have you heard any-thing about the office?" he wrote. "Uncle Harry couldn't stop smil-ing when he heard I was drafted. He brought Con into the office with him every day before I left."

Sweat-soaked on his army cot, he thought about the business and wondered if there would be anything left if he returned. His fa-ther had added a new property to their *periousia* at the time Steve had received his draft notice. When Andreas heard over the radio that the Japanese were being sent to relocation camps, he went to the Japanese farmer and bought his land. He found a neighboring farmer, an old Italian, to take care of it. Uncle Harry was attending an AHEPA regional meeting in Denver and knew nothing about it. Neither did Steve. He was clearing out his desk when his father came in with the papers, all smiles, and showed him the deed. "I got it cheap. I said to him, 'You sure now?'" Andreas reverted to English, "'When you come back you want it again?'" And he said to me, 'I never come back. I go to Japan after.'" Before the war Steve would have complained that at least he should have been informed about buying the farm, but it didn't matter what his father had done. It was all removed from him.

There were a few good guys at the base, he wrote Mary: Dan White from North Dakota, a Swede, and Johnny Leonetti, a little shrimp Italian from St. Louis. They went beer drinking when they left the base. He'd never forget them. They were good buddies. He didn't tell Mary about the first time the three of them were together. They were in a bar, blue with cigarette smoke, the smell of spilled beer, rank bodies, and sweat-stained army uniforms reminded him of the icemen and gave him a stuffed nose. He had to breathe through his mouth. He kept looking at the women at the bar, giving soldiers sultry looks through their heavily mascaraed eyelashes. They made him so angry he wanted to hit them.

Dan the Swede asked, "So, Steve, you married to a white girl or a Greek?" Steve's head jerked back, and Johnny jumped up, stuck his chin in front of Dan's red, astonished face, and said, "Say that again, you sonofabitch!"

"What'd I say? What'd I say wrong?"

"We're just as white as you are, you bastard!" Johnny made as if to spit at Dan. He and Steve sat looking at Dan, who wriggled uncomfortably on his chair and wrinkled his face, not quite looking at them. "Well, it's only an expression. I didn't mean nothin' by it."

"Okay, just so you know," Steve said. After a few wordless moments, they finished their beers and made insulting remarks about their sergeant that almost brought back their earlier camaraderie. Later Steve and Johnny talked about dumping Dan, but Dan followed them around, hurried to sit next to them at chow, listened carefully to their talk. He couldn't seem to make other friends so they let him hang around.

In his letters Steve underlined the sentence: *War brings the dregs of society together.* Day after day, night after night, he and his MP buddies went on patrol. He saw what filth people could be, in the army and out of it. Everywhere soldiers were sent, they left fatherless children, thousands, thousands of them. Radios, newspapers, and politicians talked about how noble soldiers were, soldiers, sailors, marines; all of them. They're so noble they get girls pregnant and leave kids to grow up on the streets or locked up in some whore's bedroom.

ON THE OTHER SIDE of the steel fence, girls waited for the soldiers. Steve saw them later, walking the streets, sitting on barstools. One girl could not have been more than twelve. She had painted her face and pulled her hair on top her head to look older. She was hanging onto a drunken soldier's arm. "What the hell's the matter with you?" he shouted at the girl, "you stupid little dope!" She shrank closer to the wobbly soldier. "Why aren't you home, you little shit? You want to get pregnant? Is that what you want? You damn fool!" He pulled the soldier from her. "He's going to the stockade and you better go home pronto." Mascara ran down the girl's rouged cheeks; her lipsticked mouth trembled. She turned and ran. Later, after lights were out, he wondered what would happen to her. Maybe she'd die having a baby—he remembered Mary's long labor with Andrew—probably end up on welfare, raising five kids with different fathers.

Steve carried on silent monologues: Men in high places get people into war. They didn't cut off Hitler's piss when they should have. There are maniacs in the world. They don't care how many people they kill, how many villages and cities they destroy. They don't care. War feeds their ego.

Steve, Dan, and Johnny drank too much when they were off duty; they said it was because they were so damn lonesome. Steve sometimes thought he ought to cry to relieve the pressure behind his eyes; he thought of Mary and the baby before he fell asleep.

One Saturday night he knew he had to get off the base or explode. The next morning he took an army bus to Los Angeles and then a city bus to look for the Greek church listed in the telephone book. He had trouble finding the right street and had to walk several blocks, asking people on the way for directions. He was eager to get there—he, who since becoming an adult had attended church only on Easter.

Not many people were in the church. Mothers and grandmothers were lighting candles before the icons and praying. Steve breathed in the incense, was soothed by the priest's and cantor's intoning the liturgy, by the Greek words. He had to watch the women to make certain he was making the sign of the cross at the proper times. When he joined the line of parishioners proceeding toward the priest for the cube of consecrated bread, he thought maybe he should kiss his hand, but he could not. He bowed low and took the bread. The elderly priest looked at him benignly anyway and said in Greek, "Our Lord Jesus Christ be with you."

Outside, he looked up to the blue sky and felt calmed, yet he did not want to return to the base. He thought he would walk the streets of Los Angeles. An old man approached him, peering at him with age-filmed eyes. "Can you speak Greek?" he asked in English. The irises of his brown eyes were encircled with a bluish film and minute yellow dots studded the whites of his eyeballs. When Steve said he did, a smile came to the old man's purplish lips. He looked relieved that they would not have to speak English. "Come to my house. My wife she cooked." They rode a bus for miles, transferred to another, and rode a long distance to a row of small stucco houses. The table was already set for three.

The old woman was a head shorter than her husband. Her gray hair was pulled back into a skimpy knot like Steve's mother's. His throat swelled. She wore a flower-print apron over a black silk dress. With her old hands held tightly together, she welcomed Steve, and offered him the seat at the head of the table. He thought he should take a side seat, but she insisted that he was the *mousafiris,* the guest, and that was his place.

The dining room was uncomfortably quiet. On the buffet, pictures were set on crocheted doilies, reminding Steve of every Greek house he had been in. In the center a wedding picture was enclosed in a tarnished silver frame that was exactly like his parents', but the bride's and groom's finery were of an earlier time. On one side of the wedding picture were photographs of village women wearing black headscarves. On the other side was a picture of a greatly mustached old man, wearing a white pleated *foustanella* and sitting cross-legged on a chair outside a stone house. The man was not wearing the traditional fez, but a straw boater. Steve wanted to laugh and he thought he would, but he stopped the urge by asking who the man was. His father, the old man said, from a village in the Peloponnesos. Steve said his parents came from the Peloponnesos, but at that moment he could not remember the names of their villages. No pictures of children and grandchildren were on the buffet.

The chicken needed salt, but Steve would not reach out for the shaker in front of him. In the center of the table was a cut-glass oblong plate holding a cruet of olive oil and two cut lemons. Steve wondered what they were for, then realized the old woman had forgotten the greens, yet he did not know how to say so. In between silences the old people asked him about his family, what work his father did, when he had come to America. The three ate on as if they were eating a mournful forty-day memorial dinner for a dead person. The old woman clapped her hands against her withered cheeks, got up, and hobbled into the kitchen. She returned with a bowl of boiled dandelions. "My boy, I forgot the dandelions."

"Ah!" Steve said, a little cry of pleasure that sounded strange in the quiet room. He took a large spoonful of the greens, poured olive oil on them, and then the juice of a half a lemon. He took a mouthful and ate, smiling. The old woman looked at him with kindly, faded eyes. He thought he would cry: dandelions, home, his own house, his own people.

Afterwards he stood on the cement path of the bungalow house, listened to the old man's directions for the buses, thanked the old woman, standing with her veined, splotched hands folded one on top of the other, waved good-bye, and hurried to the bus stop. He knew the old people were following the ancient edict of Greek hospitality by bringing him to the bungalow house. How sad and old they were, and he knew they would go on bringing servicemen to their house until the war ended or they were dead. He was more lonely after leaving the old people than when he had left the army base. He had to tell Mary about them.

The next day at dusk Steve called her, after waiting his turn in a long line of soldiers in front of a pay telephone. He was sweating from the lingering heat of the day and the frustration of the long wait. When he closed himself inside the telephone booth, the trapped heat and the smells of other men's sweat and cigarette smoke clogged his nose. Mary's voice came over the wire, faint, like a stranger's. Steve was nettled, self-conscious. He asked about the baby, about how she was getting along, and if his sisters had come by. He thought she was sniffing. "What's wrong? Have you got a cold?" No: he realized she was trying to keep from crying.

"It's just been a bad day. Nothing important. I took the baby to the pediatrician and three buses passed, packed full. When I got on one, I had to stand up with the baby crying and squirming. Then when I got off and hurried to the doctor's office, it was so crowded with babies and diaper bags and the doctor's wife—she's now his receptionist—wouldn't take me because we were six minutes late. I tried to tell her we'd left an hour ago, but the buses wouldn't stop. The doctor passed by the door and said, 'Don't you know there's a war on?' It was that 'Don't you know there's a war on?' that was the last straw. You hear it everywhere, but it's all right. We're getting along all right. Don't worry about us. I shouldn't have said anything."

"Why didn't the girls drive you to the doctor's?"

Static crackled, then Mary said, "I don't like to bother them."

"Bother them, hell! Those prima donnas! What about my dad? Does he come around?"

"Oh yes," Mary said and sighed. "He comes almost every morning before going to the office and has a cup of coffee and a *koulouraki,* and talks in a loud voice to wake up the baby. And every day he says the same thing to little Andrew: 'I'm your granpa, your *papou,* and your godfather. That means more special. Double special.'"

"Does he give you any money?"

"He left a twenty-dollar bill last week, but don't worry. We're getting along fine with your army checks. And with my parents' ration coupons and mine, we're all right."

Steve went back to the barracks and wrote his sisters a letter: "Why do you think I gave you my car? So you could help my wife, you spoiled bitches."

Two days later Penny and Georgia drove Mary and the baby to the grocery store. Mary could not leave the baby with her mother: her heart had become enlarged and she was in a panic over her son Alex's joining the air force.

IX

[1945]

STEVE APPLIED FOR leave three times; each one was canceled when the army base was placed on alert. War ended and he got on a train with his duffel bag over his shoulder. He hadn't telephoned anyone. If he had, it might get around, and he did not want his sisters meeting him at the train station. He wanted to see Mary and the baby alone. After sitting up all night, he got off at the depot and fought his way through the mass of people, many like him returning servicemen. With an excitement shadowed with dread, he took a taxi to his parents-in-law's house. He bounded out before the taxi had come to a complete stop. When he saw the gold star in the front window of the house, he was ashamed that Mary's brother Alex was dead and he wasn't. For a few seconds he stood at the bottom of the steps, then walked across the porch and rang the doorbell.

To his boundless relief, Mary opened the door. He kissed her solemnly, embarrassed; it had been nearly two-and-a-half years since they had seen each other. He stared, amazed at Andrew, walking about, looking at him suspiciously. He took a shower, shaved, drank a cup of coffee, and ate scrambled eggs. He walked around the small house, not knowing what to do with himself. He avoided looking at the picture of Mary's brother in uniform. It stood on a small table with a pot of basil at one side of it. He thought: *it could have been my picture on the table.*

He was uncomfortable with his mother-in-law's sad hovering over him, and her father's trying to make conversation. He telephoned his sisters to bring his car and watched at the window as they drove up. First he went to see his parents who cried, even his father. Then he went to the office.

Con was sitting at Steve's desk. He looked up, eyes wide open. Steve thought for a fraction of a second: "Ah, let him have the desk," but he knew it was a crisis. He said, "Well, Con, I guess I'll take back my desk now." Con glanced at his father. Uncle Harry said in his heavily accented English, "Stevie, you take the desk in the back. No use mixing up everything." If it had not been for Uncle Harry's calling him "Stevie" for the first time, Steve might have done so, but he knew he could not let Con keep his old desk. "No," he said, "I'm used to this desk. It's where I like it."

Uncle Harry snorted, but Con came forward and smiled. They shook hands. Steve thought that Con, now about twenty, could make a good living in Hollywood: he was that handsome.

The office had a stagnant air, yet when he later walked around town and stopped for lunch, he was surprised to see the streets crowded. There was a commotion and celebration in restaurants and stores, telephones ringing, frantic talk. Even the air seemed different to him, as if it were pulsing.

He was hesitant, but also eager, to see his house. He longed to move out of his in-law's grieving, silent house, to have his privacy again, yet he was afraid he could not get the Texas renters out of it:

wartime edicts were still in force. He had not told Mary he was going to see their house; he did not want her to get her hopes up.

He stopped in front of the house. It looked small, and the lawn was dried up, dead in spots. "Damn Texans," he said as he got out.

Cardboard boxes were stacked on the front stoop. "Gypsies," he fumed as he pressed the doorbell. The woman who came to the door, whom he barely remembered with permanented bleached hair, her face sun-wrinkled, peered at him for several seconds before she called over her shoulder, "Delbert, it's our landlord."

Steve stepped into the small living room. There was hardly space to stand: scuffed, battered suitcases and cardboard boxes tied with rope littered the room. Clothing was thrown over the couch and chairs.

"We're gittin' ready to go," the woman said abruptly.

Her scrawny, bald husband came in with his hands in his back pockets. Steve put out his hand and as if taken aback the man leaned forward and shook it.

"We're goin' back home," the woman said, looking at Steve with belligerent, faded-blue eyes.

"Yeah, back where we belong," her husband nodded.

Steve gave a quick look around—bare, dirty windows, a cigarette burn on an end table. "The arms plants is cuttin' back," the woman said and moved in front of a box she was packing with utensils.

"Your rent's not up until the first."

"Yeah," the man twitched his nose, "but we wanta git out of here."

Steve wondered if he should say anything about the pots and pans that he and Mary had left in the house and that were now being readied for Texas. No, he wouldn't want to eat out of them now. The faster the Texans got out of the house the better, and he could see they were thinking the same about him. They didn't want him to take too good a look at what they'd done to the house. "Leave the keys in the mailbox," he said. "Good luck!"

He drove off, glancing about at the greenness of the trees and the blue of the sky. *Free,* he thought, *free.*

Mary, Fanny, and Goldie scrubbed the house. The cabinets were encrusted with dirt and the scrubbing wore off the paint and left the wood showing. "Pigs!" "Gypsies!" "Hillbillies!" Goldie and Fanny shouted. Little Andrew in the corner of the living room looked up from his toys, puzzled, sometimes frightened. "Not so loud," Mary said. "Andrew isn't used to noise. My parents' house is so quiet." She picked Andrew up, placed his arms around her neck, called him *"Bebouli mou,"* my little baby, and walked through the bare rooms that smelled of raw, abrasive cleaning.

Wartime shortages continued, but construction was going on and new businesses were opening up. G.I. loans, all kinds of opportunities were there for the taking. Steve told his father and Uncle Harry that they should move the office to the uptown, three-story building that Andreas had bought twenty years previously. The building was old, musty smelling, the elevator creaky and unreliable, but Steve knew how to touch their pride: "We can't expect people to come to the Railroad Hotel to do business. One look at it and they'd turn around and you'd never see them again. We've got good properties and now's the time we can make a lot of money."

Steve and Andreas had trouble finding the plumbers and carpenters who had repaired their properties over a period of twenty and more years. They used newspaper ads, "Men want work," and this brought them an alcoholic and several men long past retirement age. Building materials were harder to get. Seasoned lumber, copper, and all kinds of metal were still in short supply. Workmen used substitutes, ersatz materials, that Steve knew would have to be replaced later. The paint and new plumbing helped the looks of the old building somewhat, but when the paint dried, the musty smell was still there.

They allowed the several small businesses to remain on the street floor: a typewriter store, a shoeshine shop, and a saltwater taffy cubicle. The second floor was rented to an insurance firm and to two new graduates of the university law school. The entire third floor became the new offices of Kallos Business Properties.

Army life had made Steve impatient; he would not let the past go unchallenged. He looked into the leases first, and as he had suspected, Uncle Harry had never followed through increasing the rents when the options came up—too busy making the rounds of bankers, attorneys, fellow Masons, and eating at Aleck's Broiler with Milt Valiotis. Steve snorted. Carrying a thick pile of leases, he walked into Uncle Harry's office. Andreas was sitting in front of the desk and Uncle Harry was leaning back in a swivel chair. They suddenly stopped talking and looked at Steve with annoyance. Steve set the leases on the desk and said, "I've looked in the books and I don't see that any of these tenants' rents were raised when their leases were up. How come?"

Uncle Harry leaned forward, eyebrows raised above his startled eyes. Andreas looked at him. Uncle Harry's face turned red as he tried to explain. "You know," he said and stumbled over a nonsensical explanation of times being bad, what with the war and—. Steve interrupted. "The war's been good for business."

Uncle Harry moved about in the swivel chair. "Well, we have to be Christians. We can't bleed these little people." He pretended to be angry. Steve kept relentless eyes on him. "What are you trying to tell me! You were away in the army! I was here working, fourteen hours a day" —Andreas looked at Heracles with his mouth pulled down at this fantasy—"You don't know how hard things were!"

"It looks to me like you forgot to keep track of the leases," Steve said in a calm voice, disguising the elation in him.

Uncle Harry began to rise from his chair. "How dare you talk to me like this, you assless bastard!" His eyes menacing, he stood up and leaned his body toward Steve, who was two heads taller and weighed at least fifty more pounds than he.

Andreas bellowed, "He's talking like that to you because you're not making sense. Neither nose nor ass to it. You're too busy taking your woman to the *Masoni* doings. From now on, Stavros will take care of the leases."

Uncle Harry put out his hands toward Andreas, his mouth open in silent demand for an explanation of this outrage. Andreas leaned his head to one side and looked at him. Uncle Harry slowly sat down. Steve picked up the leases and walked with military briskness out of the room.

The next day Aunt Myrsini came to the office during the lunch hour, walked past Steve without speaking, and left with Con and Uncle Harry. When Uncle Harry returned alone, he said as if he were spitting words, "All right. So now you doing the leases. You show Constantine so he can learn the business."

"Sure," Steve said, and wanted to ask why hadn't he been teaching his son about the leasing.

Three months after Steve's release from the army, Solly returned from Europe with news that amazed the family: he had married an American Red Cross worker in Germany and she would soon follow. She was Greek American. Marika made the sign of the cross over and over again: "I was so afraid you would bring home an *Amerikanidha,* or worse a *Germanidha.*" Then she said, "You have to quiet down. Sit still. Don't keep jumping about!" She brought out a large paper grocery sack and said, "Here, I've been saving this money. Use it for the business." The sack was heavy with silver dollars, a few gold coins, paper bills, and Solly's army checks made out to his mother.

"What the devil!" Andreas shouted. "What's the meaning of this?"

Marika did not answer. "Now," she said, "I'm giving this to you on the condition that your sisters share in the business."

"What do you mean 'share'?" Andreas yelled. "What more do you want? We give them a roof over their heads, food, clothes, send them to the university, a car to run around in? What's this shit talk? Share?"

"What I said." Marika folded her arms under her breasts.

"Okay, okay," Solly said and he winked at Steve. "We'll make so much money, there'll be plenty for everyone."

Solly's voice climbed with excitement. He showed Steve a paperback book written by Ayn Rand. The book was worn, pages creased, sentences underlined. "You've got to read this book, Steve. This woman knows what she's talking about. Capitalism! We have to take advantage of the times! Capitalists rule the world! We've got to get busy! I'm tired of being poor! Ten years of Depression and four years of war! Let's get started!"

Solly's talk brought a tingling to Steve's chest. He knew Solly was right. There was no better time to make it big, as Solly phrased it. Each evening as he drove south on Third West, he noticed small buildings: Milwaukee Tools that sold machinery and carpentry tools; Chicago Pneumatic Tools; and Skil that sold saws and planers. He thought they could turn the Japanese farm into an industrial area. Solly said he wasn't so sure about an industrial center, then decided it was a good start. Andreas said it was out of their line: what did they know about building big? They knew property. "All right," he said with a wave of his hand, as if he were letting them have their own way against his better judgment. Uncle Harry said, "We should build some more stores, like the ones we've got."

"The farm is too far away for that. Maybe in ten years, but right now it doesn't have the traffic."

Solly and Con drove Uncle Harry and Aunt Myrsini to the farm and also showed them the buildings on Third West. When they returned to the office, they sat down to discuss the industrial idea. Aunt Myrsini nodded when Solly talked, smiling at him at intervals.

Uncle Harry was against it. "Let's let the farm stay like it is for the time being and build some more shopping centers like our first one, only bigger."

"I agree with Solly," Aunt Myrsini said in English, "and I'll put in two thousand dollars to help."

Uncle Harry fell back in his swivel chair. When Marika heard about it, she said, "You know what I think? She's been stealing money from Heracles from the day they married. Saving to go back to Greece, but the war made salad out of her plans."

The evening before the bulldozers arrived, Steve and Andreas stood at the side of the road gazing at the long rows of green plants converging in the distance. Water flowed slowly between the rows, and the last vestige of a pink sunset glinted here and there on the slow-moving streams.

"I guess you'd like the farm to stay like it was," Steve said.

Andreas moved the cigar around his mouth. "Well, I didn't buy it just to look at it," he said.

Steve had a large sign put up: WILL BUILD TO SUIT TENANT. He had no idea how to get tenants and did not want to tell Solly. "We have the location," he told him and Con. "Location is everything in business." Yet he was sleepless, wondering if he had made a mistake. While Mary, pregnant again, gave Andrew lukewarm baths to bring down a high fever, Steve wondered how he should go about getting tenants. For several days he thought of finding the addresses of national firms and writing to them. He did not want to bring in real-estate people; they had never used them. His father called them *poutanes.*

A few days later, a realtor telephoned the office and asked for Steve. He said his name was Russ Hansen. "I was driving around and saw your sign." Steve made an appointment to meet him at the office. Andreas had gone to the old tobacco shop to meet a plumber, and Heracles sat next to Con and looked at the realtor darkly.

Russ Hansen was a white-haired, red-faced man with a pot belly. Even his eyelashes were white. Steve told him the farm was paid for, free and clear. "What you should do," Russ Hansen said, "is have a sketch drawn up. Now, with that and if I get you three or four tenants, you can go to the bank and get a loan. If you haven't got a draftsman, this fellow I know is purty good." Hansen wrote the name of the draftsman on the back of his card.

After Russ Hansen left the office, Uncle Harry said, "I'll bet he's a Mormon with that white hair of his. You better be careful." He gave Steve a warning look.

Steve worked with the draftsman, watching him carefully, trying not to let him know that he was a greenhorn and didn't know from up. Russ Hansen had no trouble finding tenants: a hydraulics company, a mining and construction pipe distributor, and an industrial pumps and generators factory representative. The three of them: Steve, Solly, and Con, with the sketch and Russ Hansen's commitments, got ready to go to the bank—together to give themselves confidence. Uncle Harry was not asked to go with them and he sulked. Con said at the door of the office, "I'll stay here and my dad can go with you." Uncle Harry screamed, "I don't want to go to the bank! I know everybody in the bank! I do business with them for over thirty years! When I want to go to the bank, I go. I don't need nobody!" Andreas was satisfied that others went to the bank in his place; that morning, he had been looking over the shoulders of plumbers who were repairing broken pipes in the Railroad Hotel.

At the bank, the loan officer gave them a paltry smile and looked at them as they sat opposite him. He was in his late fifties with thin shoulders, a long, wrinkled neck, and bobbing Adam's apple. A few strands of reddish hair lay firmly in place with hair oil that smelled of carnations. A photograph of his wife and eight children stood on his immaculate desk. He looked down at the sketch.

"They're big-name companies," Steve said, leaning forward, his guts strangling his stomach.

"Of course," the loan officer said, lifting his hand backwards as if he didn't need any talk coming from them. Reading slowly, he took in every word of the application, tapping the eraser of his pencil on the polished mahogany table top. At one point he looked to one side at the three desks where other hopeful men sat explaining their ventures to bank officers.

"Our dads have done business with this bank for more than twenty-five years," Steve said. He was afraid that their application would be turned down.

"Well," the loan officer said with false cheerfulness and smiled more broadly, showing two rows of small gray teeth, "how can you be sure you'll be able to finish the center with supplies so limited?"

"We'll do it, and if we don't, you've got our collateral," Steve said and Solly began a story about the general who used the word *collateral* when he was talking about soldiers. "I was his aide all through the war. A great guy."

The loan officer asked Solly a few polite questions about his war service and had them sign the loan papers. Outside Solly said, "Steve, you've got to learn to butter people up. The guy could tell you got a hard on."

"Didn't you see how he took his own sweet time going over the application? It was a form, goddamn it! He was just making us sit and squirm."

"You gotta make them think you know they're important. Flatter their egos."

"You've got your ways and I've got mine," Steve said, with a glance at Con who had not spoken a word all the time they were in the bank. "Couldn't you see he was looking down his nose at us? We were just Greeks! I'll remember that."

"Ah, so what? One of these days they'll be begging us to give them our business."

From that day Steve spent little time in the office. He had to rent heavy equipment and was lucky that many returned servicemen had learned to use it in the Army Corps of Engineers. He watched, exhilarated, when the big machines ripped up the farm.

Finding carpenters was not easy. He looked in the want ads, but carpenters just out of the army were not advertising for work: a big spurt of homebuilding had begun the moment the war ended; no houses had been built during the war, and soldiers were getting married, having families. Steve went to the AFL-CIO, but they could not help him. Coughing, he smoked throughout the day, cold inching up to his head as he thought of them, back in the office, who might find out he didn't know what he was doing.

He had noticed, driving south on Third West, two old half-ton trucks parked in front of a small building going up. As he drove past one late afternoon, he suddenly stopped and backed up into the weeded lot at the side of the building; he thought he would ask the carpenters if they knew anyone who wanted steady work. Two carpenters were pounding nails inside the shell of the building. Through the window openings, they looked at Steve making his way over the ruts and scrap lumber, but kept on pounding. The sunset had left a lingering pink brushed over the sky; the breeze was cool, yet tinged with the last warmth of the day, and the pounding of the hammers in the silent dusk echoed.

The carpenters appeared to Steve to be in their early sixties. He knew they probably had plenty of work going on while the young men were in the army, but soon they would have plenty of competition: the GIs were coming home. One of the carpenters was a tall, big man, his hair completely white; the other was dark and wiry. Steve sensed they were strong, even the small man: Wiry men who had done repairs for the family business often had unbelievable strength; they fool people.

Steve walked over the debris toward them, nearly falling against a wheelbarrow. The carpenters stopped pounding and, without looking at each other, as if a hidden signal told them it was getting too dark to see well, pushed the hammers into the slots of their white canvas aprons, picked up their saws, and walked out. Steve followed them to their trucks and talked to them while they opened the chests at the back of their pickup trucks. The wooden chests were old but sturdy with a dark brown sheen, gouged in places, the corners fitted with brass. He watched the big man put his tools away: he wiped his saw with a red rag and carefully placed it in a slot, then clasped the two hammers hanging from his tool apron on the underside of the lid. He evenly rolled up the apron with its pouch of nails inside and put it in an open space in one corner. A clean scent of oil came from the chest: claw hammers, wrenches, screwdrivers of many sizes, wire clippers—all were set in order as to size and kind. The tools were like a picture that, Steve thought, should be painted for a *Saturday Evening Post* cover. He had never known this kind of order and he saw it there in front of his eyes. He thought of telling Mary about the carpenter's box, but when he did get home, late, the baby asleep, he had too many thoughts to think through about the business.

He found the house always clean and the food ready, even when Mary had been gone most of the day taking care of her mother, now blue-lipped and bedridden. Mary would put Andrew in a cart, and steer it with one hand while holding a covered pan of food for her parents with the other. Sometimes she was late and Steve was annoyed that after his long day the house was empty. He knew he shouldn't be, but still. . . .

The carpenters came to work on the industrial park as soon as they finished the small building. Steve took the white-haired carpenter, Douglas Slater, with him when he went to supply houses. He felt more secure having a blue-eyed man by the name of Slater with him. It made him angry, but he remembered it had to be done that way. Afterwards, he took Mr. Slater to lunch. They sat in a restaurant crowded with workingmen who ate with their caps on. Steve longed to be eating in Stellios's Stadium Cafe with a bowl of greens, dandelions, endive, or spinach doused with olive oil and lemon juice, a plate of Kalamata olives and feta cheese at the side, and a lamb shank to finish it off, but he did not dare suggest it. Mr. Slater's large, pale-blue eyes, stolid face—what would he think of going to Stellios's small restaurant?

Steve asked questions to stave off Mr. Slater's reserve. Mr. Slater chewed completely before answering.

"How did you learn carpentry, Mr. Slater?"

"I was apprenticed-out in Leeds, in Yorkshire, before I came to this country." Mr. Slater cut the chicken-fried steak, which he ordered each time they ate together.

"Did you come with your parents?"

After a few seconds of chewing, Mr. Slater said, "No, they

wouldn't come. I came with mi sister." Mr. Slater looked off. "Yes," he said, "with mi sister." He cut another piece of steak.

"That's interesting, that your sister came without her parents."

Mr. Slater looked straight at Steve. "No. She had gone to the manor house to work as a maid. The lady asked her name and when mi sister said 'Hazel,' the lady said it was too good a name for a servant girl and said she would call her 'Mary' or 'Bridget.' So Hazel went down to where the Mormon missionaries were preaching and that's how we came in 1921."

"She had guts," Steve said.

After a few weeks of taking Doug Slater away from his work, which Steve could see nettled him, he went alone to the supply houses. The clerks had come to know him. Then he went to Stellios's cafe and sometimes Lefty and Perry were there. Even though he had to hurry his eating to get back to the project, he felt comfortable there and wanted to linger. He told Mary later that it was like old times.

Steve boasted to his father, Uncle Harry, Solly, and Con that the carpenters were strong as bulls. Mr. Slater and the small carpenter could work all day and hardly say more than a few words. Steve told Solly and Con, "Imagine two Greeks working like that. They'd go nuts!"

Steve carried anecdotes back to the office. He admired the carpenters, liked them. It was as if they were connected to him, in a special way, more than being his carpenters. They brought other old-timers to work on the complex: plumbers, electricians, painters, cement finishers, and laborers. They never watched the time, but worked until the light failed. The small man, Spence, could not abide people talking and working at the same time. One plasterer talked as he worked all day long. Mr. Slater just kept on working as if he wasn't listening, but Spence looked up from his work and said, "If bullshit were music, you'd be a brass band." Steve laughed so hard he had a coughing spell.

Douglas Slater was so reserved and dignified in his white carpenter's overalls that Steve never called him anything but Mr. Slater for the fifteen years he worked for him. He learned everything about building from him—to read plans, to understand specifications, foundations, sand and water content, cement, gravel, wood. Steve breathed in the scent of newly sawed wood with a deep pleasure. Much of the wood was green and quickly showed signs of warping. Pipe was especially hard to get. He hounded suppliers; they came to know him well.

Every morning he could not wait to get to the farm. He drank a cup of coffee and ate two pieces of toast, nothing more. From one day to the next he could see the progress: the framing, the joists, the brick going up, the plastering, and the painting. In the evening he would look at it just before he got back into his car and the thrill of knowing it was his was ever new.

In between scrounging for supplies, Steve stopped at the office to use the adding machine, look over bids, and have the secretaries type letters for him. Two secretaries now worked in the office. The plain young woman, whom Myrsini had approved of, had married a soldier from the Kearns army base and gone with him to his home town in Kentucky. She had been replaced by Doris Haynes, in her early twenties but already stout. Maureen, the other secretary, was pretty and plump. Once a week, Penny and Georgie came in to help type and file. Solly and Con did the bookwork, Con silently, Solly glancing at Maureen with a calculating look that disturbed Steve. "This is an office," he wanted to say to him.

At times Steve's son Andrew was in the office. Andreas often stopped by Steve's house in the morning, picked up Andrew while Mary stood at the door, looking miserable. "Go in the house, Maria," he commanded in Greek. "I know what I'm doing." In the car Andreas set Andrew on his lap and let him put his small hands on the steering wheel and pretend he was driving.

They took the freight elevator to the top floor. In a diaper and striped T-shirt, Andrew toddled about, played with bunches of keys, old bankbooks, and paperweights, and tore up trade magazines.

The paperweight that showered a miniature village with snow-flakes fascinated Andrew, but not for long. The secretaries smiled insincerely, their eyes on the wastebaskets, which Andrew liked to push over. When Andrew grew hungry and said, "Mum-mum, *Papou*," his grandfather fed him jelly beans. Andreas had one of the secretaries or the janitor Elroy take Andrew home, long after Andrew had become a nuisance or Andreas had an appointment.

Andreas also took Andrew with him to see about repairs to the family's buildings. The two of them would look on with great attention while a plumber or electrician worked, Andrew squatting with his hands on his knees like his grandfather.

Mary told Steve she didn't like it. "He brings him back filthy and sopping wet. And his idea of feeding him is stuffing jelly beans in his mouth." Steve said, "Oh, let the old guy have some fun." Mary was near her time for delivery of their second child, and as she kneeled with her swollen womb pressed against the bathtub, washing the licorice and jelly-bean dyes off Andrew's face, her mouth tightened.

One early evening, after everyone else had left, Steve came into the office to a familiar smell. Andreas had Andrew under his arm like a sack of potatoes, Andrew's brown-stained behind haphazardly wiped with Kleenexes. The tissues and filled underpants had been dropped into Maureen's wastebasket. Again Andrew had been playing so hard, he forgot to ask his grandfather to take him to the toilet, and Andreas never remembered such details.

"I'll take him home, Pa." "Nah, he want to go with me, with his *Papou*," Andreas said.

"'Bye, Andy-Pandy," Steve said. Andrew looked over his shoulder and gave a little wave, his hair matted with what looked like bits of pink taffy. The janitor Elroy and his wife stood in the hall and watched the two get into the freight elevator. Steve shook his head: Mary would complain the minute he got home. "They spoil him. They spoil him," she'd say after every visit to his grandparents' house and every visit that Andreas and Marika made to see Andrew in his own house. Marika would let no one correct Andrew. "No,"

Steve laughed and said to Mary, "But she used to chase us all over the house with the *blasti,* ready to hit us."

"No matter what goes wrong," Mary said, "they always blame me."

"You're too sensitive," Steve said.

The first Thanksgiving Day after the war, besides celebrating the holiday, the entire clan was present for a special festive dinner: Penny and Georgie had both become engaged. "At last!" Steve whispered to Solly, who appraised the two men sitting next to Penny and Georgie with a cold eye. "We're going to have them on our backs the rest of our lives." Solly said. Penny leaned toward a small man, Joe, a bookkeeper, with long, curled eyelashes. While Penny spoke in clichés, Joe watched her with great interest. Georgie's fiancé, Taki, was a recently arrived immigrant with glossy black hair that swirled back from his forehead into a high puff. Aunt Myrsini was gaily talkative, looking from Taki to Magdalene, Solly's regal wife, and paid no attention to the others around the table. Uncle Harry tried to interrogate Taki with the usual questions asked of new immigrants: "What part of Greece did you come from? What kind of work does your father do? Do you have *patriotes* here?" Aunt Myrsini interrupted to talk about Smyrna and her family, now in Athens.

A euphoric smile lingered on Marika's pale lips: At last her daughters were being married. Mary smiled, too, relieved that she would not have to hear her mother-in-law's insistent complaints that no one paid any attention to her daughters; they might as well be orphans. This self-pitying talk twice coerced Mary into giving dinner parties for the young people of the church. Penny and Georgie had sat and talked with each other while Mary and the hired waitress hurried around the tables, filled wineglasses, and brought more platters and food.

That Thanksgiving, Andreas said very little after raising his wineglass and toasting the two couples. He gave furtive, disconsolate glances toward his daughters' future husbands. Next to him, in his high chair, Andrew was using his fingers to eat small pieces of turkey that Mary had put on a red plastic plate. Andreas piled more pieces of turkey, potato, and dressing on it. "He's going to get a stomachache," she said. Andreas waved her away. "Nah, the boy's hungry."

Instead of the usual Greek pastries, Mary had made pumpkin pies. When she placed a piece in front of Andreas, he surveyed it, sampled it, and took several big bites. "Hm, what's this? Purty good."

"It's pumpkin pie, *Patera,*" Mary said.

With the back of his hand, Andreas flipped the plate from him, spilling what remained of the pie on the embroidered white cloth. "Pumpkin! Only animals and starving humans eat squash! I ate enough of it in my village! I didn't come to America to eat animal food!" Andrew looked at his grandfather, laughed, and flipped over his dish of pie. Andreas nodded at him, smiling broadly. Myrsini glanced at Taki and Magdalene with sardonic amusement. Magdalene merely continued her passive smiling and Taki lifted an eyebrow in acknowledgment, as if the two of them were in the midst of barbarians. Mary looked at Andreas with one eye crossed and in a moment took Andrew from him. "His hands are sticky," she said. "I have to wash them."

When the liqueurs were served in the living room, toasts were made again, mainly to Con. "To your wedding crowns!" Andreas and Marika said. Penny gushed, "It's your turn now, Con," and Georgie said, "Don't end up a bachelor, Con." Con said nothing. "Euripedes . . . " Aunt Myrsini began, and she looked about the seated group, "Euripedes, the Greek tragedian, said, 'Sons are the anchors of a mother's life.'" She pursed her smug mouth. "But in due time Constandinos will also marry."

"'You have to wet your ass,'" Andreas quoted the proverb while Myrsini's face hardened, "'if you want to catch fish.'"

A week later Steve was in his office rummaging through desk drawers for an estimate. He was always aware of the ominous quiet of a building when people had left it. After a few minutes, he heard a sound coming from an office down the hall. He listened; it was Con's muffled voice, speaking into a telephone. Steve closed the desk drawer carefully; he heard a tone in Con's voice like a cry, as if he were strangling. Steve leaned his head toward the door, making no sound so that he could hear better. Con's voice was stilled. A dark silence stood in the deserted offices.

Steve leaned back in his chair, thinking something was required of him, but what? Then he convinced himself that he must not have heard right, and yet that cry—he had heard it all right. He forgot about the estimate while he thought about Con, realizing that he did not know this first cousin well enough to walk into his office and ask what was the matter.

He looked up. Con was standing in the doorway. A pale-green tinge suffused his dark skin. His sleek black hair, always combed back carefully, was tousled; it looked to Steve as if he had been pulling on it. "I didn't know you were still here, Steve," Con said, without looking at him.

Steve jerked forward. "Sit down, Con. Let's shoot the bull."

Con stood a moment, a look of misery puckering his fine black eyebrows and full mouth. He moved slowly toward the big leather chair in front of Steve's desk and slumped onto it. He sat looking at his palms resting on his thighs. A few seconds passed, then Steve, impelled to speak, said, "What's bothering you, Con?" Con shook his head in a despairing motion and dropped his chin.

Now what? Steve thought. He had started it and had to go on or pretend he wasn't looking at this young, handsome cousin who was suffering. "Con, you look like you're pretty bad off." Then Con told Steve, still not looking at him, stopping to take deep breaths after every few words, that he wanted to marry a girl he had met at the university, but his mother and father were raising a storm. She was an American and they said he had to marry a Greek girl.

"Have you been taking this girl out, Con?"

"Yes, sort of sneaking around, but we don't want to go on like this."

"Aaa—go marry her. They'll cool down in a few months. That's what usually happens."

"My mother keeps screaming that it'll kill her, and my dad says he'll disown me."

Steve thought of them, Aunt Myrsini screaming and Uncle Harry roaring, and snorted. "I'll stick up for you," he said. "I know Solly will too, and I'll get my dad to go along." He knew as soon as he spoke that their approval would mean nothing to Aunt Myrsini and that it might even make it worse for Con. But he had said it. "Go marry her."

Con talked about Miriam and her parents. Her family was not too keen about it, either, he said, but they had come around because Miriam was so unhappy. Steve asked what her father did because he did not know what else to say. He was a vice president of Walker Bank, and her mother was PTA president at East High School. "They're good people, Steve," Con said, appealing to Steve. They talked for a few more minutes and left together. In the parking garage, Con said, "Thanks, Steve," looking ashamed and shaking Steve's hand.

Steve got into his car, amazed at what had happened: He had never had such a personal conversation with anyone in his life. He and his friends, Lefty and Perry, and Solly had never talked about anything so intimate, so raw. They made fun of coffeehouse Greeks, complained about Americans, especially the Mormons, but never said anything like Con's tortured confession.

He was eager to tell Mary about it. What had happened was so unusual, so unbelievable. His house was dark. He parked in the garage, unlocked the kitchen door, and turned on the light. A note was on the drainboard: "My mother died." He drove to her parents' house and demanded, "Why didn't you call me?"

"I didn't have the time to track you down," she said, her voice sharp.

In her arms Andrew looked at her and frowned. Steve tried to take him from her but he turned his head. That night Mary and Andrew began staying with her father; they returned home the day after the funeral.

Steve mused over the old man: Mary was over there every day. She had become thin, although she was pregnant. He thought he should see about getting a bigger house and have her father live with them. He wanted to say, "Mary, I grew up in a house full of kids and people. I want my peace. I don't want your dad living with us." He wouldn't say it; he thought when she had the baby, she would have to stay home; it would blow over.

Mary held little Andrew and pointed to pictures on the living room wall: "Daddy" to Steve in his military policeman's uniform— "Uncle Alex" to her brother—"Yiayia" to her mother in her 1913 wedding dress; she had never had another picture taken.

"This house is like a funeral place," Andreas said loudly one day. "Only time my little boy laughs is when he sees me. His grandpa. His godfather." That night, Mary sang and read to Andrew and played pat-a-cake with him.

While Steve still tried to find a solution of what to do about Mary's father—even outlandish ideas came to him like having him go to Chicago to live with Mary's sister—he died. For his memorial service, Mary again mixed boiled wheat, sweetened it, added currants, walnuts, parsley, pomegranate seeds, and white Jordan almonds

The death was an inconvenience to Aunt Myrsini. She would have to wait for the mourning period to end before Con's marriage could take place. Marika gave Steve the news; she heard it from the midwife: Con was engaged to the housepainter Kamberis's daughter Tessie. With a scornful sniff she served Steve coffee in her small kitchen. "Yes, *my* sons went to war. They could have been killed while she was busy finding a wife for Constantinos. And who did she pick? Not an educated girl like my daughters, but the housepainter's daughter. She wanted some poor girl she could make over. The *mami* says she took her to have her hair cut and curled a certain way. She bought her clothes. She's teaching her how to cook with all the butter and the best olive oil the simpleminded girl never had in her own house. She's teaching her the kind of manners she learned in her wonderful Smyrna. And they bought the house next door to them for the bride and groom. It has one and a half bathrooms."

Parties followed, all photographed by Penny with her Kodak: round-faced Tessie, smiling so widely her cheeks turned into two pink balls, her eyes wide, ecstatic. "I never thought anything like this could happen to me, Mary," she sighed and laughed and cried. "Oh, he's *sooo* handsome! Handsomer than any movie actor!"

Penny managed only one snapshot with Tessie and Con, but many of Aunt Myrsini, head held high and triumphant, her arm hooked through Tessie's plump elbow.

The dinner reception was held at the Hotel Utah ballroom, profusely decorated with white gladioli. Tessie's mother wore a dark blue silk dress sewed by Mary. Tessie's father wore his dark brown Sunday suit, although Aunt Myrsini had told him to rent a tuxedo. They were seated at one end of the elevated bridal table; Con's parents were at the other end. Tessie's silent father tied a napkin around his neck and proceeded to eat doggedly without looking up. "Too bad Aunt Myrsini can't see him," Solly said. Solly sat with other family members: his pretty, smiling wife Magdalene, Marika, Andreas, Penny and Georgie with their fiancés, Steve and Mary, who was worried about leaving her three-week-old baby girl for the first time. They laughed and a happy air took hold of them.

Within a few months Tessie adopted her mother-in-law's way of holding her head high when less fortunate people spoke to her. Con's telephone was altered so that no incoming calls could be made, only outgoing ones. Twice a day, Tessie reported to her mother-in-law Myrsini. At church and family gatherings, Tessie glanced apprehensively at Myrsini, who gave an almost imperceptible nod of approval or a sideways turn of her head in disapproval. If Myrsini nodded, Tessie continued talking to an old friend like Mary; if Myrsini turned her head to the side, Tessie moved away. Myrsini and Tessie did not belong to the women's church organization, the

Philoptochos. Marika said, "It isn't *high class* enough for them. Myrsini wouldn't think of putting on an apron and working in the bazaar and festivals with village women. No, the *sultana,* the *Turkissa,* can't put her white hands in hot water!" Mary asked Tessie to help with mending clothes for the poor children of the parish, but she reddened and hurried off. Mary overheard her talking to a newcomer and spoke of her father, the housepainter, as an interior decorator.

Con came to the office as before, quiet, his attention on the books. In discussions he would murmur in agreement and not look at Steve straight on. He followed Solly around, and when a decision had to be made, he looked first to see what position Solly would take. Steve shouted at him when he was outvoted by him, his father, Uncle Harry, and Solly. When his head cleared, he glanced at Con's handsome, joyless face with the look of perpetual weariness on it and new anger flared up: Why hadn't he defied his parents and married the girl he wanted to, instead of brainless Tessie?

X

[The 1950s]

THE 1950S BEGAN with a quarrel in the office that reverberated throughout the Kallos building and onto the sidewalk in front of it. Passersby looked up at the three-story building, trying to determine where the shouting was coming from. Uncle Harry had hold of Andreas's desk, his hands white-knuckled, as if he were holding himself back from striking his brother. "I want to know when this extravagance is going to stop!" he shouted. "Do you hear? Who do

you think I am to have to put up with this nonsense?" The extravagance was the preparation for Penny's and Georgie's double wedding. Con had had a wedding, the opulence of which had never
before been seen in Holy Trinity. Penny and Georgie expected the
same of everything—the flower-decorated church; the wedding
gowns to match Tessie's seed-pearl embroidered satin; the dinner in
the Hotel Utah with champagne and Metaxas liqueur; and honey-
moons in San Francisco.

Andreas looked up at Heracles and, his voice rising in competition, bellowed, "Weddings are expensive! We're not talking about
village weddings! Those don't go in America!"

"I've got one son! You have four children! Why should I be punished because I have only one child!"

"No one told you to have only one child!"

"That's what I have, one child! And you have your four bleeding
the company!"

Andreas spit out his unlighted cigar. He stood up and leaned
over his cluttered desk. "What do you mean, talking to me like this?
Your wife's spending can never match my family's! My woman was
always careful, the way Greek wives are taught! Your wife wanted
the best of everything from the minute she walked into my house!"
Andreas mimicked Myrsini's words, his voice rising an octave, "'I
want a good house! I'm not a gypsy! I came from a cultured, educated clan!' Those fancy clothes! Those AHEPA conventions! She
had to go dressed like a queen! And always *feerst cless!*"

"No, you wanted her to go like a peasant! You should be proud
that she represented the family so people would know we were
people of importance, but you're a *vlahos!* You should never have
left the village!"

"So, I'm a *vlahos!* If I hadn't left the village and worked like a
mule to send you to school and bring you here, where would you be
today?—you and your fancy wife with her nose up in the air! Shit on
your mug! I'm sick of you! I fuck your Virgin! You thankless *sonofabitch!*"

Heracles raised both fists and shook them. "I'm getting out of here before I do something and damn my soul!" He turned and stamped out of the office. The secretaries, now three, who had not moved during the shouting, went back to work. Con had disappeared into his office the moment the quarrel began, and Steve and Solly smirked and looked back at plans for a shopping center. The center would be built on property Andreas had bought before the first World War, a group of old houses and empty lots.

The quarrel between Andreas and Heracles made no difference to the money distribution. Although they now gave themselves good salaries, they replaced the old scraps of IOUs they once slipped into the cash register with checks written on the company's checking account. These sums were recorded in a separate ledger. "We'll have a reckoning one of these days," Andreas said.

Steve and Solly were building big houses miles from the city. Aunt Myrsini and Heracles bought two spacious houses, older ones, but, as Aunt Myrsini said, in the best neighborhood, where doctors and lawyers lived. She did not drive and wanted to live near the downtown stores. Steve and Solly wrote themselves checks to pay architects, bricklayers, carpenters, plumbers, and electricians. "No reason why we shouldn't," Solly said. "The Jap farm turned into a real plum!" He talked about its value as collateral. One shopping center was almost finished and they were ready to begin another. Solly was out of the office as much as Steve, getting clear title to deeds, looking at plans with architects, and going on trips with Con.

The expense accounts were high to Steve's way of thinking. "Why do you have to go all over creation looking at shopping centers? Just look through the trade magazines. Hell, they'll tell you everything you want to know."

"It's not the same. You have to look at them to get the lay of the land. It's not the same."

"I get all I need to know out of them."

"Well, we're different, Steve. You like to keep your nose to the grindstone."

"I like to keep my nose to the grindstone! If I didn't, where in hell do you think we'd have the money to do what we're doing?"

"Read Ayn Rand, Steve. You'll get a different perspective on business."

"She's full of shit!"

When leasing agents and representatives of big insurance companies came to town, Solly, Steve, and Con took them to the University Club. They had joined the club soon after the war ended. Several times, Steve heard that a representative had been in town and gone. "It was a last minute thing," Solly said. "He called and I couldn't get hold of you. So I took him to the club and got the negotiations going."

Solly wore white suede shoes; he went to the barber often; he smelled of aftershave lotion. He, Steve, and Con were leaving to meet a New York Life representative when Solly stopped at the door of the office and said, "Where'd you buy that suit? Off the rack at J. C. Penney?"

"Well, if I'm going to embarrass you, I'll go about my business," Steve said, and sat down at his desk, looked at plans, and fumed: *Bastard, sonofabitch!* Twice when he was having lunch with the president of the local carpenters' union at the club, he saw Solly and Con at the far end of the dining room with several businessmen. Solly was leaning back in his chair, relaxed, smoking leisurely, talking easily. Steve wanted to be with them; he yearned to be included. Solly and Con arrived at the office two hours later.

Solly and Con joined in the hysteria of the uranium boom on the Colorado Plateau. On the streets, in clubs, bars, and restaurants, excited men and women talked about buying and selling uranium stock. On the radio and on television, which was becoming readily available, newscasters gave daily reports on Charlie Steen and his Mi Vida holdings. They met in the University Club at lunchtime, drinking and talking with others who had invested heavily in the uranium hidden in the desert rocks of eastern Utah. They talked about *Charlie* Steen, not *Charles*, as if they were good friends of his.

Solly, his friends, and Con rented Piper Cub planes to fly them to the town of Moab, where they had guides, staked with their money and supplies, explore the desert for them. Penny and Georgie asked Solly's advice and bought penny stock. They drove to Moab to see the excitement and commotion themselves. Penny brought her new Leica camera and photographed the barren landscape, placing her husband Joe with Georgie and her husband Taki in the foreground.

For several years, uranium continued to be the topic of the day. Steve saw Solly and his friends at the club, talking, their voices loud, about new strikes, new companies, about money in the millions. He sat at a corner table. He didn't want them to see him, yet he also wished Solly would and wave him over. In the office, Solly talked about what he was buying, but did not invite Steve to get involved with him and his friends. As long as he was not asked, Steve would not join the boom. He bought some penny stock for his children as souvenirs: Eldorado, Pay Day, Majestic, and Atomic Minerals. He put them in a strong box he kept at home in a closet.

A few years later, the boom was over. The government was overstocked and there was no market for uranium. Solly's face was pulled down by a fold on either side of his mouth. "Your stock's as worthless as tits on a boar," Steve told him. Solly kept a glass of Scotch and soda on his desk.

Andreas now had more time to talk with the many Greeks dropping in to bring gossip and to argue about the Holy Trinity priest or cantor or council president. Heatedly they discussed the latest news from Greece reported in the Greek-American newspapers. The icemen came once in a while to predict the loss of the Greek language and religion in America. They had never married and had no children, yet they spouted dire prophecies. Their big faces red, their horse teeth brown, they shook their index fingers at Andreas: "The priest says there aren't as many children in the Sunday schools like when the immigrants' children were growing up! Something must be done! Our glorious language! Our great Orthodoxy! Ach. Ach." Andreas looked at them steadily and answered with proverbs: "'You know how to whistle, but you don't own any goats.' Now tell me what's the news." The icemen sat down, eyes amused, amazed, or angry, told the latest coffeehouse gossip, and after twenty minutes or so left with satisfied smiles over their big teeth.

Milt Valiotis came regularly to the office. He was still working on the city's vice squad and talked with Heracles behind his closed office door. Petty politicians stopped in "just to say hello," they always said to Harry, and a city commissioner, a fat, sweating man, who had not graduated from the eighth grade, came to "pass the time of day." They left Heracles preening as if he knew the important people who ran the city's business.

Often, when Steve's construction crews had finished for the day, he came to the office and with Solly and Con remained after their fathers had gone home. They talked about the happenings of the day. Con had little to say; he had charge of the office workers, although no one had expressly given him the task—it had gradually evolved toward him. Solly, drinking scotch, related anecdotes about business acquaintances who provided call girls for big shots from insurance companies. Twice he told a hilarious story about a leasing agent for a national company who got genital lice from a singer in a Las Vegas lounge. "Tell Steve about that guy we met at the trade show in Los Angeles, Con," he said laughing. Con shook his head. "I'm no good at telling stories," he said.

Solly told more stories while at the windows the sky changed from dusk to evening. "In Mexico City," Solly said, slurring his words.

"When were you in Mexico City?" Steve interrupted.

"Oh, we took a side trip from LA just for the weekend before we came home." He went on to describe a group of Americans being taken to a sex show where two naked girls rubbed their vulvas together until they had orgasms.

On the way home in the dark, Steve tried to ignore an uncomfortably warm excitement that took hold of his body. Icy pricks followed, stippling his back. Mary had put his food in the oven to keep warm, but it had dried out by the time he sat down to eat. "What kind of a dinner do you call this?" he asked peevishly. "Looks like dried-up leftovers." They quarreled, Mary screeching that she had been up three nights straight with the baby's teething. Steve shouted back. Then he sat down to eat the lamb shank and realized with relief that the uncomfortable excitement that had hold of him was gone.

BUSINESS WAS GROWING, the family was growing; Tessie, Penny, and Georgie were all pregnant at the same time. As more children were born, the family dinners that had been held in Marika's bungalow house were transferred to Steve 'and Mary's. Andreas did not want to go to Solly's house: Magdalene, he complained, was nice, but you didn't know what was in her head. He didn't like either Penny's or Georgie's husband, the sons-in-law, and why he didn't like them he didn't know, only that he didn't.

Yet Marika was still euphoric over her daughters' marriages. When they visited her in the evening, she hurried about to set the table with cheese and honey-nut pastries, all the while, lamenting that they had not told her they were coming so that she could have *pykilia* to serve them. Penny's husband Joe smiled as much as Solly's wife Magdalene. Penny still spoke in clichés, and he still sat with folded hands and listened intently, his long eyelashes flickering.

Myrsini was delighted with Georgie's Taki because he was Greek-born and said he was educated. He had come from Cyprus. Myrsini had been adamant that Greeks from Asia Minor, as she was, were more alert, more intelligent—"They knew why they were living"—than Greeks from the mainland. Georgie ate on while Taki expounded on Greek politics and culture. Greek poets and writers were far superior to the Americans and he would recite a few lines and press his hands over his caved-in chest. Andreas usually got up as soon as Taki began his Greek jingoism and went into his bedroom where he turned on the television news.

At least once a month Myrsini invited the family and Greek immigrants "of the better class" to have dinner and to hear her and Taki read their poetry and articles printed in Greek-language newspapers. She used immaculate white, cut-work tablecloths, which she ironed herself, unwilling to have her servant, Marighoula, a recently arrived young village woman, touch her linens. She ordered Marighoula about in icy tones. After a year Marighoula left to work in the Sweet's Candy Factory, and another hapless immigrant girl took her place, only to leave when she found work at Pullman Tailors. "That ungrateful wretch," Myrsini said. "I rescued her from the streets." Next a silent Mexican woman came who looked startled at every ring of the doorbell.

The evenings ended with the guests listening to contemporary Italianate love songs on a record player. Dressed as always like a mannequin in a store window, Con sat near a window and watched cars driving past. Tessie hurried about with trays of Turkish demitasses, *loukoum, ouzo,* and Metaxas liqueur. Andreas fidgeted: he could not abide these songs of "hearts withered by love," "crazy kisses," and "a girl wanting a light-haired man without eyeglasses." Marika looked down at her brown, blue-veined hands in embarrassment.

One evening Taki sang a song that had become popular in Greece, a lover praising his woman's body, her *kormy.* When he finished, smiling widely—his teeth were white and even—Andreas said with raised voice, "Now then! Can't we hear any of the old songs of the revolution? The guerrillas fighting the Turks! 'Old Man Demos,' 'Kitsos Mother,' 'Diakos?'"

Myrsini shook her head, her thin mouth stretched: "Andreas, you immigrants can't think of anything except the *klefts* fighting the Turks. That's a village concern. In Greek cities people are more cosmopolitan." She gave a quick glance at Taki from under her mascaraed eyelashes and he grinned.

"City people, eh? Bah, I fuck their horns!" Andreas stood up and Marika, glaring at him, got up also. All the way out of the house, into the car, on the drive to their home, she berated Andreas. He shouted back: "I said it and I'll say it again!"

Steve told Mary to make excuses when Myrsini telephoned with her invitations. "Hell, I don't have time to bowl with Perry and Lefty, and I'm going to make time for the Educated Witch!" "She's probably glad," Mary said. "She's got the kind of group she wants." The group, her *parea,* as Myrsini called it, comprised Con and Tessie, Penny and Georgie with their husbands, occasionally Solly and Magdalene, a Greek-born doctor, and two refined—like her—women who had come to America in their teens without dowries; they married men in their sixties and, fortunately for them, the men died within a few years and left them modestly wealthy. Uncle Harry sat, his ankles crossed, his hands folded under his ball of a stomach, and looked with baleful eyes at the gray-screened television set.

Myrsini tried, using her wiles, to bring Taki into the business. Andreas and Steve rebuffed Heracles, her emissary, who broached the subject to them. "What does he know how to do?" Andreas growled. "He's got the right kind of job for him, managing a cafe."

"Well, if you think that's a good enough job for your son-in-law. If you want people to talk that you left your daughter stranded with an educated husband who stands on his feet all day and shows people to a table."

"I can see your woman's been putting ideas in your head and words in your mouth."

Heracles bristled and pulled his shoulders back. "No one tells me what to say!"

Andreas narrowed his shrewd eyes. "So what do you intend to do, bring in my son-in-law so he can compete with your Con in the business?" Heracles lifted his eyebrows at the revelation.

Marika said, "If you give Taki a job, then you have to give Penelope's man a job. I treat my daughters equally. Their husbands don't make enough as it is. Why should my sons live better than my daughters? And don't forget when I gave you that sackfull of money, I told you the girls had to be part of the business."

"They *are* part of the business," Steve said. "Every month they get a check from their father's share in it."

"It isn't enough!"

"It's more than enough, but they want to live like queens."

Solly told Steve he was pig-headed. "You can find work for both Taki and Joe if you wanted to."

"Go to hell! Tomorrow you'll go about your affairs, today you're brownnosing."

The women won a halfway victory. The family set up Taki in an insurance agency and gave him their business, but not without mutterings from Andreas and Steve. The immigrants Taki had ignored as inferiors, he now courted. Andreas supplied the money for Joe to buy into a CPA firm that was rewarded with the Kallos tax work.

BY THE MIDDLE 1950s, Marika and Andreas had eleven grandchildren: Steve and Mary had two daughters born after Andrew—their grandfather Andreas patted the little girls on the head when they came running to him, then forgot them; Solly and Magdalene had a son, Tommy, and three daughters; and Penny and Georgie each had two daughters. Myrsini and Heracles had one grandchild. Con and Tessie's son Niko was named not after Heracles, as tradition would have it, but after Myrsini's father. A stillborn baby girl had come two years later.

Kallos Building Properties was doing so well that Solly, beaming, said it was following Ayn Rand's philosophy that was "putting them on the map." For himself, he bought additional acreage and built a swimming pool and a tennis court. On summer evenings, a horde of bankers, architects, attorneys, and old college friends drank and ate around the pool.

Steve also bought more land and had grass planted in a great sweep up to a wide stand of scrub oak, quaking aspen, and pines. The children often swam in Solly's pool, but more often they spent long afternoons at Steve and Mary's house. They ran over the expanse of grass, shrieking into the dark coolness of the little forest with the piquant scent of pines and the thick, springy cover of their fallen needles. In and out of the house the children ran, grabbing pieces of chicken, cookies, and soft drinks or punch. As the first-born grandchild, Andrew was their leader. He decided what games they would play. At the family dinners, he chose the board games, television programs, and the movies they were to see.

Fathers and grandfathers—Uncle Harry and his family were not always present—remained at the dinner table or sat on the patio in summer and talked about business, or gossiped about others who had failed in theirs and why. The mothers cleared the tables, scraped dishes and put them in the dishwasher, and talked about happenings in the church and the Greek women's organization, the Philoptochos. Marika insisted on covering the leftovers with plastic and exclaimed often, "What wonders there are in the world today!"

One day, the usual gleeful outbursts and shrieks from the play-room turned into shouts. Their mothers went on with setting the kitchen in order until the tearful, angry cries could not be ignored. Mary, Magdalene, Tessie, Penny, and Georgie stopped and listened, waiting for someone among them to go into the playroom to arbi-trate. The child cries came clearly.

"My dad's the boss!"

"Your dad is not!"

"My papou's the boss!"

"Your dad's always acting like he's the leader! And he's not!"

Mary hurried into the room. The children looked at her, the girls with tears running down their faces, the boys with evasive eyes. Myrsini, who had been sitting in the living room, steered her grandson Niko away.

One late summer afternoon Steve opened the door of the office to see Andreas with his arm around Andrew's shoulders. The red, yellow, and orange sunset reflected its brilliance on the windows like sheets of gold. "This is gonna be yours some day," he said. "That's what I work for." A dreamy haze was in the room. Andrew was eleven years old.

About a year later a young immigrant came to the office to speak with Andreas. His name was Theophrastos Stratopoulos and he came from the same Peloponnesian village as Andreas and Heracles. Andreas asked him about his parents, about the village. Andreas had been saying since the war ended that he would go back to see his village, ride slowly in front of the mayor's house in a good rented car, and give a dowry or two to poor girls. "And what is the great Mayor Gerontopoulos doing now?" Andreas asked. The young man wrinkled his forehead and then said, "Ah, yes, the Italian soldiers killed him by mistake when they entered the village." Andreas said, "Too bad." He was sorry he could not show the mayor his success.

Andreas told him to come back at the end of the day to speak with Steve. "I'm good with numbers," the young immigrant said. "I'll work hard."

Steve knew something of Theophrastos. "Okay," Steve said. "I'll give you a job running errands and keeping after the janitor. Help him out. He needs someone, but he thinks this is his little kingdom."

Theophrastos nodded, his eyes surprised. "First," Steve said, "you have to give up that crowd of tough guys you run around with. You can't run around with Peloponnesian bums who use brass knuckles and expect to work for us."

"Okay, okay. See, I met Angie. She's from a village near mine. Okay, okay."

"Then the next step is to cut your name. How about Theo Stratos?"

"Well, if you say so."

"Next, you have to go to night school to improve your English and learn estimating. If you're good with numbers, that's a good start."

Heracles berated Steve. "So you wouldn't bring Taki in to work in the business, but you take in this uneducated *mangas* who grew up on the streets of Piraeus! Be careful you don't groom him to take over the business!"

Marika did not know what to say: She believed in helping immigrants, but she was afraid Theophrastos might be cunning and in truth take over the *periousia*.

Steve bought a small red truck and sent Theo on errands that the office workers had previously done: picking up or returning plans to architects; getting plats at the engineer's office; making bank deposits; running errands for Elroy, the janitor, who now called himself the maintenance man. On Saturdays he did small jobs for Mary—he was good with repairs and trimmed the grass better than their regular yard crew. Mary gave him a key to the house with instructions that he look in the refrigerator for something to eat if she was not at home.

Theo took Andrew with him whenever he was in the office. Theo drove fast, but not fast enough to get tickets. He sang Greek songs, explained them to Andrew, told him about growing up on the streets of Piraeus where he had gone hoping to find work, and stopped at a just-opened *souvlaki* drive-in, where they were greeted with cries and camaraderie. One morning, they parked at an architect's firm, and Theo reached across Andrew to open the glove compartment; a pair of brass knuckles lay on some papers. "Oh, my little Virgin," Theo whispered in Greek, then in English, "Don't tell your dad, Andrew. I meant to get rid of them, like your father told me, but I kept forgetting. Don't tell your dad or I'll get fired!"

XI

As Marika and Andreas's grandchildren reached junior high school, they saw less of each other, and even less of Niko, Nick, the only grandchild of Aunt Myrsini and Uncle Harry. Their constant friends were in their neighborhoods and they attended different schools. Tessie and Con's son Nick enrolled in St. Mark's, a private school, and changed his name to Dick: His grandmother, Myrsini, said all the doctors' and lawyers' sons in her neighborhood were students there. She made mounds of Greek pastries for their teas and "back to school" nights.

[1965]

IN COLLEGE, the young people stopped coming to the family's name-day celebrations. They were busy with fraternity and sorority activities, skiing, studying, and their friends. Andrew, now in law school, still stopped at the brown brick bungalow on his grandfather's (and his) saint's day. If cars were parked in front of the house, he entered by the back door. Marika plied him with festive foods, most of which had been prepared by his mother, who was usually in the living room serving guests. Andrew ate while the women's high-pitched voices and the men's monotones went on. Marika came in at intervals. "Go back, *Yiayia*. I'm doing just fine here." Marika left but came back within a few minutes. She no longer insisted that Andrew go into the living room to greet visitors. He knew so little Greek, and besides he was too busy, a student at the university. Marika made the sign of the cross when the word *university* came into conversations. "To think," she would say, "I've lived to see my grandchildren in the *ooniversity*. Me who can't read and write."

Marika and Andreas missed Andrew's graduation services: Andreas had had an emergency gallbladder operation. While he was in the hospital, the family held its quarterly board meeting. Steve took his usual place at one end of the oval-shaped table. Uncle Harry was sitting at the head of the table in Andreas's seat. Con sat next to him, his father having pointed to the adjoining seat. Penny and Georgie in white linen suits had come directly from the hairdresser's and took seats on either side of Solly.

After the agenda had been taken care of, Solly said, "You know, Steve, we've been thinking about Andrew taking over the law work and we don't think it's the right thing to do."

"Who said he'd be taking over the law work? Who said we were going to give up Jackson and Snow? The idea was Andrew would be the liaison between our office and theirs! You knew he was going into law school and now you decide 'it wouldn't be right'!"

Uncle Harry said, tapping his pencil on the shiny mahogany table, "It's conflict of interest. That's what it is." Heracles assumed a pleased look whenever he used English words he seemed to think showed he was wise.

"Bullshit! No one said it was conflict of interest when you did the books! No one was afraid you were cooking the books! Has Con been cooking the books? You're all talking through your assholes!"

"Now, Steve," Solly said, in a judicious way, to show he was reasonable, "think about it. You'll see the logic of it. Family businesses split up over things like this."

Steve aimed the packet containing the agenda, minutes, and other documents at Solly. "You sonofabitch!" he shouted, as Solly ducked under the flying papers. He glimpsed a wry look on Solly's face as he slammed the door of the board room.

After dinner that night, Steve remained at the kitchen table gazing at Mary's rose garden in the dusk. Andrew asked about the board meeting and Steve told him how the agenda went. When his daughters had finished loading the dishwasher and gone to their rooms, he told Andrew about the quarrel. Andrew paled. Mary said in a restrained voice, "Those terrible people." Steve knew that tone; he felt weak. As soon as they were alone in the house, he would face Mary's fury.

"But I'll keep working on them, Andrew. You'll have your desk there. And when your *papou* goes back to work, he'll fix them good."

"I won't work there. It's obvious they don't want me."

"Give me a little time. A little more time."

"No."

"Think it over, Andrew. *Papou* has his heart set on it."

"No."

Steve moaned. "Oh, my God, how will we tell him?"

A few days later Andreas was back home and heard the news. "Come to the house with Andrew," he boomed into the telephone, his voice no longer stunned and weak as it had been in the hospital.

Steve stood while he tried to explain what Solly and Uncle Harry had said about conflict of interest. "Go fuck yourself!" Andreas shouted in Greek. In half-Greek, half-English he went on, "I send my grandson to be a lawyer and I'll kill anyone who tells me he can't work in the business I made with my own hands!"

"*Papou,* I won't work there now," Andrew said in a determined voice. "I can work somewhere else.

Steve said, "I never did anything behind your back."

Marika was on the telephone in the adjoining room shrilling at Solly: "Shame! Shame, Solon! You have no *filotimo,* no honor! What kind of a child did I raise! If you were here, I'd pluck your eyes out! And when I see that Constandinos with his nose up in the air like his mother, I'll spit in his face! And that Heracles! I'll make a rag of him!"

Cursing, Andreas got up carefully from the sofa and hobbled toward Steve and Andrew, his clenched fist raised as if he were holding an invisible whip, like the biblical overseer driving the Israelites into exile. Steve and Andrew quickly left the house.

Marika was certain the women in the family—not her daughters, Penny and Georgie, but Myrsini, Magdalene, and Tessie—had something to do with their men's rejecting Andrew. "That's how women are," she lectured Steve the following day. They were sitting in the small bungalow kitchen with the doors closed: his father was in his room sleeping. "They have their wiles. They know how to twist men to their designs. Don't shake your head at me!"

Steve sipped the lukewarm coffee that had stood in the pot for hours. Like you and your paper sack of money, he almost said, but his mother's swollen ankles and her gasping for air when she became excited kept him silent. Heart trouble, the doctor had said, and that she should not be trying to keep up her house. "Why should I have a woman in my house to wash the dishes and make the beds! I'm still alive!"

Penny and Georgie wanted to talk about a nursing home, but Steve said, "I'll cut your throats if you think I'll let you put Mama in a nursing home."

Penny said, "I'd take her, but I have to think about my mother-in-law. Joe won't like it if I take in Mama and Papa and ignore his mother. She's just as bad off as Mama."

Georgie said, "Well, I've got my own health problems. I'm sick half the time."

"Why don't you tell the truth! You don't want to do it. And that Greek import you married wouldn't let you anyway. Now that he's gotten everything he can out of the old folks, he forgets they're alive, the sneaky sonofabitch! You two make a great pair!"

Now there was an excuse, which seemed plausible, for letting the traditional dinners turn into occasions for each family's having its own gatherings: Marika's heart problems and Andreas's loss of strength—although his voice was still strong with demands and curses. To keep to this resolve, additional excuses abounded among the family members: Steve—that Mary's children needed her full attention; Solly—that Magdalene was having problems with her nerves; Penny and Georgie—that they were taking their children out for Thanksgiving dinner. "Aren't you ashamed," Marika scolded, "going to restaurants for *Thenksgivie* and on Christ's birth and Resurrection?"

Marika and Andreas sat at Mary's table for the holiday dinners. No matter how sumptuous the food, Theo Stratos's wife Angie always brought a big bowl of boiled greens for Andreas and Marika. The old people liked dandelions best of all; Angie dug them up in Liberty Park, where groundskeepers looked at her, baffled. Marika and Andreas often found a bundle of dandelions, cleaned and washed, at their front door in early morning. If Marika was quick enough to catch Theo, she forced him into the kitchen for coffee and sweet toasted bread. Andreas asked about Theo's new job, an estimator for a Greek-American construction company. Their talk usually ended with Andreas's outbursts about Andrew's not being taken into the business. Theo said he was angry too, a good kid like Andrew, the best of the clan's sons.

Penny and Georgie were unconcerned that Andrew had been turned away from the business. While their father was still recuperating from his gallbladder surgery, their husbands came to the office, expressly to see Steve. Solly and Con were away on one of their business trips. "We are here to represent our wives' interests," Georgie's husband Taki said, unsmiling, bringing his thick eyebrows together, which caused his face to look darker. He spoke with a twisting and pursing of his thick lips and with great attention to diction.

"So, what the hell are you doing here? Why didn't they come themselves? Why don't they open their goddamn mouths at the board meetings instead of waiting until they get home?"

"They're not satisfied they're getting what's coming to them," the little bookkeeper, Penny's husband, said, his staccato words, as if he had practiced them, belied by a flickering of his long eyelashes. "We have a right to look at the books."

"They're not satisfied or you're not satisfied? How come you wait until my dad is out of the office and you come marching in here? Get the hell out of here, you goddamn cocksuckers!"

The family talked on the telephone about Steve. They said they were sure he was ready for a breakdown. Solly offered the information that he spent a lot of time at the club and had got in with a group of cardsharps; he came late to the office and left late. Uncle Harry had his grandson, Dick, come to the office regularly and work on the books; Heracles and Con would look over Dick's shoulder. When Dick was brought in to shake Steve's hand, Steve saw Aunt Myrsini's eyes—sunken, bright, black—looking out at him. "Well, Steve," Dick said, "I know we'll get along fine."

"What's this Steve business? I'm still Uncle Steve. Only some American shitass would call his father's first cousin by his first name."

"Yes, yes, that's right, Dick," Uncle Harry said. "He didn't mean it, Steve. Just got confused."

Solly told Steve that he needed more help in looking at the rents and leases and why have an outsider do it when his son Tom now had his business degree and could just as well take care of it. Steve merely grunted and told Mary later that Solly's and Con's sons had come in through the back door.

Some mornings Steve left the house without shaving and with no attention to what he was wearing—pants that he wore around the house on weekends and white socks that Mary told him made him look like a hick. They quarreled over his coming home late. He wouldn't eat, complained that she was throwing food at him like a dog, poured himself a drink of whiskey, and sat in front of the television set. "I know you were at the club," Mary's voice rose. "Your office covers for you. Doris Haynes makes excuses for you. Telling me you're at the attorney's or at the podiatrist's. What's happened to you? You're drinking too much! What will the children think? I'm glad the girls are away at school and can't see you like this!"

After a few months, Steve stopped going to the club regularly: If the business were to progress, he knew he would have to teach Pretty Boy Tommy and Myrsini's look-alike Dick the business. Once in a while he took Dick and Tom to the club for lunch and to talk about proposals and property acquisitions that he, or Andreas, or Uncle Harry were negotiating. He hoped Andrew did not see them together.

Still, the family attended the weddings of the grandchildren and sat together to give the impression that they were a united clan. The first to marry were Steve and Mary's daughters; they had graduated from Vassar and married young men, named Young and

Fuller, who didn't mind being married in a Greek church. Connie now lived in California and Alexandra in New York. Andrew married Jeanne, who came from disaffected Mormon people, in an Episcopal church. Afterwards, Marika wiped her eyes and said she had always expected to see Andrew and a Greek girl wearing wedding crowns in the old Holy Trinity Church. She never acknowledged the suburban Prophet Elias; it was not a true Greek church to her, not a Byzantine church at all. Andreas sat very still through the ceremony and dinner that followed. Although he did not smile once, he never spoke a word to Andrew about his not having chosen a Greek girl for his wife. "Tzin" Marika called Jeanne. Andreas's conversations with Jeanne were invariably, "You okay? Tha's good."

The rest of the family's children married non-Greeks—Americans, Tessie called them. Solly's talk often veered toward his son Tom's wife. "She's a good-looking woman," he would say, and his eyes followed her as she went about, a tall, slender, blue-eyed blonde, who smiled with a gracious nod of her head to the old people and carried on superficial but pleasing talk with whomever came near her. "One look at her and Tom came to his senses," Solly would say, which reminded listeners that Tom had for a time been a hippie. He had let his hair grow to his shoulders, stopped shaving, wore clothes from the Deseret Industries, and went to San Francisco to wander the streets of Haight-Ashberry in a haze of marijuana. He returned when Solly stopped sending him money; he cut his hair and shaved his beard and soon people forgot he had ever left town.

The reports of why Tom and Dick had not served in Vietnam were conflicting: Marika was certain that Myrsini had found some way to bribe the generals to keep Dick safe, and that Solly's Tom was probably rejected because he had allergies, which was true. She retold the story of his father Solly's breathing dried oregano to keep from being beaten with the *blasti;* yes, the midwife, dead now, had told her so.

Uncle Harry died, ranting that he was too young to meet Death —Charos. "He's coming on his black horse," he screeched with his last breath. He had kept his prostate cancer a secret and it had gone into his bones. Only then did Solly and Steve remember that he had lost weight quickly and his eyes had gone dull. Aunt Myrsini took Con and Dick to Greece after the funeral. "Couldn't even wait for the forty days to be up," Marika said, which was untrue. Myrsini had done everything properly: the funeral followed by a Masonic service at the gravesite and the *parigoria,* the funeral dinner, afterwards. The day after the forty days of mourning were over, she rolled up her black dresses for the Salvation Army and took the plane for Greece. Tessie stayed at home, telling Steve and Mary that her back was giving her trouble.

The travelers returned earlier than they had expected and took Myrsini, raving and clutching her hair, from the airport directly to Holy Cross Emergency and from there to St. Joseph's Villa. "She didn't find things as she expected," Marika said with a lift of her eyebrows. There in the nursing home she remained for years, droning on to the maids about her important, wealthy family, their servants, their house with marble floors and steps, lemon and orange trees shading it, cypress trees standing like sentinels. Georgie's husband Taki visited her once and regaled whomever he saw, in church, on the street, in restaurants, with her nonsensical, meandering talk. "That's the thanks Myrsini gets for reading poems with him and singing those songs," Marika said.

No one knew how often Tessie visited her mother-in-law in the nursing home. She went to church one Sunday holding her son Dick's first child and sat next to Mary. Steve gave a *Hah!* of disgust at Tessie's saying she was keeping the baby for the weekend so Dick and his wife wouldn't have to put up with his crying. "What else did she say?"

"She said, 'Well, when it rains it pours. First my father-in-law dies, then my mother-in-law's stuck in a nursing home, and now I hear your in-laws are going downhill.'"

"They're not going downhill, they're at the bottom of the hill," Steve said.

Marika had left a pan of stew on the stove, gone out to her patch of a garden to pick a tomato, seen some weeds encroaching on the eggplants, and begun pulling them out. The fire engine arrived while she was still in the garden, oblivious to the smoke flowing out the windows. Steve said, "That's the last straw." Andrew drove to the bungalow to take his grandparents to his parents' house to live. His grandfather Andreas shuffled with a probing cane toward the car and waited for Andrew to help him onto the front seat. Mary came out, tugging at Marika's elbow. Marika wailed, "My house! My house! Catastrophe! Catastrophe! Virgin Mary, little Jesus!" Andrew drove on while his grandmother seated in the back with his mother wept and made the sign of the cross again and again. Every once in the while Andreas said in a mixture of Greek and English, *"Plug it.* Close your mouth. *It's finished."*

Steve's house was now kept with the lights on because Marika walked the nights away. She talked to herself. She wanted to help Mary in the kitchen and Mary would spread a newspaper on the table and have her pare carrots. Marika struggled, taking a long time with each carrot. She sighed deeply. "That's plenty, Mother," Mary said one day of three gouged carrots. "Go in and take a nap." She helped Marika up and watched her go slowly toward the bedroom wing. At the door, Marika stopped. "Maria, don't look so sad. It happens to everyone. You know the saying, 'There where you stand, I once stood; where I stand, you will one day.'" Mary nodded and the *thut thut thut* of the walker echoed across the floor.

Suddenly Marika began weeklong tirades at Andreas. "You had me like a slave! I was raising children, but I had that miserable Heracles and the icemen to take care of! I washed their dirty underwear! You let Heracles and that witch Myrsini decide my life! I was a slave! With no education like her! I came from poor villagers!"

As suddenly the tirades stopped. One of the family, Andrew, Steve, or Mary, would lead Marika to the bench in front of the rose garden. She sat, her eyes on Mount Olympus that rose from green slopes to a granite peak where yearlong snow filled its crags. "That mountain's called Mount Olympus, Mother. There's a mountain in Greece with the same name."

Marika looked about anxiously. "A mountain in Greece," she said, and her parchment-like forehead crinkled in puzzlement.

Theo Stratos and his wife Angie came to see her and often sat on the bench with her. She wanted them to tell her anything, anything at all, about the villages they had come from: how people were now; if they were very poor; was it still hard for girls to get dowries.

Her chest moved up and down in quick rhythm. The doctor suggested a cannister of oxygen to help her breathe. She refused: "I should have gone long ago." Andreas shook his finger at her. "The doctor knows what's best. It's not for you to decide."

"I've lived long enough," she said each time. Her grayed eyes receded deeper into their sockets as the days passed, and her myriadly wrinkled skin began to take on a transparency. In the mornings after dipping the twisted *koulourakia* cookies into a cup of coffee, Andreas read aloud to her from the Greek section of the *Orthodox Observer* or the *Greek Star.* He would take off his glasses and explain certain political or religious items. At times they would have long conversations in the television room, Andreas doing most of the talking with occasional assents or demurs from Marika. Andreas spoke in a kindly way to Marika—and to Mary.

It became harder for Marika to walk. She lay in bed. Andreas walked in and out of her bedroom. Then she could no longer speak, no longer swallow, and she died.

Andreas went into his adjoining room, sat on the bed, and cried. He ate nothing, drank a little coffee, and wept. With a fist thrust upward, he refused to talk with the figures that stood at the doorway, one tentative foot inside the room. Mary and Steve lay in bed as Andreas prowled the house, whimpering, trying to say something, as if he were explaining himself. Penny and Georgie came to discuss the funeral dinner. "No funeral dinner for everyone in the church, only the family!" Steve said, "and Theo Stratos and Angie."

"They're not family."

"No? Who's been bringing them vegetables and fruit from their garden all these years? Who's been stopping by to see them and cooking something special for them?"

At the prayer service the night before the funeral, Steve and Andrew held Andreas up, one on either side of him. When the priest concluded the service and parishioners filed past to give condolences, he pushed them off with his hand and when one woman persisted, softly telling him how good his wife had been, he told her to shut up.

The next day at the funeral, Andreas wept throughout the service. When the priest sang *Eonia y mnymy sou,* Eons be your memory, a strangled cry came from deep in his throat. Afterwards, as the family congregated for the funeral dinner in Steve and Mary's house, he went into his bedroom, lay on the bed, and refused to eat. Andrew followed and said he would bring a plate for him. Andreas shook his head: he would eat nothing, drink nothing. "You see, my boy," he said to Andrew, looking at him as if he would understand the logic of his decision, "I can die quicker."

By the third day Andreas began to moan, curled up, pressing his crossed arms against the emptiness of his stomach. Steve called the priest to speak to him, make him see what he was doing was like suicide, against church laws. The priest came and, behind the closed doors, Andreas confessed for the first time in his life, but kept to his vow, not to eat.

Andrew came daily. "Please, *Papou,*" he said. "Don't do this." Andreas lifted a wasted hand a few inches to acknowledge him, closed his eyes, and lifted his eyebrows in the irrevocable *no* of the Greeks.

Soon he did not have to be helped to the bathroom; he had dried up inside. A white sediment lined his thinned lips. Mary wiped it off continually with a moist cloth. Penny and Georgie ran in and out of their father's room, sobbing; Solly looked dubious. "The old man's lost it," he said. "He's gone off the deep end."

Penny and Georgie said they should have a big funeral dinner and have the priest invite everyone who attended the service. "After all, he was a pioneer. One of the first Greek immigrants in the state." Steve said most of their father's friends were dead, senile, or in nursing homes. "People will want to pay their last respects," Georgie said. "Everyone knew Papa, and our friends who didn't know him will come for us."

While their father lay dying, they sat in Mary's kitchen and called caterers and a rental service for extra chairs (they did not know how many parishioners would come), ordered flowers for the funeral and the dinner, went themselves to the Grecian Deli to discuss the hundreds of *baklava* and *kourambiedhes* they would need, and charged everything to Steve. "I expect your cleaning woman can bring some women to help in the kitchen," Penny said.

Two weeks later, the prayer service and funeral were held. On the way out of the cemetery, Steve accosted the young priest in his black surplice and brocaded stole. "What's this damn foolishness— a prayer service at night and the next day a funeral? It's like two funerals! Why do families have to be put through this sonofabitchin' thing twice!"

The young priest, not long out of the Orthodox seminary, tried to soothe Steve, telling him about tradition. "To hell with tradition! When I'm gone I don't want a prayer service. I don't want my kids and grandkids going through this misery twice. My daughters came for the funeral with their kids, and it's a hell of a thing for them to go through twice."

"Well, Mr. Kallos," the priest conceded, "the prayer service can be held in the mortuary just before the funeral."

"All right, then. Are you coming to the house for dinner?" The priest gave a startled "yes" at the sudden change in Steve's voice.

Tables had been set from the front lawn of the house to the little forest. The white tablecloths dazzled in the sun. Lilacs were in bloom. Under the long front porch, serving tables were laid with platters of baked ham, chicken, roast lamb; spinach and *feta pites,* meat and pasta squares. Wines, liquors, mixers, ice were set on one table; on another were coffeemakers and pyramids of pastries.

Cars choked the driveway; parishioners were forced to park on the road and walk up the long brick lane to the house. People were seated everywhere on chaise lounges, seats brought from the house, and rented chairs. Men stood by the liquor table, where two bartenders served drinks; women sat back and relaxed; young people from the choir hurried after each other, laughing. The priest and his pretty, overweight wife made the rounds, shaking hands and smiling. Talk and laughter rose; guests visited with each other, going from one group to the other; Penny and Georgie, with their husbands behind them, put gracious smiles on their lips and imparted little bits of information about their father's behavior after their mother's death. Little cries of surprise and amazement followed. Taki nodded, trying to look deeply grieved.

That night, Steve said to Mary, "It was like a wedding reception," and Mary nodded, "It certainly was different from when my parents died. Our customs aren't what they used to be."

Steve went to his desk in the television room and made out a list of instructions for his own funeral. He wanted a family funeral with the great-grandchildren—if they weren't too young—and Theo Stratos and his wife Angie. The same for the funeral dinner— only his immediate family, Theo, and Angie. "AND I MEAN IT," he wrote in large block letters and signed his name.

Steve could not sleep. About two in the morning, he got up, walked into the television room in his bare feet, and looked at his funeral instructions. He stood in thought a moment, then wrote under the block letters: *If Lefty and Perry and their wives outlive me, let them come to the funeral and the dinner.* He went back to bed, wondering what Lefty and Perry were doing now; he had not had time to say much to them at the dinner. It had been years since he had had a talk with them.

XII

AFTER ANDREAS AND Heracles, the grandfathers, died, their grandsons, Steve's Andrew, Solly's Tom, and Con's Dick, were put on the board of the Kallos family business. Penny and Georgie sulked for a while because their husbands had been ignored. At their first board meeting, Dick and Tom talked about civic participation. They brought tickets to charity events, paid for by the company, to distribute to the board; their wives belonged to the Junior League, the Symphony, and the Ballet West guilds. Steve said he couldn't use them. "You ought to get out, Uncle Steve. You have to socialize," Dick said, as if he were talking to a child. "It's good business to get close to important people."

"I've been in this business since I was a kid, and I never kissed nobody's ass!"

"If the company," Tom said, "had got on the good side of that jackass chairman of the planning board, we would have got that easement on Ninetieth South without a delay."

"The company? You mean me, so say so!"

Soon after, in 1972, they bought a six-story building, renovated it, and reserved the top story for themselves. Steve saw no reason to buy new furniture and machines. "What's wrong with what we've got? My mahogany table is as good as new."

"Because we're big now," Solly said and shook his head to convey Steve's obtuseness. "Important people come here. We have to impress them."

"Up to now we've impressed them with the location of our buildings and the service we give."

"That goes without saying," Solly said, and Steve cut in, "Sure it goes without saying because you knew someone, me, would take care of it." Solly gave a little snort and continued, looking around the table at Penny, Georgie, and the three new board members, "I think the girls and the kids feel the same way. Everything old goes out." It was put to a vote and Solly won. Only Andrew voted with his father.

"Okay," Steve grumbled and waved the vote away. "Furniture isn't important. If you want to throw money away, okay."

IT HAD TAKEN Steve a few weeks to become accustomed to the change in the board and to the new offices—"the suite," as the others called it. A glass wall marked the entrance. The glass doors in the center opened electronically with a touch on big brass knobs. The aging janitor, Elroy, who reminded everyone that he had been with the family business since the earliest years, polished the glass and the knobs every morning. A short distance inside, a young, red-haired receptionist sat at a high desk. Behind her was a large oil painting: against a greenish background, black, zigzag flashes aimed at the bottom left corner toward a round ball, which on second glance was the planet Earth. The painting was the work of Dick's wife. "Goddamn trash," Steve told Mary, after seeing the painting for the first time. Mary said it wasn't worth making a fuss about; there were more important things than that.

The large, round conference room was to the right of the receptionist's desk; in the center of it was a heavy teakwood table. A floor-to-ceiling glass wall looked over the city, and on the cherry-wood walls hung paintings in green and black by Dick's wife.

A wide hall bisected the row of offices. More greenish-black paintings hung on the walls. On the left side of the hall, in a large room, four secretaries used computers under the office manager Doris Haynes's surveillance. There were also offices for two CPAs, the sales manager, and the head of maintenance for all the properties except the renovated building. That was Elroy's domain: Steve had given him a desk and a telephone in one corner, neither of which he really needed.

There were two wide windows in Steve's office. His desk was placed so that he could look through the west window beyond the railyards to the Oquirrh Mountains, whose seasonal changes—spring and summer green, autumnal oranges and yellows, and snow—gave order to the year for him. He had chosen the office, liking it especially because it was the last one down the hall and had relative privacy in the humming and clacking of machines, telephones, and voices blurting over the intercom. No one had a desk in the office across the hall. It was used for file cabinets, old documents, blueprints, and the walk-in safe.

One of the first board meetings in the costly suite was of great importance to the Kallos family. It was held on a spring day in 1973. Seated around the teakwood table, they discussed building an upscale shopping complex, to be called the Silver Rails Plaza. Dick's wife had chosen the name—but what the hell, Steve told Andrew later, it was a good name. They had had the land since Andreas had begun buying it before the 1920s: the old Railroad Hotel, boarded up for a decade by the Board of Health, and a street of pioneer houses, some also closed up, the others rented out by the month to Mexican railroad workers.

Solly had spread preliminary sketches on the table. His face sagged, the dark puffs under his unnaturally shiny eyes were almost black, yet his voice was hoarse with excitement. "Our properties have been bringing in money by the bucketful. We're itching to spend it. We're going to have ethnic restaurants on the ground floor. Then shops on the mezzanine, featuring Italian suits and shoes for men. Next to it will be designer dresses and evening wear for women. There'll be a real high-class leather store—handmade leather belts, purses, billfolds. A shop will carry bath soaps, salts, towels. Another one will have linens embroidered by Portuguese nuns. Imported chocolates, gelato, fancy stationery, paintings by nationally known artists. Now this small hotel here," he pointed forcefully on the sketch, "has two-hundred rooms, made up entirely of luxury suites. It'll have everything—swimming pool, saunas, exercise gym, gourmet food. Corporations would put their VIPs there."

Steve said, "You're thinking big. What tenant have you got that the bank will lend you that kind of money?"

"No big department store. These are boutiques. This is how the exclusive strips in California are. We can be our own bank."

"We own our properties outright," Steve interrupted. "You'd risk them on this kind of gamble?"

"The economy is going great! The Jews know what they're doing. They don't throw their money around. We saw this in California."

"We're not California. We need an anchor," Steve said. "And no big department store is going to come in the middle of nowhere. Sit on your eggs."

"This is a businessman's risk. We've got the properties and we've got the zoning. If we don't do this, some guy down the street will, then you can sit forever on your goddamn properties!"

"No one's going to come to an out-of-the-way shopping complex to buy do-dads! We need an anchor store, like Auerbach's."

"They'll come," Solly said with an emphatic nod.

Penny and Georgie said they would certainly go out of their way to shop there and they knew their friends would, too. Several scents emanated about them: winey and lilac from their dyed bouffant hair. Tom said people liked to eat out and that would be a magnet. "Yeah," Steve said, "they eat out all the time and expect Social Security to take care of them in their old age. They got a surprise coming to them."

Tom, smiling a movie-actor smile, brilliant against his dark suntan, said, "It sounds great."

"How many men do you know who have a wardrobe of thousand-dollar suits?" Steve asked Tom.

Dick interrupted. "You'd be surprised, Uncle Steve. There are plenty."

"Why are you questioning me?" Solly demanded, jutting out

his chin. "I've got the expertise for this. You don't. If we listened to you, we'd still be a dime operation."

"What the hell are you talking about? You've got the expertise! Those last two deals you brought in ended up costing us two million bucks to get out of! Is that your idea of expertise?"

"Listen, goddamn you, you know the situation!" Solly's red-veined eyes bulged. "Nobody could have done better! You know the economy went through a slump!"

"I know you got involved with some fly-by-night drinking buddies, that's what I know! And don't talk to me about expertise! When you came home from the army, you weren't too thrilled about me turning the Japanese farm into an industrial complex!"

"That's a goddamn lie!"

Their faces red, bloated, they jumped up and leaned over the table. Penny made ineffectual sounds, "Now—you're brothers. Now—don't! Don't!"

Con spoke. All heads turned toward him. In a low voice he said, "This isn't going to get us anywhere. Let's not talk about the past."

Steve sat in his office for a long time, worrying, but not knowing exactly why. It seemed the past was being lost sight of—forgotten. Yet there was plenty of money. Maybe they did know more than he did about boutique shopping complexes: he saw them only in magazines. The hotel, too, would be a drawing card.

They put up the industrial park as collateral and got a twenty-million-dollar loan. Steve again took over as project manager, and as the red sandstone walls went up, as fountains were cemented and tiled, and rock walks and a courtyard laid out, the old enthusiasm came back to him for working with carpenters, painters, rock masons, plumbers, and even plasterers, for whom he had early developed the prejudice that they were all drinkers and adulterers.

Steve brought Andrew's seven-year-old son Jim to watch backhoes and dump trucks excavating the earth, uncovering boulders, piling up hillocks of dirt. He explained to him the great number of workers with the tools of their trade, Skilsaws moving effortlessly, paintbrushes gliding down plastered walls, the buzz of work, talk, and laughter making conversation almost impossible. Jim was a quiet little boy who, Mary said, saw a lot and said little. Steve took him to the old Denver & Rio Grande depot lunchroom to eat. Jim looked across the table at his grandfather, gobbling a taco with lettuce, ground meat, and *salsa* falling around his plate. "Jim," Steve said, "how would you like to be in your old grandfather's shoes someday? And run this business?"

Jim looked at his grandfather for a moment and said, his forehead wrinkling, "Gramps, I want to play my violin in an orchestra."

Steve and Jim looked into each other's eyes. The seconds passed. Steve's lips spread into an artificial smile. "Well, maybe you could learn to play my clarinet, too."

Jim wrinkled his forehead, and Steve thought, *Even little kids can worry.* "Gramps," Jim said, "can I just have it for a keepsake?"

"Okay. Hell, everybody's got to do what they want. I never wanted to do anything but what I've been doing for fifty years." He thought he should correct himself: It was more like thirty years. Mary told him not to exaggerate and tell lies, especially to the grandchildren. They would catch on to him some day, she said.

"Why didn't Daddy work for you?"

Steve looked back at his plate, a mess of beans, rice, guacamole, and sour cream. His face was red. "Yes, your father should have been in the business," Steve said and was silent for the rest of the meal.

The adornments went up: chandeliers from Czechoslovakia, marble and tile from Italy, brass from Spain, but nothing from Greece. Each morning he stood on the sidewalk and looked at the Plaza, noted the progress, and felt a deep pleasure, with flashes of exhilaration, as he had had years ago when the Japanese farm had been turned into an industrial complex.

The opening of the Silver Rails Plaza was big news on television and in the newspapers. Teenage girls handed out balloons, prizes, miniature pizzas, soft drinks, and candy. Solly was interviewed on television. "How did you come up with the idea of the Plaza?" a pretty reporter asked him. "I had my eye on the property for a long time," Solly said, "and just waited until it got more valuable. I knew the city was ready for just this kind of operation."

At the grand opening, Steve took Jim's hand and pushed through the crowd of people walking about on the grounds, now turned into flower gardens interspersed with enormous trees, re-planted from elsewhere. The excited crowd ate in the various restaurants, climbed the spiraling staircases, dawdled in front of the stores, and sampled perfumes, looking about with gasps of admiration. Both male and female models displayed the clothing to be found in the designer shops.

The opening occurred in summer when Jim was out of school. At least twice a week Steve picked him up, sometimes with his little sister Liesa. He drove them to the Plaza where they ate in one of the ethnic restaurants, and then he drove them back to their house. By the end of summer, the crowds had thinned. The promotional work was stepped up. Contests, big prizes, free lunches gave little spurts of business, then settled back to even fewer people, mostly window shoppers. The hotel was never more than half full. The Mormons who came to the twice-a-year church conferences could not afford such luxury—they usually stayed with relatives any way—and corporations kept to their old habits.

Steve began to hate the little boutiques with their lavender soaps and bath salts, imported linen mats, Godiva chocolates, gelato, children's books, leather goods displaying two-hundred-dollar belts, the filmy dresses beginning at eight hundred dollars, the Italian men's suits laid carelessly over chairs, and the Chinese, Thai, Italian, French, and Greek cafés with college students waiting on tables and never pronouncing the names of the foreign foods correctly. Wafting throughout was the acrid-yet-sweetish scent of eucalyptus that caused Steve's nose to swell.

Christmas came, but the crowds of shoppers didn't. The small shops started to fail.

XIII

THE TABLES AND chairs that had stood on the tiled outdoor patios had vanished, as had the crowds of people who had eaten, talked, and laughed under the blue skies. The board met to discuss ways to salvage the Plaza. Looking around the table with an exaggerated seriousness, Solly said, "We've got to find new tenants."

Steve snorted. "The Plaza is damaged goods. What tenants are going to sign leases for a center that's a failure? Who's going to buy the goddamn place when it's empty?"

"Con and I can go to LA and talk to our connections there. We've got to salvage it. We've got to start looking."

"Yeah, like the people who told you a boutique plaza would go! Salt Lake City was ready for one! You wouldn't need an anchor store!"

"Nobody dragged you into it by the nose!"

Andrew had not attended the meeting. Con, Dick, and Tom sat at the table, saying nothing, every once in a while glancing at Steve as he stared at the designs in the teakwood table as if hypnotized.

"Steve," Con said, "tell me what I can do."

Steve waved his hand in dismissal, got up, and walked out of the conference room, past the receptionist who, he realized, had heard everything that had gone on in the conference room. He walked down the hall and stood in his office; his head seemed to have swelled into a big solid ball. He stared at the west window that looked over the railyards and the nearby Silver Rails Plaza north of it. He lifted the receiver and pressed a button below it. "Elroy, get Jay Lambert for me. Tell him to come to my office."

Jay Lambert appeared within an hour. "What's up, Steve?" he asked, a short man with white hair and eyelashes and a big stomach.

"I want this window bricked up and plastered over."

"Hell, Steve, you sure you want to do that? That's a real good view, and besides the office would be dark."

"That's what I want."

"Okay, you're the boss."

The bricked-up window shut off the railyards, the Plaza, the Oquirrh Mountains, and the change of seasons. Lights had to be on all day. After the wall was painted a grayish white, Steve had a large Charles M. Russell reproduction, "The Exalted Ruler," hung in the center of it. It was his favorite picture: a herd of elk grazed among sagebrush; in the distance were snow-covered mountains; in the foreground the great buck leader with lifted head surveyed his herd.

Solly and Con took planes to Los Angeles, San Francisco, and San Diego. When they returned, they went off to lunch as if, Steve fumed, they were the most successful businessmen in town. Steve often forgot to eat lunch. He stayed at his desk, read the *Wall Street Journal,* business magazines, and made hundreds of telephone calls. He thought of the family's going through the company money like a flash flood disappearing into a deep crevice of the desert. His head began to buzz with something the doctor told him was tinnitus and that he would have to learn to live with. He was furious that that, too, had been inflicted on him. He called the board together, told them they had lost the industrial park and the Plaza, but they still had their other properties. "We can survive if we don't let loose cannons go off in all directions." No one questioned him; no one spoke. Solly looked at him, his eyes bloodshot. Steve had smelled whiskey on his breath when he had walked in, twenty minutes late for the meeting.

One night soon after, Steve was awakened by Tom calling to tell him he had taken his father to Emergency. In a bed cordoned off by curtains, Solly lay babbling nonsense: "Phoenix. Nine-thirty-five plane. First class. What time is it? Call Brad Johnson." He rolled his head back and forth and they looked down on him: Magdalene, now stout, her hair short and gray; Tom, without his usual smile; and his two younger sisters, sniffing and dabbing their eyes.

A stroke, the young doctor said, the damage extensive. Steve left Magdalene and Tom sitting in the waiting room, talking back and forth in quiet voices as if they were discussing the weather. They were expecting the priest. Mary had told him that Magdalene did all kinds of volunteer work for the priests; she practically lived in the church. It was three in the morning when Steve drove home. Aloud he said to the black windshield, "Goddamn you, Solly. You left me with your Pretty Boy Tommy."

From then on, Steve became aware that Tom spent a good portion of the day in Dick's office, usually with the door closed. Steve never saw Con enter his son's office. For a year after Solly's stroke, Con wandered about the suite with a slight frown on his still-handsome face as if he were not certain what he should be doing. He stopped going to the nursing home when Solly kept asking who he was. One late winter day he had a heart attack at his desk. "It's a shame," Steve told Mary, "and he wasn't even sixty years old."

Besides working with the CPAs, Dick took over his father's job as personnel manager. When Steve noticed a new secretary one morning and asked about her, Dick said, offhand, "Oh, I hired her. Doris okayed her. I knew you were too busy with the Plaza business."

"I see she's good looking, but she better know her work," Steve said. Dick smiled, a mocking smile it seemed to Steve. "Slick Dick" Steve thought of him from then on.

Soon after Con's funeral, Tessie, the new widow, bought Dick a Mercedes and promised Dick's four children BMWs or whatever when they got their drivers' licenses at sixteen. "What a family!" Steve told Mary. "Pretty Boy Tommy, Slick Dick, the Religious Fanatic, and Diamond Tessie, who doesn't give a good goddamn that we lost the industrial park and the fucking Plaza."

"Don't use that word," Mary said.

PART 3

XIV

STEVE READ THE newspaper item again: Western Enterprises, Dick Kallos, president. He touched his hot face and knew he should take his blood pressure. Mary was still in the rose garden. He strained forward, yearning to tell her about what he had read, but he was afraid. she might burst out, raving at him as she'd done ten years ago, when he had come home cursing Solly over something, he could no longer remember what. She had stood a few feet from him; until then her criticism of the family had always been mild; she began shouting, while he stood there, shocked at the wild look in her eyes. "You fight with him, but in the end you go along! Why you want to be close to him, I don't know! He ignores you! He thinks more of his alcoholic friends than he does of you!

"When the children were teenagers and made remarks about his drinking and giving women the eye, you yelled at them, told them you never wanted to hear his name on their lips again! He never said hello to me when he walked into my house, ate my food! He kept you on the phone gossiping for an hour or more while he was drinking! And you wouldn't hang up!

"You never helped me when the children were babies! You never changed a diaper, never got up at night with them even when I was sick! Business always came first with you! You kill yourself to make money for a bunch of relatives who don't give a darn about you! You didn't stand up for Andrew against them! You wouldn't even take off to go to Greece with me! We lost our friends! We never went any place! Solly and Con went, but not you! You and your idea of family! But who am I? Only your wife!" She hurried out of the room. They ate dinner without speaking for three nights.

With a jolt of his head, Steve picked up the cellular telephone and called Andrew's office. "Meet me at the Hilton," he said.

"Why so far? Why not Lamb's?"

"No, I don't want anyone walking in on us." He hung up, tore off the corner of the newspaper, and replaced his reading glasses with thick ones from his shirt pocket.

He walked on the toes of his shoes to the side entrance of the house and, looking over his shoulder, pressed a button that automatically lifted the garage door. To his relief the sprinklers were on and concealed the slight noise of the rising door. As he backed the car out of the garage, he glanced at the far end of his property, east of the grove of aspens and pines to the field-stone wall. On the other side of the wall, tall, straggly cottonwood trees grew. A rush of relief: he was getting away without being seen. Mary had not yet gone over to the stone wall to talk with their old neighbor Mrs. Sorensen, who had sold them three acres of her farmland more than fifty years ago.

He turned on the ignition and pushed the automatic garage control on the visor. As the door came down, he saw that a cabinet at the back of the garage was open, showing empty shelves. A month or more ago Mary had begun cleaning out decades of accumulation.

This cleaning out the house, what was it for? Steve asked himself. Earlier when he had gone to the kitchen for coffee, he had noticed a grocery-sized box of snapshots on the floor and had wondered what Mary intended doing with them. He did not like the interruption in the routine of the house; it had a bleakness to it. He lifted a hand in dismissal. At the moment he had the Western Enterprises business to take care of.

A black bird stood on the circular brick-paved driveway, its glossy wings catching a ray of the sun. Its solid black eye watched Steve, but he did not see it.

He drove carefully over the tree-lined brick lane. It would be another hot August day, he knew, and September seemed long in coming. As the car traveled over the familiar streets, he was unaware of the small pleasures he usually took in driving: tires humming over cement; the encircling distant mountains; the sky, blue that morning, although he liked all skies, whether blue, pale gray, cold steel, or with white rolling cumulus clouds.

He passed his parents' old brick bungalow. The present owners had pulled out the aged phitzers and other bushes and enclosed the grass with a low wall of red brick. A new red-tiled roof gave the house a top-heavy look. The house meant nothing to him. He drove on into a half-residential, half-commercial district, slowing down while passing a row of one-story, tan brick buildings. A few cars were parked in the asphalt lot. It was the first strip center his father and Uncle Harry had built before the Wall Street crash of 1929.

Steve gave the stores a cursory glance: Benson's Tax Service, the sign faded and inexpertly painted in blue; Shirlee's Nail Salon, walls, chairs, artificial flowers, all in pink; Ed's Appliance Sales and Service—even from the street Steve could see the hodgepodge of waffle irons, lamps, microwave ovens, clocks.

When the Plaza failed, Steve had thought the six small centers should be torn down; the land had become valuable and they could build and lease space. He had not pursued it because, then, what would he do with Tom who had made messes of the jobs he'd been given. Putting him in charge of the strip centers had solved the problem. Steve seldom thought of him as Pretty Boy Tommy anymore, even though he was still a good-looking man, in spite of the suspicion of a potbelly. He wondered as he passed the row of buildings if Tom ever went to the nursing home to see his father Solly. *Solly,* Steve snorted the name, beat his johnny too much and look where it landed him.

Trying to see better, Steve squinted, then opened his eyes wide. He reached a main artery. Few cars at midmorning were speeding, but he drove in the slow lane, filled his cheeks with air and blew out with relief when he turned into the Hilton Hotel parking lot. He was already perspiring when he got out of the car. The morning was beginning to gather the heat of August and he had forgotten to turn on the air conditioning.

The coffeeshop was quiet, almost empty at that time of day; a few people sat at scattered tables in the beige-and-brown room, eating late breakfasts. The scent of bacon and coffee lingered.

Andrew was sitting in a back booth, against a brick ledge that ran the length of the dining room. Plants on the ledge cast a darkness over the tables and chairs. Andrew held a cup of coffee and watched his father approach. Each long, heavy footstep knifed Steve's arthritic hip. He tried not to wince. Andrew was wearing a dark-gray summer suit with a shirt that looked fresh from its wrappings and a navy-blue tie with a small red pattern. Steve realized he had not put on a coat jacket—had not shaved that morning.

Andrew stood up as if ready to help Steve. He waited for his father to reach the booth. A wary look came into his slightly bulging eyes. "Didn't Mom drive you down?"

Steve waved his right palm back and forth, a trait his children had learned from childhood meant he was not to be questioned.

"And where's your cane?"

"How the hell do I know?" Steve avoided Andrew's eyes: he had left canes all over the city.

"What's wrong, Dad?"

Steve slumped on the brown vinyl seat. Andrew picked up a carafe of coffee, but Steve pushed the empty cup to one side. He exchanged the glasses he was wearing for the pair in his breastpocket and took the torn piece of newspaper from his wallet. Breathing heavily, he slapped the newspaper fragment in front of Andrew. "You ever hear of Western Enterprises?" he demanded. Andrew shook his head, and Steve pointed to the article. Andrew read it and a slow pink suffused his olive skin. He looked to the side of Steve's head, then cupped his chin as if to give himself time to think of a reply. "I'll bet this goes all the way back to Uncle Harry," he said in a cold voice.

Steve raised his right hand to dismiss getting into that kind of talk. "I want you to go to the state registrar of business properties and find out when the sale of this property was done. Then go to the county recorder and look at the deed, find out when it was recorded. Look at the stamps to give us an idea of the value. Don't send one of your legal aides. Go yourself. Find out when this shitty Western Enterprises was incorporated." He leaned across the table and tapped his forefinger on the table. Andrew looked at the tapping finger. "We got to keep it quiet for the time being. Don't tell anyone. I mean *anyone*. We can't let this get out."

"I won't tell Jeanne if that's what you mean. What about Mom? Aren't you going to tell her?"

Steve's eyes moved sideways. "No, and maybe I'll never tell her. It'll only upset her."

Andrew quirked the corner of his lips. "If you can keep that away from her, I'll be surprised."

"Why can't I? Unless you go tell her. And when you come to the house, watch what you say."

Andrew lifted his shoulders in a shrug. "Dad, this kind of thing is all over town by now. You can't keep it quiet. What about Theo? I'll bet he already knows. Are you going to tell him?"

Steve jerked his head and looked away. "Maybe I will and maybe I won't." A few seconds passed in silence. "I'd go see Theo, but I've got to sign the weekly checks." He looked at Andrew as if he had defied him. "I'm not giving that up to those bastards! That's what they want! Then they could do what they goddamned well please!"

Andrew said, faintly sharp, "So when you see Dick in the office, you're not going to say anything about this?"

"Not yet. Dick Kallos, president of Western Enterprises," Steve said sarcastically, "that bastard cocksucker. Sitting in his fancy gold room. Spoiled, rotten little sonofabitch! Probably on another vacation. You work like a jackass and you hear this little bastard talk about having to get away because the poor guy works so hard!"

Andrew kept his eyes on his father, his lips pulled inward, a habit he had developed in childhood from trying to decide whether to speak his thoughts or not. Still looking at Steve with his intense dark eyes, he said, "Sure I wasn't allowed to do the law work for the company. Conflict of interest, inexperienced they said, but Dick comes in and before you know it, he's vice president. Evidently he was experienced enough to get his agenda going." In the silence, Steve looked out the window. Andrew kept his relentless eyes on Steve. "I see it now. They were afraid if I were in the office, I'd find out about their hanky-panky. That's the reason they didn't want me in there, the bastards."

Steve looked at the plants set on the ledge. "What could I do? They were against me. They had a point."

"The only point they had was to take away some of your power."

"Oh, maybe Uncle Con, a cousin, but not Uncle Solly. Solly, my brother? No, not Solly."

"What do you mean 'Con'? Con never did anything but what his mother and father and Uncle Solly wanted him to. You'll defend Uncle Solly to the bitter end. And my poor *Papou,* told me to get a law degree so no one could take advantage of the business. 'Watch over the business,' he said." Andrew stopped talking for a moment, then said, "And what will you do when I get you the details?"

"I don't know what the Christ I'm gonna do! Right now I'm mad as hell!"

They walked out of the restaurant. In the parking lot, the heat struck them with sudden force; the asphalt was spongelike under the pressure of their shoes. "I'll get to work on it as soon as I can, Dad," Andrew said.

Steve pushed his face close to Andrew's. "Listen, I want you to get on this right away, goddamn it! I want to have this all figured out by the next board meeting."

"Dad, I'm in court all day today." Andrew spoke with a slightly admonishing tone. Then he looked guilty. Steve thought the tone had crept into Andrew's voice since he, Steve, had begun losing his sight. Andrew quickly added, "I'll get on it right away, Dad. You're going to bring it up at the board meeting?"

"I don't know what in hell I'm going to do, I said. I want it *done*. I want to *know*."

"Dad, don't do anything until we get the facts. Then we'll decide how to handle it. At your age you have to be careful. You can't keep losing your temper. You don't want to end up like Uncle Solly."

Steve looked at him with widened eyes.

Andrew opened the door of Steve's Suburban. Neither spoke as Steve got in and drove off. Steve looked in the rearview mirror as he backed out of the parking space. Andrew was standing, watching him, and his lips were moving. Steve's heart gave a thump: *What is he saying?*

He drove toward the city center with careful attention to the traffic lights, constantly looking to the right and left, afraid he might be too close to cars. He no longer went through yellow caution lights. The steering wheel was hot, yet he clutched it and his heart beat erratically at the thought of getting a ticket and having to take the eye test. Not to be able to get in his car and drive off! It had happened to his father. He turned on the air conditioner. It had a new, slightly grating sound and the hissing in Steve's ears was too much. He turned it off, put down the window although that barely helped, and kept driving in the stifling heat.

He drove into the underground parking of the Kallos building and sat in the coolness for a few minutes until his breathing settled evenly. He stumbled as he got out, but went on, watching his feet, and took the elevator to the sixth floor. As he stepped off the elevator, he grunted a good-morning to Tom, who was standing nearby talking to a thin, handsome man. The man was giving Tom a long smile.

"Oh, hi, Uncle Steve!" Tom said, raising his hand as if he were hailing him. Steve continued toward the glass entrance, wondering who the man was; he had seen them having lunch at the Baci.

Elroy was working with one of the large brass knobs on the

glass door. "Morning, Steve," Elroy said. His baggy orange coveralls were faded and spotted with black oil; the baseball cap, pulled low on his forehead, was greasy, the major-league baseball team logo on it smudged beyond recognition. "Well, what I'm doin' here, Steve," Elroy said, looking away from his work and smiling at Steve—his narrow, wrinkled face suddenly animated—"is oilin' this here knob to see if I can stop the squeakin'. The gals say it gits on their nerves." For a minute or so, the two talked, the same kind of conversation they had had for fifty-four years: it was always about what had gone wrong with the building and how Elroy had fixed it.

"See you later, Elroy," Steve said, giving him a pat high up on his shoulder where the orange fabric was reasonably clean. He stepped into the air-conditioned coolness, liking it, even though it might stir up his arthritis later. He gave a dignified nod to the frizzy-haired receptionist's "Good morning." A bouquet of red roses was on her polished desk. She was not really pretty, but being young was enough. He looked ahead quickly, not wanting to acknowledge the red roses: it could be Secretaries Day—an asinine promotion of florists. He had told Dick when the stupid celebration started to give the women money for a nice lunch, but no, Dick had to give them flowers and take them to the New Yorker. Steve had been more friendly with the secretaries when he was a younger man, but he had learned, after one became flirtatious that, as he told Mary, "If you give an inch, they'll take a mile."

He walked toward the hall. The receptionist and a young woman who spent her work days at the filing cabinets and making certain the coffeemaker was filled at all times, exchanged amused looks under lifted eyebrows. Steve did not see this silent communication and walked on. "Uncle Steve," Tom called, hurrying after him.

"Yeah? Who's that guy you were talking to?" Even as he said this, he frowned: Mary had nagged him from the time they married not to be so curious about people.

"Oh, that's the comptroller for the Perkins Company. I didn't introduce you because you looked like you were in a hurry."

"I thought he was another of your fraternity brothers 'passing through town.'"

Tom reddened. Without glancing into the offices on either side of him, Steve walked down the hall thinking: *You dumb shit Tommy.*

"Just a minute, Uncle Steve. I renewed Imogene's lease for another ten years with a five-year option."

"Who's this Imogene?" Steve stopped and faced Tom, scowling.

"She's got the antique store on Twentieth. Real nice lady."

"You mean that old bag with the dyed hair on top of her head? I'll bet you didn't take her to the club for lunch."

Tommy laughed. "No, I took her to Riley's." He smiled affably.

Steve looked at Tom's white, even teeth. "I've told you before, you waste your time taking tenants to lunch. I never took a tenant to lunch. You don't get familiar with tenants. But," Steve lapsed into a Greek proverb, "'Does the wall hear?'"

"Times are different now," Tom said, still smiling.

"Well, okay, so you renewed her lease."

"I increased the rent like you said, ten percent. I'm doing that with all the tenants as their leases expire. Cost-of-living increase."

"That's good," Steve said, then mildly scoffing, "Did you take into consideration the maintenance?" Tom's smile faded and Steve's voice slid into a hard staccato. "That building's old. It needs a new roof and the parking lot has to be resurfaced. What about the future increase in taxes? Did you take that into consideration when you gave her the option?" With an abrupt turn, Steve almost lost his footing.

"Hi there, Uncle Steve!" Dick called out and ran his hand over his almost bald head. His heart jumping, Steve gave a quick glance toward Dick, sitting at his hand-carved rosewood desk. Dick's cheerful voice was at odds now with the cold apprehension in his Myrsini eyes. Steve raised his hand to acknowledge him: He didn't want Dick to know anything yet, but he had to say something. "Morning, Nick," he said and was pleased at Dick's surprised look. The dark, skimpy hair at the back of Dick's head had grown long and curled at the base of his neck. Looking over his shoulder, Steve raised his voice into a shout. "Did you see where Theo Stratos got that big award from the state home builders? And he did it all by himself. Pulled himself up by his own bootstraps." Pig, Steve thought as he walked heavily into his office. "Asshole," he said to himself with bitter disgust. And to think, he berated himself, there had been times when he had wished Andrew and Dick had been friends.

Now that he was over eighty, he knew his time was limited. And after he was gone, what would happen to his one-third share? He had never thought of it when he, Solly, and Con were working together. Con dead, Solly in the nursing home, and their sons more and more trying to take over. They called it, "We didn't want to bother you with this."

The beating of his heart was like a jagged huffing. He took a deep breath as he sat at his desk and felt safe at last. He thought of Dick, bald and smiling, then those cold, distrusting eyes. This was new and Steve realized he must not have paid attention to Dick for a long time. He remembered that Dick's eyes had been eager when he first came into the business. And he had to train him, just as he had to train Pretty Boy Tommy, because he was always *there.* Yes, Dick's eyes had been eager at first, then later there was fear in them at times, but this hard look—this was new. For several seconds, he sat with his palms on either side of his head to steady it. Then he sat up straight with his shoulders pulled back.

He knew Dick didn't like his talking about Theo Stratos. At lunch once, when they needed some help with a remodeling and carpenters had gone on strike, Tommy and Dick had made fun of Theo's ordering a French dish. Theo, who worked like a dog. Had worn clothes he bought at the Salvation Army. Tommy, the spoiled dummy. In college, ski trips, London, Paris, fancy sports car—all of it handed to him—said he knew how business was run in the 1990s. Bastard, always hinting that his father Solly had been the brains of the business. And Dick. He thought of himself rushing into Dick's office and grabbing him by the lapels of his hand-tailored suit. *West-*

ern Enterprises. Steve tried to think of anything that could give him an explanation for Dick's treachery.

He held his head again: it was so heavy it kept falling forward. He looked at the soft, brownish-red corduroy sofa his daughters had bought him twenty years ago, urging him to take naps. He could never lie there for more than a few minutes. He felt guilty stretched out during business hours and was also afraid that someone would find him there.

He stared at his desk; the solid oak had become as nicked and scarred now as his old mahogany had been. On top of it were a collection of pen holders in marble stands; leather boxes, supposedly to hold papers and documents, but empty; two brass nameplates; and several sayings burned into wooden scrolls, all Christmas gifts from secretaries. He had given the gifts cursory glances and then pushed them to one end of the desk, where those at the edge eventually toppled into the wastepaper basket. One of the scrolls read: "A soft answer turneth away wrath: but grievous words stir up anger: Proverbs xv 1." He could not remember the secretary who gave it to him the day she left for another job.

He then looked at the wall on which a black cork panel had been mounted. It was covered with yellowed newspaper clippings; obituaries, snapshots of the grandchildren when they were of grade school age; several of their Father's Day crayon drawings; a 1958 photograph of a long-dead mayor shaking his hand on the day he, Solly, and Con remodeled their first big downtown building.

His father's old rolltop desk stood in the corner next to the window. The top was down; and several pieces of paper protruded from under it. He thought that somewhere in that jammed desk, hidden by the rolltop, there might be something his father hadn't paid attention to, something that would tell him how his Uncle Harry and Con had bought Block 325 secretly. He rubbed his dry hands back and forth: If only he could see well enough to go through the papers, but he resigned himself to sit where he was. He had the sensation that his head was made of compacted cardboard.

The telephone rang. Doris Haynes said, "Steve, Theo Stratos is on the line." Steve lifted the telephone. "How's it going, Theo?"

"I'm okay. How about you?" Theo had never lost the Greek tinge to his pronunciation of English words.

"Eh, *gheramata,*" Steve said, using the Greek word for old age.

"Yeah, me too. This arthritis in my hands is killing me."

"Just take Motrin and do those exercises I told you about. You know, with a rubber ball. While you're watching television, knead the ball." Steve's internist had prescribed this ten years ago. Steve had kneaded the ball once.

Theo lowered his voice. "You wanna go to lunch? Have coffee? Come to my office?"

He knows: Steve also lowered his voice. "I better go home. I don't feel so hot. I'll call you. Want to talk to you about your award and something else."

"Okay. Pretty good me getting the award ahead of those Mormon builders, eh? I showed them."

"You sure did, Theo." Steve hung up, wondering what else Theo had learned about Western Enterprises.

Doris Haynes came in with a stack of checks: payroll, subcontractors, and maintenance services. "There are two in there you probably won't want to sign," she said as she placed the stack in front of him. He glanced at her: She knew him well. "Okay," he said as she walked out.

Doris Haynes had been with the Kallos Company almost forty years; next to Elroy, she was their longest-serving employee. Other secretaries asked her to take reports into Steve's office; and Dick and Tom were also in the habit of handing her documents for him and hurrying out to lunch. With a sardonic look on her plump, wrinkled face, she would watch them take quick steps toward the elevator.

Steve looked at each check carefully, glowered at several, and put them on his left, unsigned. He then read a long lease, crossed out words, and wrote in the margins: "Why are we paying for this?" "Not our responsibility." "Tell him to go to hell."

When he finished, he sat back in his chair and breathed hard. He stood up, took the checks and the lease into Dick's office, and dropped them on his desk. Dick looked up, his eyes cautious. "These three checks on top," Steve said. "I'm not signing them. Tell the bastards I want itemized statements. And you better start getting a better bid list. These guys are robbing you blind."

A dark red covered Dick's face and bald head. As Steve walked out, he relished the guarded look in Dick's eyes; probably, he thought, his mentioning Theo Stratos's write-up in the newspaper had given him qualms that Steve had also read the paragraph about Western Enterprises. He wanted very much to drive to Theo's office, but the heaviness in his head worried him. He was also breathing too fast. He had to get home.

He reached his house, parked the car in the garage, and walked into the kitchen. Mary angrily lectured him for taking the car when he knew he shouldn't have, besides going without his cane. Her right eye moved toward the inner corner of her eye. Steve looked away. He took the corned-beef sandwich she had ready, a can of beer, and went into the television room, which used to be called his den and, before that, the playroom. The sandwich lay in the pit of his stomach, with no intention of moving on. He listened to the news, thinking any minute Andrew might telephone, and fell asleep, cursing the newscaster: "Aw, shut up, you bastard! Another pretty boy, goddamn you!"

XV

MARY WAS READY to leave the house for church. She was holding a shoebox, her purse, and a gingham apron, and she was aware that Steve wanted her out of the house. He was walking around the kitchen, hitting the floor with the rubber tip of his cane, and had drunk only a half-cup of coffee. The morning paper was open to the sports page, but she had noticed earlier that he had not read it. "Why are you so nervous, Steve?"

"Nervous? Who says I'm nervous? Can't I walk around my own kitchen without you asking if I'm nervous?"

Their grandson Jim called from the front of the house. Mary smiled. "Jim's here." She turned to Andrew's now-grown son, standing at the doorway. "Jim, I didn't know you were coming."

"I came as soon as Gramps called me." There was something of his father in Jim's face, but it was softened, not chiseled; his eyes were a lighter brown and almost always animated as if he expected something interesting to happen. He was a musician, a teacher at the university. Maybe that was how he looked at his students, Mary thought.

"Oh?" She turned to Steve, who gave an exasperated sigh. "Well, sit down, honey. The coffee's ready and I have some *koulourakia* on the table.

Steve waved his palm back and forth. "No, we haven't got time. Jim's going to drop me off at Theo's office."

"Why take Jim from his work? I could have dropped you off at Theo's on my way to church."

"It's okay, Gran. I'm glad to do it."

"Well, all right. I'm on my way to help with the food for the festival. I'm head of the *dolmadhes* committee." She turned to Steve. "I've made you a plate for lunch. The bread's already cut in the basket. There's plenty to eat for both of you."

"Aaa!" Steve gave her a wave of dismissal. "We'll probably have lunch at the Grecian Deli—stupid name." He took two steps forward, his way of hurrying people out, but Mary would not leave. Then she set down her purse, apron, and the shoebox, took out a cup and saucer from a cabinet, and poured coffee for Jim.

"I can get it, Gran," Jim said with a laugh. "When are you going to stop waiting on me?" Mary did not answer; she was looking into the refrigerator, then the freezer, for something else to serve Jim.

"You look tired, Gramps. Didn't you sleep well?"

"I'm okay."

"How about going to a Buzz game tonight? We can see that pitcher they sent down from the majors." Jim was scrutinizing his grandfather.

"I dunno. I get chilled pretty quick at night."

"Don't give up, Gramps. Everything I know about sports I learned from you. All those times we sat in the television room and you'd tell me those anecdotes about Red Grange, Knute Rockne, Jack Dempsey. I haven't forgotten a one." Steve looked pleased. Jim dipped a *koulouraki* into his coffee. Mary had turned on the microwave oven, and when it stopped she brought a plate of Danish pastry to the table.

"Oh, Gran," Jim said and proceeded to eat the pastry. "Gramps did you read in the paper yesterday that the old Franklin School was being demolished? Isn't that the school you went to?"

Steve took a big bite of pastry, and as he chewed, he looked straight ahead with half-closed eyes. "I saw it!" Steve exploded with bits of pastry flying from his mouth. "It made me sick! All those former students," he shouted, "making a big noise about their poor old school being torn down! As far as I'm concerned it should have been burned down the minute it was built! The worst years of my life were spent there! All through grade school we were branded. Us kids with immigrant parents! Teachers, principals, especially the so-called 'white' kids!" He gave a hooting laugh. "We weren't considered white. We were treated like dirt." He breathed heavily in the quiet room. "I was nine years old when the Ku Klux Klan burned crosses and marched down Main Street, wearing their goddamn white sheets."

"Burned crosses?" Jim leaned forward, looking intently at his grandfather as if trying to bring him back to reality.

"That's what I said. Up on Ensign Peak, they burned crosses. They wanted the 'foreigners out!' It didn't matter that we were born in America. I was ashamed to go to school. I played hookey.

Then I got it twice, once from the principal with his rubber hose and then from my mother with her goddamn *blasti!*"

Mary said, "Steve, you're making Jim uncomfortable."

"Ah, he knows I'm not talking about his mother's folks." Steve snorted. "Of course, who knows what his other grandfather was up to in those days?"

"Oh, Steve, for heaven's sake!"

Steve barely glanced at Mary, enough to see her warning looks. "It's water under the bridge, Jimbo." Steve looked at Mary and said in a conciliatory tone, "If they've got any *pites* ready down at the church, the spinach kind, sneak one for me."

"I'll do no such thing. If everybody took here and there, we wouldn't have enough for the festival. I've got some *pites* in the freezer. I can take some out when I come back."

Mary began walking toward the side door that led to the garage. Steve said, "Why don't you take a pair of house slippers? So you can be comfortable."

"We sit down, Steve. At those big long tables. We don't stand up."

"Don't take Third West. There's too much traffic now. Take Fifth East. No, maybe Seventh would be better. There aren't as many lights on Seventh. Stay on the inside lane."

"Steve, you don't have to be in charge of everything. Should I pick you up at Theo's or what?"

"No, Theo'll bring me home. Or Elroy. Go about your business."

Jim opened the door for Mary and kissed her. "Tell Paulie hello," she said.

As she got into the car, she heard Steve say, "Gran's got some goodies for her committee in that shoe box."

She backed out of the garage, trying to control her anger at Steve. "Jim doesn't come that often," she thought she would tell him later, "now that he's married. Why do you have to carry on like that?" A black bird was standing at the edge of the lawn, just out of reach of water spraying from sprinklers. As the car passed close to it, the bird turned its head to watch. Its wings were glossy. She drove on, into the already hot day that was momentarily disguised by the cascading water. When she left the brick-paved lane, the heat pressed on the windows. She turned on the air conditioning. The glossiness of the small black bird reminded her of a song her father and his friends had often sung. She knew now they had been young fathers, not old as she had then thought.

After a nameday dinner, they had leaned back and sung *traghou-dhia tou trapeziou*, songs of the table. They keened for the guerrillas who went to their deaths, rushing at Turks with swords and giant pistols. Slowly rising to a plateau and falling ominously, the voices sang of heroic darkness. From a battlefield an eagle clutches a sev-ered head in its talons and soars upward. Head and eagle carry on a conversation. The eagle calls the head foolish, asking what it was searching for. The head replies, "Eagle, take my youth, my manli-ness, to gloss your wings, to sharpen your claws."

Since then, Mary had never seen a bird with glossy black wings without remembering the young fathers, singing with eyes closed, the song of the eagle. With longing for her quiet father, she thought of the solace those guerrilla songs must have given him after the long hours in his small grocery store. The men had sung as if the battles, the martyrdom, the cruelty had happened but recently, not centuries ago. Her father had looked rested afterwards. "A nice little guy," Steve said of her father, and she never knew why his words an-noyed her.

At the door of the church hall, Mary breathed the acrid scent of grape leaves in brine. She glimpsed Magdalene on the mezzanine floor walking awkwardly toward the priests' offices. Sitting at a long table, she worked silently, hearing the women's talk and laughter, and wishing she were back home. Most of their complaints that day were about the movies: when they were growing up the movies were about love, now it was all sex, sex, sex. They hated that open-mouth kissing that went on and on—"like they're eating corn on the cob," one of the women said. Tessie came for a short while, out of place in a fine navy-blue suit among the women, dressed in cottons and denims, for practical work. Mary closed her ears to her boasting.

Mary wasn't sure why she was tired so early in the day and she thought of leaving after lunch, but she was the head of the committee; she couldn't. She stayed until five o'clock and accepted the women's offer to supervise the cleaning up.

She had barely entered the house when Steve left a baseball game on television and came into the kitchen. "Well, what went on?"

"Same old people working."

"Did you see the Religious Fanatic?"

"I saw her on the mezzanine going into the priests' offices. The women were praising her for doing all that church work for nothing and felt sorry for her because Solly was in a nursing home."

"Does she still look like hell?"

"And Tessie came doused with perfume and wearing a fancy suit that she said cost two thousand dollars with tax. And then," Mary said grimly, "when she got up to leave, she had powdered sugar all over the back of her skirt. Someone had spilled powdered sugar on the seat. She walked out of the door that way and no one told her. I should have gone after her."

"Oh, hell, don't always feel so guilty."

XVI

WHILE MARY BACKED out of the driveway on her way to church, Steve and Jim sat in the kitchen, drinking a cup of coffee. Steve listened for the sound of Mary's car, uncertain if the hissing in his ears deceived him into thinking the car had reached the road. He waited a few more seconds, then said, "Jimbo, I just remembered a telephone call I have to make." He hurried, losing his balance once, cursing his lost cane, knowing Jim was aware that he did not want to use the cellular telephone on the kitchen table. In his bedroom he dialed Andrew's office. "What did you find out?" he whispered loudly into the telephone receiver and sat on the bed.

Andrew's steady voice, as if from a far distance said, "Western Enterprises was incorporated in 1958 with Uncle Harry as president, Con as vice president, and Aunt Myrsini as secretary-treasurer."

"1958!"

"1958. I haven't had a minute to go over to the recorder's office, to look up Block 325, but—"

"Well, get on it first thing in the morning." Steve knew his voice was rough. To his surprise Andrew said in his usual calm voice, "Dad, that happened thirty-seven years ago. Give me a little time."

Steve sat for a few minutes, looking at the shelves of books next to his television set—one even larger than the one in the family room. He wiped the perspiration from his head and face. His armpits were wet and he knew he should change his shirt. He wanted instead to sit in the big chair in front of the television set and let the hissing in his head subside a little. Then he thought he ought to take his blood pressure, but after another moment's indecision, he stood up and returned to the kitchen.

Jim said, "Is it okay if I bring the guys in my quartet sometime over the weekend to practice?"

"What the hell! Do you have to ask?" This kind of asking for permission reminded Steve that Jim's mother was a blonde, blue-eyed Episcopalian. He liked it that Jim looked like his father Andrew, but handsomer, and even taller.

Jim laughed. "I've been trained by a mother who had all these rules about telephoning before dropping in on people."

"We're not people," Steve said sourly, "we're your grandparents. What kind of bullshit is that—calling up your grandparents for permission to come by?" He wanted to say more, something about his mother being raised differently from Greeks, but he did not want to get started on anything like that. She was all right, Jeanne, but he should end that talk right then or he would end up thinking about Andrew not being a happy man and as he often did, he would wonder why.

Jim waited a moment. "Do you feel all right, Gramps? Do you still want to make the rounds and go to lunch?"

"I feel lousy, Jim. I better stay home. Make yourself a snack. There's chicken. You can heat it in the microwave."

"I'm really not hungry yet. Are you sure you're okay?"

"Goddamn it! Of course I'm okay. I think my blood pressure's a little high. On your way. If I need you, I'll call your office."

Jim walked to the door, stopped, and looked back at Steve. "I'll call you later, Gramps," he said, but Steve did not hear him. He was looking into his coffee cup. The minutes passed while he sat there, the hissing loud in his head.

With a sudden push of the unyielding teakwood table, he stood up and, steadying himself with his palms against the wall, made his way to the garage. He took the streets he knew so well to the nursing home. As he turned too fast into the parking lot, the front wheels hit a dip at the entrance and his body jerked forward. Pain screamed up his back. He sat for several seconds with his foot on the brake, disgusted with himself: he always forgot the dip, and as usual he had not put on the seat belt.

The parking lot was completely filled. Just then a car backed out of a space near the entrance; a good sign, Steve thought, and drove into it. He got out; the arthritic pain in his back, stirred up when he had hit the dip, took his breath away. He looked in the back seat of the car for his cane. He had forgotten it again. For a few seconds, he stood on the asphalt paving and looked up to the fifth floor of the pale brick building. Behind the windows patients were languishing in two-hundred-dollar-a-day rooms; he took a deep breath, hoping he would not someday be one of them. Something moved from his throat to the pit of his stomach. He pressed his fist into the small of his back where the pain was receding.

Then a rush of energy sent him hobbling through the wide glass doors, across the potted-plant entrance to the elevators. He pressed the UP button and waited. The door slid open and exposed the dim, square cave. He turned quickly, a shimmer in his chest, to the door a few feet away with a lighted green STAIRWAY sign above it. He would go slow, he told himself, and rest every few steps. In the quiet he trudged and stopped, trudged and stopped until he reached the fifth floor, relieved that he had met no one on the stairs. At the landing he stood for several minutes, breathing heavily before opening the door to the long, wide-aisled floor.

A woman seated at the nurses' station did not look up as he walked past. He did not know if she were a registered nurse, a practical nurse, or an aide. It annoyed him: if they'd wear their caps as nurses once did, you'd know who the hell they were. Most doors were open and he looked into them—how Mary hated his doing this. People lay propped against elevated headrests, white skeletal faces with their sunken eyes trained on the doorways. A fully dressed man sat in a chair padded with sheepskins and gazed through reddened eyes as Steve passed. Steve averted his face; he hadn't expected anyone to look at him. From behind a closed door, a fecal smell came. *Oh, God, or whatever,* he said to himself, *give me one big blow and let it be over.* His mother had talked like that, but it hadn't turned out that way for her.

The door to Solly's pink room was open. Solly's wife was talking to a fat nurse whose blue uniform pulled at the line of buttons down the front. Steve had not seen Magdalene for over a year, but as he looked at her, he felt no interest in her—nothing at all. She looked more stout than he remembered. Her gray hair was cut even shorter, almost like a man's, and her face was smooth like dough. She was wearing a white cotton dress with long sleeves and a black patent leather belt around her thick waist. They exchanged hellos. Steve felt guilty, as if he had done something to her that was bad.

Magdalene said, smiling, "Well, I'll leave you two." She left the room without saying good-bye to Solly or even looking at him. The nurse accompanied her, explaining in a defensive tone, "It was done on the night shift, I'm sure."

Steve wondered what Magdalene thought when she saw him. In the attorney's office a year ago, they had met to discuss Solly's nursing-care expenses. Magdalene's placid expression then and a few minutes ago were no different. He was offended at how she had let herself go—she looked like one of the hospital aides. He hadn't noticed if she carried a Bible with her; he had heard she took one everywhere. When Solly had been brought to the nursing home after his stroke, Steve had found her trying to read biblical verses to him. "Shut up!" Solly had shouted. "You crazy woman! Get out of here!" Maybe, Steve thought, she had been trying to make him ask God for forgiveness. Above the bed on the pink wall was an icon of Saint Stephen, the first martyr—so Mary had told him.

He remembered the Magdalene who had been young and pretty with a perpetual smile. When she arrived, she was wearing her Red Cross uniform. She had been released at the end of the war and her mother, who died soon afterwards, sent her clothes by train. The train was clogged with returning soldiers and an overflow of delayed packages. After the business had begun to make money, she looked queenly in her spacious living room near sideboards stacked with whiskeys, mixers, liqueurs; smiling, she had pointed out platters and bowls of Greek delicacies on massive dining-room buffets. A pretty little woman guest had squealed, "Ooh, look at all this nice Italian food!"

After ten years of Magdalene's parties, Mary had balked at going. She asked Steve one night when he was churlish about her not wanting to attend a party—one of the children had a fever— "Do you ever see any of these people again?" He had thought about it: they seldom saw any of the guests twice, but he thought they had to go; they were family. A few years later, he was the one who made excuses to stay home.

Solly was looking at him, his lips pressed together as if he were toothless. His eyes were watery, hazy, reddish pouches scalloped under them. His sparse hair had been brushed across his skeletal head. "How are you, Solly?"

In a creaky, bewildered voice Solly asked, "Who were those two women in my room? What am I doing here? I can't get up."

Steve sat down in the same chair as on the first day Solly had been brought to the airy pink room from the ambulance. His doctor reminded them that Solly had been having problems for some time; the stroke had done irreversible damage. Magdalene, their daughters, and Tommy left the room to talk with the doctor down the hall. As soon as they left the room and closed the door, Steve put his head in his hands and cried. He could not stop, though he tried desperately, afraid they would come back and see him crying like a child.

Now he looked through the wide window at the top of the trees. They appeared to him like the rainforest trees he saw on television nature programs. Then he looked at Solly. You sonofabitch, he thought, she should have left you years ago and I should have helped her to. His heart tripped: he didn't want to think about the old days. "Well, Solly, how've you been?" he repeated. It was the question he asked each time he sat in the pink room. It came with a dry despair.

Solly began a monologue, his lips pulled back to show his worn-down stubs of teeth. "I saw Jack Burns on Main Street. Said he made a bundle when Pacific Corp split. You know who came into my room last night? I don't know if it was my dad or the general I was aide to. He was mad about something. Wouldn't even sit down. Was with him all through the war. I'm going to Vegas tomorrow. Told the doctor I'd take him with me. There were two women here and they had their nerve. Strange women coming into my room. Women—only good for fucking. Not even good for that sometimes. What did you say your name was?"

"I'm your brother Steve, goddamn you!" Steve did not know how to begin his questioning and he gazed at the plastic tube running under the sheets to a urine bottle on the floor under the bed. "Solly, you ever hear of Western Enterprises?"

Solly lifted his red eyes, contemplating the ceiling. "Solly, you ever hear about Western Enterprises?" Solly looked at the door. "They should be bringing my breakfast pretty soon," he said.

"You already had breakfast. Think, Solly. You ever hear of Western Enterprises? Con, and Uncle Harry, Aunt Myrsini, they were all involved in Western Enterprises. *Did you ever hear of Western Enterprises?*"

"Why are you hollering at me? I'll tell the doctor you're hollering at me."

"Okay, so you don't know anything about Western Enterprises?"

In a creaky voice, Solly said, "Saw Milton Berl's show. Last night she couldn't open the window to get in. Yelling. Yelling at me. Forty-nine percent." He closed his eyes, and Steve did not know if he were feigning sleep.

Solly's head was sunk into the fluffed pillows, his sagging face drained of purpose. His sparse hair had been recently cut. Steve could smell the aftershave lotion on his jowls. Steve's eyes narrowed as he looked at Solly: the cost of keeping him bathed, shaved, pedicured, his pillows fluffed in the $200-a day room could keep how many families going? And you're not worth it, he said silently to the freshly shaved face, because you're a goddamn sonofabitch and always were. You took credit for everything we did. You know damn well I'm the one who supplied you with the money on the financial statements to show the banks. Me, the workhorse. You wined and dined the bigwigs from back East and most of the time you kept it from me. You and that expense-account business. You were a selfish, egotistical bastard and you were that way from the time we were kids. You'd get into trouble and worm yourself out of it with that snake tongue of yours. You even twisted things around to make me out the guilty one. Like a goddamn fool, I always came to your rescue.

"You wanted to be so rich you'd be listed in the Forbes Five

Hundred. You bastard. Those deals you made with bums like yourself. Whoremongers. You cheated on your wife and I knew it. All those stories about your friends and Las Vegas call girls, they were you, you no-good bastard. Your great friends! All of them ended up alcoholics or dead, but you preferred them to me. You never turned to look at me at your parties. You couldn't leave your great buddies for a minute. And Con. He was so grateful to have a friend his mother approved of, you led him around by the nose. And I know as sure as I'm sitting here that you were involved in Western Enterprises. You shit! Look at you. As useless as tits on a boar."

Steve stood up and gave Solly one last malevolent look. On the way back to his house, he almost hit a car parked on a residential street. He opened his eyes wide, told himself to stop fuming, and he did for a few blocks. Then the anger came back and he could not will it away: Why had he wasted so much of his time—his life— fighting with Solly and wanting to be close to him? Solly with his grandiose ideas. Solly, who had been rotten to his wife and he had never told him so. Solly who had got Con to go along with his scheme for the Silver Rails Mall. And he went along too.

When he drove up the brick lane, Mary was hosing down the driveway. The little black bird was standing on the grass, unmoving, watching. Mary stood aside to let Steve drive into the garage. He thought he would go into the kitchen without saying anything, but she turned off the nozzle and said, "Where did you go?"

"What are you doing?" Steve pretended anger. "We've got a whole crew of morons taking care of the grounds. Why the hell are you standing on your feet like that?"

"Don't change the subject," Mary said and followed him into the kitchen. "Why did you sneak off like that?"

"I didn't sneak off. You're getting so damn suspicious. Paranoid. That's what you are."

"If so, you made me that way."

Steve tried to look angry as he opened the big refrigerator and took out a bottle of beer. Mary reached for a lemonade. Steve sat at his usual place, facing the garden, and Mary filled a glass with ice and lemonade and sat opposite Steve. "Well, where did you go? I don't want to hear any lies."

"To see Solly." Steve took a long swallow of beer.

"You saw him this past Monday. How come you went there again?"

"I just went, that's all. I got cabin fever sitting in this house."

"So you had cabin fever and you couldn't think of a better place to go than a nursing home? What's bothering you, anyway?"

Steve flung out his arms. "Nothing's bothering me! You're getting so paranoid."

"Since you learned that word, you've been using it a lot." Mary kept her gaze on Steve. "One of these days you're going to hit someone. Maybe a child. Why do I have to keep nagging you about it?"

Steve hit his left palm with a slicing motion of his right hand. Mary said, "Don't act like your father used to, telling your mother to shut up."

"She was there. Magdalene. No makeup. Smiling." He grimaced. "That goddamn smile. Fifty some years that same goddamn smile. You don't know what the hell's behind it."

"I think it's tranquilizers."

"When she left the room, she didn't even say good-bye to him. She could have him home for what it's costing. She hates him."

"Did she ask about us?"

"No."

"I wonder what kind of a life she has."

"I don't know and I don't give a good goddamn what kind of a life she has."

"She knows that," Mary said. "From the day Solly was taken to the nursing home, you put her out of your mind. You never telephoned her."

"All she had to do was call me if she needed something. I told her so." Steve drained the beer and stood up. "She looked awful and like she didn't give a damn what she looked like, the stupid religious fanatic. I'm gonna take a nap," he said and tried to hurry out of the kitchen, to get away because the impulse to tell Mary about Western Enterprises was in his mouth.

"Where's your cane?" Mary called after him.

XVII

TWO EVENINGS LATER Mary set out for church. She did not tell Steve she intended going to confession. "Where you off to?" he asked. He was watching a baseball game on television and turned to her with an accusing frown.

Mary looked back at him and hesitated: he did not like to be alone in the house, even though he had a full schedule of television sports events to watch: he could not just sit back and enjoy the games he had looked forward to. When she returned, she would find bread crumbs, cheese parings, smears of jam on the drainboard, a jar of peanut butter left out, and cupboard doors open. She must be careful, she often told herself, to outlive him, he could not be alone—their daughters were too far away.

"There's church tonight for *Panaghias*," she said, which was not much of a lie: there were no services, but confessions were being heard before August the Fifteenth, the Dormition of the Virgin. If she told him the truth, he would try to find out what she had to confess. There was no privacy at all with him. No, he never attended church, never read the church bulletins; he would not know that she had lied.

As she backed out of the garage, she noticed again the little black bird. She could not find pleasure in the warm evening, the sky a lingering pink left in the wake of the red and orange sunset, because she was uncertain about facing Father Symeon. What she wanted to confess was hard to put into words, and Father Symeon was well-meaning and dense.

A dozen or so cars were parked in the asphalt lot. Mary got out with some difficulty—her legs felt like wood—and pressed the automatic lock on her car key. She intended to walk quickly toward the old immigrant church, but her legs would not respond. She had not really loved the church until she had been married several decades. It became her refuge, and remembering that Father Symeon would soon retire, she took a deep breath of relief.

Fanny and Goldie were ahead of her, climbing the cement steps. They leaned forward, pulling one heavy leg after the other as they made their way upward. At the top they stopped and panted, laughing at their predicament.

Mary reached them and they rested a moment before Goldie opened the heavy oak doors. "Well," she said, "you're doing better than Fanny and me. You're not even out of breath." Mary, out of breath, demurred.

"We're meeting Lefty and Perry after, at Little America for pie and coffee," Fanny said with an encouraging nod. "Come with us."

"I'd like to, but Steve's not feeling too well, so I should go straight home." She wanted to be with them, but without Steve she thought she might feel out of place.

"Tell him we asked about him and *perastika*," Fanny said, and Goldie echoed *"perastika."*

"Well, *perastika* to all our ailments," Mary said. When they were young, they had spoken far more Greek with their English than they now did. *Perastika:* "May the sickness be gone." Mary liked those Greek words that popped up in conversations and forgot Father Symeon until she followed Fanny and Goldie into the narthex. A council member they knew from Greek-school days stood behind the tall table and greeted them. They took turns placing money into a basket, taking candles from a full tray, lighting them, pushing them into a sand-filled tray, and making the sign of the cross before the icons. No more than twenty people sat on the pews: two were young people; the rest were like them, the elderly children of immigrants.

Fanny led the way to a front pew. Parishioners turned to look at them and nodded, all waiting to enter the small confessional room to the right of the icon screen. It was late evening and the great stained-glass windows were gray, devoid of the brilliant reds, yellows, and blues of daytime, when the rays of the sun sent colored motes toward the altar screen. In the gloom, the icons on the altar screen were barely lit by the votive lights in dark-red glasses above them. The coolness was touched with incense.

The parishioners were gazing at the altar screen, their lips moving, or were reading the confessional prayer at the back of the liturgy book. Mary wondered if she could get up and walk out without attracting attention, but she did not know how to explain this to Fanny and Goldie. She had made the decision to confess and had practiced what she would say: I failed in keeping the women of the family together. I should have tried harder. I was the first married, the oldest. It was my responsibility. They are all lonely (she had wondered if she should say that she was lonely at times). I let the men with their feuds influence me. We all did. I should have seen the women alone; I should have overlooked some of the things about them that bothered me.

Parishioners took their turns. When someone left the confessional room, another stood up and walked slowly toward the closed door. Fanny had gone in, soon emerged, and held the door open for Goldie. She returned to the pew with resolute steps. Still Mary wanted to leave. She felt no warmth for the priest, as she had for others she had known from the time she was unmarried and had taught Sunday school.

Sometimes during liturgies she felt a pain, an anginal clutch in her chest when the choir softly finished the Amens and the We beseech Thees and the priest climbed ponderously to the podium. Pinching his rose-brocaded phelonion, he raised it and revealed white socks. He hurumphed before beginning his sermons. She had tried not to look at him: overweight, big, gray-headed, his phelonion wrinkled—when he put it away he evidently hung it sloppily. Then the sermon, using the text for the day, but he wandered off to condemn people with AIDS, or some unnamed member of the church council who had insulted him, or—Mary let him go on while she thought of her grandchildren, their coming birthdays, a family dinner.

She knew she could not go into the confessional. She half rose from the pew with a glance over her shoulder to see how many people sat behind her. There were about ten, ten who would see her leave and conjecture over it. Then raising her head, she looked at the painted Christ in the great dome, at his scowling eyebrows and piercing black eyes, and sat down.

In black cassock the priest opened the door of the confessional for a woman, older than Mary, about eighty-five, she thought, one of the first of the immigrant children to be born in America. The old woman left the confessional with her head down. She was wearing black for her dead husband and wiping her eyes. Her thin hands pulled a large purse high onto her chest. Like a chastened, wrinkled child, she walked down the aisle. The priest motioned Mary forward. "The older people first," Father Symeon ("Father Sam-Sam," wags called him) said to a teenage boy who had stood up. Mary walked toward Father Symeon, her feet heavy, unwilling.

In the small, windowless, but brightly lighted room, two straight-backed chairs next to the wall faced each other. On the wall was a shelf with a pot of basil and an icon of the Virgin and Child. The scent of basil gave Mary a moment's wonder: How could basil grow without sunlight? She crossed herself before the icon and sat down.

Father Symeon raised his arms in a gesture of impatience; the big cassock sleeves fell to his elbows and revealed the frayed cuffs of his white shirt. "These old ladies, I keep telling them I don't want to hear every little bad thought or word or quarrel, but they go on and on." This surprised Mary: Father Symeon was the most gossipy priest they'd ever had. He placed a freckled hand against the bulge of his stomach, inadequately hidden by his cassock. "It's not easy listening when you're fasting and just plain hungry."

"Oh, Father," Mary said in sympathy. Her mother had felt sad for hungry people and so did she.

"So, what did you come to confess? You read the confessional prayer?"

Mary nodded, blinking her eyes: she had not read the prayer. The room now looked smaller, grayer, and something in it was suffocating her. She had to hurry and get out of there. A little out of breath, she realized there was a small pain in her breast bone. She was afraid that if it worsened, she would have to open her purse and unscrew the small bottle of nitroglycerin tablets she took everywhere with her. She glanced at the priest, gray eyes, gray jowls, thick, colorless lips, and blurted, "Father, I just feel I haven't done my," she could not think of the English word *duty* and said it in Greek, "my *kathikon* to my family. I'm the oldest of the women and I should have kept them together. We haven't had anything to do with each other for years."

Father Symeon frowned as if he did not know what in the world she was talking about. Mary thought of the elderly woman hurrying out of the confessional and down the aisle. "You mean your children and you don't get along? Well, that's nothing new."

"No, I mean—. You know our husbands and the sisters-in-law were all involved in the business and in a family business there are always upsets." Mary saw she was not making herself understood. "The women in the family drifted apart."

"Yeah, well, that's life." Father Symeon raised his left hand slightly until his wristwatch showed. He glanced at it and then at Mary.

"It's my husband's brother Solly," Mary burst out. "I try not to hate him, but I can't help it!"

A little spark of interest came into Father Symeon's eyes. "Just go to him and tell him you're sorry you've hated him in the past and you'll feel better."

"He's in a nursing home. His mind's not quite right."

"Yes, I know. Go anyway. You'll feel better. And here are some prayers that will help you. Read them often, say the Lord's Prayer several times a day, and you'll get over it. 'Forgive us our trespasses as we forgive theirs,'" Father Symeon intoned as he stood up.

Mary said, "Thank you, Father Symeon," and stepped out of the room. She hurried down the side aisle, head down, and waited until she stood at the other side of the heavy oak doors. "The damn fool," she said. She had never used the word *damn* before.

As she drove home, she wondered why she had been so stupid as to go to confession and try to explain the feelings she could not quite put into words—and then explode over Solly. She was still angry with herself when she reached her house. "Who'd you see in church?" Steve asked.

"I don't know why you always ask me that question. Why don't you go yourself if you're so interested in who's there?"

"Well, I won't. So who'd you see?"

"The usual people and Fanny and Goldie."

"Yeah? What'd they say? Did they ask about me?"

"Yes, they asked about you. They said the usual *perastika.*" Mary drew out the words: "They were going to meet Lefty and Perry afterwards at Little America for pie and coffee."

Steve said nothing, his eyes on the television screen. "Ah," he said, and his drooping cheeks lifted into a smile that, though yellow-toothed, was wide and youthful. "You know what I just thought about when you mentioned Fanny and Goldie? I thought about the Harvest Dance we had when we were juniors in high school. We went to Old Man Olsen's farm to make apple cider for the dance. We just gave it out free. They did things like that in those days."

"I wouldn't know," Mary said. "I was home embroidering dish-towels for my trousseau."

Mary let Steve again tell the story about the Harvest Dance, Mr.

Olsen, the manual arts teacher, and the farm. "I wish I'd a thought to buy the farm after the war. Now it's all industrial properties and factories. Used to be all farms. Farms from pioneer days, not great for farming, but great for industry."

Mary thought of what good friends the three of them, Steve, Lefty, and Perry, had been. He should have kept in touch with them. She had told him often enough years ago. He had not made real friends in his work. She said, "I've decided I'll invite your sisters and Magdalene and Tessie for coffee and give them the old family pictures that have piled up. It's ridiculous. We're a family and never see each other."

"Maybe you don't, but I've always seen too goddamn much of them."

"That's just it," Mary said, and she walked into the kitchen; where she turned on the light and sat at the table. It had come out without her thinking about it—that she would invite them. There would be five of them if they all came: She, Magdalene, Tessie, Penny, and Georgie. She stood up and went to the window. For a while she looked at the rose garden in the waning dusk. The little black bird was standing between a Peace rose, her favorite, with its creamy pink-tipped petals, and the red Tiffany, darkening as the light faded.

An old restlessness surfaced; it had come and gone at intervals for decades and then diminished into an occasional bout. She had learned it could be quelled only by work like clearing out the garage. She decided she would look at the snapshots once more before giving them away. Some might bring back memories better left alone.

The north end of the kitchen was lined with closets, long drawers for table linens, and cabinets for canned goods. There were also manila envelopes containing warranties for kitchen and laundry appliances, and cookbooks of all sizes and ages. One was her first cookbook, *Women's Home Companion*. Its loose cover was held together with a thick rubber band and several pages of the index had come loose. Every time she used the book, she knew she should throw it away. She decided she would do it that moment before she changed her mind.

In a corner of the garage were three cardboard boxes into which she had been placing books she knew no one would ever read: coffee-table travel books, and best-sellers of decades past like *Gone with the Wind*, *The Thibaults*, and *Rebecca*. She intended giving them to the city library or to the veterans' hospital. In a separate box she had put cartoon books like Feifer's *Boy, Girl, Boy, Girl* and light titles about family life: *"Where did you go?" "Out." "What did you do?" "Nothing."* Hospitals and nursing homes might like them, she had thought. The third box was reserved for books she had come to think of as superficial, even nonsensical; they were destined for the trash collector. *Elegance* was the first to be thrown into it. Mary remembered the absurdity of its advice: "If you haven't the courage to walk past a building under construction where twenty workmen are sure to whistle at you, there is no point in buying the stunning red hat that is so becoming to you." Further on, a new negligee was suggested to relieve the boredom of home evenings. The book still annoyed her; she thought of the women's magazines of the fifties telling women how to pamper their husbands when they came home from work: have a delicious dinner ready; take time to rest; refresh your makeup; put a ribbon through your hair; be cheerful; get the house in order; teach the children to be quiet; speak in a low, soft, soothing, and pleasant voice.

She had been about to throw *Amy Vanderbilt's Complete Book of Etiquette* in with *Elegance* because the book's advice had been completely erased by the 1960s revolution. She still used the correspondence section, though, for the correct forms of address and lately, more than once, had thought of writing to the archbishop: "The Most Reverend Archbishop Spyridon: Your Eminence: I am disturbed. . . ."

Mary returned to the kitchen. She took out five large, bulging manila envelopes she had stacked next to the cookbooks, lined them on the table, took out the snapshots and pictures from each one, and placed them in orderly piles. The television noise erupted into rabid screams. Steve walked in. "God, what a touchdown! Fourth down and by hell that little pipsqueak quarterback jumped over those big galoots and made a touchdown." He sat down, looked around the kitchen, and picked up a snapshot. "I'll be goddamned! My godfather. Look at him! That goose-egg head of his. Too bad we didn't give him this picture to take back to Greece."

Steve watched Mary for a few seconds. "I think I'll take my blood pressure," he said. He took the machine out of a cabinet and kept talking, nervously, Mary noticed. He kept on talking while he wrapped the blood pressure band about his upper arm. Mary thought, but didn't remind him, that he should not talk while taking his blood pressure. Steve took off the cuff and gave a deep sigh. He said, "Do you know what my pressure is or don't you give a good goddamn? It's one-ninety over ninety-eight."

"It always shoots up when you've got something on your mind."

"What the hell have I got on my mind!"

Mary did not look up as Steve walked, more heavily than usual, into the television room. At the door he said, "You're wasting your time with those pictures."

Mary pursed her lips and began going through the snapshots. Steve's cursing came from the other room without stop: "You god damn bastard! I read all that in this morning's newspaper! You get paid two-hundred thousand a year to tell us what we already read in the morning newspaper! Acting like you're telling us something new, you pisspot! You ought to have your prick cut off! And there she is, Miss Prissy, telling us about a murder with that big smile! Those great big twinkling eyes. You bitch! Someone ought to tape that big mouth of yours shut!"

Mary thought Steve was keeping whatever was bothering him to himself longer than usual. It was no use her trying to talk with him about it; it had to come from him—when he chose to tell it. As she looked through the snapshots, she thought with sad wonder that the years had gone by so quickly. More than eighty years of family history was in the piles: weddings, baptisms, lodge banquets, picnics, Christmases, Easters—celebrations both "American" and Greek, the Dormition of the Virgin, Mothers' and Fathers' Days. . . .

The lodge pictures showed a progression of youngish immigrant men in their Sunday-best suits, wearing tasseled fezzes, some with the stoles of office across their chests, smiling, eyes alert; later in their forties, graying; in their fifties, bald or skimpy-haired; in their sixties and seventies, fewer of them, slumped shoulders, big stomached, pouched dark skin under patient eyes mirroring decline.

Methodically, Mary went through the snapshots, most of them Penny's work, and tried to place them in chronological order. The earliest showed Andreas and Uncle Harry, each squatting at either end of a spitted lamb. They were men on the verge of middle age, both with considerable hair but with their graying temples shaved, the barber-shop routine of the twenties and thirties. Their eyes were half-closed against the heat of the hot ashes. Their mouths were opened slightly. Mary knew they were singing the old laments of the guerrilla Greeks stealthily moving from their mountain lair in the night to pounce on the Turkish conquerors. The children of the family stood in a circle around the two fathers, looking on: Steve, about eight years old; Solly; Penny holding Georgie's hand; and at a short distance, Aunt Myrsini with Con, a toddler, in her arms.

Mary lingered over several pictures. In one Aunt Myrsini wore a dress with a geometric pattern, sleeveless, that must have shocked Steve's mother; Uncle Harry was wearing his Masonic fez. Two pictures of Steve's mother were in the jumble. In one she was standing in her Greek Town garden, a frown puckering her forehead as if she had been interrupted in her work. She was wearing a bib apron over a cotton dress, and her hair had loosened from the bun at the nape of her neck. In the other snapshot, in a dark Sunday dress and wearing a slanted hat with a white flower on the center of the brim, she leaned straight backwards. Her shoes were close together. She was standing at attention for the photographer—probably Penny.

Mary was unsure about many snapshots: who should have them when members of different families were pictured together? The young Steve, Solly, Con, and sometimes Penny and Georgie at mountain picnics and backyard barbecues, Solly making faces and striking silly poses, Con looking on. Aunt Myrsini was often in the background. A snapshot taken in a mountain canyon showed her seated at the head of the table. Mary shook her head and put the snapshot in Tessie's envelope. Another showed Tessie standing next to Aunt Myrsini. Mary remembered the occasion, a dinner she had given for Tessie and Con's engagement. Penny had probably had them stand up from the table. Tessie's mouth was opened foolishly wide as if in surprise, her eyes staring. She was wearing a long, pink dress—the picture was in black and white, but Mary remembered the expensive pink georgette. Next to her, Aunt Myrsini was smiling smugly, her head lifted.

Mary looked up from the snapshots. She thought of herself and Tessie, living next door to each other in Greek Town in the row of old houses behind the church. All day and night, trains chugged from the Denver & Rio Grande Western and the Union Pacific railyards, black smoke billowing up to the sky. On Saturdays, Mary and her sister, who too soon would be married off at seventeen to a much older immigrant in Chicago, helped their mother wash the smoke-smudged curtains and stretch them on wooden frames to dry. Tessie, who was younger than Mary by a few years, was often with them, dark-blue bruises on her arms from her mother's beatings.

Mary and Tessie held hands on their way to public school and, later in the day, to Greek school. In summer, after they had mopped the worn-out linoleum, ironed, and washed dishes, they sat on the porch steps and fanned themselves with folded Greek newspapers. The smell of acrid engine smoke and of rotting vegetables and fruit came from the Growers' Market a few blocks away. Tessie talked without stop about all the things she was going to do when she grew up. Mary would shake her head at her foolishness. In winter, they walked through stinging wind, rain, and snow, which numbed their feet in their cheap shoes. Greek school in the church basement was so cold they had to keep their coats on. No matter how cold the day, though, they were glad to watch passenger trains go by and admire the people sitting in the club cars and eating at the tables with white tablecloths. Black men served the passengers, holding plates and silver pitchers.

Mary went back to her work. Many pictures had been taken around Solly's swimming pool: The flat-chested little girls posed close together in one-piece bathing suits; Grade-school Andrew poised to throw a ball to Dick, at that time called Nick; Andrew and Dick, hands raised to hit each other; Tommy on the diving board, one elbow crooked, pretending he had muscle rather than the puny bulge on his upper arm; another snapshot showed Tom, a little boy, bat raised to hit a ball, looking at his father Solly, whose back was turned from him. Foolish Steve, Mary thought—how much he had wanted the grown Dick and Tom to like him.

Mary paused while sorting through the many photographs of brides and bridesmaids. She had forgotten who some of them were, and Penny had not written their names on the backs. She put them in Penny's envelope. Penny would remember who everyone was; she never forgot names or the dates of weddings, baptisms, and funerals.

The little flat-chested girls were later snapped in bikinis that they were not allowed to wear around the grandparents. Solly was in a number of the pool pictures, lounging, either in swimming trunks or dressed in slacks and sports shirts: Solly sprawled on a chaise lounge, wearing dark glasses; Solly talking to friends of his daughters, holding a cigarette in one hand, a drink in the other. Solly was absent from the pictures of the swimming parties Tom gave for the young men he said were his fraternity brothers. Mary realized that no girls were in the snapshots.

She lifted her head and looked at the rose garden, now dark except for the white roses. The only picture of Tom's mother, Magdalene, showed her sitting on the side of a chaise lounge looking toward Solly, who was talking to a pretty blonde with breasts barely contained in the skimpy top of her bikini. Solly was standing so close to the girl that only a few inches separated their faces. Mary dropped the snapshot into the wastepaper basket.

She would keep the next picture for herself. She gazed a long time at her twenty-three-year-old self with Andrew in her arms. He was wearing the white cap with the blue *V* and inside it the letters *USA*. She breathed in sadly, remembering her mother, who embroidered the cap before Steve left for the army. Those terrible war years moving back to her small, dull bedroom in her parents' house with barely room for Andrew's crib nearby; the crowds on the street; the confusion; the buses that would not stop to take her on, hurrying with Andrew in one arm, the diaper bag in another, on the way to the stern pediatrician—"Don't you know there's a war on?" Sometimes she had an additional burden, a package of cookies to mail to Steve because he complained about army food. Her parents tried not to let her know how little money they had. The ration coupons. Worst of all, the Jewish girl who refused to take her clothes off to walk naked to the Nazi ovens and was thrown into the flames alive; she had thought about her for years, agonized for her.

She went back to her work. Not one snapshot of Andrew and his wife Jeanne were among the hundreds on the table, not even one of their wedding day. She remembered staring at the back of Andrew's head as he and Jeanne stood at the altar in the Episcopal church, flanked with white stephanotis. Andrew did not smile or even look at Jeanne when he pushed the wedding band on her finger. Blonde, blue-eyed Jeanne smiled happily throughout the service. "They make a darling couple," women said afterwards.

It puzzled Mary that Jeanne's twice-a-year dinners were unsatisfying. After eating, she still felt a little hungry, even though the food was adequate. The house always seemed cold, too. Mary still resented Jeanne's not standing up when the old people, Andreas and Marika, entered her house. But Jeanne couldn't be all bad; her children, Jim and his sister Liesa, were so good to her and Steve.

Andrew had met Jeanne several weeks before they married.

Why hadn't he waited, Mary had wondered on their wedding day as she sat in the church? Too much had gone wrong in the family at the time. His grandfather Andreas had not stopped fuming at the board for refusing to take Andrew into the business. His father Steve had taken to staying at the club after lunch, playing gin rummy, drinking too much. Mary's heart began a frenzied beating. At that moment she realized that Andreas's wrath, Andrew's quick marriage, and Steve's deserting his office for long hours at the club were connected. She waited patiently for her heart to quieten and then she made a decision: the day after her luncheon she would go to Andrew's office and tell him how hurt Steve had been by the board's decision. He had cared so much, he almost became a bum, she would tell him. Maybe, she thought, some of that feeling they once had for each other would come back. She was angry with Steve. He should have told Andrew how he felt, but, no, he let it pass as if Andrew would magically know how much he cared.

She rested for several melancholy minutes before returning to the snapshots. The first one she picked up was of her and Steve a few days before their marriage. Mary looked a long time at their youngness. The picture did not show how tired she had been. She had worked at Woolworth's until the day before her Sunday wedding. Her sister and her two children had come from Chicago by coach. When they arrived, the younger boy had a high fever. The three of them: grandmother, mother, and she, the aunt, bathed him in tepid water, put a small amount of aspirin crushed with sugar into his slack mouth, and rubbed his small body with alcohol. The commotion in the house, the children, the wedding preparations, and her lunchhour meetings with Steve to buy a few pieces of furniture for the small house he had rented—his father had given him two hundred dollars as a wedding present—had left her worn out. And Steve wanted to park behind the state capitol on the few nights they went out. They almost went too far one night.

She laughed outright at the next two pictures, but she knew Steve could not hear her; the blare of television news had been replaced by excited sports commentary. In one, Steve's father Andreas and Uncle Harry were facing each other; their pregnant-looking stomachs almost touched. In the second snapshot, they were stretched out on chaise lounges, sleeping on Mary's patio. On the nearby table, plates were strewn with the leavings of lamb ribs and corn on the cob. Mary recalled Penny's laughing inordinately while she photographed the old men. She thought it was too bad Uncle Harry was in the snapshots or she would give them to Andrew; maybe she would cut out Uncle Harry.

Then she looked at Tessie and Myrsini, both decades older than in the engagement picture. Tessie leaned away from her mother-in-law, looking disgruntled as if she were being unwillingly photographed. Aunt Myrsini's mouth was a thin, lipsticked line.

She wasn't sure what to do about the Greek-school pictures of girls in junior high and high school dressed in the pleated kilts worn by men in the 1821 Revolution against the Turks. One snapshot showed them in the play *Esme,* about a Turkish girl who was in love with a *kleft,* a young Greek guerrilla. Even then, Fanny had been hefty and had been chosen to take the part of the hero. Georgie was Esme and wore full, voile trousers and a veil, sewed by Mary's mother. When they practiced the play, boys stood around whispering and nudging each other. The schoolteacher, "the assless dandy," chased them outside. One of them had been Steve. The girls took all parts because it would not have been right, according to immigrant ways, for girls and boys to mingle. When the Star Theatrical Club put on plays, men were made up to look like women.

Mary thought of that lost immigrant world. Now young people lived together before they married. The girls even wore white dresses at their weddings.

She finished sorting the snapshots, but she was still restless. She knew that if she went to bed, she would not be able to sleep. She should not have looked at the pictures late at night. She decided to make a grocery list for the luncheon and brought a pencil and pad from a drawer, sat down, and looked at the black window that cut off the rose garden from her view. She shivered at the profound blackness. They should have, she thought, installed lights so that the garden would be there, alive in the night. It was too late for that now.

She wondered whether to serve the luncheon in the living room or the dining room. Two decades ago they would have sat in the kitchen with a good view of the roses, but now it might seem to the women that she did not think they were worth the trouble of being served either in the living room or dining room. Better the dining room, she decided. Then she considered her china, crystal, and sterling that she had not used for at least ten years, maybe more. They would need washing by hand: she could not put them into the dishwasher. In the past, when the sisters-in-law had sat at the kitchen table, she had used either a set of Dansk her daughters had bought or simple, inexpensive bone china.

Also, she mused, the linens would need touching up. She imagined the open linen cabinet showing the shelves of tablecloths in rows with tissue paper placed in the folds and stacks of matching napkins next to them, wondering what would happen to her linens when she died. Her daughters would never use them. They had told her so: they were too much trouble; no-iron place mats were easy and just as good.

She decided on the white cut-work tablecloth. Her mother had made it for her while Mary was in high school. Her mother had worked on it in her small living room with her few treasures, the Chinese dragon vase her son had bought for her with his first paycheck as a grocery clerk and a cut-glass bowl, a gift from the best man at her wedding. On either side of the sofa on small end tables were two pink glass bud vases—Depression glassware they were now called.

Mary's heart began the irregular rhythm that she hated: what would they talk about? She, Tessie, and Magdalene had never spoken about the business. After the family dinners had faded away, whenever they saw each other in church, in a department store, on a downtown street, they talked about their children and grandchildren, never their husbands. They kept to this policy long before Dick and Tom came into the business. It was also possible that Penny and Georgie might say something unsettling about the business. She did not know what to expect from them.

As she thought about the luncheon, Mary became unsure of herself, afraid she had become rusty after the many years' lack of formal entertaining. That she would have to be in charge of the table talk gave her the odd feeling that her brain might stop working. She tried to force herself to think, and then it came to her: she would tell the women about the bowl and the Depression vases she would place on the table. It would start the conversation off. It could lead to less personal, more general topics, like the Depression they used to talk about. Relieved to have solved the problem, she visualized how the dining room table would look. She thought with distant nostalgia of her mother's cut-work cloth with the glass bowl and the pink vases in the center.

Early in the morning of the luncheon, she would cut pink and white roses, or perhaps yellow would be a good contrast. Next she mulled over the menu, forgetting that she had intended to serve only coffee and dessert. She was now back in her old pattern of hospitality, wanting to serve her guests beautifully prepared food that would look appealing on plates as well. She stopped, worried; she had no idea if the women watched their cholesterol, and she had forgotten their likes and dislikes. She did remember that Penny was allergic to strawberries. She would not cook red meat; too many people were cutting down on it, and she was tired of chicken.

She thought of taking one of her cookbooks from the cabinet, then recalled the favorite menu of her early married years when she and friends took turns giving luncheons. Now the women served only coffee and dessert. Her daughters had jobs and took friends out for lunch. So much had changed in her lifetime.

Her favorite menu consisted of crabcakes, new potatoes, asparagus, fruit salad, and either pie or cake. She hoped it wasn't too late for asparagus. She was pleased that she had taken care of the important details, the table and the menu. In the morning, she would make the telephone calls. This deflated her enthusiasm and she slept badly.

THEY SAID THEY would come, although Magdalene hesitated before agreeing. She echoed Tessie's, Penny's, and Georgie's, "Oh, why go to all that trouble? Why don't we just go out?" Mary said, "I *want* to do it. I have a lot of snapshots to give you."

Mary would not trust her cleaning woman Sandy to touch the crystal, china, and sterling. She washed them herself when she was alone in the kitchen and Steve was watching a game in the television room. They looked brand new. During the Depression, her friends had worked in J. C. Penney's or as cashiers in their fathers' or godfathers' restaurants and candy stores and paid weekly amounts on lay-aways for china, crystal, even sterling. She had not: there was so little money in those years that if she had not bought a little fish, meat, and fruit with her meager salary at Woolworth's, they would have lived on beans, rice, and pasta. An image intruded, her father raking the grass of the City and County Building under the WPA of the Depression years. He had tried to hold onto his small grocery store, but people could not pay their accounts. She had avoided taking the streetcar that went past the grounds, unwilling to see him in an old black suit and hat, his face sorrowing. Not until the early fifties when the Kallos business was feverishly building, buying, and leasing did she replace the flatware, ordinary glassware, and heavy dishes bought in the first years of her marriage. She had cared for the new treasures herself, always aware of their expense and that she must pass them on to her daughters in good condition. She gave a little sigh: her daughters would use nothing that could not go into the dishwasher.

It took more than an hour to wash the dishes and crystal; she also had to remove tarnish on the forks. Part way through pressing out the creases on the linen tablecloth, she began to take short breaths and looked with alarm at her greatly swollen ankles. She hoped Steve would not notice.

THE NEXT MORNING, the day before the luncheon, she made the crabcakes, cooked the asparagus, scrubbed the new potatoes, pared and cut a pineapple into spears, washed raspberries, and made a lime-and-honey dressing. Fortunately, Steve had gone to Andrew's office and she did not have to listen to his jeers. She had to go to bed while Sandy, in a green janitor's jumpsuit, dusted, vacuumed, and scrubbed the bathrooms.

"Will you wear a dress tomorrow?" Mary asked later as Sandy was leaving. Sandy shrugged, pursed her lips, deepening the rays of wrinkles around them, and shook her short bleached and perma-nented hair. "Well, I guess I can hustle something up," she said, work-ing her lips about and looking past Mary. Alarm ruffled Mary's heart. She was afraid Sandy might appear in one of the short, full, sequined skirts she wore to the Saturday night country music dances at a bar near the airport. She had come in once wearing such an outfit, and from the look of her smudged lipstick and bleary eyes Mary knew she had probably not gone home but had come straight to work.

That evening, as Mary got ready for bed, Steve called, "Mary!" and again, insistently, "Mary!" Mary put on a robe and hurried down the hall and into Steve's room. She turned on the light. "What's wrong?"

"My shoulder hurts. I can't sleep. Put some Capsolin on it."

"Oh, Steve, I thought something terrible had happened."

"Well, isn't a bad pain in the shoulder that won't let you sleep terrible?"

"All right. Unbutton your pajamas." Mary opened the drawer of the bedside table and searched among various tubes and prescrip-tion bottles for the Capsolin ointment. "The right shoulder?"

"Yeah. I guess so."

"Don't you know?"

"Yes, I know! My right."

With the fingers of her left hand, because her right ones were more arthritic, Mary began making circles of the white ointment up and down and across Steve's shoulder. It seemed strange to her that Steve's stomach was still good sized and yet his shoulders were bony. While her fingers automatically made the circles, she looked around the room: clumps of underclothes, pants, shirts, and socks on the floor; the morning newspaper that Steve took to his room to finish reading flung across the carpet; eyedrop and prescription bottles on the small bedside table—also a coffee cup she had overlooked that morning when she had hung up the clothes and put everything away before Sandy came to clean. A smile was on Steve's lips. She thought of saying something sardonic like, "Well, the Capsolin sure worked in a hurry," but she didn't. Instead she said, "Is that enough?"

"Uh! That feels better. But do the other shoulder while you're at it."

When she finished, Mary looked at Steve. His eyes were closed and the small smile was on his lips. She felt sorry for him: he had never had much of a childhood, so little attention from his overworked mother. She covered him and returned to her room, so fatigued she could not sleep. It was old age, she knew. When she was a young wife, she had given large parties and done everything herself, besides taking care of the children who ran around, complained, and hit each other. She would stop whatever she was doing to have dinner ready the moment Steve came through the door and then stay up beyond midnight to shell shrimp, wash and tear lettuce, do as much preparation for the dinner as she could while the house was quiet.

Down the hall, Steve talked in his sleep.

XVIII

Steve had telephoned Elroy to take him to the Grecian Deli. Although Mary told him the women were not coming for lunch until noon, he wanted to get out of the house by ten o'clock. The Deli was a stucco building painted a sky blue, the color of the Greek flag. Under the eaves a discolored, yellow Greek-key design encircled the walls.

As Elroy drove into the parking lot, he made his usual comment: "Goddamn potholes." The potholes had been there for the past fifteen years, since Theo's friend from Piraeus had opened the delicatessen. Theo had explained his friend Stavros's venture as "we were tough guys in the crazy times, then we got too old and got married, and were forced to settle down."

Steve liked the scents of roasting meats, cheeses, and olives that met a person the moment the door opened. On one side of the store were displays of bottles and cans of imported olives of all kinds, artichokes, pepperoncini, Turkish *loukoum,* anchovies, even snails for Italian customers. A refrigerated display case enclosed feta cheese from Bulgaria, Greece, and France, olives in bulk, and slabs of dried yellow cod. Next to it another display case featured honey-nut pastries. Behind the counter were shelves of bread in large rounds and more pastries.

In an adjoining room a dozen tables were covered with blue-and-white checked oilcloth, each with a bottle of olive oil, vinegar, and steak sauce in the center. The room was empty, except for Theo sitting at a corner table with Stavros. On seeing Steve, Stavros stood up, pulled his tomato-splattered apron tighter by bringing the ties to the front of it, and waved heartily. "What you like Steve? Coffee? Ouzo?" Stavros did not have a liquor license—his delicatessen was too close to a school—but he managed. His body was spare, and in the last several years his hair had thinned; he was now half-bald. He had been a sailor who had jumped ship in San Francisco five years following the Second World War and made his way to Theo. After years of Stavros's furtive anxiety, Steve convinced him to have Andrew send a petition to the immigration officials. He had lived an impeccable life, Andrew had written, leaving out any mention of his first eight years as a *mangas,* as Andreas called the toughs from the Piraeus seaport. The Immigration Services sent Stavros back to Greece and after a few months allowed him to return as a legal alien.

Stavros brought a cup and saucer, a carafe of coffee, and a plate of round honey cookies sprinkled with crushed walnuts. "Toula, she send them. She make them today." Steve glanced toward the counter. Behind it, in the open kitchen Stavros's plump wife waved, and Steve raised his hand in thanks. She turned back to the stove. With a vague salute Stavros joined her to prepare the food for the lunch crowd.

The first day Stavros met Steve, he had said, "Why you changed your name to Steve? Ashamed because Stavros is a Greek name? I never changed my name. You're born Stavros, you stay Stavros."

Steve had told him to plug his mouth. He was never ashamed of being Greek. He didn't even know who changed his name. "If you grew up in America like I did, you'd change your name, too. Even teachers made it hard for immigrant children." Stavros had shaken his head, refusing the explanation.

Steve said, "Good article about you in the *Tribune,* Theo."

Theo looked at him without smiling. He was sitting to one side, his short legs crossed. He looked older than his sixty years, although his curly hair had only a few highlights of gray. His face had become round from cortisone injections for arthritis. "What about this Western Enterprises business? You didn't know anything about it, eh?" he said. Theo leaned over the oilcloth, while Steve took a bite of the *melomacarona* to give himself time. Theo waited. Steve took a sip of coffee, so hot his tongue lost the sense of taste. He looked at Theo, ashamed. "No, I didn't know a goddamn thing about it."

"That's what I thought." Theo's eyes pierced into Steve's. He gave a disgusted snort. "I heard it a week ago and I thought: 'How come Steve didn't say something? Something fishy.'"

"Yes."

"You're mad, huh?"

"I'm goddamn mad."

"What you gonna do?"

"I don't know. We never had anything on paper. Let's see what Andrew says when he comes in."

Theo leaned farther over the table. "So where do you think they got all that money to buy that property? And you didn't know about it?" While Steve fingered the walnut crumbs on the oilcloth, Theo said in a rasping voice, "You know that Greek saying, 'You pee in the sea, you eat it in the salt.'"

Steve's eyebrows went up in surprise. He didn't know if this was a criticism of himself or a prediction of what would happen to Dick and Tommy. He would not ask Theo to explain. Could he have seen or heard something? He wavered between wanting and not wanting to know.

Theo said, "That Uncle Harry of yours and that wife of his, they hated my guts because your old man was nice to me. Afraid I'd get in the business. And Solly should have given me encouragement because I was born in the same village as your old man and Harry. You know all that.

"Tommy—he's not real bad, just puffed up and thinks he's a big businessman, but Con's side of the family—" Theo shook his head. "Con's father and that Myrsini he married, they were the most egotistical people I ever saw. Con was just scared to do anything on his own, but that son of his, that Dick, he's bad—a no-good sonofabitch. When Mary stopped giving those big family dinners, I was glad. I went to them, me and Angie, because out of respect for you and Mary, but to tell the truth, I didn't enjoy them one bit. Me, I was just a poor, uneducated Greek. And they, they used to make remarks about you, kinda like you didn't have it." Theo tapped his temple. "I got mad once and said to them, 'Steve's worked like a mule. I was there. I saw it with my own eyes.'

"Now that I've made lots of money, working like a mule like you and your Dad, now they don't make fun of the way I talk. The way I dress. Not to my face, anyway. No, they want to be friends. They want to take me to lunch. They want me to be on committees to ask people for money for the symphony, things like that. They can all go to hell! I don't even put my hand out to shake their hands." Breathing heavily, he rested, took a sip of cold coffee, poured what was left of it into the saucer, and filled the cup from the carafe. He looked at Steve. "They better not get away with it."

Steve sat, a blunted look in his eyes. He shook his head to alert himself. "Yes," he said, "They hate my guts. Dick especially. I see it in their eyes. They didn't get the reports out last week and I told them they needed a shot of kerosene up their asshole."

Theo burst out laughing. "Greeks say that all the time. *'Petrelion ano ton kolo.'*"

Andrew came up to the table and sat down. "What's funny?" he asked, although Steve was not laughing. Theo repeated what Steve had said, then the Greek words, as if Andrew knew them. He lifted his arms up and let them drop. "What can your dad do about this monkey business?"

"They're within their rights," Andrew said. "They never had contracts among themselves."

"It was understood," Steve said with a thump on the table that rattled the cups. "It was understood. We were a family."

Theo and Andrew looked at each other. Theo said, "So, where are we? We know all about Block 325."

"We don't know where the bastards got the money." Steve clamped his mouth, his face a deep red.

"How you gonna find out?" Theo asked.

Andrew pulled on his chin. His voice was weary. "Dad thinks we might find something in *Papou's* old rolltop desk. And then there are the files."

"How you go about goin' through the desk and the files with those assholes Tommy and Dick down the hall?"

"We'd have to do it at night," Andrew said.

Andrew's tired voice and the pulled-down folds on either side of his mouth bewildered Steve. A faint, yet familiar clutching began in his stomach. He did not know what to think. He raised his voice. "Don't you give a good goddamn about finding out what those goons did?"

"I care, Dad, but I also know we can go through everything and spend weeks on the books and not find a thing."

"There's got to be something there!"

"Dad, you know as much as I do that a lot of your business was talked out and not put on paper."

"What the hell! Do I have to defend myself?"

Theo signaled to Steve, palms down, telling him to lower his voice. Andrew said, "My theory is they did it under the table. And it all started with Uncle Harry. When they bought or sold, he'd make deals, part paid to him in cash. The same with the leases. He made deals. He had a front man."

Steve lifted his hands and let them drop on the table. It came to him: Uncle Harry and the shady detective Milt Valiotis who knew everybody in the City and County Building, knew all the politicians. Milt was the front man. Yes, that's how it had all come about. And they were dead. He couldn't go to them and grab them by the throat and scare the Jesus out of them. He lifted his head. He could not tell Andrew and Theo that he had never looked into their friendship— Uncle Harry standing on the sidewalk, handing Milt a wad of money; Milt coming to see Uncle Harry in his office and closing the door behind him. Aloud he said to Andrew, "Why the hell didn't you tell me you suspected this shit was going on?"

"Because I didn't know about Block 325 until Monday morning."

Steve put his elbows on the table and rested his head in his upraised palms. "Oh, my God! That's how it happened. I knew Uncle Harry was a no-good sonofabitch, but never, never did I think he'd go that far." He waited a moment before he said, "It was him and Milt Valiotis."

"What about Con? After his old man died—his soul be cursed," Theo said in Greek, "what about Con?"

Both Steve and Andrew shook their heads at the same time. "We'll never know," Steve said. "But Uncle Harry trained Dick. He was under orders from Aunt Myrsini. He bypassed Con—knew Con couldn't cut the mustard—and trained his little shitass grandson. He had him in the office when he was still in junior high."

Theo nodded, pulling down the corners of his mouth.

"I'm not taking this lying down," Steve said in a loud voice that brought Stavros to the pass-through window. "I'm not going to my grave without getting revenge. I don't know how or where, but I'll get my revenge."

"You better be careful, Dad. That's just a theory. I could be wrong."

"How could it be wrong? That's the only explanation."

"How about Uncle Solly?"

"That sonofabitch! That bastard!"

"It's too far in the past, Dad."

In his village dialect, Theo intoned an old proverb: "'After the fox is in the vineyard, it's too late to close the gate.'"

Steve's face reddened, darkened. "One of you take me home. I got to get home."

"I said I'd take you home," Theo said, barely glancing at Steve, as if he regretted casting the criticism, "and I'll take you home."

Outside, just before he closed the door to Theo's car, Andrew leaned down and said, "Dad, don't let this get to you." He lowered his voice: "We want you alive."

Steve jerked his head forward and looked straight ahead while Theo drove block after block. "We'll find something, Steve. Don't worry. We'll find something."

Steve did not answer for a few minutes. "You work like a jackass all your life. Bust your guts. Think you're doing the right thing. And it all ends up *skata*. You know what I mean, Theo? *Skata*."

"Don't let them make you sick. They're not worth it."

"Oh, God, if I were twenty years younger! Even fifteen."

As they drove up the long brick lane, Theo said, "I won't come in. Go to bed. We'll have another meeting tomorrow. It's not over."

Steve groaned: Magdalene's old Buick, Penny's Cadillac, and Tessie's Mercedes were parked in the circular driveway. "Jesus Christ! I forgot Mary's got my sisters and Tessie and Magdalene visiting."

"Okay. I'll take you back to my office. You can look at the TV and rest on the couch."

"No, I can't. I'll sneak in the back way and go to my room." Steve raised his hand in good-bye, took a few steps toward the side entrance to the house, realized his legs were unsteady and that he had forgotten his cane in Theo's car. He looked at the little black bird and the bird looked at him. He was afraid to go into the house: the women might see him and he could not stand the thought. He made his way around the garage, pressing his palm on the brick, walked to the rose garden, and sat on the redwood bench.

Noise buzzed in his head, heavy as if his neck could not hold it up. He thought he would vomit, thought of Andrew's hesitancy to go forward, of Theo's old proverb about the fox in the vineyard that pointed blame at him. Another Greek proverb Theo often used came to him: "The fish stinks from the head." He gave a sob: did Theo think he was like the fishhead?

XIX

THE MORNING OF the luncheon, Mary was tired when she woke up. She showered and sat with Sandy to drink decaffeinated tea and eat a Danish pastry. Sandy was wearing an orange-satin cowboy shirt and a bright green skirt that came above her wrinkled knees. Mary then went out to the rose garden with a basket and scissors. Sparkles of dew were on the roses and the freshness of moist grass was in the clear air. Her fatigue vanished. She cut a bouquet of pink daylilies for the tall vase on the living room coffee table, yellow roses for the cut-glass bowl, and white ones for the Depression vases. As she returned to the kitchen, she thought she saw the little black bird at the far end of the rose garden. She arranged the flowers, the scent of roses pleasing, satisfying to her, then walked through the house, looking about to make certain everything was in order.

As soon as Steve left with Elroy, she had hung up his clothes, made the bed, and put the underwear, strewn over the floor, into the hamper in the adjoining bathroom. Mary knew the women would not go into Steve's room, but she could not feel free to attend to the luncheon with a vision of Steve's room in disorder.

She went back to the kitchen, reheated the crabcakes in the top oven on low heat, and roasted the boiled new potatoes in the bottom one. She asked Sandy to stay until after the luncheon and had her fill a pitcher with ice water, prepare the decaffeinated coffee, and defrost an applesauce cake she had stored in the freezer. She baked the cakes regularly for Andrew and Jim. Looking at the cake, she decided it did not seem festive enough and told Sandy to drive to a grocery store to buy several packages of cream cheese. When Sandy returned, Mary whipped the cheese with milk. "Place a dollop on each slice of cake just before you serve it," she told Sandy and reminded her to serve from the left and remove from the right. "Well, what'd yuh know?" Sandy said in her rough voice, forgetting that Mary had given her the same instructions the day before. "Never heard nothin' like that when I waited tables at the Cowboys and Rustlers."

Mary arranged the pineapple spears with sprinkles of raspberries on plates and put them into the refrigerator. By the time the potatoes were ready, the doorbell rang. She hurried, her breath coming in short pants, and reminded herself as she walked that everything was ready and looked inviting. She opened the door: Penny and Georgie walked in, giving Mary the usual cheek-to-cheek greeting. Penny's hair was dyed a silvery blonde; and Georgie's a jet-black. Mary thought they looked as if they had just stepped out of a hairdresser's shop—so many women looked like that to her lately. Penny and Georgie no longer seemed to have waists under the silk shirtdresses they were wearing.

"It's been a long time since we've been here," Penny said, her cheeks sagging at the corners of her mouth. Mary saw she was in one of her depressed moods and ignored the tone of blame. Georgie said nothing, merely looked about with her black, crazy eyes, as Steve called them. Her face, the facelift notwithstanding, looked drawn forward—minimized, like a little animal's.

Mary remained in the doorway. "Sit down, girls," Mary said— Steve's sisters were still referred to as "the girls." "Tessie's parking her car."

Georgie said sharply, "The Mercedes?" Mary nodded.

Tessie got out of her shiny, bronze-colored Mercedes. She waited for Magdalene to drive up the lane in her ten-year-old Buick and park next to her car. Tessie was wearing a green-silk suit with a long jacket that concealed her protruding stomach skillfully. As Tessie waited for Magdalene to get out of the car, her face looked sad or, Mary thought, just old. We're all old, she thought. Dyed hair and facelifts can't change that.

"Is Steve here?" Georgie demanded, behind her.

Mary turned her head to answer. "No, he's having lunch with Theo."

"Oh, lunch with Theo," Georgie repeated with faint insolence —so faint that a person had to have learned to recognize it, as Mary had.

Magdalene had trouble getting out of her car, and Mary thought that if she lost weight it would be easier for her. Also she was dressed as if she were getting ready to garden or use a hose on her patio. Magdalene's wide face, almost without a wrinkle or dewlap, had her perpetual smile stuck on it. Mary had often wondered if she smiled when she was alone. Magdalene's hair was cut shorter than when she had seen her on the mezzanine floor of the church; it was still straight, with a little bang.

She went out to meet Magdalene and Tessie. A whiff of sweet perfume accompanied Tessie. The three of them gave each other half-hugs and Mary led them into the living room. The four women greeted each other with warm little cries as if they were friends. Tessie was vivacious; Magdalene kept her smiling reserve on her face, which still showed a vestige of having been beautiful.

"The house looks nice," Tessie said, giving a swift look about as she sat on a chair with needlepointed tapestry. Mary had worked on it decades previously. Magdalene sat on a companion chair on the other side of the sofa.

"I haven't bought new furniture since 1968," Mary said with a rueful look around the living room. "Christine and Alexandra make a few changes here and there when they come to visit in the summer." Her daughters had taken down the reproduction of lilacs in a brass bowl and replaced it with an oil by a local artist, a grove of autumn-gold aspen at the foot of Mount Olympus. They gave several pieces of furniture to the Disabled American Veterans: a thick-legged cherrywood coffee table, end tables, and all the heavy chairs except their father's favorite. Tall Chinese vases appeared on the marble mantel and on the grand piano. The Spanish shawl on the piano became a Halloween costume for one of the granddaughters. Mary allowed her daughters to do what they pleased: she thought that as college graduates they had better taste than she. She did feel a pang when the pink-shaded bisque lamps of a little boy in pantaloons holding hands with a small girl had been given to one of her cleaning women; in their stead stood glass columns with plain, white-silk shades.

Tessie waved her hand across her face. "I just redid my entire living room. I'm just exhausted working with my interior decorator. Finally I just said to him, 'Jon, you have such good taste. Just do what you want.'" Her dark eyes glinted merrily, reminding Mary of Tessie as a child in Greek Town. "Of course, he charged me plenty, but if you want the best, you pay for it."

Magdalene asked her, "What kind of furniture did you get?"

Tessie again waved her right hand, diamonds on three fingers: her large engagement ring, which had been traded in for a larger one three times, and two smaller ones that had belonged to her mother-in-law Aunt Myrsini. The women would not look at her hand. "This time, I just said to Jon, 'Jon, I'm tired of this period stuff. Let's do something different.' And he did. All Danish furniture. And then, you know, the vases and lamps and things didn't go with the furniture!" Tessie leaned forward and with upraised hands made a motion as if she were throwing a basketball from the free-throw line; she meant to convey the inevitable—that nothing could be done but to get all new finery. "You'll all have to come and see it."

Georgie's eyebrows met. "What's that perfume you're wearing?"

"It's—it's, oh, I've forgotten the name and I just bought it two days ago. . . ." She turned to Mary. "After helping with the festival, when I picked up Samantha, we stopped at Nordstrom's and I even bought an ounce for her, too."

Penny looked at Tessie with dull eyes. "Isn't Dick's wife good at interior decorating? I think I saw something on her in the Sunday paper."

Tessie stopped talking and looked away, blinking.

Penny and Georgie leaned their heads toward each other. Magdalene kept her eyes on Tessie. Mary wondered how her face could look so placid after having been married to Solly for fifty-five years. "How are your grandchildren, Tessie?" Magdalene asked.

Tessie began a long litany, jiggling as she talked, of her grand-children's accomplishments. Mary glanced at Tessie with her usual annoyance, but it quickly softened into indulgence: Tessie hadn't changed since they were girls. "Why don't we go into the dining room and continue our visit there," Mary said. The women stood up, Penny struggling. "This awful arthritis," she said.

Mary took Penny's elbow and helped her to her feet. "I guess we all have *gherammata*," Mary said, and the women chimed in: "I'm wearing trifocals now," from Penny; "I don't sleep more than three or four hours a night," from Georgie; "I can't wear real high heels anymore," from Tessie; "We have to be philosophical," from Magdalene.

The women looked at the table for several seconds before tak-ing their seats. Mary had told Sandy to serve ten minutes after the women arrived, and the gold-banded Lenox plates with the crab-cakes, asparagus, and new potatoes were in place. Near the tip of each fork was a fruit salad. Sandy had filled the Baccarat goblets with ice water and the wineglasses held Merlot—Mary had heard that Merlot was the wine of the moment. "What a beautiful table," Magdalene said, "the flowers and everything. You've gone to so much trouble."

Tessie's perfume overcame the delicate scent of the roses. It piqued Mary, this alien intrusion. She asked the women to sit wher-ever they liked, and then she felt a squeeze in her chest. She had not thought about whether they should say a prayer. They might think her old-fashioned. She glanced at Magdalene, wishing she would make the decision. Magdalene's lips were moving, then she made the sign of the cross. In Greek, Mary said the traditional *"Kalos erthate,"*—You've come well—and Magdalene and Tessie answered, *"Kalos sus vrikame,"*—We find you well. All except Georgie made the sign of the cross. The women began eating. "I haven't had crab-cakes in ages," Magdalene said, her voice pleasant but remote.

Tessie said, "The New Yorker makes the best in town." Then a lull descended on the room.

Quickly Mary said, "This glass bowl was given to my mother by her best man at her wedding and the little vases are what they call Depression glass."

Georgie turned to Penny. "What happened to the Depression dishes we got Mama? Those green dishes?"

Penny shrugged. "I have no idea."

They both turned their heads and looked at Mary, who said, her voice light, "Don't look at me. I didn't take them."

"Well," Georgie kept her eyes on Mary, "when Mama and Papa moved in with you, what happened to the dishes?"

"They didn't bring anything with them," Mary said, then realizing her voice had sharpened, she smiled. "You know your mother was giving things away for years before she came to live with us."

"I don't remember that." Penny wrinkled her forehead and cocked her head as if she were trying to remember.

"She gave a lot of things to some Greek families who came here after the war," Magdalene said, and Penny and Georgie gave her peevish looks as if she, a daughter-in-law, knew something that they, the daughters, were unaware of.

"Now I remember!" Mary said. "When we started having the big festivals at church, we had that white-elephant booth. Yes, I remember." She nodded to Penny and Georgie, "That's where the Depression dishes ended up."

"I don't remember anything about that," Georgie said with a stab at a crabcake. "I'd liked them for my girls."

Magdalene nodded and smiled. "We don't think about those things at the time, then wish we had."

Georgie frowned at her. Another lull followed. "I've enjoyed going through the old snapshots," Mary said. "But it's kind of sad to see the kids in the family grown up and having children of their own. You think of all the things that can happen to them."

"Like growing old and dying," Penny said.

Magdalene smiled. "They used to have so much fun when they were little, playing together." She looked forlorn to Mary. "But time doesn't stand still."

Georgie's voice turned harsh like her mother's as she grew older. "Now the kids never see each other."

"Well," Tessie said, "Dick sees Tommy every day, and he sees Andrew once in a while downtown."

Penny leaned over her plate with a sudden show of interest. "You mean Dick and Andrew have lunch together?"

"Oh, you know, they sometimes eat in the same restaurants."

"But not together?" Georgie said with a glare.

Mary remembered Georgie's old complaints that her children had "always been left out." She said, "I forgot to pass the dressing for the salad. You might want a little more." She handed a small cut-glass pitcher to Magdalene. "It's very good. What's in it?" Magdalene asked.

"Olive oil, lime juice, and honey."

"I'll have to remember that."

Penny took the pitcher from Magdalene. "What are we going to do with all the things we've accumulated? Young people won't use them. They won't bother with anything that can't go into the dishwasher."

Magdalene gave a benign, sideways nod. "Maybe some of the grandchildren will. What's that saying: 'What the children discard, the grandchildren take up?' Something like that."

"That means culture," Penny said, and Magdalene smiled and said, "Oh."

"No, the grandchildren won't want our china and sterling or anything else." Penny's voice turned strident. "It's the sixties that did it. All those hippies supposedly living off the land. Driving all over the country in vans bought by their stupid parents. I didn't put up with any of that sexual liberation and that feminist stuff. Marijuana. Sleeping all over the place like dogs."

"Anyway, it's nice to sit down and be served like this." Tessie smiled warmly at Mary. "Like we used to. Our best china and every-thing."

Mary laughed from the strain of keeping the conversation going and within bounds. "I sometimes can't believe the entertain-ing we did. All that cooking for the freezer. I started a month before Steve's nameday and all of the holidays. And getting the house and the tableclcoths and silver ready!" She laughed. "I'm certainly out of practice."

"We're just too old to do that kind of entertaining." Tessie shrugged her shoulders. "No matter how much help we have."

Georgie sneered. "You were all nuts. I got the drift after a few years and gave it up."

Penny turned to her. "We know, Georgie, we know, but you still went to everybody else's dinners."

Georgie snorted. "Oh, you."

Mary let not a second elapse. "If you're all finished we'll have dessert."

"Dessert, too? This is a banquet." Tessie clasped her diamond-studded hands and glanced happily at the others around the table.

Mary picked up a few plates and returned with Sandy. "Sandy, these ladies are my sisters-in-law. Sandy is a big help to me."

"Hi," Sandy said, and reached to take Magdalene's plate from the left, remembered, clicked her teeth, and removed it from the right. Sandy then brought in the plates of applesauce cake topped with artful swirls of whipped cream cheese on top—she had worked up to being in charge of desserts at the Cowboys and Rustlers. The women said they shouldn't be eating the cake, what with their cholesterol, but they ate it all. They then talked about where the best pastries could be bought; no decision was reached. For a while, the women drank their decaffeinated coffee without talking.

Then Georgie said that she heard Tina Livadias's husband was carrying on with his secretary. None of the others had heard any-thing about it and Georgie looked disappointed.

Penny said she would not contribute any money to the new church addition. "I'm just not going to. Last Holy Week on Good Friday afternoon services, I was appalled at the way the kids were dressed. Girls in Levi's. Two of them in shorts! Chewing gum. Talking to each other. And some mothers, younger than us, of course, in pantsuits. I couldn't believe it."

In a quiet voice, Magdalene said, "The children come right from school. The priests tell them to come as they are for this one service."

"Well, that did it for me. I'm not giving them a dime for the addition."

Mary reverted to her patient manner when talking with Steve's sisters. "But, Penny, we've never given individually. The company always makes the big donations."

"Well! There's not going to be much of a Greek church left, if that's how the kids act."

Georgie snapped. "I hear Father Symeon makes a big fuss about homosexuals."

"Yes." Mary sighed. "He lumps them together—sin and homosexuals."

Penny scoffed. "What else do they teach them in seminary anyway?"

Tessie looked uncertain. Magdalene said nothing.

They finished the coffee and the lull came down hard and long. They talked about the weather.

Mary stood up. "Let's go into the living room where it's more comfortable."

Tessie said she had to leave: she had promised Samantha she would buy her new outfits for school and the stores had just brought in their fall clothes. "They bring in the school clothes earlier and earlier each year. I hate to leave, but Samantha is waiting for me and you know how impatient children are."

As if this were a signal, everyone rose and each said she should leave also. Magdalene had to stop at the nursing home; Penny and Georgie wanted to see a movie. Mary handed them the bulging manila envelopes. Tessie put her envelope down while she stirred the contents of her purse for car keys, then she walked out behind Magdalene, Penny, and Georgie. Mary picked up the envelope and followed the women to their cars. As Tessie unlocked the door of her Mercedes, Mary handed her the envelope. "Gee! I'm getting so absent-minded," Tessie said.

As one car after the other turned onto the brick lane, Mary waved. She stood looking down the long drive: the women hadn't thanked her for the snapshots. Her body felt hollowed out and empty. All her work had meant nothing. The little black bird had come within a few feet of her. She wondered what the women were thinking, what they would do with the snapshots.

PENNY HAD PLACED her manila envelope on the floor in the back of the car. She had taken most of the snapshots herself, first with the little Brownie Kodak and then with increasingly more expensive cameras, the last one a Leica. She did not want to look at the snapshots: they would make her remember her young years, when her mother called her a cow whenever she fell or dropped things. Worse, when Aunt Myrsini was around, pretending she was showing her how to present herself as a refined young woman, but a moment later, looking at her with disgust, saying, "You're hopeless. Look at Gheorghia. Look at your sister. Why can she learn and you can't? Not even a peasant would want you for a wife."

She didn't want to see pictures of old Greek Town, especially their lean-to house. She was ashamed to have lived there, cooped up with her parents, brothers, sister, Uncle Harry, and the icemen. She had wanted to take piano lessons, but she had never said a word about it. The money had to go into the business, the buying of property. Maybe her mother would have seen to it, but she wasn't sure. It was always "getting married," "getting married," "getting married" from her. How stupid she'd been with her snapshots no one looked at a second time. At least her yardman was pleased with the Leica she'd given him one Christmas.

At Mary's house, Penny had risen out of her gray listlessness for most of the hour and a half, but now she slid back into it. Everything had become an ordeal: a telephone call from a neighbor who had moved away; what she should eat for dinner; a letter she should write. Her colorless daily routine nauseated her, but she preferred her colorless existence. She had thought that when her husband Joe died, life would be fun: she would give dinner parties; she would go on trips without the bland little man she had married. Instead, she slid into the grayness so deeply she could not get out. She did not want to get out. She did not want to look at snapshots and remember. She thought the food she had eaten at Mary's had dumped undigested into her bowels. She thought of it fizzing, churning. What, she thought, if she did not make it to the bathroom? It had happened twice. Oh, she wailed silently, old age, this awful old age. As soon as she got home, she would throw the envelope into the trash can.

WHILE PENNY DROVE, Georgie rummaged through her envelope. "All these old snapshots," she said with a bitter hiss. "Nothing's turned out the way I thought it would. The children grow up and have their own lives and think we're such a burden. Oh, they don't say it, but that's what they think." She became silent, thinking of the stuck-up man she had married who thought she was a peasant —Taki, thinking that his Greek education made him so superior to her and her family.

She did not want to see the pictures of the old house with its outdoor bread oven, the rabbit hutches, the chicken pen, the privy. She did not want to remember the icemen who used the new lean-to bathroom as part of the family. She had abhorred their using the toilet; the bathtub they infrequently filled up. Their smell disgusted her; she sometimes threw up when she had to use the toilet. She'd balk, refuse to go in, then suffer horrible pains inside and her mother would force her to swallow tablespoonsful of olive oil. There was no reason that they had to live with the icemen. And her mother took it; didn't say a word about the icemen living with them, taking away their privacy. All so her father could buy more property. The property —that's what was important.

She had intended asking Penny to stop at the bank to cash a check, but she did not want to do that now, and she did not want to go to a movie. She wanted to return to her house immediately. With frantic eagerness she wanted to look at the snapshots. They would give her fodder to prove that they, Steve, Mary, Solly, Magdalene, Tessie, and Con, had taken advantage of the business. They had a bigger share in the profits. Taki used to say it, and though she was glad he was dead, in this one area he was right. The snapshots would give her clues.

Besides, the snapshots would show forty, no, fifty-year-old mountain picnics, celebrations in the church basement and later in the memorial hall. She would see herself all dressed up, trying to pretend she was above having some boy—"dippy," she and Penny had called the young men they had attended Greek school with—come loping over to ask for a dance, looking ashamed, prodded no doubt by mothers and grandmothers. There certainly would be pictures of family dinners in the backyard that included a young man, a stranger from New York, Chicago, or San Francisco, who'd come to look her over. Afterwards, her mother would scream at her for thinking she was too good for the stranger. "Your nose up in the air. You'll be left an old maid! No daughter to care for you in your old age. People will say we haven't done our duty by you, hadn't found you a husband! If they only knew what a twisted stick you are!" But she would not and Penny could not—their pride would not let them—be looked at, evaluated, matched up, and married off as if they were merchandise. Oh, but Steve and Solly could go out, stay late, while she and Penny had to listen to the *Hit Parade* for their entertainment.

No, better not, Georgie decided; she did not want to look at the snapshots to see herself young and pretty and remind her of her old age. She did not want to see Taki and herself as they had been forty, fifty years ago, when she thought Taki knew what he was talking about. She had been so easily convinced by his derogatory remarks about people, usually men like Steve who had done well, who had made money. Because she knew now that all the excuses Taki had made for his not getting ahead were just that—excuses. He would never have done better, no matter what. And those snide remarks he made about her parents, smiling as he said them so that when she confronted him he could say he was only teasing. Better to throw the snapshots in the garbage.

MAGDALENE THOUGHT she would not give Tom any of the snapshots. She wouldn't even look at them. All the pictures taken in the houses of Solly's parents, sisters, and brothers when she came as a bride in her Red Cross uniform would remind her of how naive she had been. They would remind her that she had left her parents' orderly house and married into a shouting, warring family of people who thought they were special because they had made money—people who stretched the truth when it suited them, who condemned outsiders for no good reason, and who spoke village Greek. She would remember that dinner table, erupting in bombast, with scatological talk from Solly's father—and Solly's mother, so sure that the daughters-in-law would get more of everything than her daughters.

Solly had liked to have Penny take his picture and there would be plenty of him in the envelope, especially around the pool. She thought she had forgiven him for all the humiliations he had inflicted on her, for all the insults he thought she had been ignorant of. She hadn't been able to tell anyone, not even the priests. She went to Christ. He had said, "Come unto me, all ye that are heavy laden, and I will give you rest." From then on she attended every Sunday liturgy, every saint's day service listed in the church bulletin; she fasted the forty days of Lent as her grandmother had done—no dairy foods, meat, or fish. She attended the church and a neighborhood nondenominational Bible Study class. She had led the neighborhood class for the last five years.

After saying the Lord's Prayer at her icons each night, she went to bed and three times repeated the Jesus prayer: "Lord Jesus Christ, Son of God, have mercy on me a sinner." She made generous contributions to all the church organizations, both important and unimportant to her: collections for famines, earthquakes, and genocides far off; choir, Sunday school programs, junior and senior oratory contests, summer camps, and the Greek school, which she knew could never last another generation.

Whenever Solly's sisters had told funny anecdotes about him, she smiled and told herself to cleanse herself of hate: She must be righteous in all things if she wanted to become Christ-like. She reminded herself that Jesus said we must forgive not seven times, but seventy times seven. Even while telling herself that she had forgiven Solly, she despised the sight of him. She worked to become a true Christian and she kept repeating this aim to herself. She took tranquilizers.

After Solly was put in a nursing home, she stopped taking the tranquilizers, but the respite was short. Tommy's wife Sally came to her, screeching, pulling her hair, her howling mouth revealing flawless teeth and a pink, curled tongue. Tom had a lover, a young man. Magdalene was not surprised; she had wondered if Sally knew. Ten years back, Magdalene had seen Tommy kiss a young man on the mouth at a family Christmas party. She had seen the look in Tommy's eyes as he pulled back and gazed at the other man.

That day ten years ago Magdalene had held her daughter-in-law's beautifully cared for hands as she cried. "And I thought it was my fault! All the time it was my fault he didn't come near me! I went to the gym every day! I had the pouches under my eyes fixed! I went to the hairdresser's twice a week! But it was him! Him! And he let me think it was me! Me!"

Magdalene said nothing while Sally sobbed. When she quieted, she asked what she would do. She would not divorce him. The children loved him. "What will you do with your life?" Magdalene asked. Sally shook her head, her tear-reddened face looking suddenly old. Magdalene put an arm around Sally's shoulders. "Then do what I always did. Take tranquilizers."

She would throw the envelope into the trash can when she got home. Then she would light the vigil taper before the icon of the Virgin and Child. She would ask forgiveness, look into their Semitic eyes, and as she did every day, beg Them to help her believe in Them.

TESSIE INTENDED to do more than throw the manila envelope into the trash: she would burn it in the fireplace. She would even take out the snapshots so she could see the flames devour her parents-in-law, especially her mother-in-law—she, who had made her tremble, who had made all the decisions. Only once did she defy her; she had said she would not go to Greece with her, Con, and Dick after Heracles died. Myrsini did not insist. Of course not, she was ashamed of her. She didn't want to introduce her to her Athenian family. Dick was ashamed of her, too. Who knows what Con thought?

Tessie's cheeks trembled; her eyes blurred. They hadn't asked her, not Con's mother and father, nor Con. They came into her private room on the maternity floor and told her about the baby. Myrsini did all the talking while Heracles nodded and Con looked stunned. The baby was a girl; her brain was not like other babies. The doctor said Down's Syndrome babies did not live long. What they had done, Myrsini said, was have the priest baptize the baby and then put her in a foster home. They would tell people that the baby was stillborn. "It's not as if you don't have a child already. You have one and a boy at that."

Tessie had seen the baby once: she had shiny black hair and red cheeks; her little tongue protruded. Tessie made no reply to her mother-in-law; her head was frozen. When she returned home from the hospital, she began to think. She thought about the baby throughout the days and sleepless nights. She wondered if she were being cared for, if she were left to cry, in soiled diapers, never picked up, never held. She wondered what name the baby had been given at baptism; surely not the name of the father's mother, as was the custom. No, Myrsini would not give the defective baby her own name. She had wanted to tell Mary, tell her everything, but she was so afraid Con's mother would find out.

On holidays she could not get out of bed, no matter that her mother-in-law came into her room and said in patrician Greek, "Get up! What is the meaning of this? You have your little Niko to take care of. Hurry. The table is set." Tessie would turn her weeping face away from Myrsini. Each year on the baby's birthday, she wanted to kill herself, to take pills or cut herself, but only God could take a life, the priests said again and again. Her fear of Myrsini turned into a hard knot of hate and she tended it as a gift for her nameless little girl.

She began shopping every day and it helped, while she went from store to store. Often, though, she saw a child like hers with slanted eyes, thick tongue, and little nose. If the child had shiny black hair, she followed, trying to get a better look, furtively glancing at the mother: Other mothers had kept such babies. She returned to her house and sobbed in her closed bedroom.

Con had begun sleeping in the guest bedroom even before she came back from the hospital. The first night, she howled in the darkness and Con came to the door. The hall light behind him outlined his slender figure in a dressing gown. "What is it?" "Nothing. Leave me alone!" and he did. Tessie pressed on the gas pedal. She could hardly wait to get to her house to burn her mother-in-law's pictures in the fireplace, watch that face curl and char in the flames.

XX

MARY WAS STANDING in front of him. "Are the women gone?"

"What's wrong, Steve?"

"Are the women gone?"

"Yes."

"Were they glad to get the pictures you spent all that time on?" Steve's voice began with sarcasm, but ended in a whisper.

"Better tell me what's wrong. I know something's bothering you and has been for days." Mary sat next to him on the bench. She repeated, but in a lighter tone of voice, "Steve, what's bothering you?"

A torrent of garbled words burst from Steve's mouth: "Western Enterprises . . . Uncle Harry . . . Educated Witch . . . Con . . . Dick . . . Block 325, since 1958, before, before from the thirties, even the twenties . . . Milt Valiotis, five million dollars . . . Synoris . . . sneakysonofbitchinbastards, maybe Solly, Tommy too." Then he sat back, his face drained, gray, sweat stippling his forehead, dripping down the sides of his face.

He waited for the words: "You wouldn't listen. Anyone could see. But who am I? Only a woman, only your wife, not even a blood relative!" The words did not come. Steve waited, looking at Mary as she sat with her hands folded on her lap, a pensive look on her face. Still she said nothing and he needed to hear the bitter, abusive words. Then she lifted her head and said quietly, "It's too late, Steve."

He stood up with such force that the redwood bench moved. If he had a pebble he would have thrown it at the little black bird a short distance away, looking at them. "That's not what I want to hear," he shouted with a sob in his voice. He tottered.

"Where's your cane?" Mary screamed.

"That's it! I'm going to catch Dick in the office! I'm gonna tell him I know all about his sonofabitchin' Western Enterprises! Either buy me out or I'll buy them out! That's what I'll tell him! I'll kick his ass from here to Timbucktoo! Get your car out!" With his hands held out in front of him, as if he were walking in the dark, he made his way to the kitchen. Mary followed, her arms reaching, ready to support him.

At the kitchen table he collapsed on a chair and dialed Andrew on the cellular telephone. "I'm going down to the office to have it out with Dick! Either they buy me out or I buy them out!"

"Dad, you know that's easier said than done. Anyway, Dick has a standing golf game this afternoon with his friend the judge. Remember? You told me you could never find him on Wednesday afternoons. Let's talk about it before you do anything."

"What's there to talk about! You said yourself there's nothing in black and white. You couldn't find anything to nail the bastard! What can we prove? Everybody's dead."

Steve was gasping for air when he hung up. "Mary! Something's wrong with me. I can't breathe! Take me to Emergency."

Mary opened a kitchen drawer and took out a paper sack. "That won't help," Steve said, his chest moving up and down in shallow rises and falls.

"Here. Breathe into this bag. You know, how the doctor told you." She gathered the top of the bag, leaving an opening.

"That won't help, I tell you!"

Mary put the bag against Steve's mouth. "Breathe into it, in and out. In and out."

Steve glared at her but took the bag and began breathing into it. His hands shook. After several minutes he put the bag on the table and wiped his forehead and face with tissues Mary held out to him. "It's getting old. That's what it is." He would not look at Mary. "I can't take this shit. I'll go lay down for a while." Mary filled a glass with ice water for him.

He couldn't sleep. After a half hour, he returned to the kitchen, opened a drawer where he kept pads and pencils, and took writing materials to the table. Mary was cooking and glancing at him. "I'm gonna be prepared, Mary. Anything he brings up, I've got the answers. Him and that asshole Tommy." He filled pages, and as he wrote, he began to smile, to relish what he was doing.

Mary said, "Let it go, Steve. You'll end up with a stroke or something."

"Get off my back!"

Andrew walked in. "Once and for all I'm gonna have it out with those bastards!" Steve shouted at him.

"You can't pin anything on them, Dad. The days when people shook hands over a deal are gone."

"We didn't have to shake hands! It was understood! We were family! How many times do I have to tell you that?"

Andrew leaned against the back of the chair, crossed his arms, looked at his father, but said nothing. Steve flared up. "At least I'll have the satisfaction of telling them to go to hell! After I've told them I know all the underhanded shitty things they had going!"

"That's history. If you were going to do something, you had to do it fifty years back. Not now when you're more than eighty years old."

Steve clamped his hands on his head and rocked back and forth, then sideways. "We were family! Don't you understand what I'm telling you? Are you that thick-headed?"

Andrew did not answer. "Better forget the idea of buying each other out." he said. "Sure, if you cashed in all your investments. And God knows they're in no position to buy you out. If either of you go to the bank to borrow—oh, Dad, all that takes time."

"I'm not going to put up with those shitasses one more minute! Do you hear what I'm saying!"

"Dad, you have to remember your age. You can't take over at your age. If you were twenty years younger, it'd still be hard."

"I don't want to hear another word from you!" Steve shouted and struggled to his feet.

"Theo and Jim and I are having lunch at the Grecian Deli tomorrow morning at eleven thirty. We want to talk about it some more. See you there, Dad."

"That depends, goddamn it!" Steve plunged out of the kitchen. In his room, he picked up the yellow-lined pad and wrote more accusations, more recriminations. When Mary called him to come to the table, he said nothing; his brain was sparking epiphanies: Uncle Harry . . . his father, a workhorse like himself . . . Aunt Myrsini . . . the nephews. . . .

They watched television, a rerun of a country-music program, and the late news. "Look at those Serbs and Croats, those Bosnians," Steve said, breaking the silence, "always at each other's throats. They haven't any sense." Medicare was going bankrupt an official warned. A man had been badly beaten outside his house. No sign of robbery. Police would not identify the man or speculate further. "Probably carrying on with someone else's wife," Steve said with a snort.

The next morning, they quarreled. "Don't go!" Mary said in a begging tone Steve had never heard before. "You'll lose your temper and end up sick. You'll end up in an ambulance."

"Are you gonna drive me or should I call Elroy?"

Mary turned her face from Steve and after a moment said, "I'll drive you."

When Steve came out of the house, Mary was sprinkling bread crumbs on the front walk. "What are you doing?"

"I'm putting out some breads crumbs for that little black bird that's been about."

"Well, I don't see him. I guess he's lost and can't get his bearings."

"There he is. By that grove of scrub oak."

Mary clasped her hands against her waist. Her eyes were afraid.

"Well, what?" Steve said, frowning, his face red.

"It's too late, Steve. It's water under the bridge."

"When I show them these facts," Steve patted the yellow notebook, "they won't have a leg to stand on. It's all here in black and white. All their mistakes. All their failures. I'll save their fucking Western Enterprises for last. I'll hit them with it!"

"Don't use that word to me. Maybe they have some grievances against you they can trot out."

"Me! What can they say about me? I've worked like a jackass all these years! That's what they can say about me. The investments I've made are giving them all a pretty good living. Let them contradict me on that! Those bastards! Them and their fancy consultants. Wouldn't think of picking up the telephone to make a few calls and save the company money. No, they have to have someone else make them. They're too important to do that themselves. And that's my money they're spending!"

"All right. Get in the car."

Mary drove, leaning forward in relentless silence. After a few miles, the silence overwhelmed Steve. He said, "Better get in the left lane so you can make the turn on Second."

"I'm going to Third."

"Okay, then."

When she stopped the car in front of the Kallos building, Mary said, "Take your cane."

"Don't come and get me. I'll get a ride home." He wanted to show her he was angry with her—that talk about them having grievances against him! He walked as slowly as he could toward the door, waiting, wanting her to call out to him. As he reached the elevators, he turned to look outside. Mary was gone, and he was sorry he had shown his resentment.

His heart beat with a good excitement as he walked into the office suite. He nodded to the receptionist and her friend at the coffee machine. The women glanced at each other as he went down the hall. He walked into Dick's office. Dick was at his desk, his jaws looking odd, like he had had them wired shut. His head was wrapped in gauze, and his frightened eyes stared out from purplish skin encircling them. "What the hell?" Steve shouted, taking a few steps closer. He peered closely at Dick. "You're the guy who got clobbered on TV last night!" Another few steps and he looked into Dick's wary eyes. "Whyn't you stay home, for Chrissake?"

Dick picked up a pencil and began writing on a note pad, then leaned back in his chair with a despondent hiss. Steve walked to the door and looked over his shoulder at him. "You know, I came in here to tell you, you were a no-good-sonofabitchin' pig, you and your Western Enterprises, but I'll just think about it some more while you recuperate." Smiling, he walked down the hall to his office. He knew for sure; brass knuckles had done the job.

He sat in the swivel chair and luxuriated in being there with nothing pressing, nothing that needed immediate attention. He decided he would give himself fifteen minutes to savor the peace that had stilled the past days' turmoil. Moving the chair from side to side, he glanced at his father's old roll-top desk with the papers sticking out. He admitted to himself that there were no magic documents there or in the file cabinets across the hall—none to give him clues to the treason; he had been grasping at straws.

He was looking forward to meeting Andrew, Jim, and Theo at the Deli. They would celebrate. They would have a good lunch and laugh. He thought of Theo with a smile. With an energy he thought he had lost, he went through the mail and the overnight faxes. He hoped to feel just as good at the Deli; he'd enjoy himself.

He pressed the button for Elroy. The janitor said, "You betcha, I can give you a ride. I'll stop for lunch somewheres on the way back." He wasn't sure, Elroy said, as he drove his dirty pickup truck erratically from lane to lane, what he would do with his time now that he was retiring. "Me and the wife never had much to say to each other, and she's already complainin' about havin' me under her feet all day." Then Elroy talked about problems in the building. "There's this here faucet in the ladies restroom on my third floor needs replacin'. The stem's stripped. I'll git a new one from Moen tomorrow. You know that there door I told you about on my second floor, the one that's warped. Well, I took it down and sanded it and all, but it's no go. I'll call Martin's to come over and install another one. Other than that, all my offices are shipshape. I don't know what I'm gonna do, Steve. I'm thinkin' of gittin' a trailer and hitchin' it to my truck. Maybe just drive around. See some of the parks. Visit the kids and grandkids, but hell, they're scattered from here to hell, and busy with their own lives."

"Well, Elroy, you better ask Mrs. Elroy what she thinks about getting a trailer before you go out and buy one."

"Yeah, she don't want to do nothin' but sit in front of the TV and watch sappy soap operas. God o mighty, Steve, them soaps are pretty racy."

Elroy bumped over the potholes in the Deli parking lot. "For hell's sake, what kind of people run this here place? People don't want to come to a place with a rotten parkin' lot!" The lot was almost filled. "You come here often? Well, how come you haven't put a bee in the guy's bonnet? Like you do at my buildin'? Christ, Steve, sometimes I don't understand you." Elroy stepped on the brakes, jolting the truck unnecessarily. Steve got out of the truck and thanked him. Elroy said, "Now, don't worry about my buildin'. I'll leave it in A1 condition before I git my last paycheck."

"Okay, Elroy," Steve said, surprised at the beseeching look in Elroy's eyes.

The Deli buzzed. Steve waved to several Greek Americans seated in a corner. Business-suited men, truck drivers wearing caps with logos stamped on them, and young people from the nearby high school filled all the tables except two near the kitchen. Steve wove through the crowded room as best he could, but was not fast enough to get to the table he wanted before it was taken. He swayed, realized he had forgotten his cane in Elroy's truck, and fell onto a chair at another table with a happy relief that he had not made a fool of himself.

While Stavros hurried back and forth with trays and pitchers of ice water and his plump daughter took orders, no, his granddaughter, of course, helping with the noon rush, Steve leaned back and smiled, satisfied. Americans were eating and relishing the food in the small restaurant with its tantalizing scents—roasting meat, piquant sauces, herbs, and spices. He remembered how the American, mostly Mormon, children at noon recess made fun of the immigrant kids' food: "What's in your lunch pail, some of that wop spaghetti?"; "You gonna eat some baa-baa sandwiches?"; "Did yuh bring your Chink chopsticks with you?"

Stavros called out to Steve, who raised his hand in a gesture, meaning he was in no hurry. Within a few minutes, Theo walked in, went over to the Greek Americans who greeted him with voluble cries, then came to Steve's table. He said nothing to Steve, merely looked, his mouth open, ready to give way to laughter. The rays at the corners of his eyes were deep. Steve also did not speak, but gave a short nod. "Eh, Steve," Theo said heartily. "That poor guy on television who got beat up." He winked.

Steve winked back. "They got *kalamaria* today," he said, laughing softly. He lifted his hand high and waved. "There's Andrew, and Jim's with him." He felt wonderfully happy and didn't know what to do with this happiness. To be sitting at the table with three people who meant so much to him! As his old father used to say when a name from the past came up, the name of one of the Greeks he had met during his early days crisscrossing the country looking for work, "Yes, I remember him. We ate bread and salt together." It meant more, much more than food for the stomach.

The four of them greeted each other in high spirits, as if they were meeting after a long absence. They looked at the menu and the chalked specials on the blackboard above the pass-through window. The plump granddaughter came to take orders in a little-girl voice, and smiled at Jim.

"I'll order for all of us," Steve said. *"Koukla,"*—the girl giggled at the Greek word for *doll*—"tell your grandmother to make us a big platter, *moussaka, pastitsio, kalamaria,* and bring some *avgolemono* soup to start with."

Andrew said, "Dad, we've got to go back to work. We can't eat all that food."

Steve waved his hand, "It won't go to waste. Jim, you take home what's left."

"I better not, Gramps, Paulie can't eat that heavy food now."

"Don't worry," Theo said, throwing his hands out sideways, "if no one wants it, I'll take it to my office for a snack."

They had a great deal to say. Steve told them about Dick, bandaged and wired up. Jim looked at him, then at Theo. Both were chuckling, shaking their heads. Jim glanced at his father. Andrew was contemplating them, nodding with a quirk of a smile: "Did you ever get rid of your brass knuckles, Theo?" A festive mood took over. Stavros stopped by. "You having a party or what?"

"It'd be a party if we had something good to drink," Steve said.

"I'll fix that," Stavros said, and returned with four coffee cups filled with illegal red wine.

Stavros's granddaughter, whose name was Tiffany, served the soup. Steve and Theo stooped over theirs and ate noisily. Andrew turned to Jim and said, "You should have heard *Papou* whoosh his soup. You could hear it at the other end of the house. A great guy," he said.

"I have two memories of *Papou* and *Yiayia* myself," Jim said. "I heard *Papou* whoosh his soup once. It was in their old house before they came to live with Gran and Gramps. Their kitchen was so small, the noise *Papou* made with his soup sounded like a waterfall. And *Yiayia*. Every time Gran took us to her house, *Yiayia*'d go downstairs to her freezer and bring us popsicles, even in winter."

Stavros brought the large platter, bountifully crowded with delicacies. "Ah!" Steve, Andrew, and Theo said in unison, and Jim gave a short, appreciative whistle. "You celebrating?" Stavros demanded, as if he, as host, should be so informed. "Someone's nameday? What?"

Steve and Theo looked at each other, and Andrew said, "We're just glad to be together, Stavros. You know how you feel when you get together with your friends and relatives."

"Friends, yes. Relatives—eh, sometimes yes, sometimes no." Stavros nodded toward the coffee cups and said loudly, "You want some more coffee?"

Andrew laughed, Jim looking pleased at his father's light-heartedness. "We have to go back to work," Andrew said. "Too much coffee'll keep us from working."

"'And manure on cabbages,'" Stavros said in Greek.

Steve explained the proverb to Jim. "It means that's a lot of bull-shit."

Theo shook his head and, his mouth full, said, "It means 'don't tell me something I know, like when two things go together.'"

They ate too much. Theo jumped up and called through the pass-through window, "Toula, the best food you ever did cook."

"Yeah, yeah," she answered.

Stavros served demitasses of Turkish coffee and a plate of honey-nut pastries. "This is on the house," Stavros said. "It make me happy to see other people happy."

In the parking lot, Jim said he had time to drive Steve home, but Theo insisted he would do it; he had one of Steve's canes in his car. Besides, he was going to the Parade of Homes to check on his men. He'd found one of them asleep on opening day. "One more time I catch him, I'll kick his ass out of the door."

In Theo's car, Steve made himself comfortable. Now that he had spent an enjoyable lunch hour, he wanted to hurry home to tell Mary about Dick. Neither Steve nor Theo was inclined to talk. Once in a while they looked at each other and laughed. "I know you want to get going," Steve said at the house. "So long. See you." They looked at each other with quirky smiles.

Leaning heavily on his cane, Steve walked across the grass to the side door of the house. The bread crumbs on the brick path remained untouched. Drowsy from the wine and heavy food, he thought how pleasant a nap would be. The house was quiet, in order, the kitchen counters cleaned off. He sensed Mary was not in the house. He walked to the window and saw her sitting on the red-wood bench. She was leaning back, her head to one side. He knew she was dead.

XXI

STEVE THOUGHT his arms and legs had been broken into pieces. Rooted in the kitchen, he stared, his mouth slack, at Mary's thrown back head. A profound pity suffocated him and he looked away for a few moments. Then he hobbled to the telephone. His fingers were trembling and he had to tighten his left hand over his right wrist to punch in Andrew's office number. "Come home," he said. "Your mother's dead." He hung up and sat down with his back to the window. He thought of her body there without her and his lungs tightened, forced him to gasp for air, but he would not reach for the ventilator in his pocket.

A darkness settled over the kitchen and he turned to face the window. It was bright, midafternoon, yet it looked grayed. It occurred to him that the little black bird might come back and perch on her head or her shoulder. He could not have that.

Several times he tried to get up, but his legs were not strong enough. Once more he grasped the edge of the table and with great determination pulled himself up. Gasping, he opened several drawers, found a tablecloth, and probing with his cane slowly made his way to the redwood bench. He placed his cane against the bench, tried not to look at her dead, shook out the tablecloth, and lifted it over her. With a sob he sat on the bench next to her and a strangled sound, a groan, a cry, a howl, came from his depths. He hugged his body.

A BLURRED FIGURE leaned over Mary. Andrew lifted the tablecloth. "Mom, Mom," he said as he stroked her cheek. Her mouth had fallen open. He pushed her chin upwards, but it fell back again. He covered her head and sat down on the bench. Heads bowed, he and his father cried silently, sitting a foot apart.

Two men in orange uniforms walked around the corner of the

house. One of them said, "Oh, there you are. We've been ringing the doorbell." To the younger man with him whose excited eyes flitted about, he ordered, "Get the gurney."

"She loved her garden, Andrew. How can she leave it?"

Andrew took Steve's elbow and tried to move him toward the house. Steve watched, slowly shaking his head as the men placed Mary's body on the gurney. The young man watched them eagerly while the scrawny older man gave instructions.

"I'll follow them, Dad. Don't come."

Steve whispered hoarsely, "What do you mean 'Don't come?' I got to."

They drove behind the ambulance to the hospital. "Why are they taking her there? Can't they see she's dead?"

"Dad, when people die outside a hospital, an autopsy has to be done."

"Don't let them do that to your mother! Do you hear? I don't want them cutting her up."

"She did sign a donor card." Andrew glanced at his father. "When she signed the 'no life-sustaining procedures' document. She said she didn't want to live tied to tubes. She said her organs probably weren't any good, but her skin could be used for burn patients."

After a moment Steve said, "Yes, that's what she said."

At the hospital, Steve signed forms and Andrew telephoned Theo. Then they sat in the crowded reception center in Emergency, not speaking, Steve looking ahead, his eyes hazy. People turned the pages of old magazines. An old man whispered loudly to his angry wife. A child of about twelve months with a cast on one leg from his toes to his hip pushed himself toward them, looked at them, and waited. Andrew smiled weakly. The child turned toward another patient, a teenage boy with a scanty beard and several gold loops in each ear. The child looked at the boy, again waiting, then went on pulling his stiff, injured leg like an ant struggling with a much larger insect. A commotion at the desk: a youngish, muscular Hispanic with blood streaming down one side of his face was steadied by two boys, no older than ten or eleven, while a woman screeched at him. A young mother rushed in shouting, holding a limp baby.

Steve cupped his hands over his ears. Andrew got up to call the mortuary, the same one to which his grandparents, his *papou* and *yiayia,* had been taken. He dialed his sisters; they were not at home and he left messages. When he returned, he said, "Dad, I called Alexandra and Christine." Steve did not reply but kept gazing at the worn blue carpeting. Twice Andrew asked his father if he wanted a cup of coffee. Steve shook his head. A gray-haired woman, wearing a doctor's jacket, stood before them and told them softly that they could leave. Andrew again took Steve's elbow. At the entrance Steve stood stolidly, his feet refusing to move. Andrew pulled him until Steve started walking.

In the car Steve said, "Did you call the girls?"

"The girls? Your sisters?"

"No," Steve's voice rose slightly, "*your* sisters. *My* daughters."

"I left messages on their machines." They said nothing the rest of the way to the house. At the end of the lane, Theo's dirty Suburban and Angie's shiny black Lexus were parked in front of the house. Andrew said, "Well, Theo and Angie are already here. I'm glad they have a key."

As Andrew's car entered the driveway, Theo rushed out. Angie, short and square, ran out with him, her eyes red and swollen. "Oh, Steve!" she burst out, wailed and pulled on her hands. "All right now, Angie," Theo said. He had been crying.

Theo helped Steve into the house and to the kitchen. Steve stopped and sniffed with repugnance the scent of cooked food and coffee. "Sit down," Angie said, as if she were now in charge, "and I'll serve the coffee." The men sat down. Angie had already set the table with the better cups and saucers Mary had used for kitchen visitors. She poured the coffee. "Andrew, pass around that basket of *paximadhia* and biscotti. I made them yesterday because I was getting low and—." Angie cried soundlessly, her shoulders moving.

Steve turned to Theo. As if he owed him an explanation, he

said, "What happened was, after you dropped me off, I came into the house and I knew Mary wasn't inside. So I look out of the window and I see her sitting on the bench. I could tell the way her head was turned back that she was dead."

The kitchen was quiet; no one lifted a coffee cup. Steve looked down, drew in a long breath, held it, and the escaping sigh fluttered in the still room. After a long moment, he said, with a touch of his old authority, "Who's gonna meet the girls at the airport? The priest, someone's got to call the priest." He could not maintain the pattern of control and his voice became faint.

"Christine, she already called," Theo said, "She's coming seven-forty-three, Delta. I'll go get her."

"You stay with Dad," Andrew said. "I'll meet the girls."

"I called Father Symeon," Angie said. "He's coming around seven."

Steve sighed. "Call him back, Angie. Tell him to wait until to-morrow when Alexandra and Christine get here."

"Mom told me what she wanted," Andrew said. "Don't worry, we'll take care of it."

Steve shook his head. "I never talked to her about any of that. I never thought she'd go first."

Angie went into the television room and telephoned the priest. Her voice sounded querulous as if she were arguing with him. When she returned, she said, "I told him. He said okay. I've got lamb with artichokes ready. And I boiled a chicken and put some orzo in the broth if you don't feel like having the lamb, Steve. You know, if you think it's too heavy. Any time you want to eat, just tell me."

Steve waved his hand. "You go ahead and eat. I'm not hungry."

Andrew pulled his lips inward. "Don't pull a *Papou* on us and starve yourself," he said.

"No. I haven't got the guts the old man had." Steve stood up. Theo handed him the cane and he walked into the bedroom wing of the house. He went into the room that had been Andrew's and had been inherited by his children, Jim and Liesa, when they were little and it was an adventure to stay in their grandparents' house. Steve looked at the icon of the Virgin and Child. He had not said prayers before an icon in fifty years. He wanted to say something, but he stood mute. The votive taper floating in the glass of water had gone out, and a thin line of olive oil lay on the water. He looked behind the icon for a fresh taper and olive oil, but he could not see them there or on the dresser or the bed table. He thought Mary had put them somewhere in the room, but he could not think where. He sat on the bed and stared at the icon.

The telephone rang at the other end of the house. He got up slowly, took his cane, and returned to the kitchen. "Was that Alexandra?" he asked.

Andrew nodded, looking relieved. "She's coming tomorrow at ten in the morning. She couldn't get on tonight."

"I'm gonna lay down." Steve said.

"Dad, have some coffee and a *paximadhi.*"

Steve shook his head and went back to the bedroom wing. He stopped outside Mary's room and looked in. He had an intense desire to rest there on her bed, but he thought: What would they think if they came in and saw me. "What the hell?" he said, closed the door, and walked to the bed. He lay down heavily on it, then remembered he had not taken off his shoes. He sat up, untied them, let himself fall back, and felt his muscles relax. He closed his eyes but he could not sleep. And he did not want to sleep. He wanted to think, but he could not. Instead a feeling so dull it was welcome filled his head.

He heard voices from the other end of the house—his sisters' and his grandson Jim's. He would not go out to see Penny and Georgie, but he wished Jim would walk into the room and sit on the bed beside him. He thought of him as a little boy with a round face, big eyes, and bangs. Every so often, light footsteps came down the hall and stopped, then retreated. The room darkened.

He started, surprised. He had slept, and someone was tapping on the door. "Daddy, it's Christine. Let me come in."

"Okay, Doll." He tried to lift himself but lay back again.

The door opened and Christine came in, the youngest of his children. "Daddy," she had said. Andrew and Alexandra had teased her in high school over her still calling him Daddy until she began saying Dad to stop their heckling. She leaned over, her head against his face. "Oh, Daddy, I can't believe she's gone. My little Mom." She sobbed and Steve put his hand on her head.

After a few moments, she stood up and wiped her eyes with a tissue. "Let's go into the kitchen. Only Theo and Angie are still here. Angie wants to see that you eat something before she goes." Christine took Steve's right hand and tugged.

"Don't do that. You'll get tendonitis."

"I won't."

They walked down the long hallway and across to the kitchen. Angie had a place set for him. She apologized. "The rest of us had to eat and Jim had to go home and see his wife."

"What's wrong with her?" Steve's voice was thin. He wished he hadn't been told about Paula. He didn't want to think about anything right then.

"I don't think there's a thing wrong. It's just how people are with a first baby coming. And you know these young kids. They help their wives and get involved. They even change diapers."

Christine sat next to her father. "I would have had a breakdown if Mom hadn't come to help me when Ricky was born. I was so afraid to give him a bath." She lowered her head and tears dropped on her cheeks.

"Now, Steve," Angie said, "I'll serve you some chicken soup with orzo. Just a little and if you want more, Christine can get it for you."

"Just a little," Steve said, not looking at her: She had been so good to Mary. He didn't want to cry again. He took a few spoonfuls, nodded to show it was good, although it had no taste. Christine hovered over him, brought a bowl of crackers. "Maybe you'd rather have crackers, Daddy." He took one to please her and with a glance saw a few long strands of gray in her brown hair. He had trouble swallowing.

The doorbell rang and Steve's body gave a jolt. Theo hurried to the front door and suddenly the house was filled with horrible cries that grew louder as Theo appeared with an arm around Tessie's heaving shoulders. "Steve, Steve, I can't stand it! I can't stand it!"

Steve's heavy eyebrows shot up, startled. Theo carefully pushed Tessie down on a chair while Angie gave both of them a dark look. Theo looked at Angie, lifted his shoulders and put out his hands as if to say, "What else could I do?" Christine stood up and with an arm around Tessie spoke soothing words that no one could hear. Tessie cried louder, mascara running down her rouged face; her hair, moist around the temples, lost its careful sculpting and hung limply. Her lipstick had smeared. "I can't stand it! She was like a big sister to me! We went everywhere together! My mother was so mean and I'd run to Mary! Oh, Mary! Mary! We watched the trains go by! Mary, I wanted to tell you! I wanted to tell you. You were the only one I could trust. I wanted to, Mary!" Tessie shrieked and bent over, then began again, the silk over her chest trembling as she tried to catch her breath. Taking advantage of a lull, Christine patted her shoulder and said, "We know, Aunt Tessie. She cared a lot about you." New explosive cries followed, and everyone except her father gave Christine warning looks.

Steve got up, unsteady. Andrew quickly stood up and helped Steve to the bedroom wing. "I'll sleep here," he said at the door of Mary's bedroom. "It's closer to the kitchen." Andrew helped him remove his sweater and untied his shoes. "Okay, that's good. Tell Christine I'm gonna sleep and not to let no one bother me."

At the door Andrew looked back. "I'll be here first thing in the morning, Dad."

"No. Go about your business. I'm okay."

Andrew gave his father another long look and shut the door. Steve got under the covers and burrowed his face into Mary's pillow. The closed door muffled Tessie's howls and Angie's high-pitched commands. After a while, Tessie slid into a loud weeping. Steve thought of Christine's strands of gray hair. Mary, who would not have thought of dyeing her own hair, had said one morning while they were drinking coffee that she wished Christine would dye hers. He thought of other little incidents to keep from thinking of Mary's body being flayed. Perhaps now at the mortuary. Alone.

He had slept in his clothes. The scent of coffee came to him as he quietly opened the door and went down the hall to his own room. He thought of taking a shower: Mary had always nagged him to take daily showers when their daughters came for visits. He asked Mary's forgiveness. "I can't right now," he said.

Father Symeon was seated at the table with Jim and Theo. Angie was serving them scrambled eggs and toast. Jim jumped up and hugged Steve tightly. "Gramps," he said. Steve looked into Jim's reddened eyes. "It's okay, Jimbo," he said.

Father Symeon shook his hand and said, "My *sylipitiria*, Mr. Kallos."

Steve waved them to sit down. "Where's Christine?"

"She and Andrew, they went to pick up Alexandra," Theo said.

Angie hovered over Steve, "Steve, I can make you a feta omelet in just one second."

"Just a piece of toast, Angie." But a gnawing in his stomach told him he had to eat something or get an ulcer like he'd had when he was a young man working day and night. "All right, but not too much."

Angie happily poured the beaten eggs into a pan. Father Symeon began explaining to Jim, "As I was saying, that's what the church says. It doesn't matter if a person pays dues all his life, if he isn't married in the church, he can't take communion or be buried in the church."

Steve thought of saying "bullshit," but he didn't care. Jim said, "It bothers my friend because he was an altar boy."

"Nevertheless—" Father Symeon began to object while Jim looked at him, his fine black eyebrows coming together.

Alexandra ran in from the side door that led to the garage.

Andrew and Christine followed. She put her arms around Steve, said nothing, and disengaged her arms slowly. She nodded to the priest. "Let's go into the living room, Father, and discuss the service." As the priest, his daughters, and Andrew reached the doorway, Steve lifted his head, "One thing, Father," he said, his voice suddenly strong even though the tone was quiet. "I don't want a prayer service the night before."

Father Symeon objected, "That's how it's always done."

"No. When my dad died, I told our young priest at the time that it was like having two funerals and he said if I felt like that we could have the prayer service just before the funeral at the mortuary."

"But everybody liked Mary. They'd want to pay their respects."

"They can pay their respects at the funeral."

"People work. They—"

Steve waved him to be silent. "All her friends in the Philoptochos are too old to be working. And that's how I want it."

The priest turned and followed Alexandra into the living room. Angie said in a whisper, "Steve, I gotta listen. See what they're saying. Mary didn't like big fancy funeral dinners. I'll be in charge. We'll have a fish dinner like it's supposed to be. Halibut *plaki*. Not all those meats and *dolmadhes* and *pites*. We can have it in the church hall and invite the Philoptochos and their husbands." She sniffed. "They're just about all widows anyway."

"Go ahead," Steve said. He drank the rest of his coffee with Theo's assuring him he didn't have to worry about anything. Between him and Angie and Andrew and the girls, they would do everything right.

THE NAVE WAS cool; the incense, blue and acrid, hovered against the icon screen and over Mary's open casket. Great bouquets of flowers surrounded the casket, their scent overpowered by the blue incense. Steve sat on the front pew between Andrew and Alexandra. As the congregation sat down after the opening prayers, he leaned slightly forward, beyond his daughters, to catch sight of Jim. He could hardly breathe while the priest intoned the supplications to God, to Christ, and to the Virgin. Then his thoughts stopped; he sat numbed and unthinking while the priest's mouth moved, while the cantor droned, while the choir sang, while the congregation stood and sat, stood and sat. His head dropped toward his chest. With a start he lifted it and heard the priest's supplication: "Lord, give rest to thy departed servant Mary in a place of brightness, in a place of greenness, a place of repose, whence all sicknesss, sorrow, and sighing have fled."

"Eternal be thy memory," Father Symeon called out; "Eternal be thy memory," the cantor echoed; "Eternal be thy memory," the choir sang. Steve's heart gave a clutch of pain. The priest poured a few drops of oil from a small bottle and a spoonful of ashes into the casket.

Steve kept his head down while people passed to kiss the icon laid on Mary's chest. He felt the pressure of people's hands on his knees, but he would not look up. Then Theo and Angie and others went up, one by one to cross themselves and kiss the icon. Tessie muffled her cries; Magdalene's pale lips moved in silent prayer. Penny and Georgie stared down at Mary's face, made the sign of the cross, and returned to their pew; Dick and Tom, with their wives, bowed. Tom patted Mary's hand. Andrew's wife Jeanne and Liesa were next, Liesa looking at her grandmother with a faint smile and a shake of her head. Jim escorted his aunts, Alexandra and Christine, forward and stood with his arms about their waists as they wept. Then Andrew grasped his father's elbow, and Steve, with a terrible pounding in his heart, let himself be led to join his daughters and Jim. He reached over, not looking at Mary, and kissed her cold forehead. His shoulders shook. Andrew and Jim helped him back to the pew. Steve thought he would cry "No!" when Father Symeon swung the censer and the men from the mortuary closed the lid.

It was worse at the cemetery when her casket was lowered into the ground. He thought he would die on the spot, wanted to die, the hurt was so great. He wanted to go home that moment to lie on Mary's bed, but instead he was driven back to the church hall for the traditional fish dinner. A crowd of people filed by the table where he sat, pressed his hand, said the traditional, "Life is the Word," and told him Mary was a wonderful woman. An ancient, wrinkled woman said that she would see Mary soon and give her his regards.

Lefty and Perry sat with him while their wives prepared the food. In the kitchen, Goldie filled plates with halibut and a macedoine of green beans, new potatoes, and zucchini. Fanny mixed the green salad and distributed it onto the salad dishes. Theo and his two sons poured wine and Angie gave orders to the granddaughters of Philoptochos members, who hurried back and forth from the kitchen to the hall with plates. Their hair was long and shiny, their faces young and smooth. Steve lifted his eyes and looked about the hall at the crowd of dark-dressed people seated at the tables—so few men, so many women. His eyebrows came together: how was it he was alive and Mary was dead?

The priest gave the prayer and soon a subdued din filled the hall. Steve ate a little; he remembered his mother having said that by eating the funeral meal, the dead and the living forgave each other, in the same way as it was with the memorial wheat eaten forty days after death. He looked around the table at his solemn family: to his surprise, Sandy was there, her hair freshly hennaed, earrings dangling, wearing something bright green, her head lifted proudly. His voice hoarse, Steve said, "Gran said people had to eat the funeral dinner to forgive each other." As if by his permission, the family picked up their forks and ate, saying little. Steve wanted to go home.

On a table at the right of the kitchen door were platters of honey-nut pastries and a coffeemaker. Perspiring and bustling, Angie brought a plate of pastries and a cup of coffee for him. He nodded his thanks and took a sip of the coffee. "Jim, drive me home," he said. "Sure, Gramps." They had been seated at a table near the basketball court, and while his daughters whispered that they would stay—the old propriety their mother had taught them—Andrew, Steve, and Jim went into the gym and out to the parking lot. Jim helped his grandfather into the passenger side of the front seat. Andrew sat in the back. Jim drove slowly.

After several blocks of silence, touched only by the hum of the car's engine, Jim said, "Gramps, it was a good service."

Steve spoke carefully, as if the words were hard to bring out, "Why were there flowers? Gran didn't like people spending money on flowers. 'Give to the poor,' she used to say."

Andrew leaned forward. "Dad, we put it in the obituary: donations to the church in lieu of flowers, but you know people do what they want."

"People do what they want," Steve echoed. "And why was her casket open? She didn't like open caskets."

"I think," Jim said, "the mortuary people misunderstood the priest. He made some kind of motion with his hand."

"At least," Andrew said, "we got it through Father Symeon's head that Mom didn't want a eulogy. He tried to convince us to let him give a talk, but we said no."

"The sonofabitch," Steve said, and they were silent until they arrived home. Steve blinked as if his eyes were pained at the sight of the long drainboards covered with platters and bowls. "I'm going to my room," he said. "I don't want to see nobody."

In Mary's room, he took off his dark suit and stiff white shirt and got under the covers. He did not sleep. He did not want to think, but images came to him, then fled, foolish images: Sandy and her dangling earrings; the little wrinkled woman who talked in his face; women and girls scurrying with plates like a revved-up old movie. But he could not keep away the image of Mary in the casket being lowered into the ground. He wept, then slept from exhaustion.

FOR A WEEK, women came with food: Tessie, eyes puffed and red, carried in bakery boxes; Penny and Georgie brought nothing. "We knew you'd have too much stuff," Georgie said. Afterwards, Alexandra, the one who never let anything get by her—her mother's assessment—said, "The aunts acted like they were, well, superfluous." Delivery florists brought plants, mainly azaleas. Alexandra and Christine went about the house, talking to each other in low voices.

During the second week, few visitors came, and Steve sat in the family room with the television on, the sound turned off, and stared at it. His daughters talked in the other rooms: "Remember this little wine measure we got Mom for Mother's Day when we were in grade school. Do you care if I take it with me?" "No. I'm going to ask Dad if I can have that little vase she got when she went to Greece, the one she always put a rose in."

When they came into the family room to cajole Steve into having lunch, he said, "Take what you want. Then when you come back for the forty-day service, divide her good dishes and glasses. The silver things. Give Jim some."

"All right, Daddy," Christine said, and then hesitated. "What about Mom's clothes?"

Days had passed since he had cried and he was afraid he would start again, but he said, "After the forty days, give them to the Philoptochos for those Albanian refugees."

His daughters, Andrew, and Jim wanted to take him in the car, to get some air, they said. "No, I'm gonna stay home until the forty days are up. Just like the old folks used to do."

"Dad," Alexandra said, carefully exasperated, "nobody does that anymore. All that wearing black and not going anywhere for forty days, that's all past."

"I'm gonna stay in my house and yard for forty days," Steve said.

Christine gave a little wail, "But what will you do for forty days, Daddy—Dad?"

"I'll sit in my chair and sort things out."

"What things?" Alexandra asked.

"Things. Now go home to your families. Just show me how to use the coffeemaker."

"Dad, we can't leave you here so soon."

"I want you to go home. And I won't be alone. I've got Andrew and Jim. Theo, Angie," he paused. "Lefty and Perry."

"You can't live here alone!"

Steve raised his voice. "I don't want to hear any of that talk from you, Alexandra. I'm gonna live here 'til they take me out feet first. Sandy can come in every day or so. Angie'll ride herd on her."

Cowed, his daughters served the food and later made plane reservations. The first night in the house after they had gone, he felt bereft, as he knew he would, and he paced through the rooms, turning on many lamps to dispel the dark. He thought some giant hand had taken a sickle and cut out the lungs, heart, and guts from his body. His head was like a piece of lead and he realized that he had not taken his blood-pressure tablets. His feet would not lie still. They rubbed against the sheets and wore him out until he was breathless with fatigue. His eyelids closed against his will.

He awoke groggy, knowing he had dreamed an important dream, but he could not remember it. No coffee scent came from the kitchen, and he remembered that Mary was gone. The refrigerator, full of covered dishes, repelled him. When hunger kneaded his stomach, he made himself a ham sandwich and ate it in front of the television set, but he could not keep his attention on the programs he had always watched. The newscasters' voices hurt his ears, baseballs flew into the grandstand and he didn't care. He turned off the sound, then the set, and sat in the quiet house while the mantel clock ticked on.

Each morning he knew he had dreamed forgotten dreams. Then one morning he awoke and recalled a dream clearly: all the toilets in the house had overflowed with fecal sludge. He ate nothing the entire day and a thought nagged at him, that he had done something wrong, that he was unworthy.

A few nights later, he dreamed of his mother. It was a gray day. He was crossing the street on Main Street halfway between Third and Fourth South where First Security Bank had had its offices years ago. His mother came toward him, a youngish mother, and as they passed each other she smiled as if they shared a secret. The dream was puzzling, but it left him feeling peaceful, seeing his mother, her face round and smiling.

He had not yet seen Mary in a dream. Before going to bed each night, he crossed himself at the icon. A week after the funeral he had found a box of votive lights and a bottle of olive oil on the closet shelf; after a few fumbles, he was able to light the icon taper. Then after crossing himself at the icon, he lay down thinking he would see her that night. He dreamed another night that he stood in his parents' brown brick house. He was standing in the empty dining room and he was holding his grandson Jim's hand—Jim a little boy. A woman stood at one side and said, "Your father's asleep in the back bedroom." Yet even in the dream he knew that his father was dead. The woman's voice continued, "I'll take the front bedroom and you and Jim sleep in the middle bedroom." The next morning he thought that maybe the shadowy figure who spoke was Mary, and if so, that was not the kind of dream he wanted to see her in. But why was Jim there in a house with dead people? He walked from room to room, circling the house until he tired himself out. When he sat down at the kitchen table, he thought of a day the three of them were drinking coffee and Jim and Mary talked about dreams. Mary had read something and Jim said he had read it, too. They talked back and forth, forgetting all about him sitting there. He got up and went into the television room. If Mary were alive, he could tell her about the dreams he was having.

He should have gone to Greece with her. At least he should have done that. Most of the people on the church tour were long-married couples, Mary said, all of them going back to see their parents' birthplaces. She took a bus alone to his parents' villages. His mother Marika's house had come down through the generations to her brother's granddaughter. The middle-aged woman referred to Mary as "Aunt Marika's bride," and had her sit at a roughly made wooden table covered with a crocheted cloth. Mary had taken a small camera with her, but Steve had wanted to know all the details of the visit, not just look at the snapshots. "Of course, you couldn't take the time to see for yourself," Mary said, but she described the small stone house. On the ground floor, animals were penned. The top floor was one room where the entire family lived, a fireplace at one end, next to it a raised bench-like bed with an embroidered sheet as a drape, evidently for the parents, a few old chairs, nails in one wall where the family's wardrobe hung; the floor of weathered planks had several loomed rag rugs over it.

Mary had brought chocolates from Athens, and the hospitality tray was brought out. The woman gave her hands a clap and lamented that her husband was down in the steep valley working his fields.

Steve looked at the picture Mary had taken of his father's house and sputtered, "You sure this is my old man's house?" The house was a hut built into a mountain side; it was used as a goatshed when Mary took pictures of it. The next time Steve complained that his father never gave him a dime for cleaning the Railroad Hotel, Mary said, "If you saw where they came from, you'd understand the way they were."

She could not visit her own parents' village. It was the time of the Cyprus invasion and airplane travel was halted between Greece and Turkey.

SOME DAYS STEVE sat in the family room for hours; sometimes, when Sandy was cleaning, he went out to the redwood bench in front of the rose garden and looked at Mount Olympus. He wondered what Mary had been thinking of when she had sat so still and gazed at the mountain.

Out of nowhere, thoughts came to bedevil him. His mother bent over the washboard, scrubbing Uncle Harry's and the icemen's underwear—as a boy, he had never given her a thought, and he called himself an ass, a thoughtless ass. The icemen didn't leave the house until he was fifteen years old and yet it had never occurred to him to do something about it, to tell his father it was wrong. She was the *mother;* she wasn't a slave. So what if his father beat him? He should have tried. It would have made his mother glad to know that she wasn't alone.

Once when he was a boy, while walking to school beyond Greek Town, he had seen a mother standing on a porch, leaning down to kiss her two children, one who was in his second-grade class. Then she waved good-bye to them. He tried it once, stood by his mother with his school lunch of leftover spinach and rice between two slices of thick bread wrapped in a Greek newspaper. He hung around her, waiting. "Go! What are you doing here, getting in my way?" Yet she gave him a bottle of wine, thinking the teacher would be nicer to him. His throat ached.

And he didn't grieve when his father died, even though by the time he and his mother came to live with them, his father had mellowed, as people said. Once his father had hit him with a piece of heavy kindling because Uncle Harry had tattled on him, and his father took Uncle Harry's word, never asked him about it. Mary had explained early injustices, "It was the culture they brought with them, Steve. Stop thinking about it."

Often, in the television room, he would doze off and the images would come. Solly was in some of them. In one dream he was running down the alleys after he had been caught in mischief, Penny and Georgie laughing, happy at his escape. A puzzling kind of sadness came to Steve thinking of teen-aged Penny and Georgie sitting on the front porch and nowhere to go.

When he woke up he continued to think about Solly. Mary had told him once that his mind was cluttered with big and little things, most of them better thrown away, and he had laughed at her—but scenes came from that cluttered mind of his: memories of Solly slighting him, showing he preferred some drunk to him. Why couldn't he have realized that he had wasted time with Solly? He didn't know why Solly was like he was; he should have let him go on his way.

And yes, that's where he made his big mistake—hanging on to

the business all those years when it was obvious that the family should have separated long ago. His father had finally caught on to Uncle Harry, and yet with those old Greek ideas about the family, they went on for three generations, battling each other, so sure they could make more money staying together. They wouldn't let Andrew do any legal work for the business, plain meanness. His dad had counted on it so much and Andrew held it against him, his father. . . .

Steve would doze off again, then open his eyes, stare at the silent television screen, and after a while remember something else. When the doorbell rang, he was relieved to open the door to Andrew, Jim, Theo, or Perry and Lefty. Andrew and Jim often brought pastries from Leslie's Bakery and made coffee. Theo, Lefty, and Perry brought cooked food: feta pita; artichokes in oil and lemon juice; bean soup that Angie knew he liked. Steve had learned to use the coffeemaker and the men sat around the kitchen table and talked. Perry's voice had gotten thin, too—he'd be the next to go, and Lefty was always going to the bathroom and afraid to have his prostate removed.

He talked to himself as his mother used to talk to herself: Mary, Mary, you were right. I should have kept up with them. They cared about me, but I was no different than my dad. Money meant everything. I wanted to show the bankers, kids I'd gone to school with, I wanted the world to know that I could make money.

Perry and Lefty sat forward and told the old stories of their growing up: Greek school; making cider for the Harvest Dance; Steve learning to play the clarinet; priests and Greek school teachers; bachelor Greeks who got old and peculiar in coffeehouses that had long disappeared, high rise buildings in their place. They avoided talking about the three of them and the "girls," as they called their wives, in the days of their engagements and early marriages just before the Second World War. Steve wanted to hear about those days, wanted to remember that there were good days, and he said one afternoon, "And we ate a lot of popcorn in the Depression." They talked and laughed then about those days when they couldn't afford doing anything more than seeing an occasional movie and mostly sat around the radio and ate popcorn. Lefty's voice boomed out; he had forgotten nothing and he remembered the very night when Steve took Mary home after they had dinner on the mezzanine floor of the China Gardens and "next thing we hear, the two of you was engaged." They laughed over putting drops in Steve's wine at his wedding that turned his urine red.

They talked about how things were once; how things were now, and mostly how they used to be better long ago. When they left, Steve watched old movies and replays of situation comedies on television. This way he expected he would be tired enough to get a few hours' sleep. His eyes remained unblinking on the set, yet memory took over his thoughts. They began orderly enough, then became mixed up, senseless: the elderly carpenters who worked on the industrial complex where the Japanese farm had been; his mother holding the sack of silver dollars and Solly's GI checks; Uncle Harry, Aunt Myrsini; the telephone booth at the army base; the two soldiers he thought he would never forget and did; Dick, Pretty Boy Tommy, the women in the family. He clicked off the television around two in the morning, turned on the burglar alarm, and left only one light burning in the living room. He then went into Andrew's old room. One night he looked at the icon there and said, "That's enough. I did a lot of things wrong. There were reasons, but it's all done and gone. No use beating a dead horse. It's okay."

WHEN HIS DAUGHTERS returned for the forty-days memorial service, he was glad to see them. In the kitchen, Angie prepared the memorial wheat, the *kolyva,* for the service. She boiled the wheat until it puffed and had Alexandra and Christine chop walnuts and parsley and open pomegranates and remove the seeds. Angie spread the wheat on towels to remove the moisture. Alexandra asked if they could sit down for coffee, but Angie said, "No, first the *kolyva,* then we can enjoy the coffee better." Angie transferred the wheat to several enormous brown earthenware bowls, then added the nuts, pomegranate seeds, Jordan almonds, parsley, currants, and powdered sugar. "What significance does everything have, Aunt Angie?" Christine asked.

"Significance? What do you mean significance?"

"Well, the nuts and the parsley and the pomegranate seeds. What do they mean?"

Angie frowned. "That's how they always make it, that's all." She knew no more than Christine and Alexandra that wheat, nuts, and pomegranate seeds were symbols of immortality; parsley represented the greenness of the other world, and sugar and currants its sweetness.

They filled small plastic bags with the memorial wheat and stapled them shut. Only after they had stacked trays of the bags in the large refrigerator did Angie allow them to sit down to coffee and pastries.

A larger than usual congregation attended the memorial service. Afterwards, the family and Angie, Theo, and Perry and Lefty with their wives had lunch in a restaurant; Andrew had made reservations for a private room. Steve was quiet, but he made certain that everyone had either rib roast or salmon, a choice of wines, and several kinds of desserts to choose from.

At home, Steve's children and his grandson Jim talked about the future. Andrew asked, tentatively, "Do you want to just stay here for a while, Dad, then we could look into retirement homes?"

"No, I'm gonna stay here. You kids can take what you want, the good dishes, the glassware, all of her doodads. Just leave me the kitchen things so I can have coffee with my friends."

"About your driving, Dad . . ." Andrew began.

"I'm not gonna drive anymore. Jim, you choose one of the cars and give the other to the priest. He drives a rattletrap."

The sighs were audible. "You girls, take charge of your mother's clothes and all the things she's got in the bathroom and in the dressers." Steve stood up, walked into the television room, and turned on the news. First in the kitchen then in the living room, Alexandra and Christine talked with their brother Andrew and Jim.

Jim found him sitting in front of the almost soundless television set and sat next to him, but several moments went by before Steve realized he was there. "I want you to take something of your grandmother's, Jimbo," Steve said.

"I did, Gramps. I chose that painting over the sofa. But I don't know how I'll feel about driving around in a fancy car."

"You'll get used to it."

Jim rubbed his chin. "Just take it," Steve said mildly, "and sell the damn thing if you can't get used to it."

They sat for a long while, talking a little about the news and sports. After Jim left, Andrew walked in. Steve had been hoping he would. "I made a lot of mistakes in my life, Andrew," he began, looking out the window. "For one thing, your mother didn't think I tried hard enough to see that you did the legal work for the company. It bothered her a lot, but I didn't think about her, I just thought of myself."

"It was circumstances, Dad. There were too many of us involved in the business."

Steve grunted, but gave a little laugh, "That's why the Greeks have this proverb, 'Eat with your family, do business with strangers.'"

They both nodded in appreciation of the saying.

Steve coughed and gave Andrew a quick glance, "I wasn't a great husband, Andrew. I'm not sure I even spent much time with you kids when you were growing up. And a lot of the problems in the company were my fault. But it's over with. No use beating a dead horse."

Andrew reached over and put his hand on Steve's for a moment. "I've made lots of mistakes, too, Dad." Steve looked at the hand Andrew had touched. "I'll bring some papers over tomorrow," Andrew said. He stood up. "There's a board meeting, on Wednesday. You don't have to go if you don't want to."

"I'll be there."

"I'll pick you up."

"No, because you always leave the meetings early."

"No more, Dad."

"Okay, then, and I'm not gonna bring up that other stuff."

"It's better. And any time you change your mind about the house, I'll take care of it."

Steve waved his palm back and forth. After Andrew's car drove off, he sat without moving and stared ahead until the clock struck on the half hour. Then he pulled himself up and taking his cane went out to sit on the redwood bench. As he gazed at Mount Olympus in the dusk, the snow in the crevices took on a blue tint. On the green slopes, a few scrub-oak bushes were tinged with autumn red. Then the music of a clarinet began soaring, pealing in his head, and it went on for a long time.